KILLING GROUND

Created by MIKE MIGNOLA

ABE SAPIEN

An amphibious man discovered in a primitive stasis chamber in a long-forgotten subbasement beneath a Washington, D.C. hospital. Recent events have confirmed a previous life, dating back to the Civil War, as scientist and occult investigator Langdon Everett Caul.

CAPTAIN BENJAMIN DAIMIO

A United States Marine whose distinguished thirteen-year career ended in June of 2001 when he and the platoon he was leading were all killed during a mission. The details of his death remain classified. Exactly how it was that he came back to life is an outright mystery.

LIZ SHERMAN

A fire-starter since the age of eleven, when she accidentally burned her entire family to death. She has been a ward of the B.P.R.D. since then, learning to control her pyrokinetic abilities and cope with the trauma those abilities have wrought.

DR. KATE CORRIGAN

A former professor at New York University and an authority on folklore and occult history. Dr. Corrigan has been a B.P.R.D. consultant for over ten years and now serves as Special Liaison to the enhanced-talents task force.

JOHANN KRAUS

A medium whose physical form was destroyed while his ectoplasmic projection was out-of-body. A psychic empath, Johann can create tem-

MIKE MIGNOLA'S

B.P.R.D.™
KILLING GROUND

Story by
MIKE MIGNOLA and JOHN ARCUDI

Art by
GUY DAVIS

Colors by
DAVE STEWART

Letters by
CLEM ROBINS

Editor
SCOTT ALLIE

Assistant Editor
RACHEL EDIDIN

Collection Designer
AMY ARENDTS

Publisher
MIKE RICHARDSON

DARK HORSE BOOKS®

NEIL HANKERSON ♦ *executive vice president*
TOM WEDDLE ♦ *chief financial officer*
RANDY STRADLEY ♦ *vice president of publishing*
MICHAEL MARTENS ♦ *vice president of business development*
ANITA NELSON ♦ *vice president of marketing, sales & licensing*
DAVID SCROGGY ♦ *vice president of product development*
DALE LaFOUNTAIN ♦ *vice president of information technology*
DARLENE VOGEL ♦ *director of purchasing*
KEN LIZZI ♦ *general counsel*
DAVEY ESTRADA ♦ *editorial director*
SCOTT ALLIE ♦ *senior managing editor*
CHRIS WARNER ♦ *senior books editor, Dark Horse Books*
ROB SIMPSON ♦ *senior books editor, M Press/DH Press*
DIANA SCHUTZ ♦ *executive editor*
CARY GRAZZINI ♦ *director of design & production*
LIA RIBACCHI ♦ *art director*
CARA NIECE ♦ *director of scheduling*

Special thanks to Jason Hvam

www.hellboy.com

Published by Dark Horse Books
A division of Dark Horse Comics, Inc.
10956 SE Main Street
Milwaukie, OR 97222

First Edition: May 2008
ISBN: 978-1-59307-956-7

1 3 5 7 9 10 8 6 4 2

Printed in China

This book collects the *B.P.R.D.: Killing Ground* comic-book series, issues 1–5,
published by Dark Horse Comics.

CHAPTER ONE

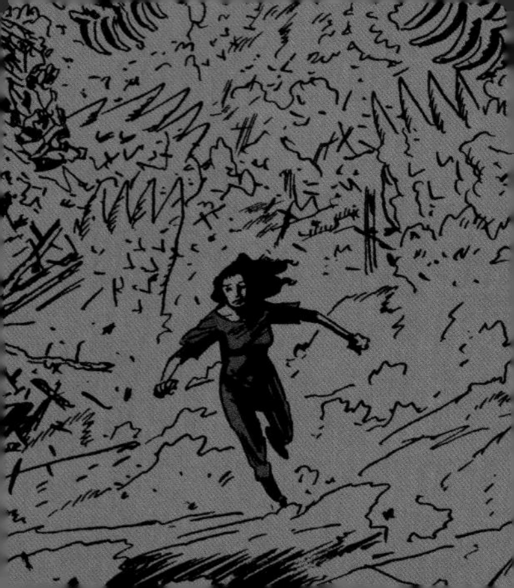

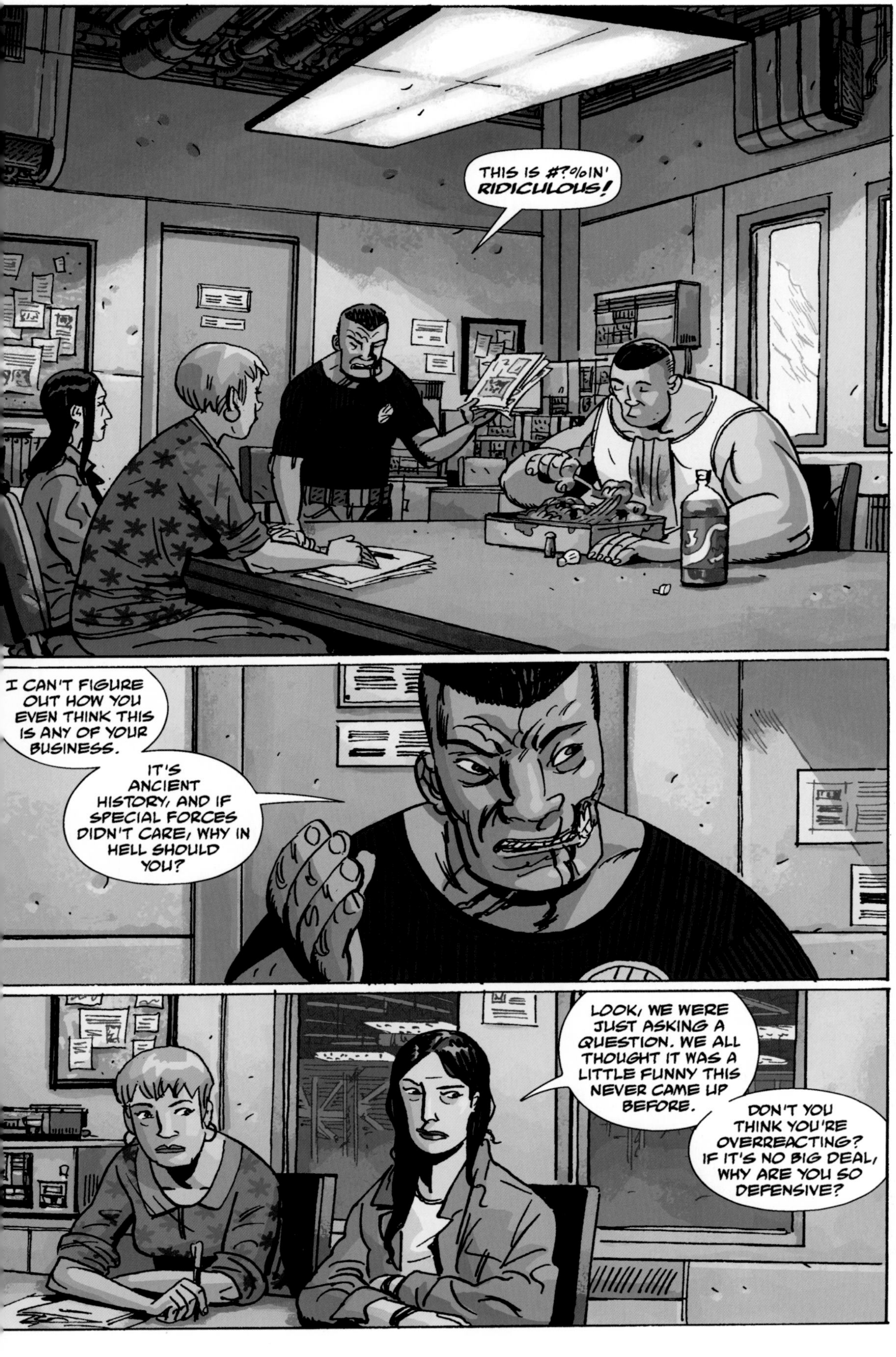
THIS IS #?%IN' RIDICULOUS!
I CAN'T FIGURE OUT HOW YOU EVEN THINK THIS IS ANY OF YOUR BUSINESS.
IT'S ANCIENT HISTORY, AND IF SPECIAL FORCES DIDN'T CARE, WHY IN HELL SHOULD YOU?
LOOK, WE WERE JUST ASKING A QUESTION. WE ALL THOUGHT IT WAS A LITTLE FUNNY THIS NEVER CAME UP BEFORE.
DON'T YOU THINK YOU'RE OVERREACTING? IF IT'S NO BIG DEAL, WHY ARE YOU SO DEFENSIVE?

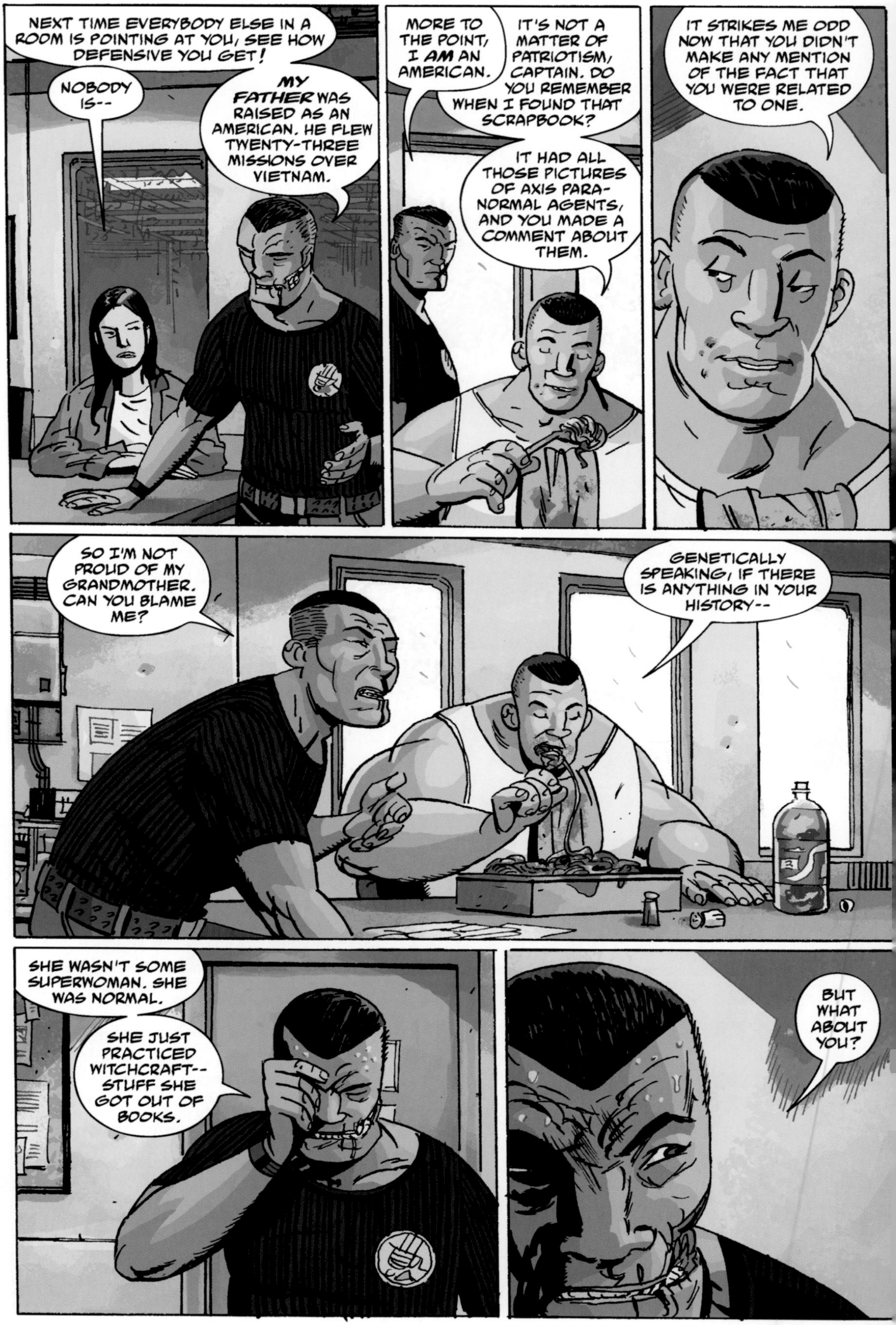
NEXT TIME EVERYBODY ELSE IN A ROOM IS POINTING AT YOU, SEE HOW DEFENSIVE YOU GET!
NOBODY IS--
MY FATHER WAS RAISED AS AN AMERICAN. HE FLEW TWENTY-THREE MISSIONS OVER VIETNAM.
MORE TO THE POINT, I AM AN AMERICAN.
IT'S NOT A MATTER OF PATRIOTISM, CAPTAIN. DO YOU REMEMBER WHEN I FOUND THAT SCRAPBOOK?
IT HAD ALL THOSE PICTURES OF AXIS PARA-NORMAL AGENTS, AND YOU MADE A COMMENT ABOUT THEM.
IT STRIKES ME ODD NOW THAT YOU DIDN'T MAKE ANY MENTION OF THE FACT THAT YOU WERE RELATED TO ONE.
SO I'M NOT PROUD OF MY GRANDMOTHER. CAN YOU BLAME ME?
GENETICALLY SPEAKING, IF THERE IS ANYTHING IN YOUR HISTORY--
SHE WASN'T SOME SUPERWOMAN. SHE WAS NORMAL.
SHE JUST PRACTICED WITCHCRAFT--STUFF SHE GOT OUT OF BOOKS.
BUT WHAT ABOUT YOU?

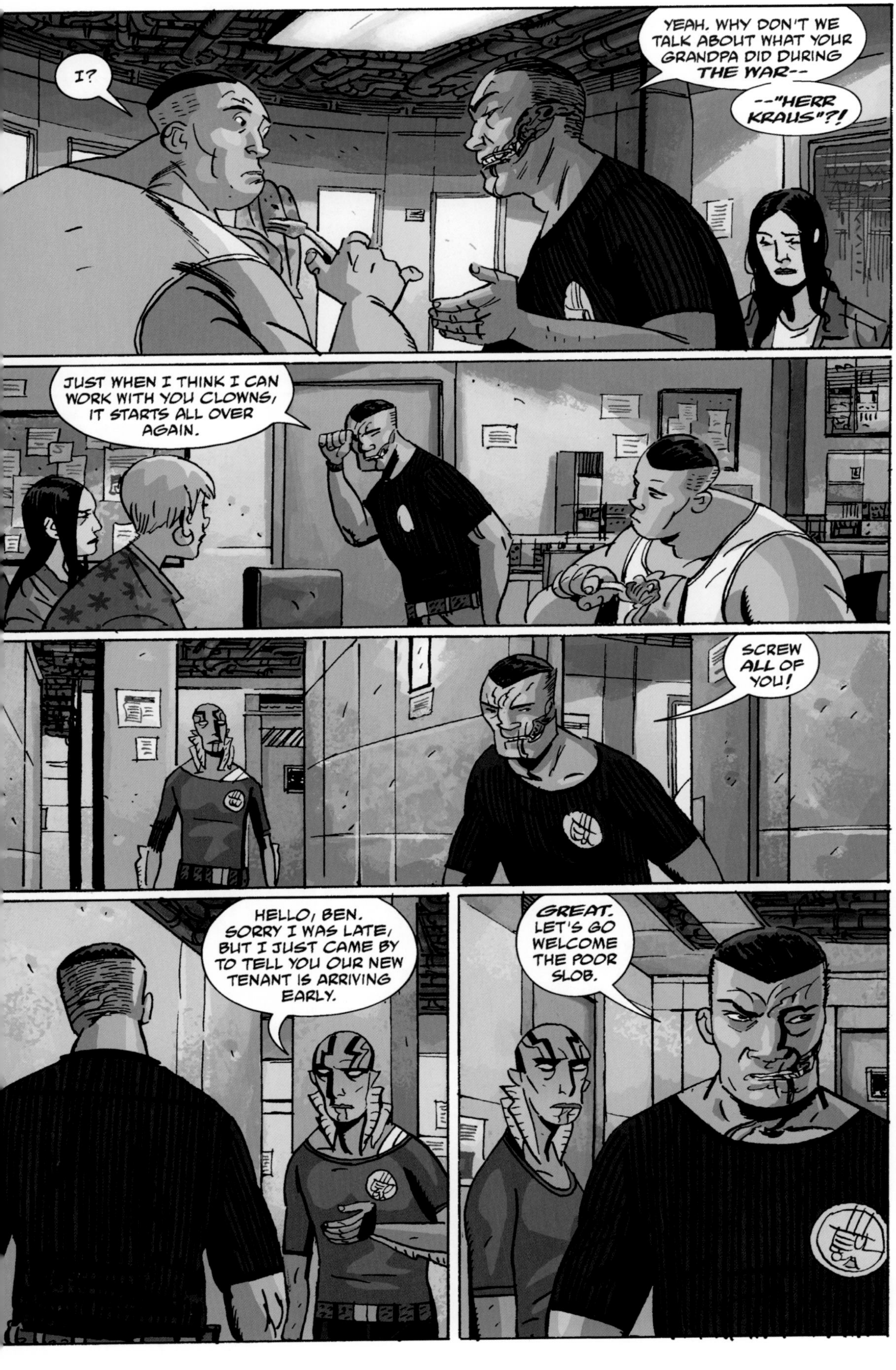
I?
YEAH. WHY DON'T WE TALK ABOUT WHAT YOUR GRANDPA DID DURING THE WAR--
--"HERR KRAUS"?!
JUST WHEN I THINK I CAN WORK WITH YOU CLOWNS, IT STARTS ALL OVER AGAIN.
SCREW ALL OF YOU!
HELLO, BEN. SORRY I WAS LATE, BUT I JUST CAME BY TO TELL YOU OUR NEW TENANT IS ARRIVING EARLY.
GREAT. LET'S GO WELCOME THE POOR SLOB.

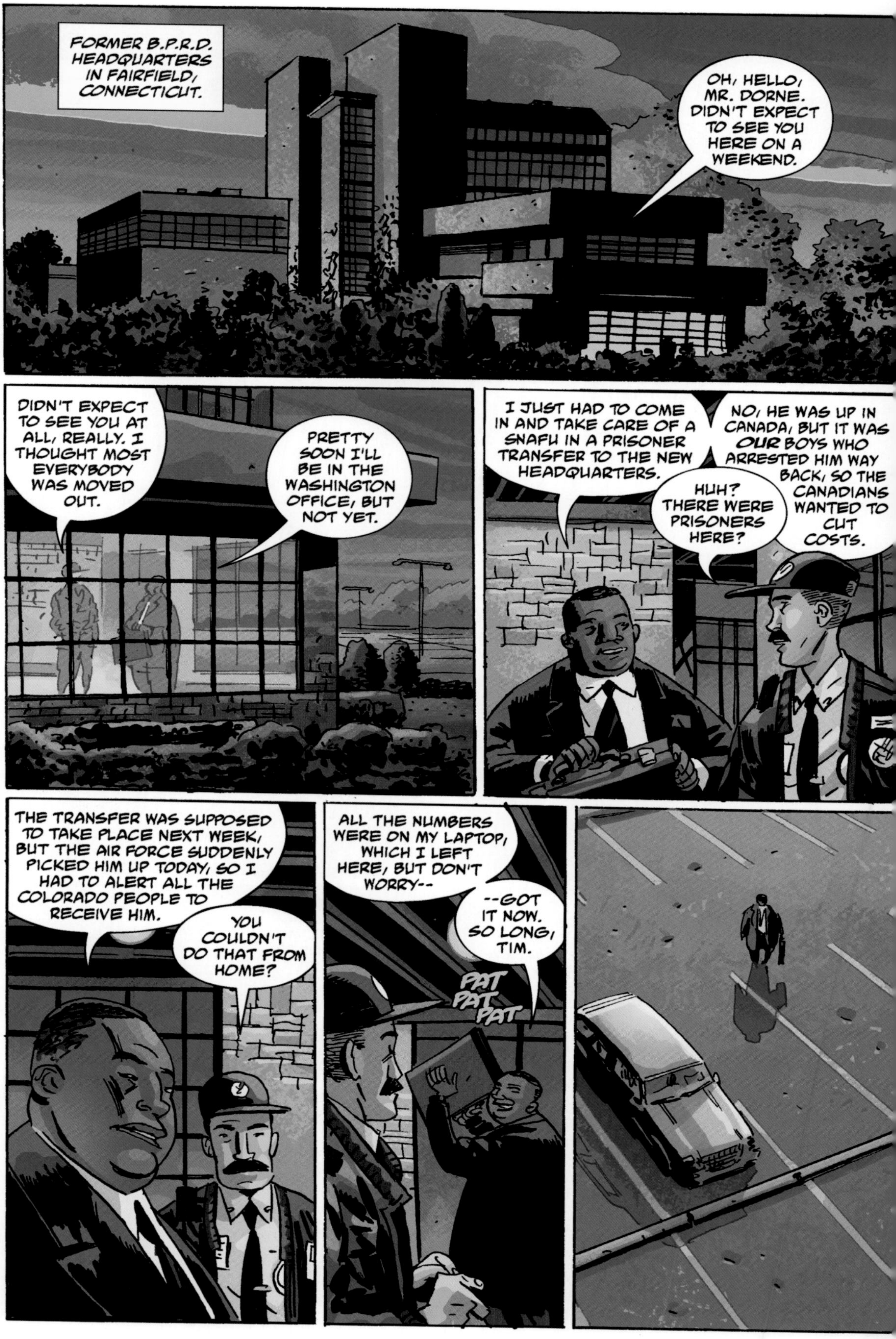
FORMER B.P.R.D. HEADQUARTERS IN FAIRFIELD, CONNECTICUT.
OH, HELLO, MR. DORNE. DIDN'T EXPECT TO SEE YOU HERE ON A WEEKEND.
DIDN'T EXPECT TO SEE YOU AT ALL, REALLY. I THOUGHT MOST EVERYBODY WAS MOVED OUT.
PRETTY SOON I'LL BE IN THE WASHINGTON OFFICE, BUT NOT YET.
I JUST HAD TO COME IN AND TAKE CARE OF A SNAFU IN A PRISONER TRANSFER TO THE NEW HEADQUARTERS.
HUH? THERE WERE PRISONERS HERE?
NO, HE WAS UP IN CANADA, BUT IT WAS OUR BOYS WHO ARRESTED HIM WAY BACK, SO THE CANADIANS WANTED TO CUT COSTS.
THE TRANSFER WAS SUPPOSED TO TAKE PLACE NEXT WEEK, BUT THE AIR FORCE SUDDENLY PICKED HIM UP TODAY, SO I HAD TO ALERT ALL THE COLORADO PEOPLE TO RECEIVE HIM.
YOU COULDN'T DO THAT FROM HOME?
ALL THE NUMBERS WERE ON MY LAPTOP, WHICH I LEFT HERE, BUT DON'T WORRY--
--GOT IT NOW. SO LONG, TIM.
PAT PAT PAT

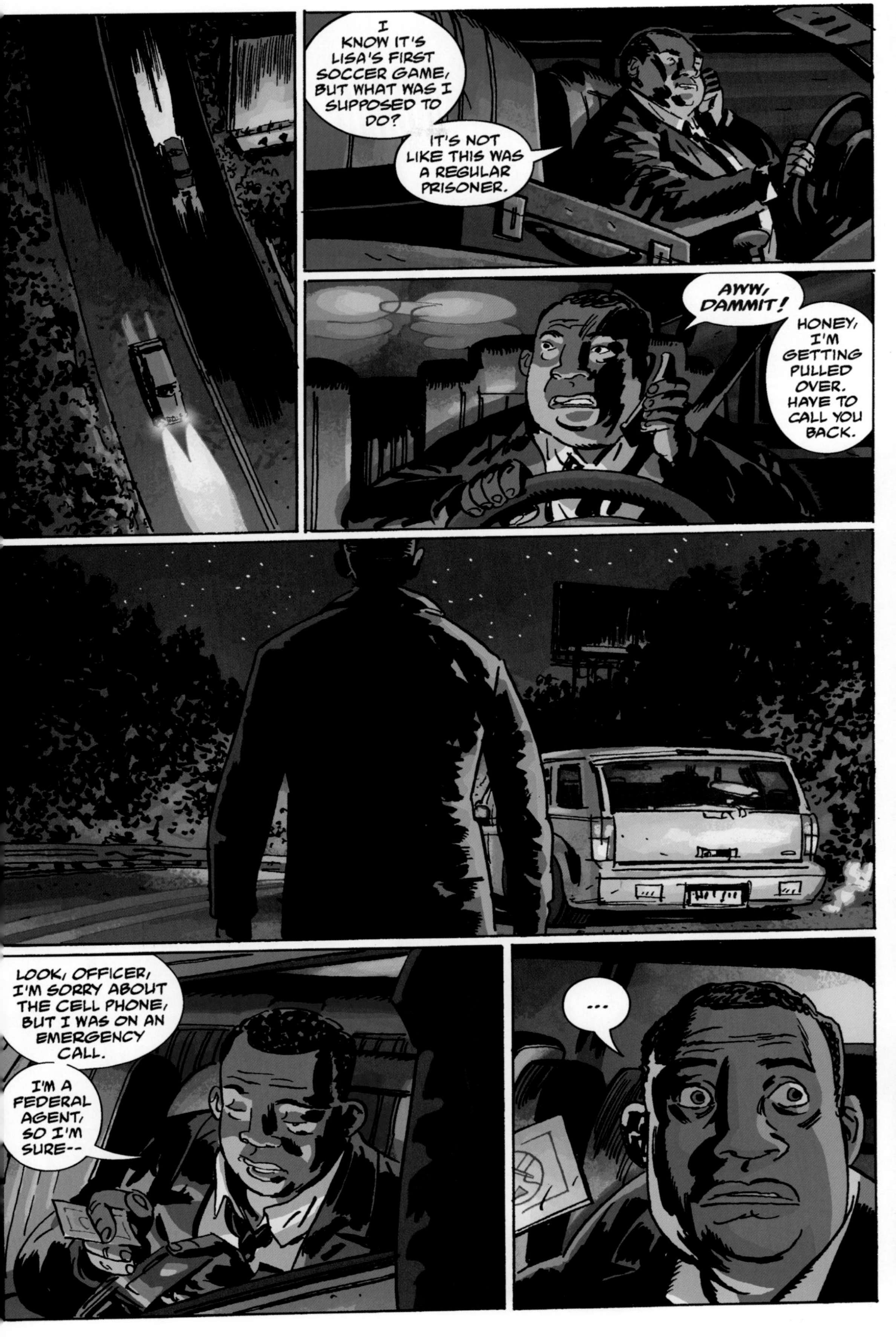
I KNOW IT'S LISA'S FIRST SOCCER GAME, BUT WHAT WAS I SUPPOSED TO DO?
IT'S NOT LIKE THIS WAS A REGULAR PRISONER.
AWW, DAMMIT!
HONEY, I'M GETTING PULLED OVER. HAVE TO CALL YOU BACK.
LOOK, OFFICER, I'M SORRY ABOUT THE CELL PHONE, BUT I WAS ON AN EMERGENCY CALL.
I'M A FEDERAL AGENT, SO I'M SURE--
...

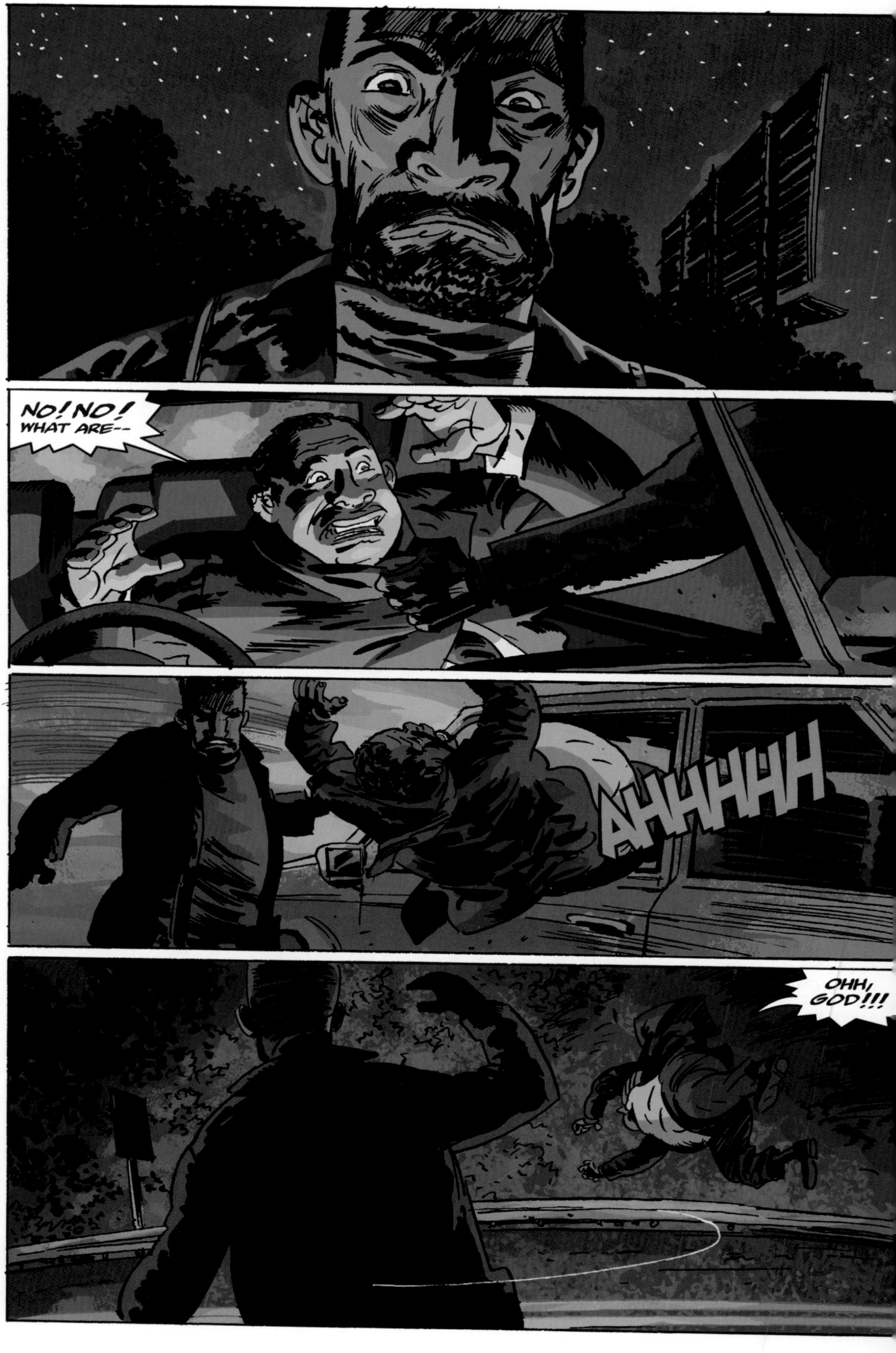
NO! NO! WHAT ARE--
AHHHHH
OHH, GOD!!!

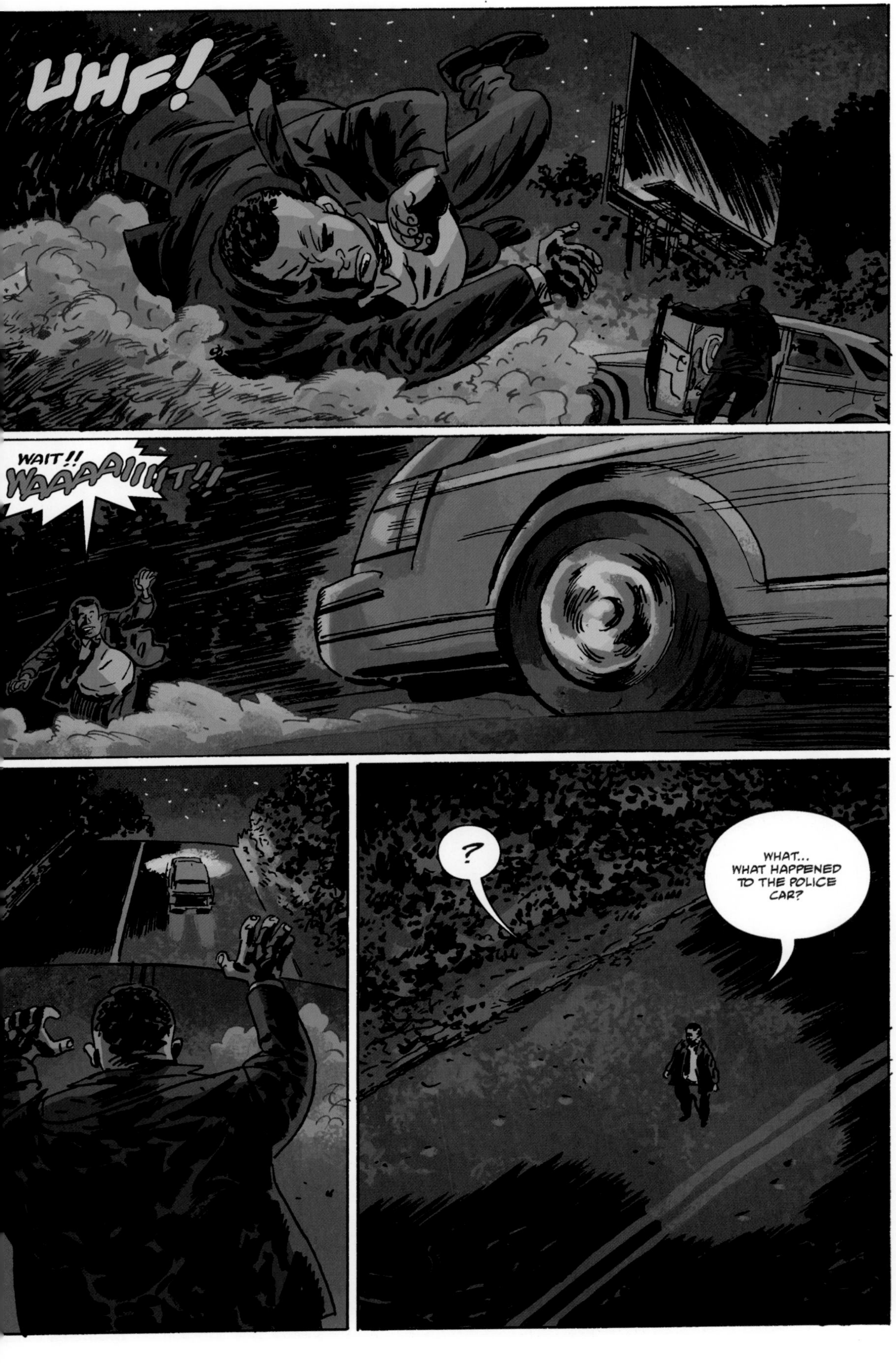
UHF!
WAIT!! WAAAAIIIIIT!!
?
WHAT... WHAT HAPPENED TO THE POLICE CAR?

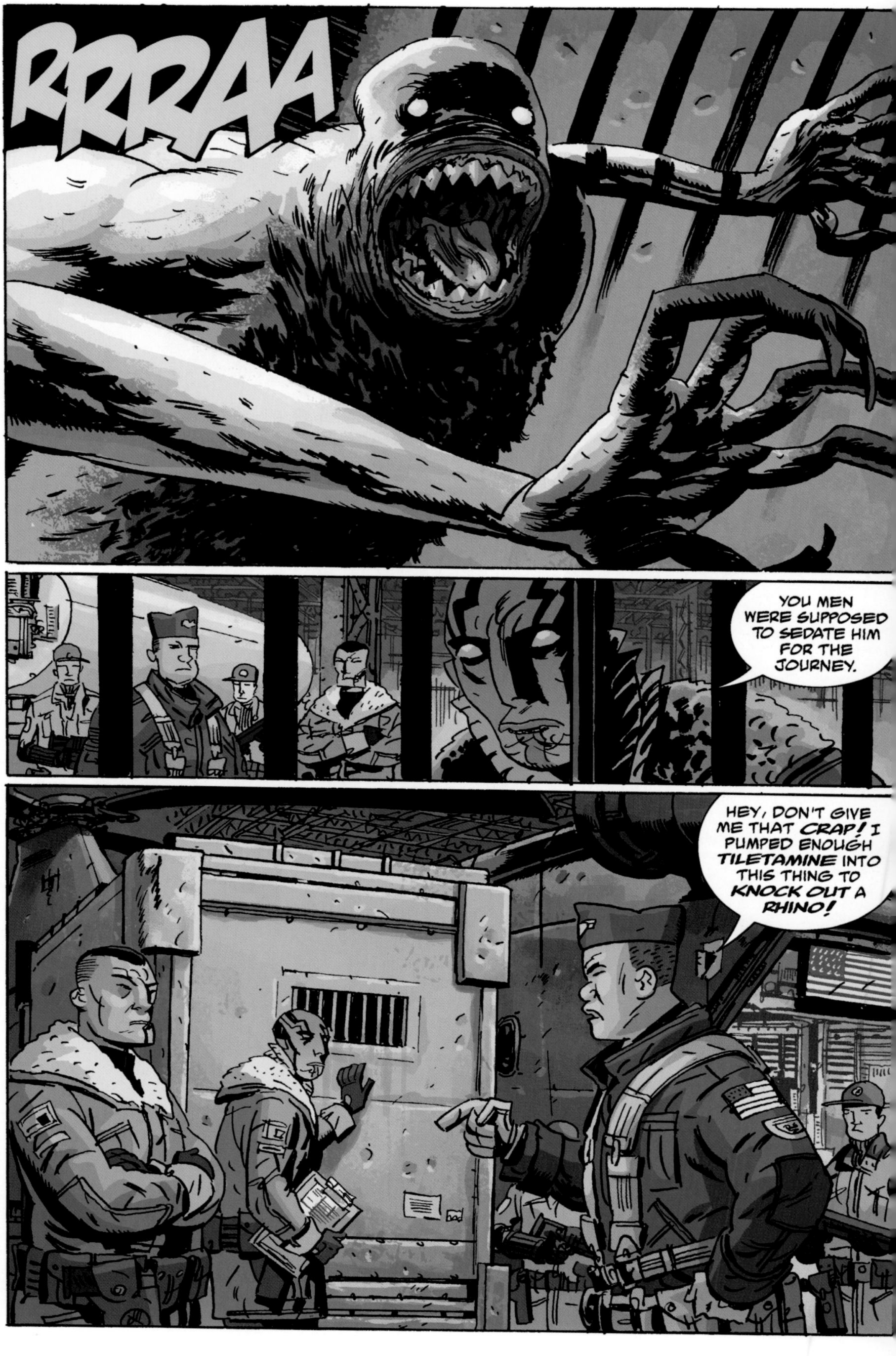
RRRAA
YOU MEN WERE SUPPOSED TO SEDATE HIM FOR THE JOURNEY.
HEY, DON'T GIVE ME THAT CRAP! I PUMPED ENOUGH TILETAMINE INTO THIS THING TO KNOCK OUT A RHINO!

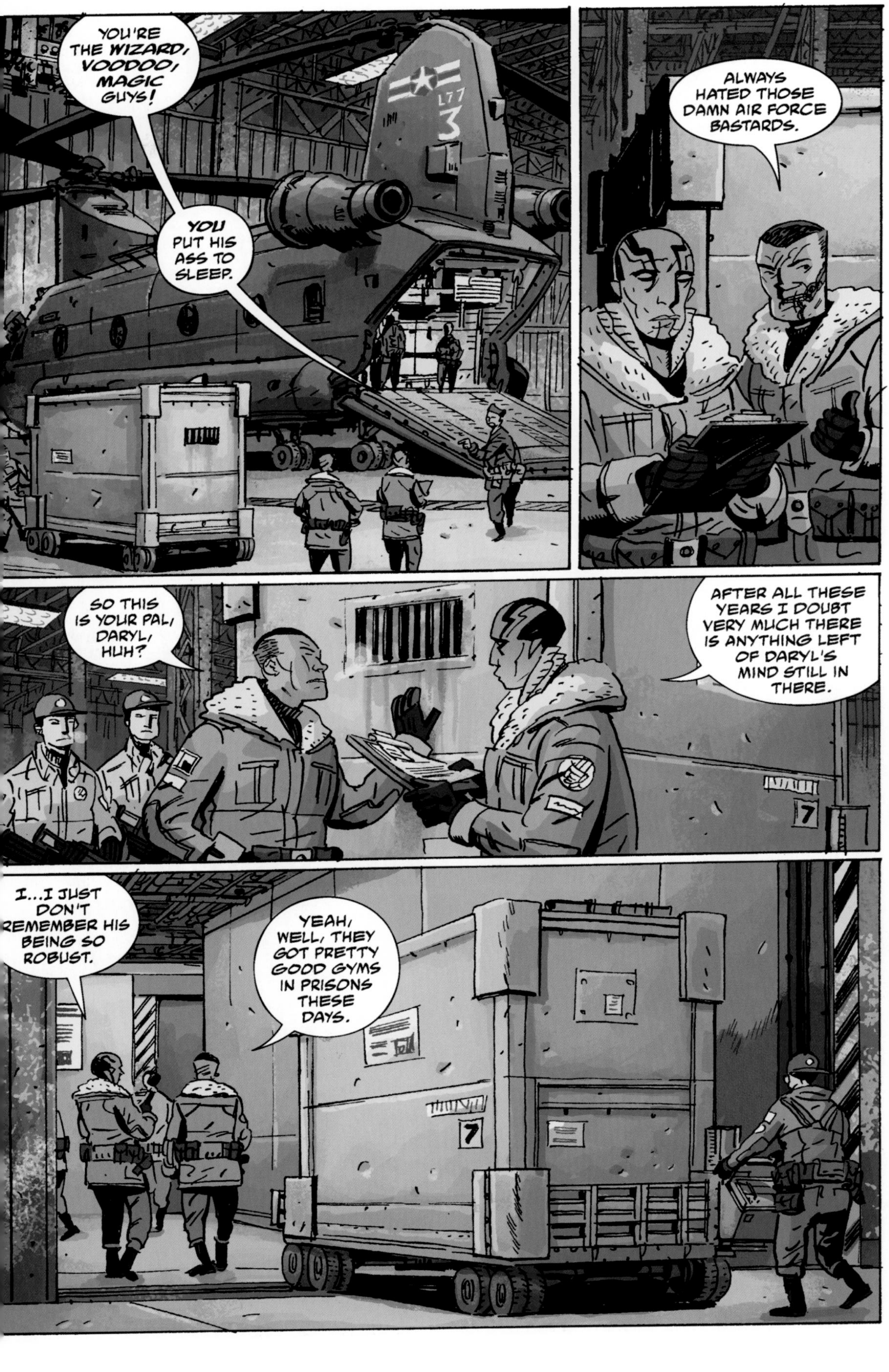
YOU'RE THE WIZARD, VOODOO, MAGIC GUYS!
YOU PUT HIS ASS TO SLEEP.
ALWAYS HATED THOSE DAMN AIR FORCE BASTARDS.
SO THIS IS YOUR PAL, DARYL, HUH?
AFTER ALL THESE YEARS I DOUBT VERY MUCH THERE IS ANYTHING LEFT OF DARYL'S MIND STILL IN THERE.
I...I JUST DON'T REMEMBER HIS BEING SO ROBUST.
YEAH, WELL, THEY GOT PRETTY GOOD GYMS IN PRISONS THESE DAYS.

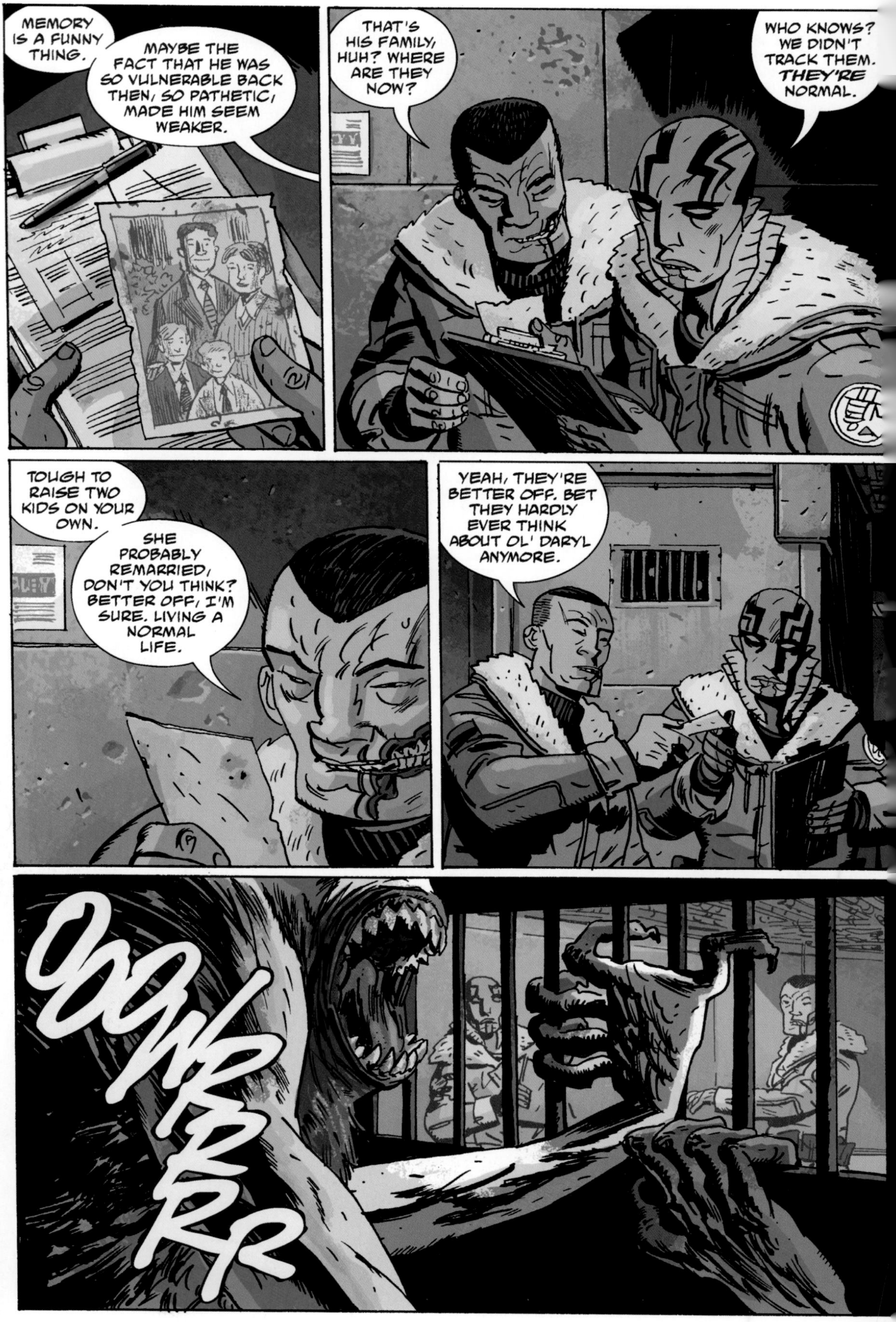
MEMORY IS A FUNNY THING.
MAYBE THE FACT THAT HE WAS SO VULNERABLE BACK THEN, SO PATHETIC, MADE HIM SEEM WEAKER.
THAT'S HIS FAMILY, HUH? WHERE ARE THEY NOW?
WHO KNOWS? WE DIDN'T TRACK THEM. *THEY'RE* NORMAL.
TOUGH TO RAISE TWO KIDS ON YOUR OWN.
SHE PROBABLY REMARRIED, DON'T YOU THINK? BETTER OFF, I'M SURE. LIVING A NORMAL LIFE.
YEAH, THEY'RE BETTER OFF. BET THEY HARDLY EVER THINK ABOUT OL' DARYL ANYMORE.
OOWRRRR

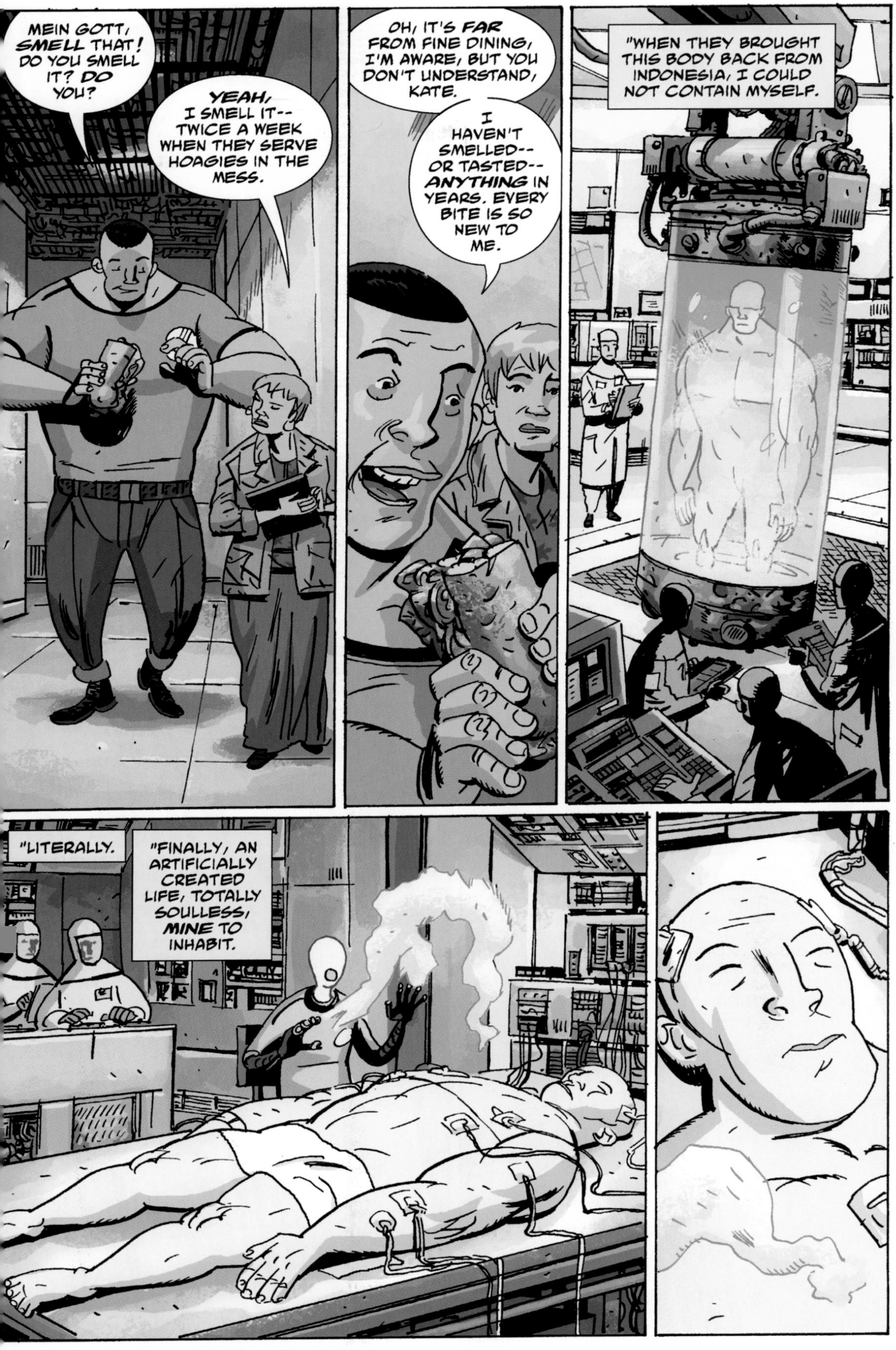
MEIN GOTT, SMELL THAT! DO YOU SMELL IT? DO YOU?
YEAH, I SMELL IT-- TWICE A WEEK WHEN THEY SERVE HOAGIES IN THE MESS.
OH, IT'S FAR FROM FINE DINING, I'M AWARE, BUT YOU DON'T UNDERSTAND, KATE.
I HAVEN'T SMELLED-- OR TASTED-- ANYTHING IN YEARS. EVERY BITE IS SO NEW TO ME.
"WHEN THEY BROUGHT THIS BODY BACK FROM INDONESIA, I COULD NOT CONTAIN MYSELF.
"LITERALLY.
"FINALLY, AN ARTIFICIALLY CREATED LIFE, TOTALLY SOULLESS, MINE TO INHABIT.

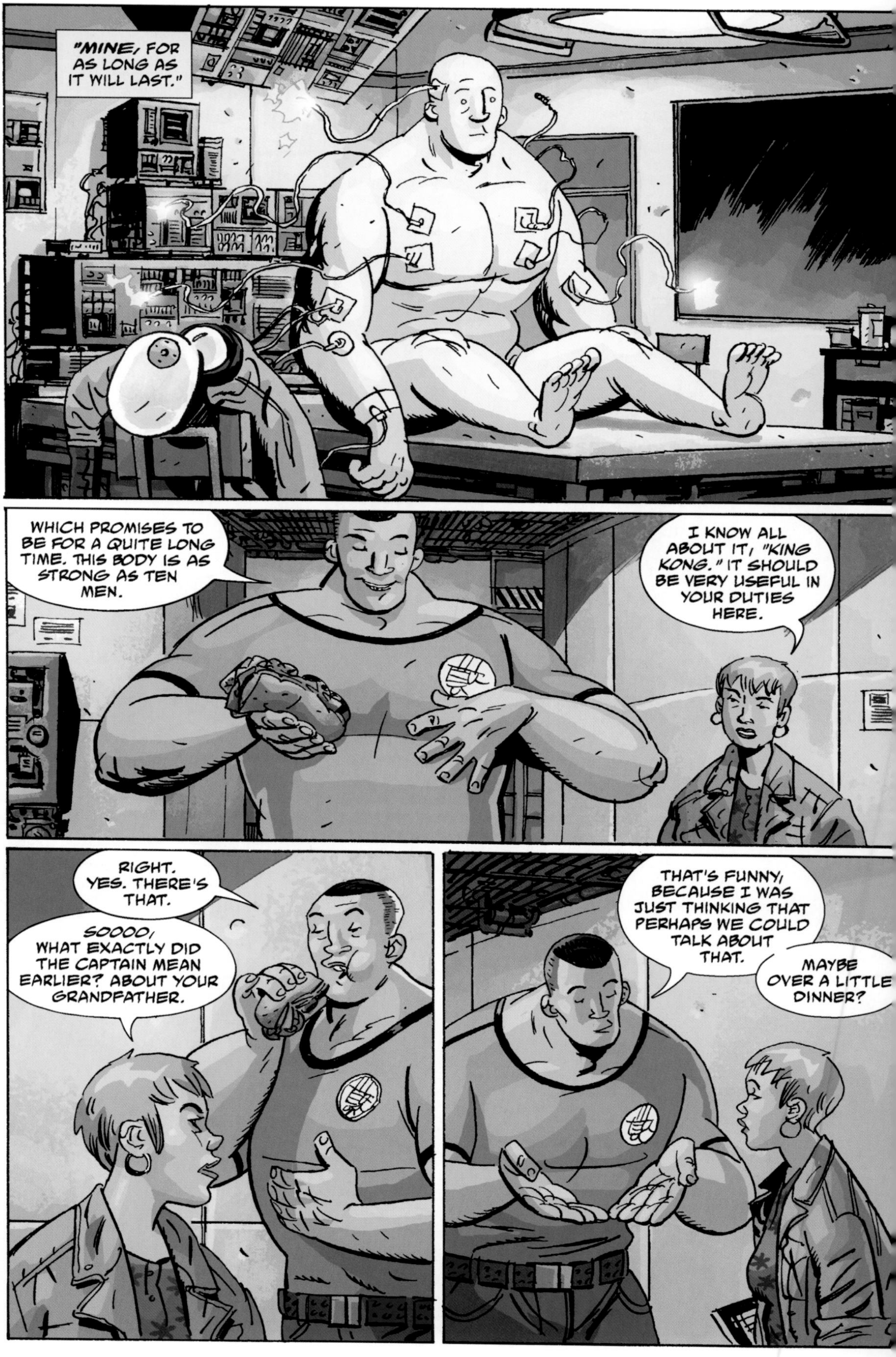
"MINE, FOR AS LONG AS IT WILL LAST."
WHICH PROMISES TO BE FOR A QUITE LONG TIME. THIS BODY IS AS STRONG AS TEN MEN.
I KNOW ALL ABOUT IT, "KING KONG." IT SHOULD BE VERY USEFUL IN YOUR DUTIES HERE.
RIGHT. YES. THERE'S THAT.
SOOOO, WHAT EXACTLY DID THE CAPTAIN MEAN EARLIER? ABOUT YOUR GRANDFATHER.
THAT'S FUNNY, BECAUSE I WAS JUST THINKING THAT PERHAPS WE COULD TALK ABOUT THAT.
MAYBE OVER A LITTLE DINNER?

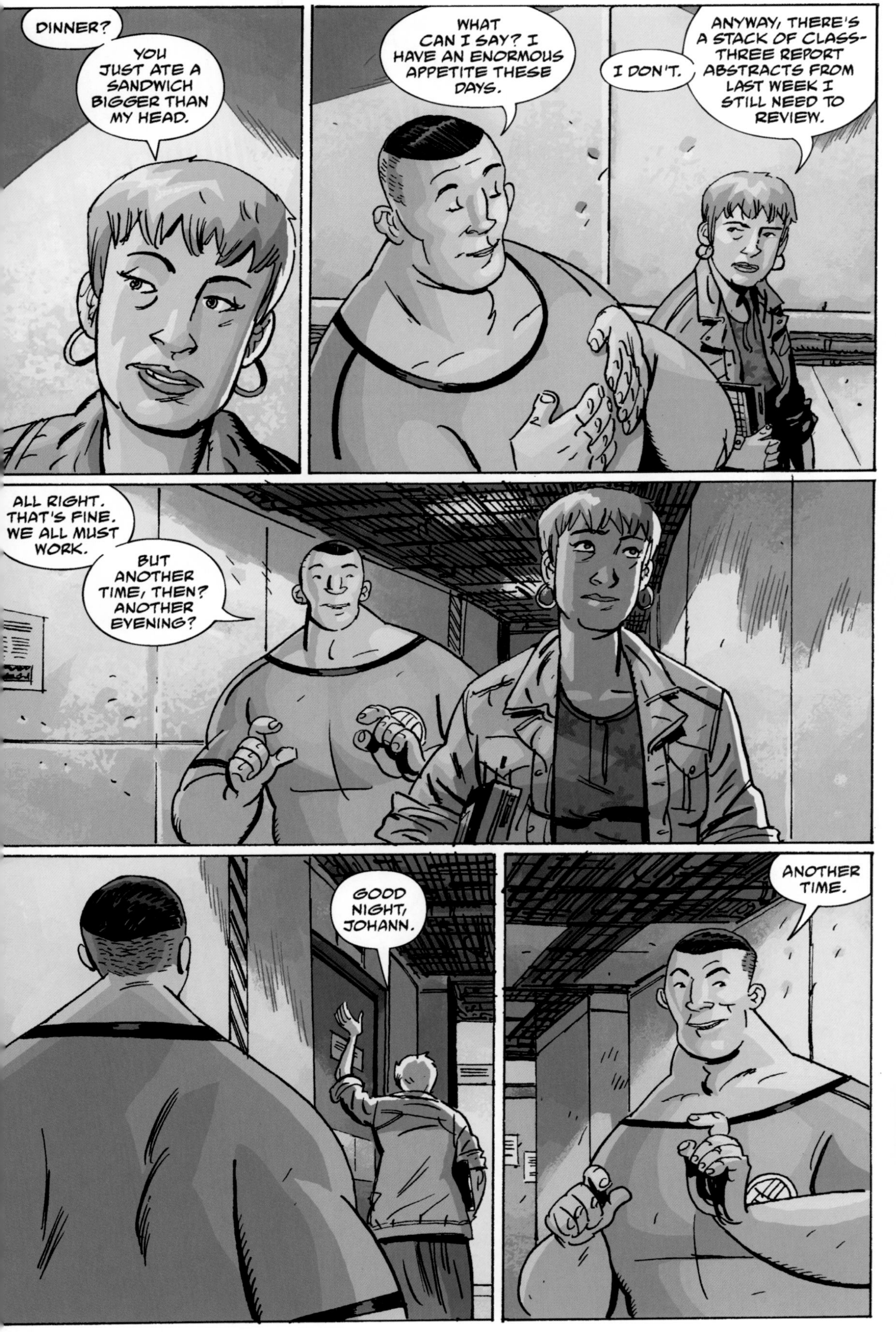
DINNER?
YOU JUST ATE A SANDWICH BIGGER THAN MY HEAD.
WHAT CAN I SAY? I HAVE AN ENORMOUS APPETITE THESE DAYS.
I DON'T.
ANYWAY, THERE'S A STACK OF CLASS-THREE REPORT ABSTRACTS FROM LAST WEEK I STILL NEED TO REVIEW.
ALL RIGHT. THAT'S FINE. WE ALL MUST WORK.
BUT ANOTHER TIME, THEN? ANOTHER EVENING?
GOOD NIGHT, JOHANN.
ANOTHER TIME.

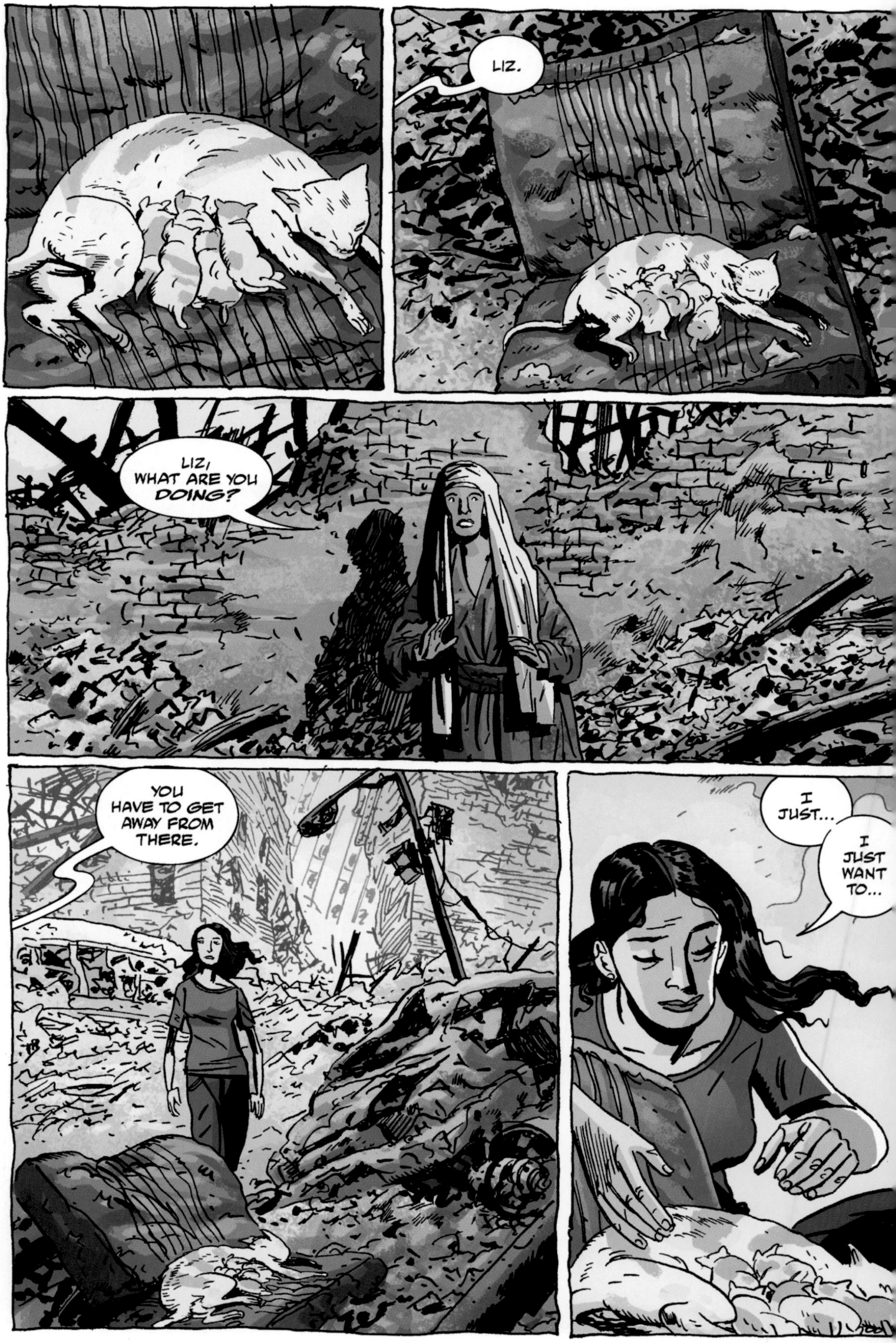
LIZ.
LIZ, WHAT ARE YOU DOING?
YOU HAVE TO GET AWAY FROM THERE.
I JUST...
I JUST WANT TO...

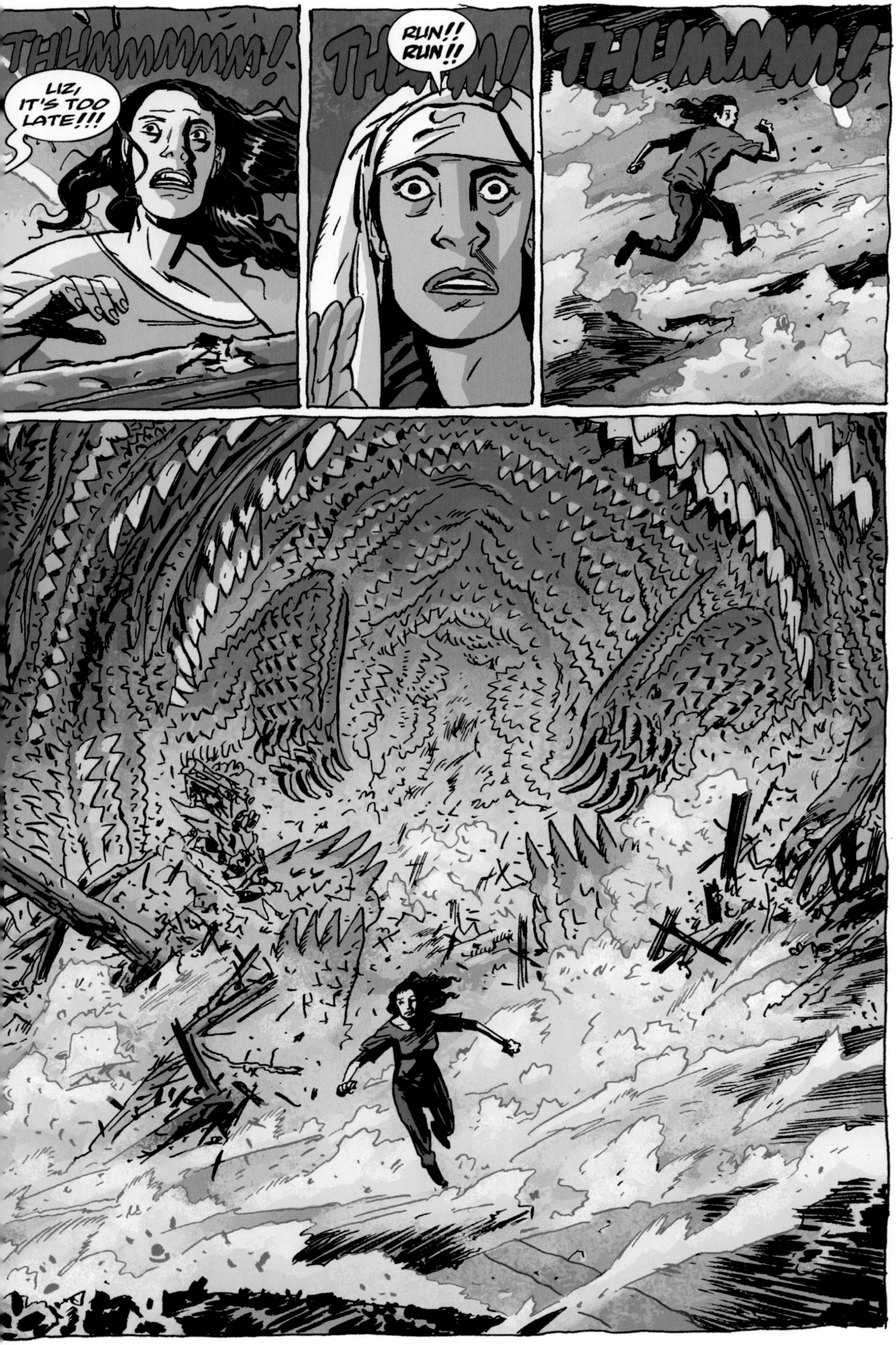
THUMMMMM!
LIZ, IT'S TOO LATE!!!
THUM!
RUN!! RUN!!
THUMMM!

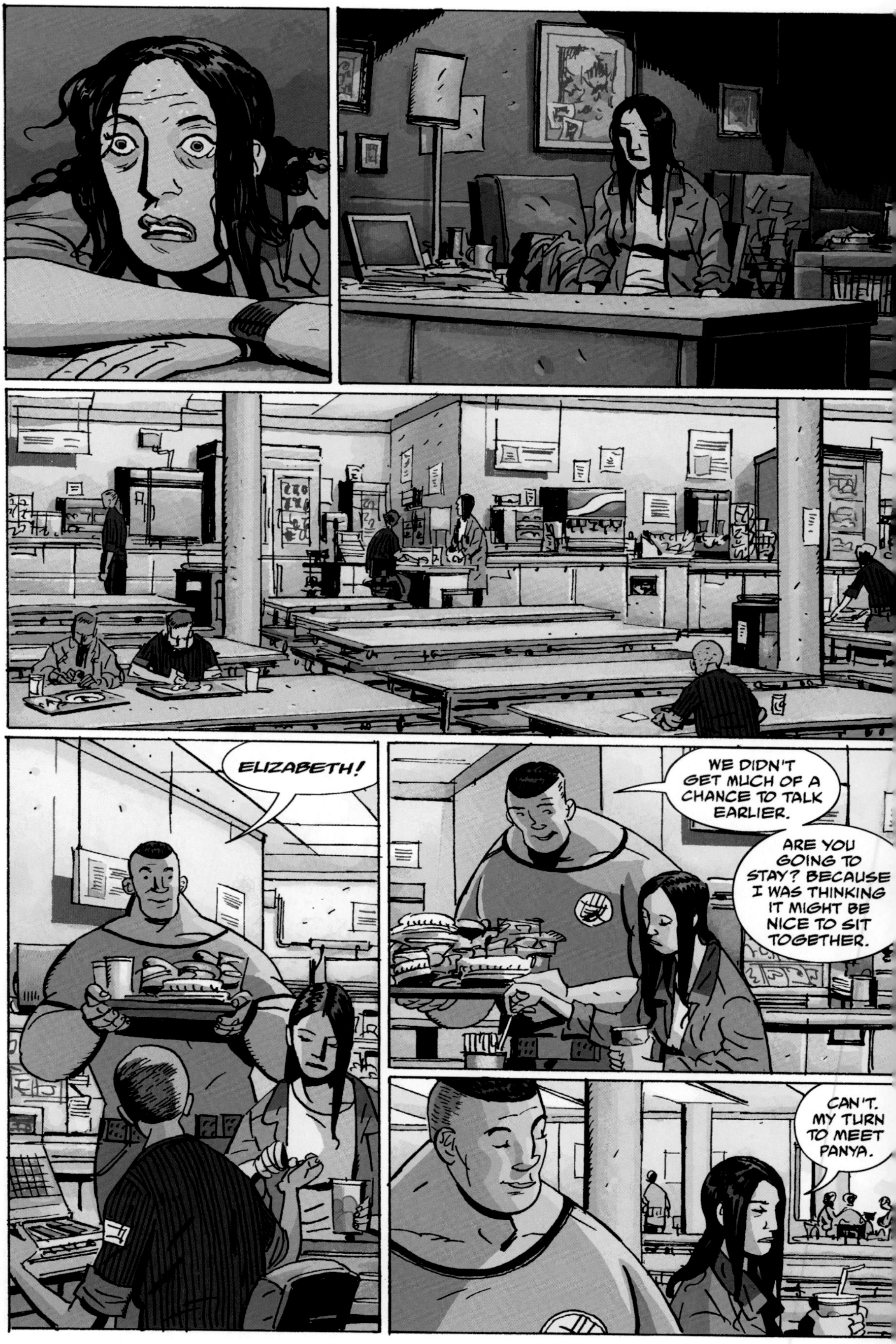
ELIZABETH!
WE DIDN'T GET MUCH OF A CHANCE TO TALK EARLIER.
ARE YOU GOING TO STAY? BECAUSE I WAS THINKING IT MIGHT BE NICE TO SIT TOGETHER.
CAN'T. MY TURN TO MEET PANYA.

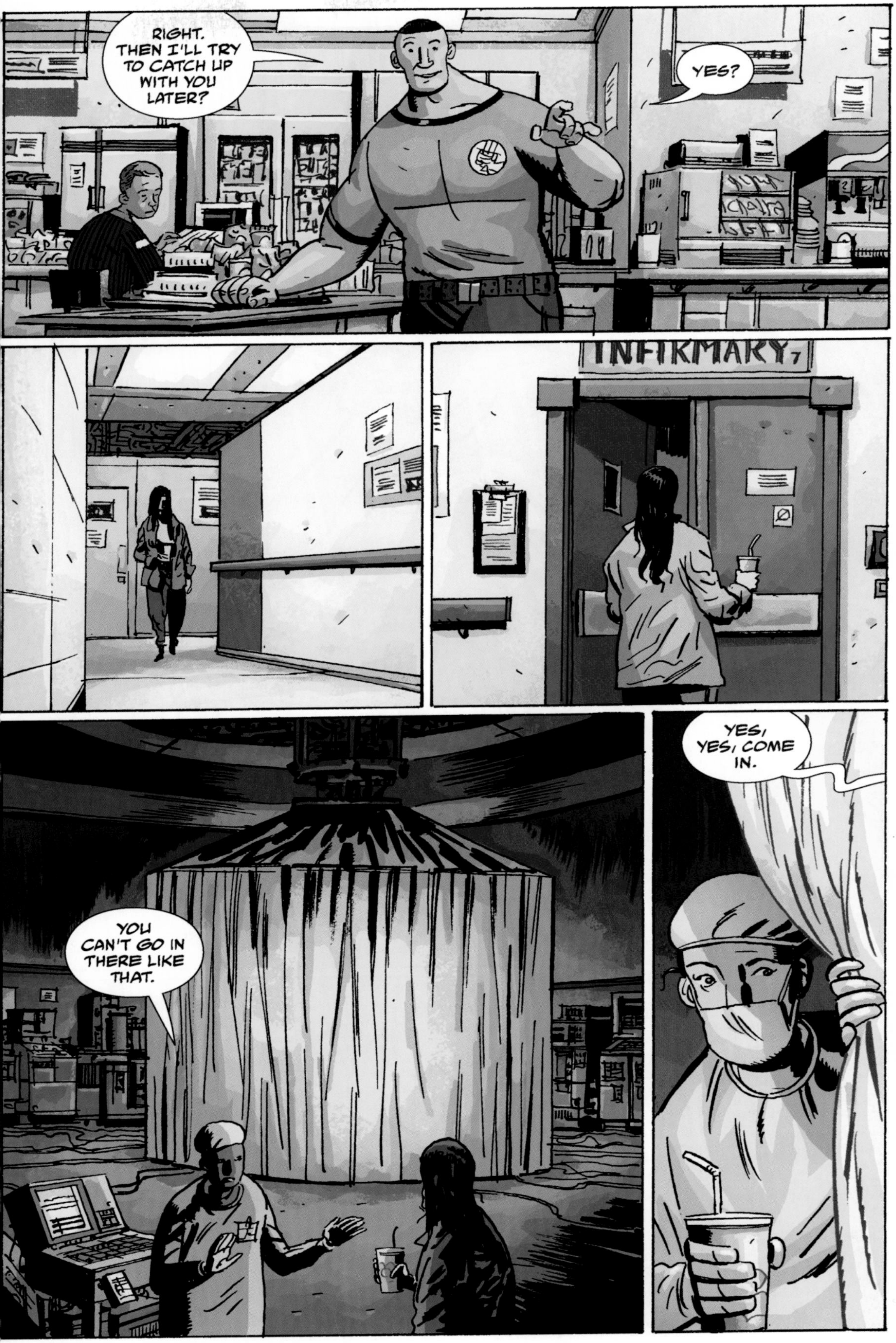
RIGHT. THEN I'LL TRY TO CATCH UP WITH YOU LATER?
YES?
INFIRMARY
YOU CAN'T GO IN THERE LIKE THAT.
YES, YES, COME IN.

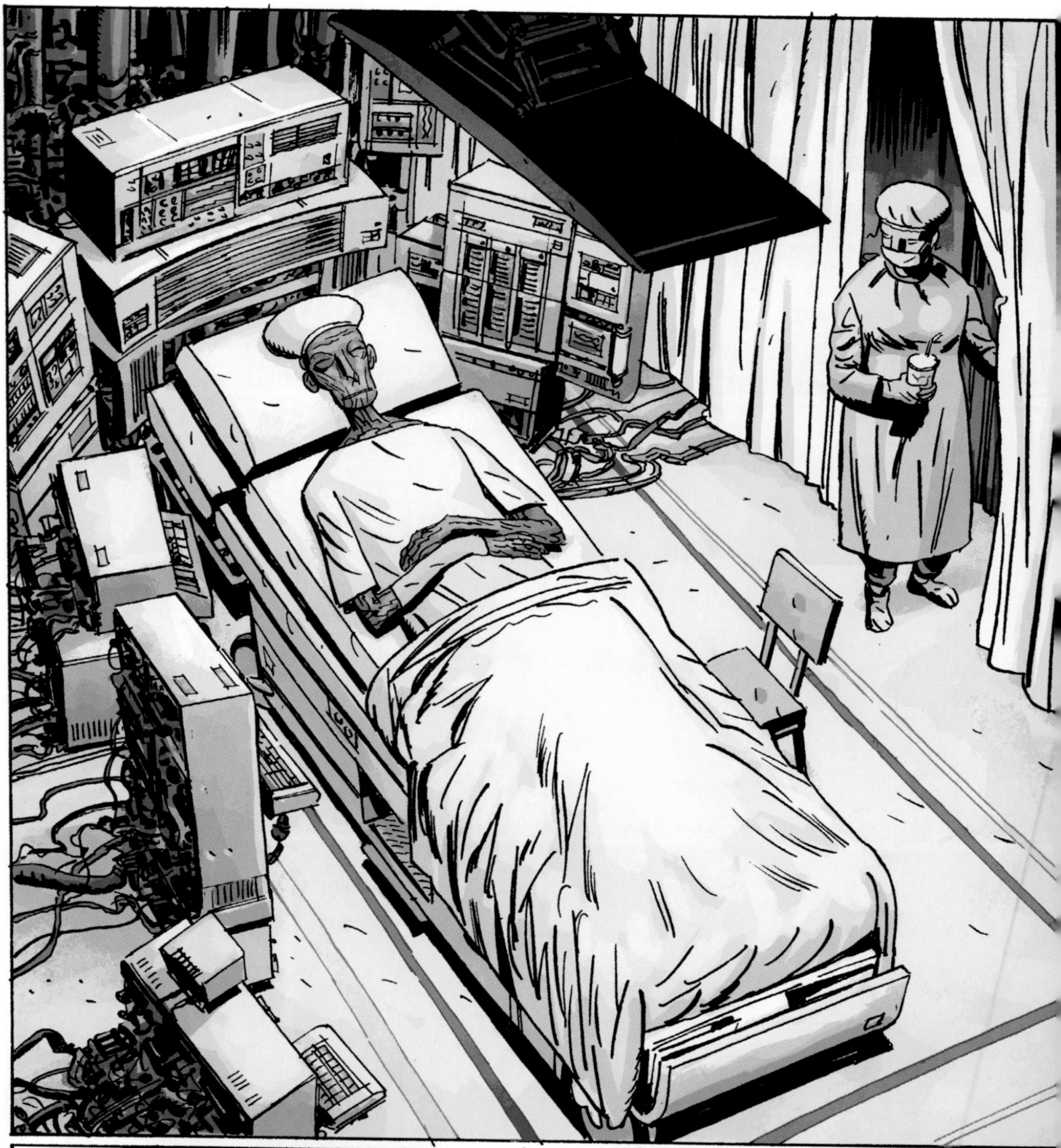

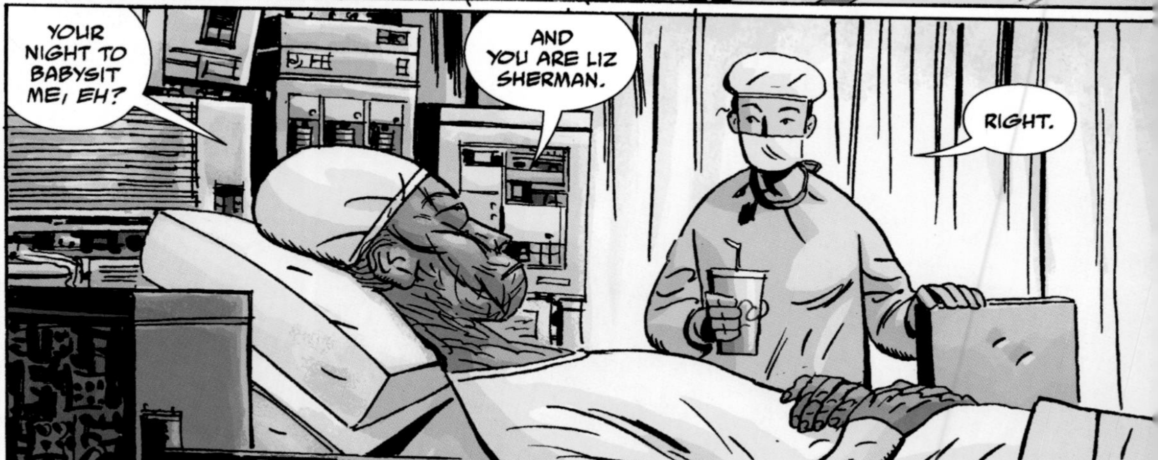
YOUR NIGHT TO BABYSIT ME, EH?
AND YOU ARE LIZ SHERMAN.
RIGHT.

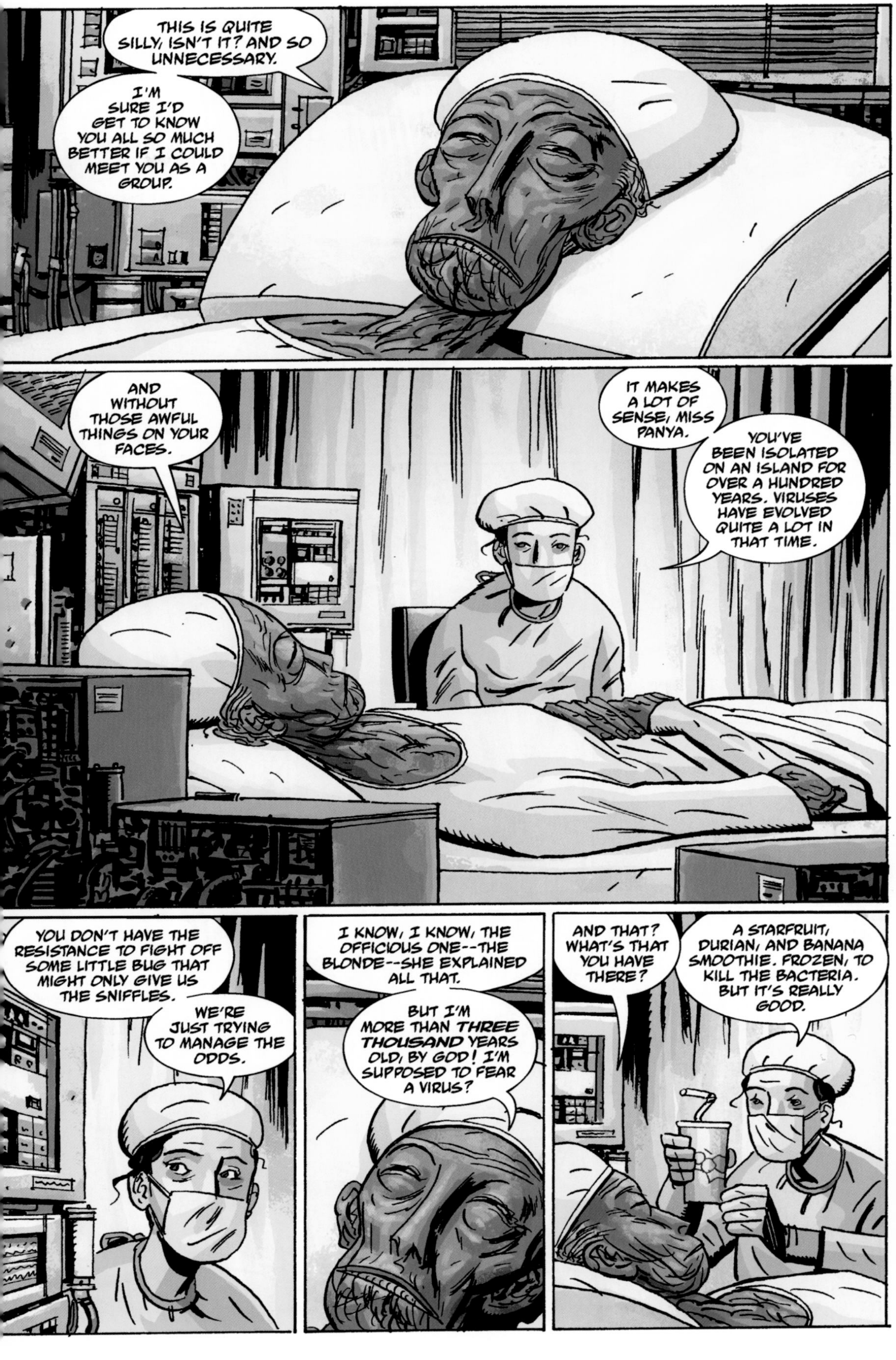
THIS IS QUITE SILLY, ISN'T IT? AND SO UNNECESSARY.
I'M SURE I'D GET TO KNOW YOU ALL SO MUCH BETTER IF I COULD MEET YOU AS A GROUP.
AND WITHOUT THOSE AWFUL THINGS ON YOUR FACES.
IT MAKES A LOT OF SENSE, MISS PANYA.
YOU'VE BEEN ISOLATED ON AN ISLAND FOR OVER A HUNDRED YEARS. VIRUSES HAVE EVOLVED QUITE A LOT IN THAT TIME.
YOU DON'T HAVE THE RESISTANCE TO FIGHT OFF SOME LITTLE BUG THAT MIGHT ONLY GIVE US THE SNIFFLES.
WE'RE JUST TRYING TO MANAGE THE ODDS.
I KNOW, I KNOW, THE OFFICIOUS ONE--THE BLONDE--SHE EXPLAINED ALL THAT.
BUT I'M MORE THAN *THREE THOUSAND* YEARS OLD, BY GOD! I'M SUPPOSED TO FEAR A VIRUS?
AND THAT? WHAT'S THAT YOU HAVE THERE?
A STARFRUIT, DURIAN, AND BANANA SMOOTHIE. FROZEN, TO KILL THE BACTERIA. BUT IT'S REALLY GOOD.

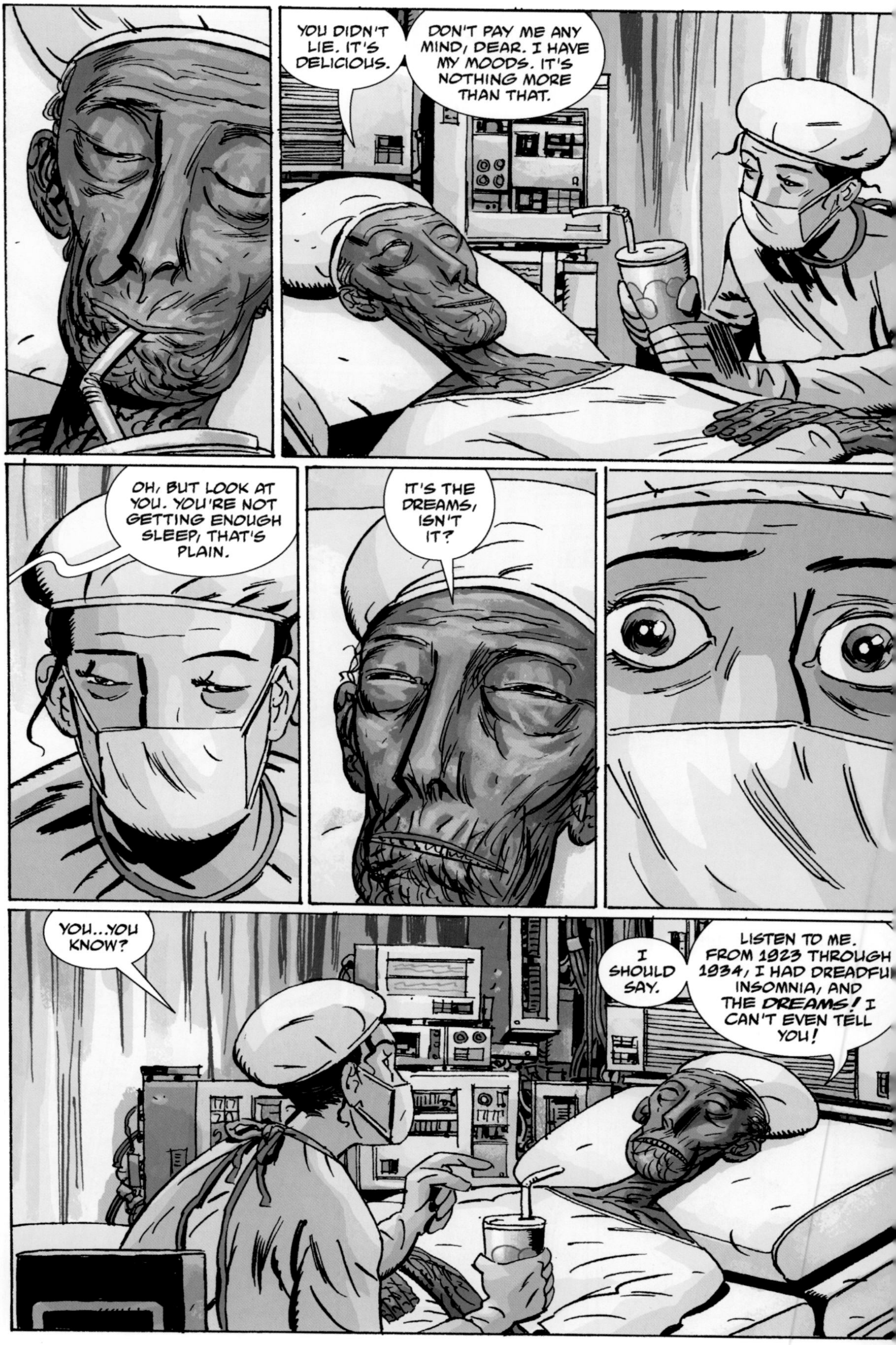
YOU DIDN'T LIE. IT'S DELICIOUS.
DON'T PAY ME ANY MIND, DEAR. I HAVE MY MOODS. IT'S NOTHING MORE THAN THAT.
OH, BUT LOOK AT YOU. YOU'RE NOT GETTING ENOUGH SLEEP, THAT'S PLAIN.
IT'S THE DREAMS, ISN'T IT?
YOU...YOU KNOW?
I SHOULD SAY.
LISTEN TO ME. FROM 1923 THROUGH 1934, I HAD DREADFUL INSOMNIA, AND THE DREAMS! I CAN'T EVEN TELL YOU!

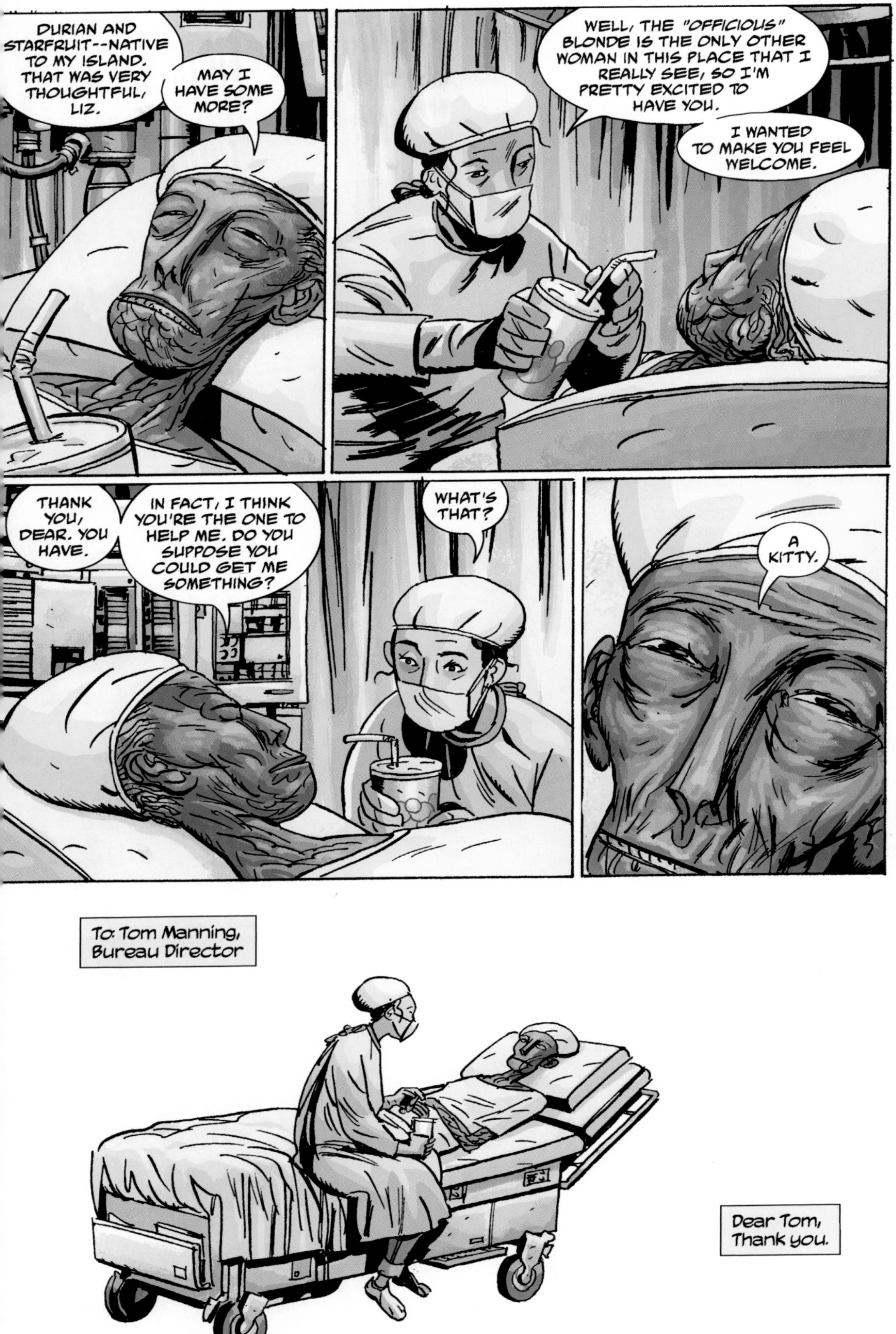
DURIAN AND STARFRUIT--NATIVE TO MY ISLAND. THAT WAS VERY THOUGHTFUL, LIZ.
MAY I HAVE SOME MORE?
WELL, THE "OFFICIOUS" BLONDE IS THE ONLY OTHER WOMAN IN THIS PLACE THAT I REALLY SEE, SO I'M PRETTY EXCITED TO HAVE YOU.
I WANTED TO MAKE YOU FEEL WELCOME.
THANK YOU, DEAR. YOU HAVE.
IN FACT, I THINK YOU'RE THE ONE TO HELP ME. DO YOU SUPPOSE YOU COULD GET ME SOMETHING?
WHAT'S THAT?
A KITTY.
To: Tom Manning, Bureau Director
Dear Tom, Thank you.

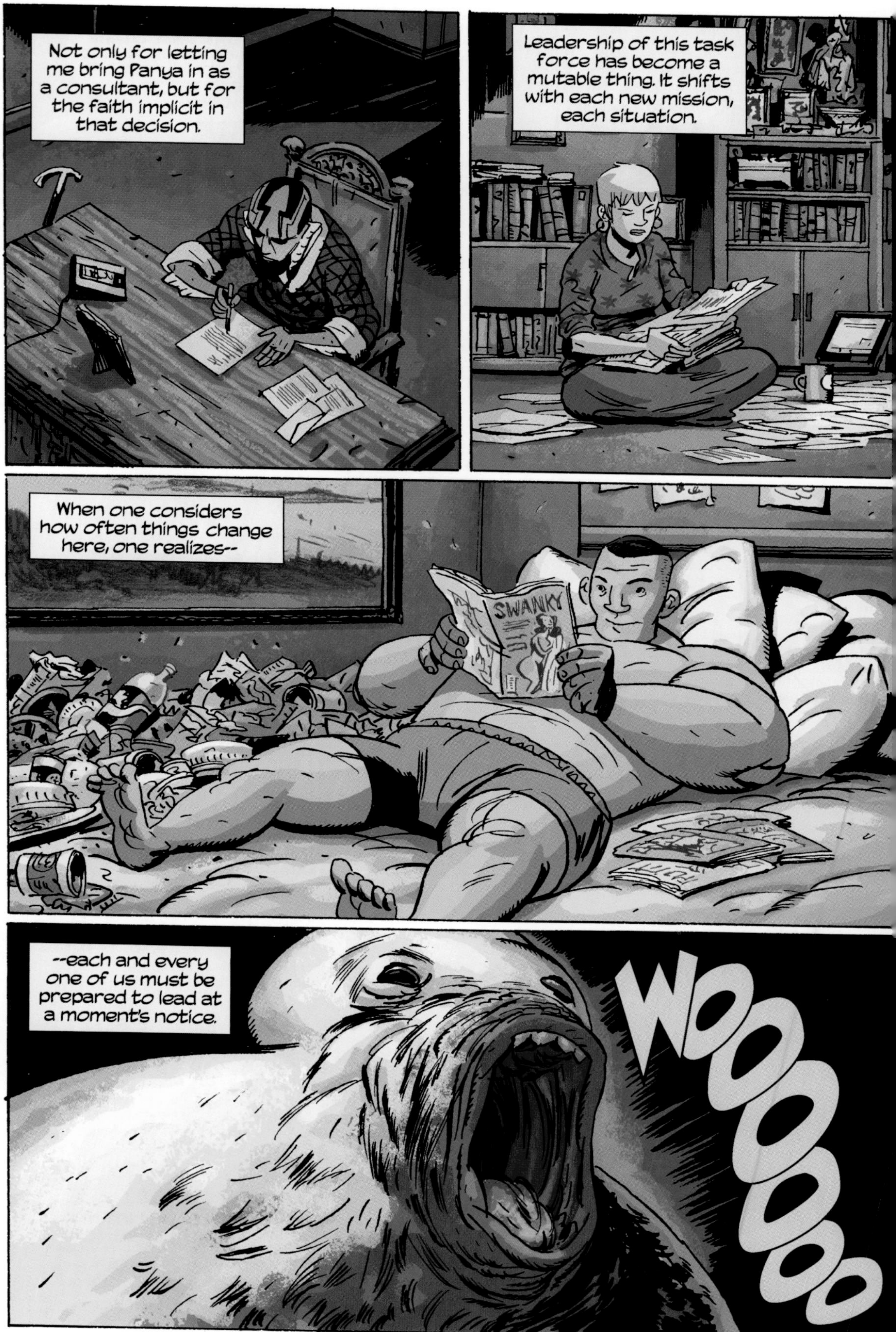
Not only for letting me bring Panya in as a consultant, but for the faith implicit in that decision.
Leadership of this task force has become a mutable thing. It shifts with each new mission, each situation.
When one considers how often things change here, one realizes--
SWANKY
--each and every one of us must be prepared to lead at a moment's notice.
WOOOOOOO

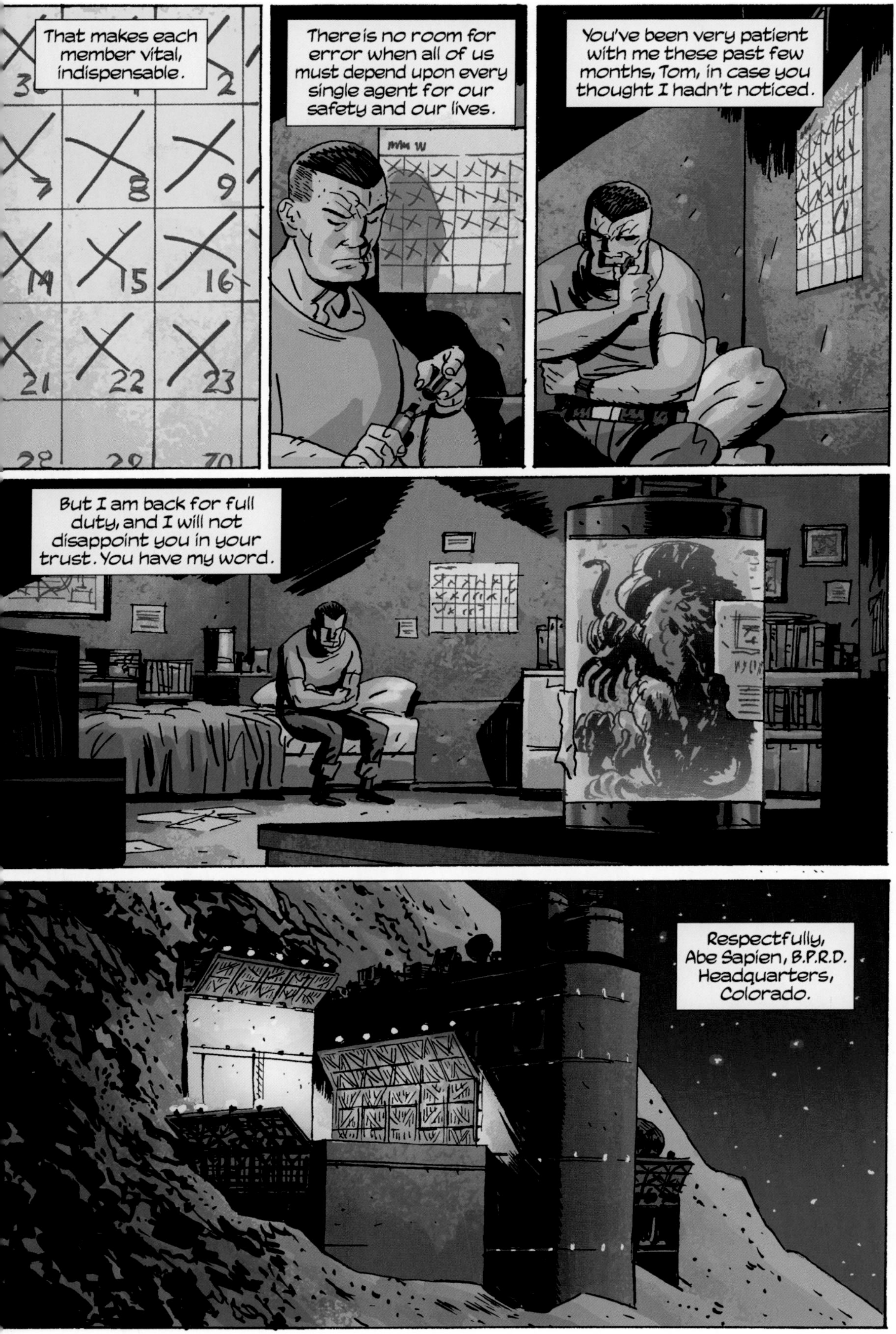
That makes each member vital, indispensable.
There is no room for error when all of us must depend upon every single agent for our safety and our lives.
You've been very patient with me these past few months, Tom, in case you thought I hadn't noticed.
But I am back for full duty, and I will not disappoint you in your trust. You have my word.
Respectfully, Abe Sapien, B.P.R.D. Headquarters, Colorado.

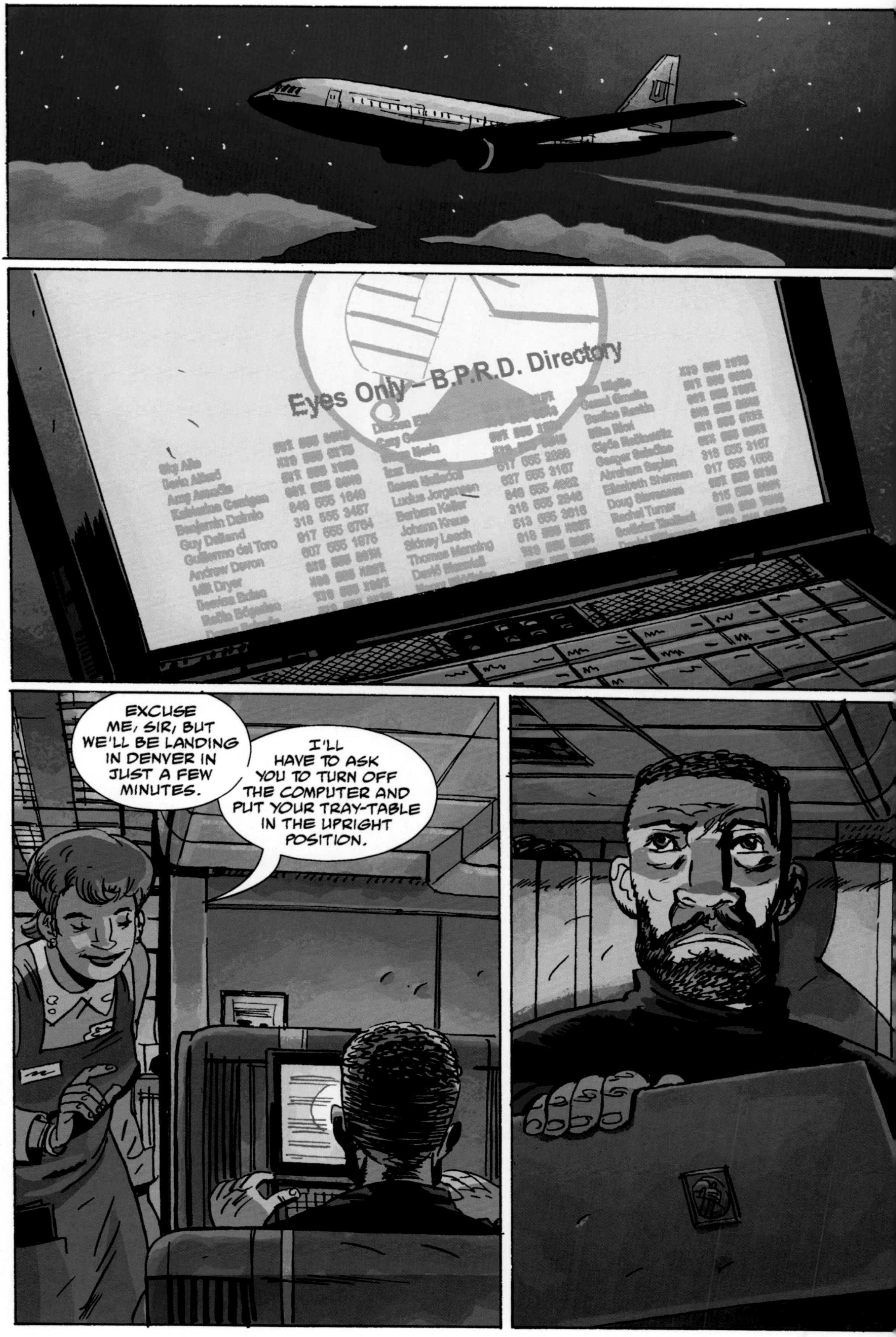

Eyes Only – B.P.R.D. Directory
EXCUSE ME, SIR, BUT WE'LL BE LANDING IN DENVER IN JUST A FEW MINUTES.
I'LL HAVE TO ASK YOU TO TURN OFF THE COMPUTER AND PUT YOUR TRAY-TABLE IN THE UPRIGHT POSITION.

Chapter Two

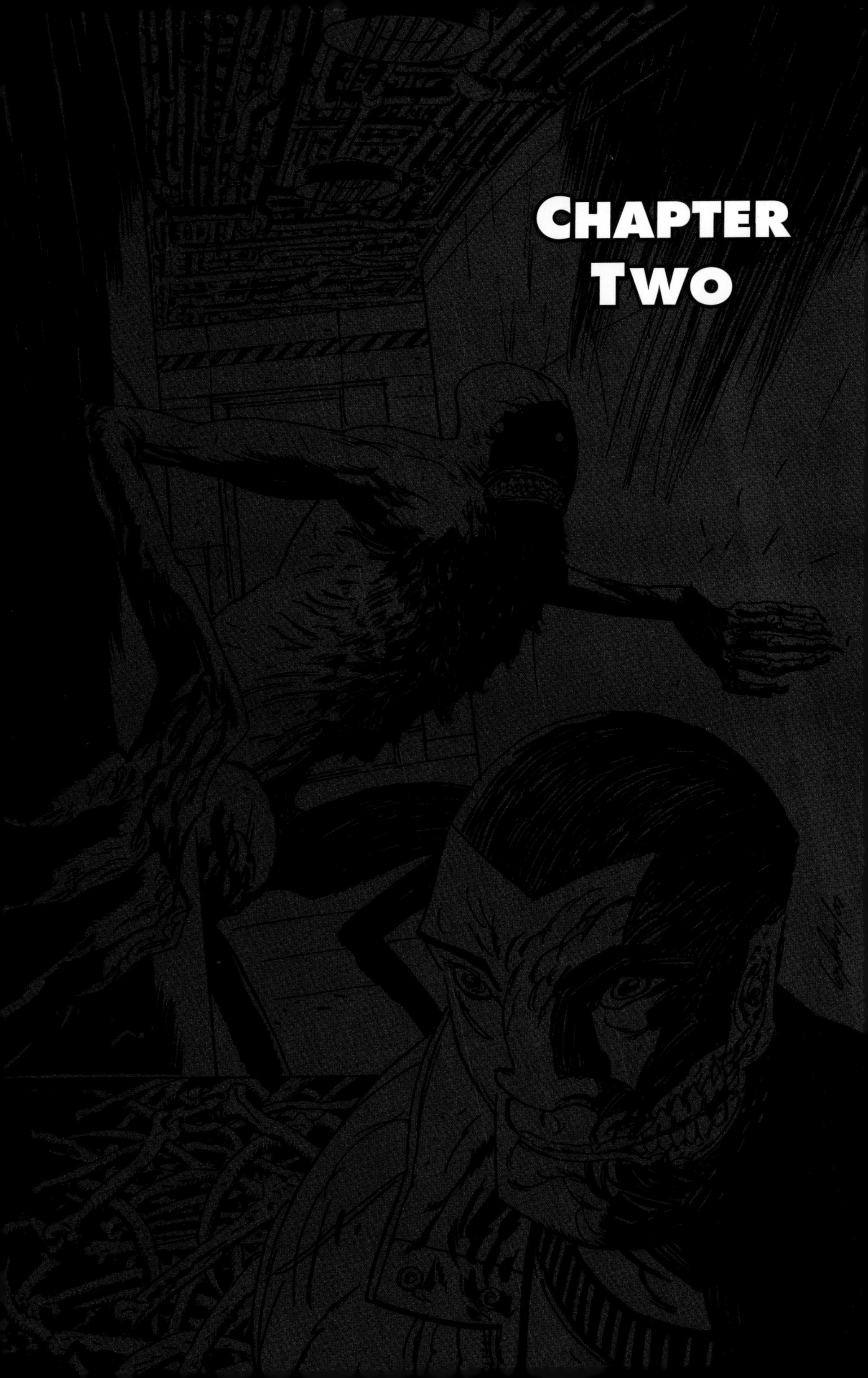

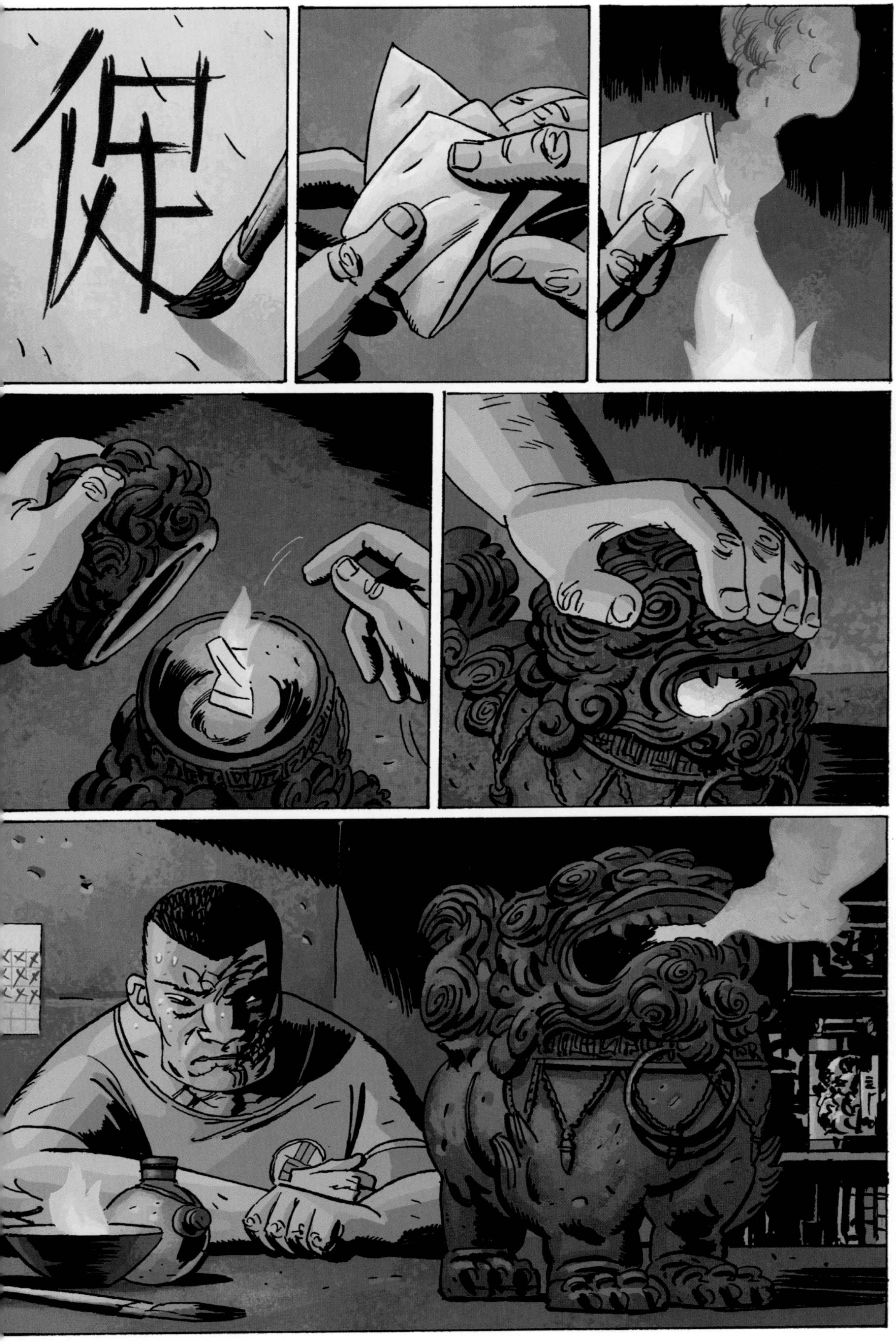
促

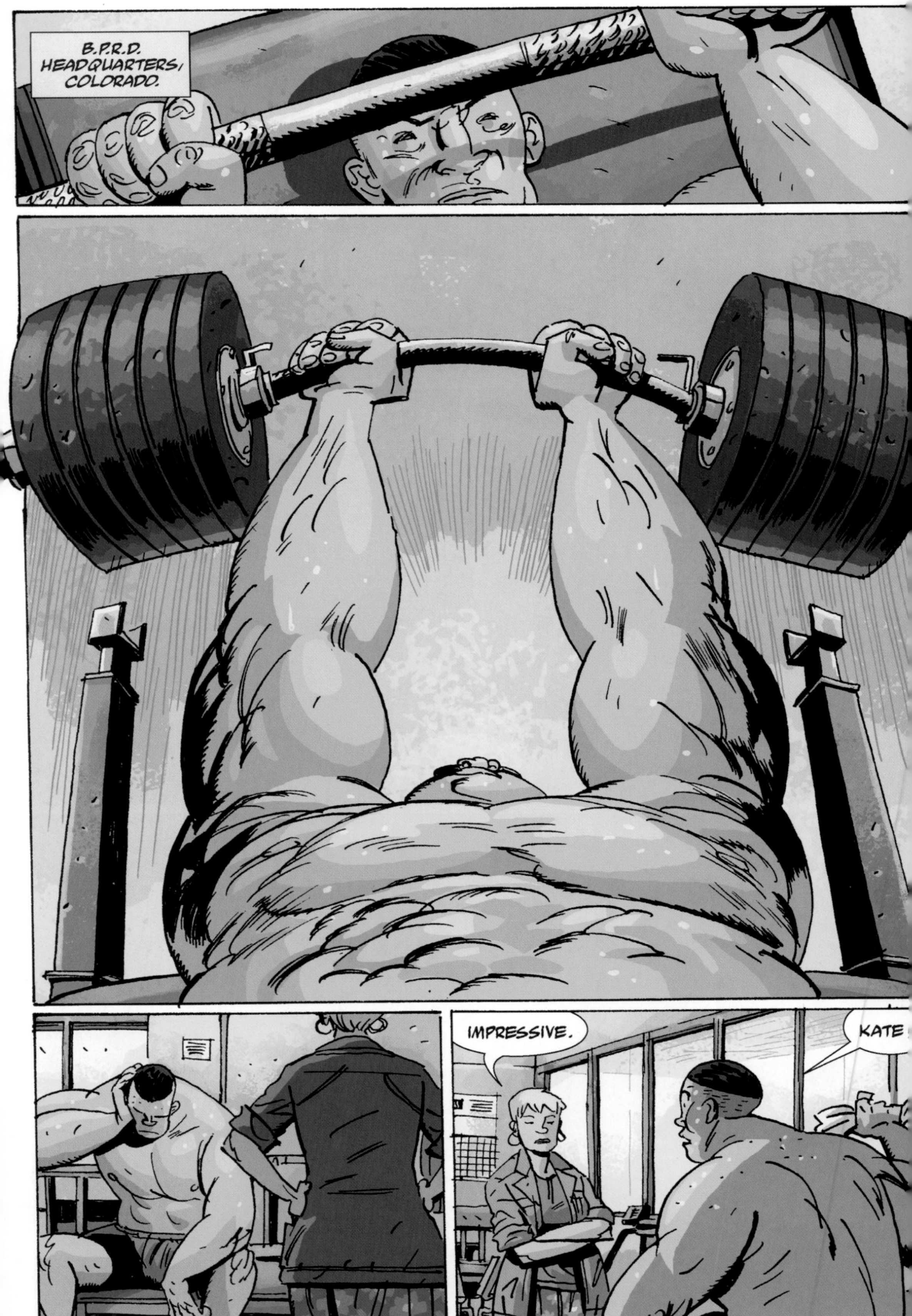
B.P.R.D. HEADQUARTERS, COLORADO.
IMPRESSIVE.
KATE

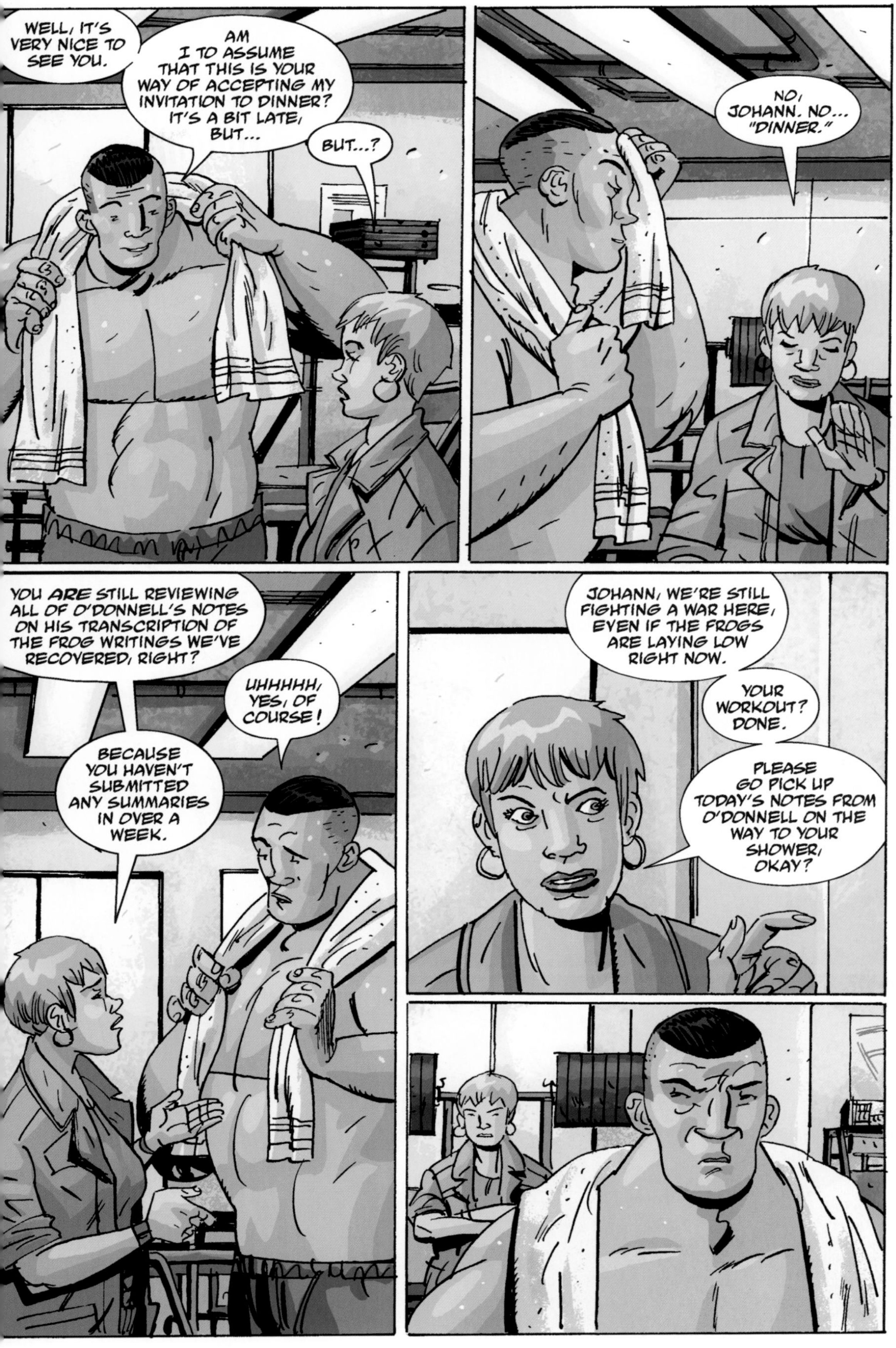
WELL, IT'S VERY NICE TO SEE YOU.
AM I TO ASSUME THAT THIS IS YOUR WAY OF ACCEPTING MY INVITATION TO DINNER? IT'S A BIT LATE, BUT...
BUT...?
NO, JOHANN. NO... "DINNER."
YOU ARE STILL REVIEWING ALL OF O'DONNELL'S NOTES ON HIS TRANSCRIPTION OF THE FROG WRITINGS WE'VE RECOVERED, RIGHT?
UHHHHH, YES, OF COURSE!
BECAUSE YOU HAVEN'T SUBMITTED ANY SUMMARIES IN OVER A WEEK.
JOHANN, WE'RE STILL FIGHTING A WAR HERE, EVEN IF THE FROGS ARE LAYING LOW RIGHT NOW.
YOUR WORKOUT? DONE.
PLEASE GO PICK UP TODAY'S NOTES FROM O'DONNELL ON THE WAY TO YOUR SHOWER, OKAY?

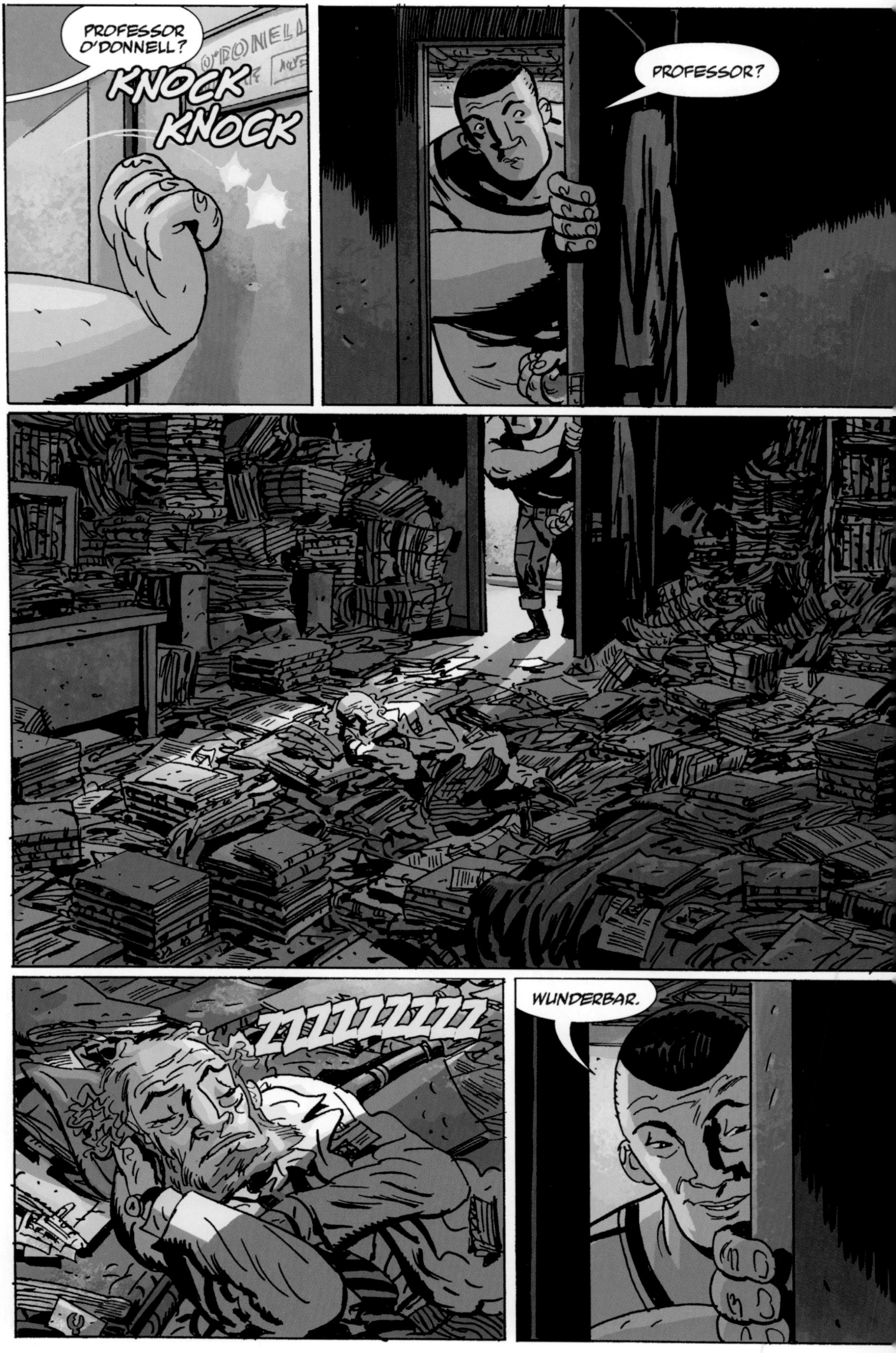
PROFESSOR O'DONNELL?
KNOCK KNOCK
PROFESSOR?
ZZZZZZZZZZ
WUNDERBAR.

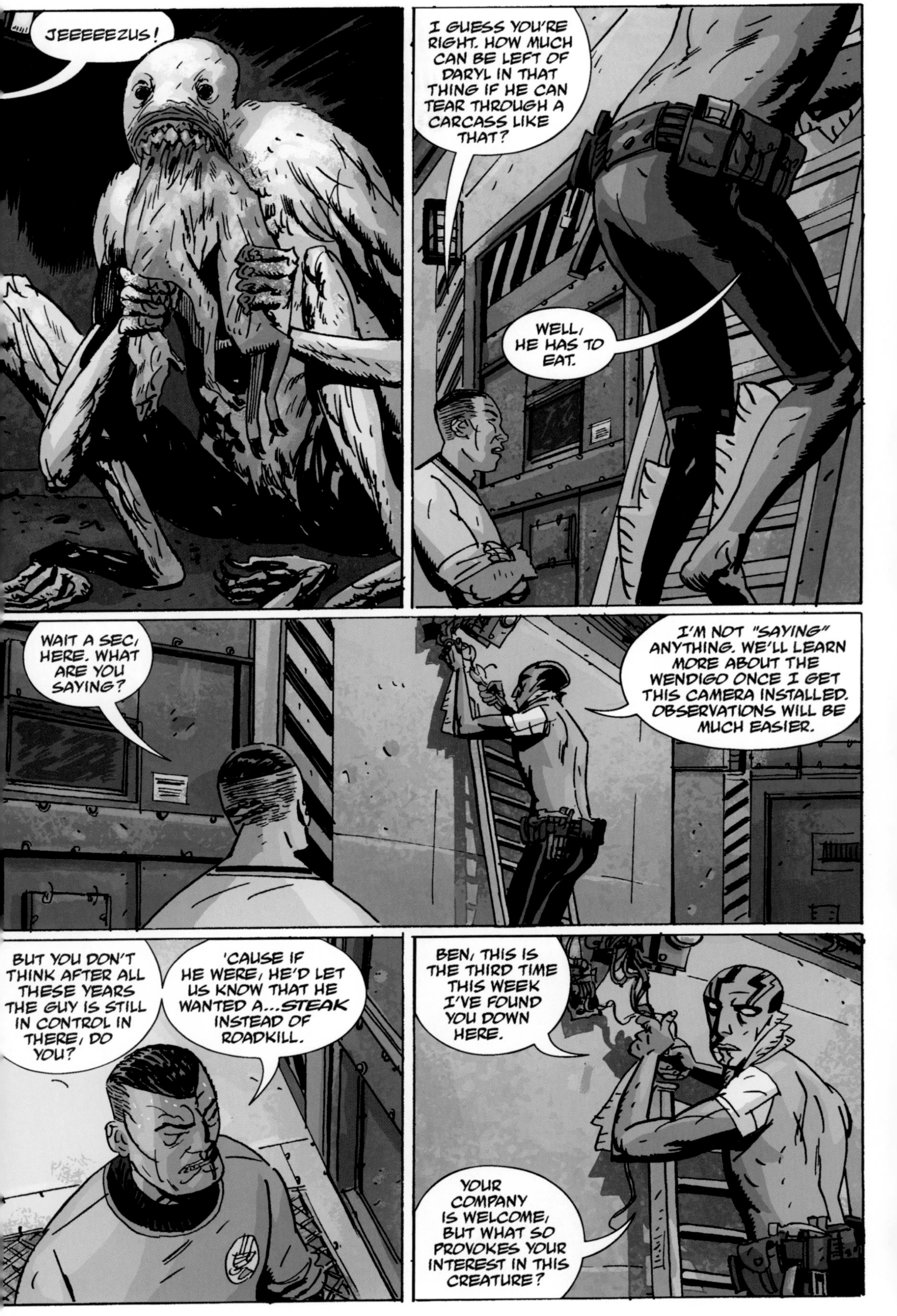
JEEEEEZUS!
I GUESS YOU'RE RIGHT. HOW MUCH CAN BE LEFT OF DARYL IN THAT THING IF HE CAN TEAR THROUGH A CARCASS LIKE THAT?
WELL, HE HAS TO EAT.
WAIT A SEC, HERE. WHAT ARE YOU SAYING?
I'M NOT "SAYING" ANYTHING. WE'LL LEARN MORE ABOUT THE WENDIGO ONCE I GET THIS CAMERA INSTALLED. OBSERVATIONS WILL BE MUCH EASIER.
BUT YOU DON'T THINK AFTER ALL THESE YEARS THE GUY IS STILL IN CONTROL IN THERE, DO YOU?
'CAUSE IF HE WERE, HE'D LET US KNOW THAT HE WANTED A...STEAK INSTEAD OF ROADKILL.
BEN, THIS IS THE THIRD TIME THIS WEEK I'VE FOUND YOU DOWN HERE.
YOUR COMPANY IS WELCOME, BUT WHAT SO PROVOKES YOUR INTEREST IN THIS CREATURE?

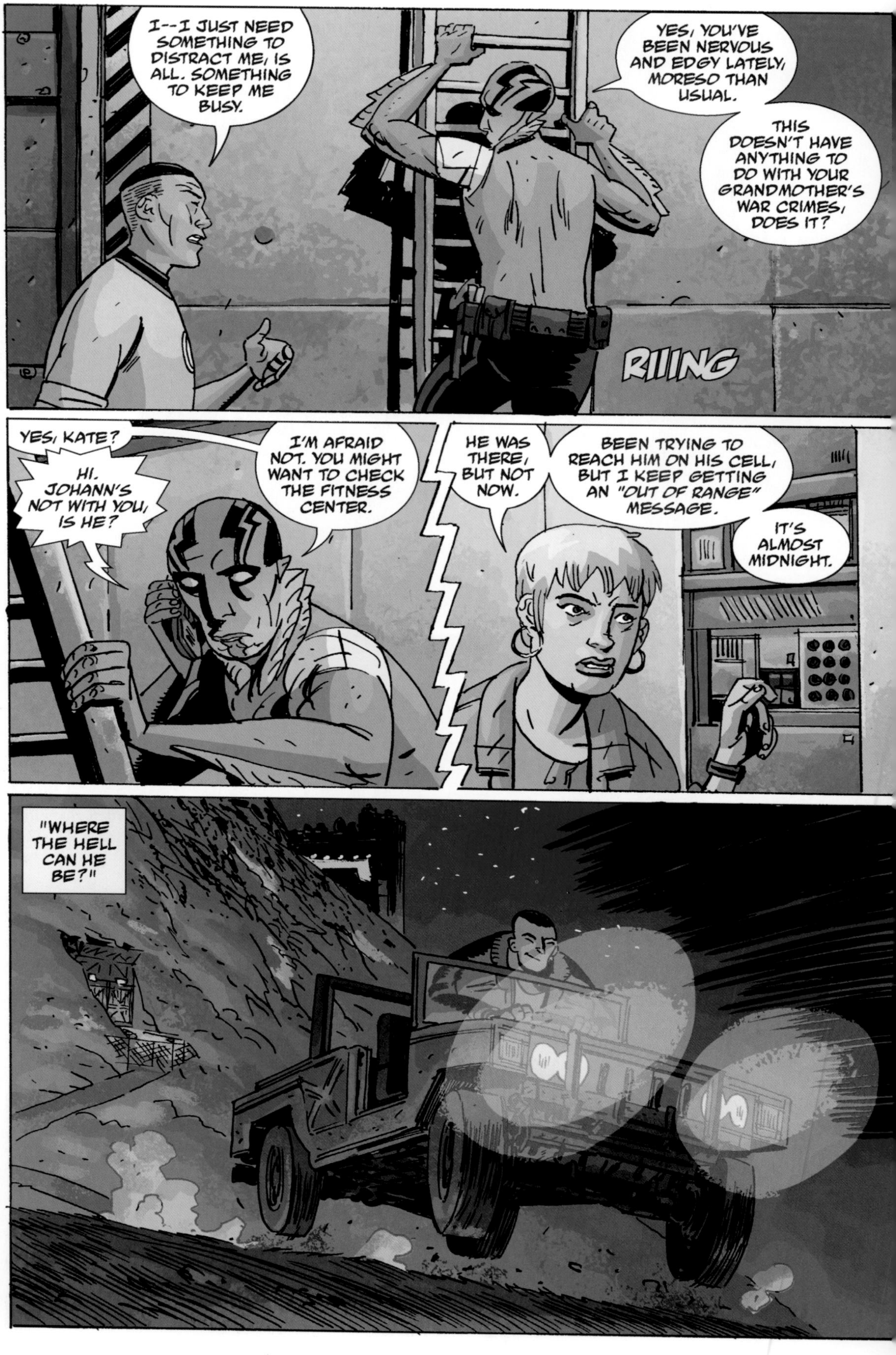
I--I JUST NEED SOMETHING TO DISTRACT ME, IS ALL. SOMETHING TO KEEP ME BUSY.
YES, YOU'VE BEEN NERVOUS AND EDGY LATELY, MORESO THAN USUAL.
THIS DOESN'T HAVE ANYTHING TO DO WITH YOUR GRANDMOTHER'S WAR CRIMES, DOES IT?
RIIING
YES, KATE?
HI. JOHANN'S NOT WITH YOU, IS HE?
I'M AFRAID NOT. YOU MIGHT WANT TO CHECK THE FITNESS CENTER.
HE WAS THERE, BUT NOT NOW.
BEEN TRYING TO REACH HIM ON HIS CELL, BUT I KEEP GETTING AN "OUT OF RANGE" MESSAGE.
IT'S ALMOST MIDNIGHT.
"WHERE THE HELL CAN HE BE?"

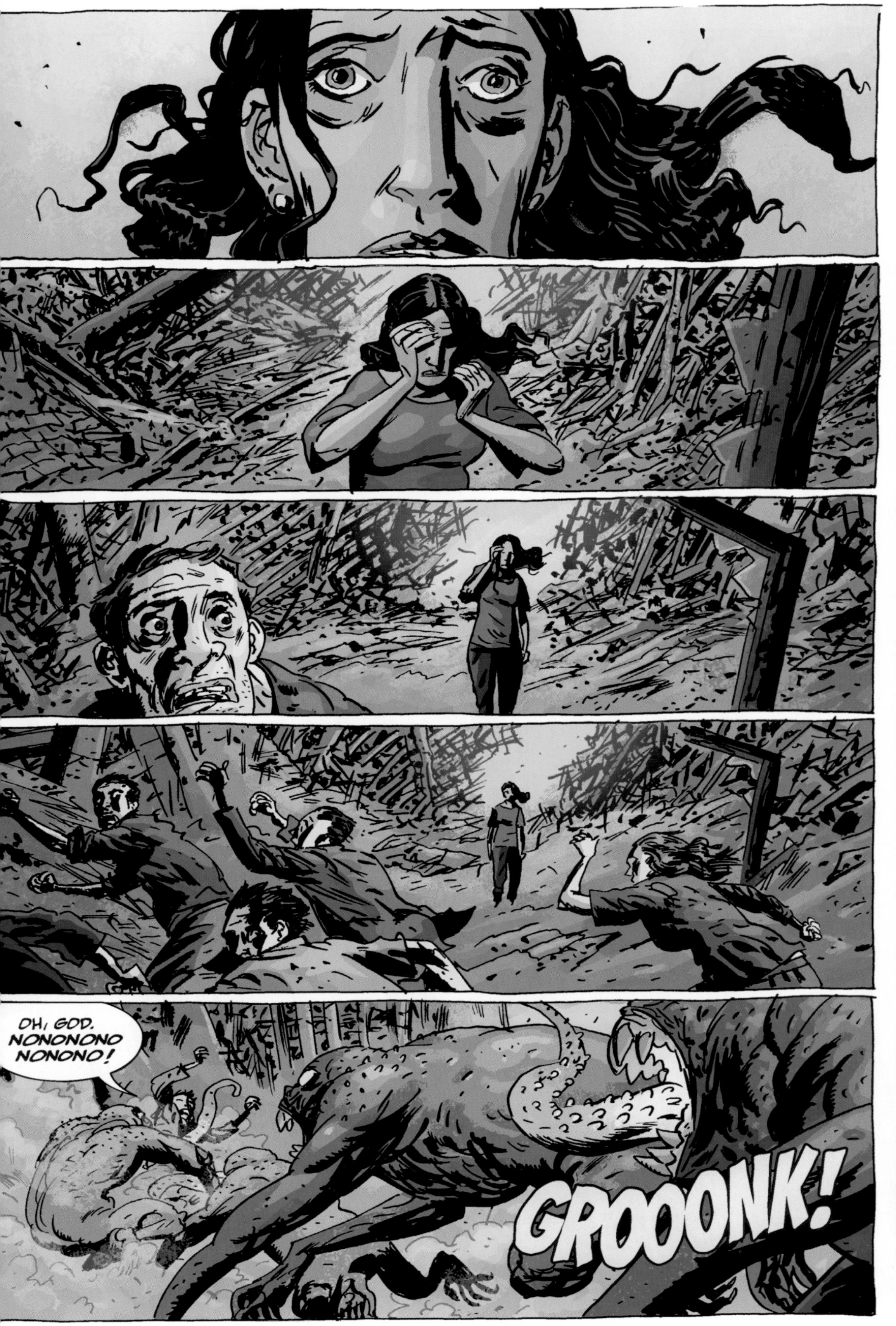
OH, GOD. NONONONO NONONO!
GROOONK!

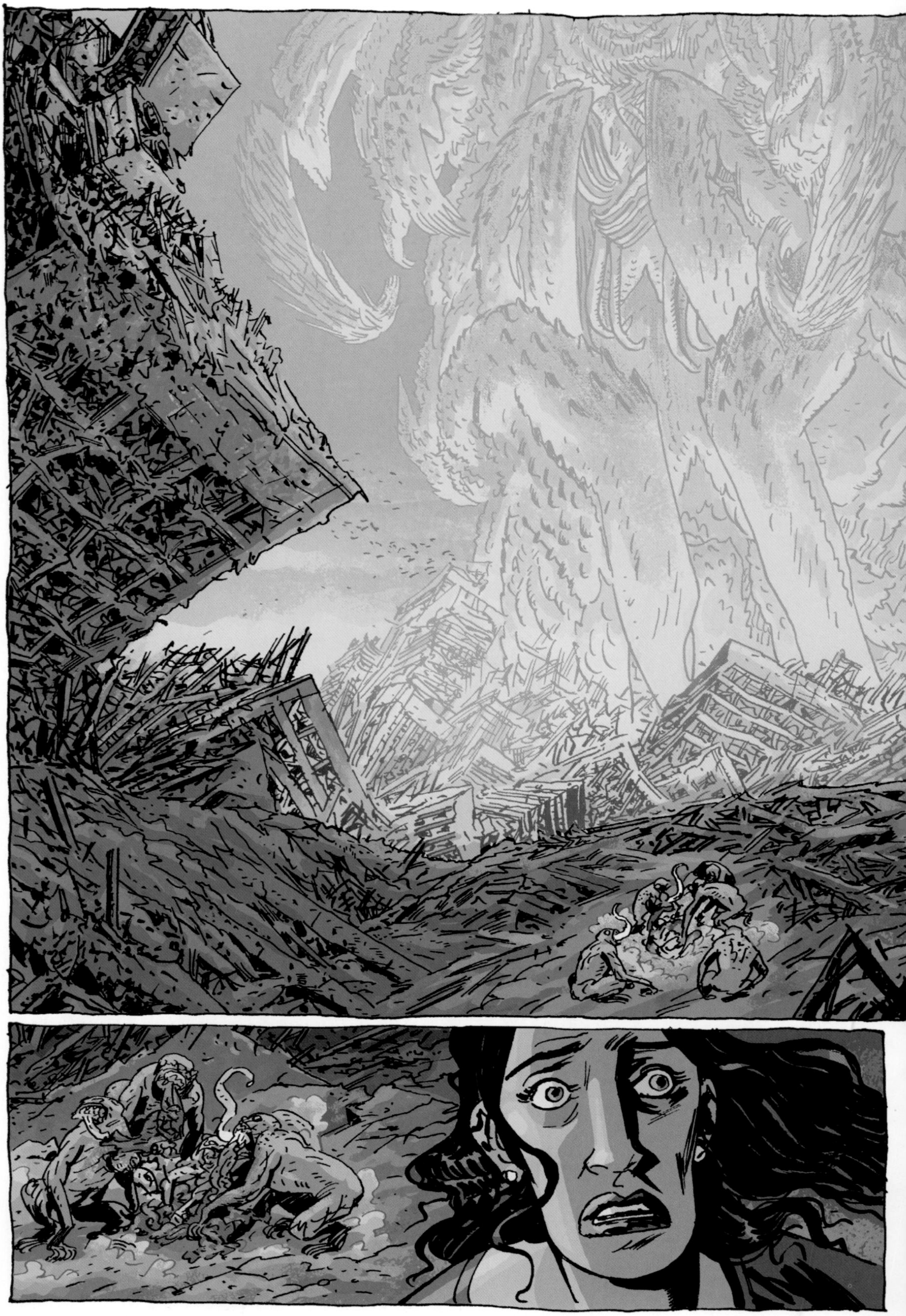

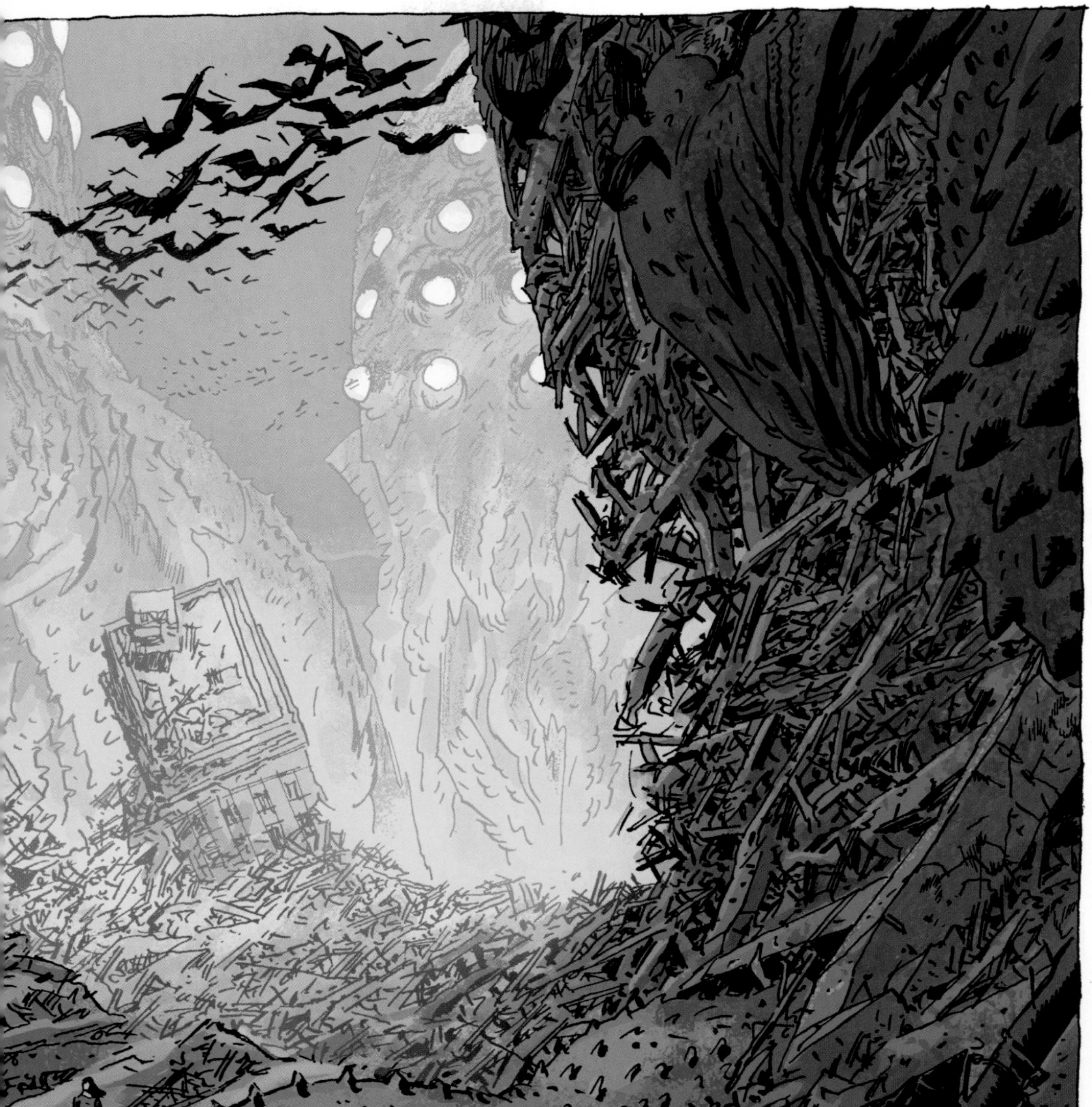

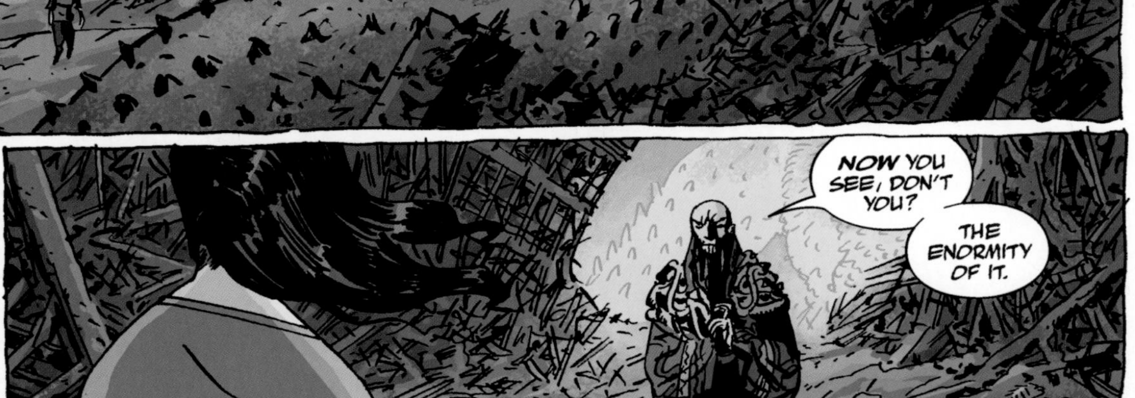
NOW YOU SEE, DON'T YOU?
THE ENORMITY OF IT.

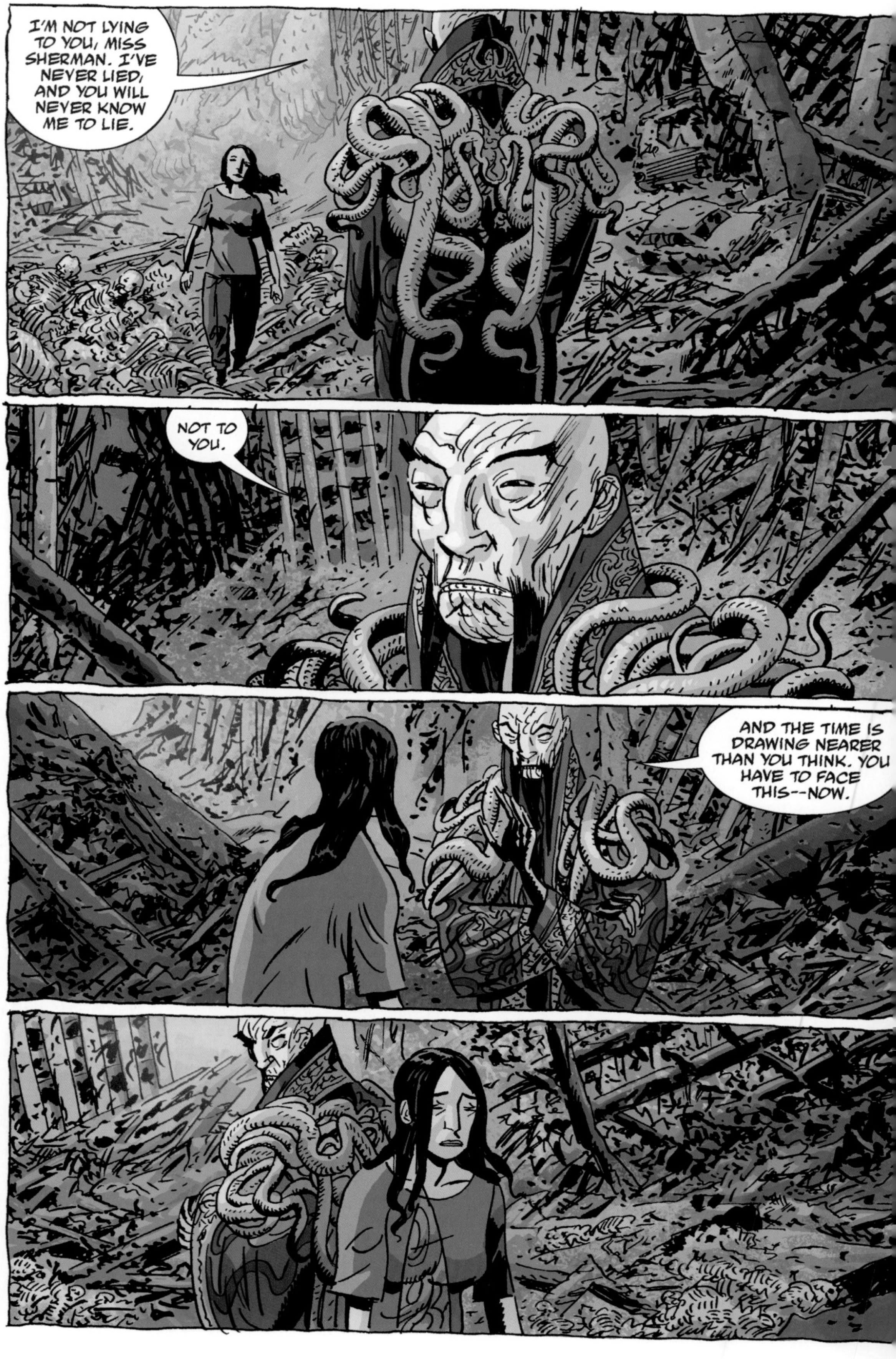
I'M NOT LYING TO YOU, MISS SHERMAN. I'VE NEVER LIED, AND YOU WILL NEVER KNOW ME TO LIE.
NOT TO YOU.
AND THE TIME IS DRAWING NEARER THAN YOU THINK. YOU HAVE TO FACE THIS--NOW.

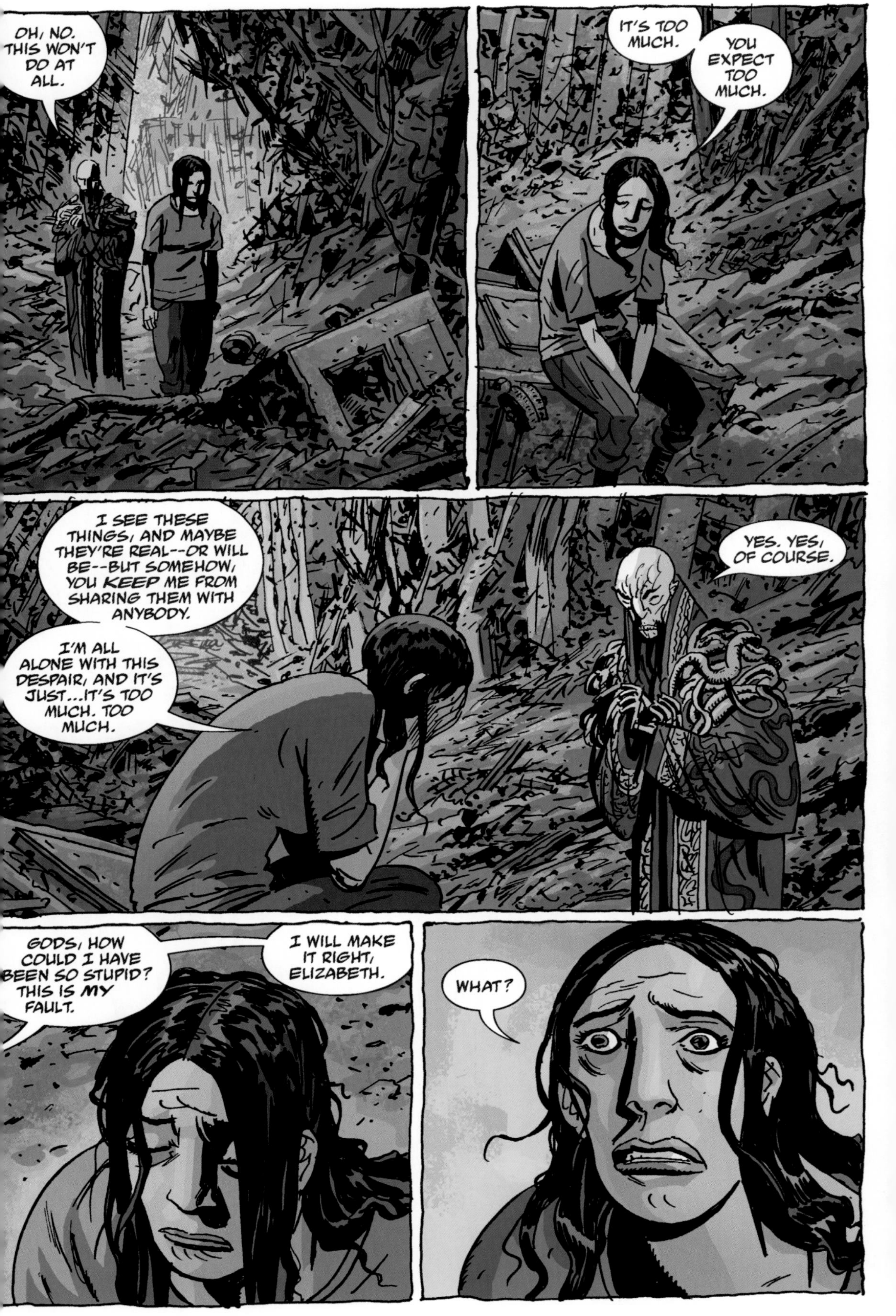
OH, NO. THIS WON'T DO AT ALL.
IT'S TOO MUCH.
YOU EXPECT TOO MUCH.
I SEE THESE THINGS, AND MAYBE THEY'RE REAL--OR WILL BE--BUT SOMEHOW, YOU KEEP ME FROM SHARING THEM WITH ANYBODY.
I'M ALL ALONE WITH THIS DESPAIR, AND IT'S JUST...IT'S TOO MUCH. TOO MUCH.
YES. YES, OF COURSE.
GODS, HOW COULD I HAVE BEEN SO STUPID? THIS IS MY FAULT.
I WILL MAKE IT RIGHT, ELIZABETH.
WHAT?

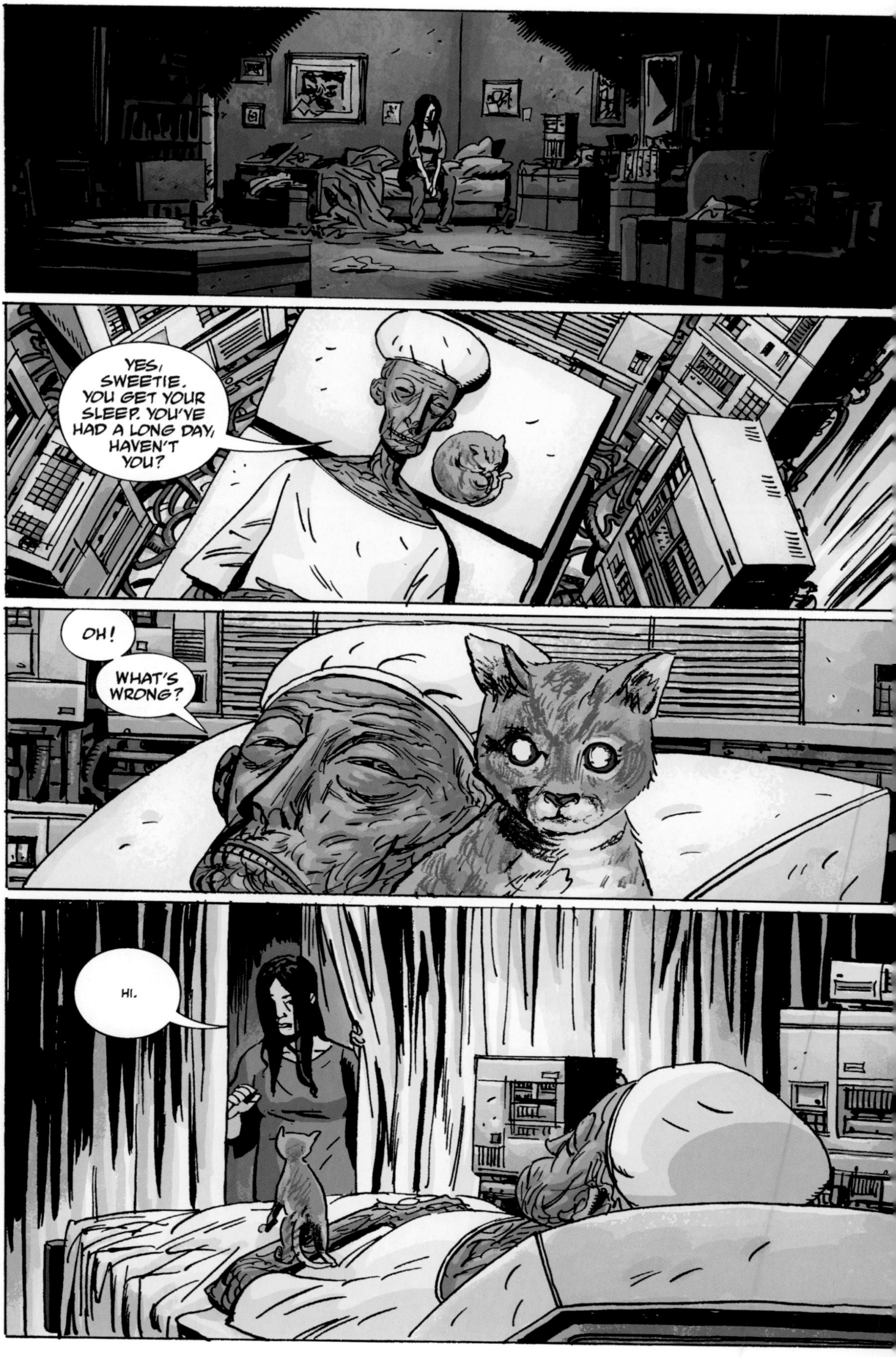
YES, SWEETIE. YOU GET YOUR SLEEP. YOU'VE HAD A LONG DAY, HAVEN'T YOU?
OH!
WHAT'S WRONG?
HI.

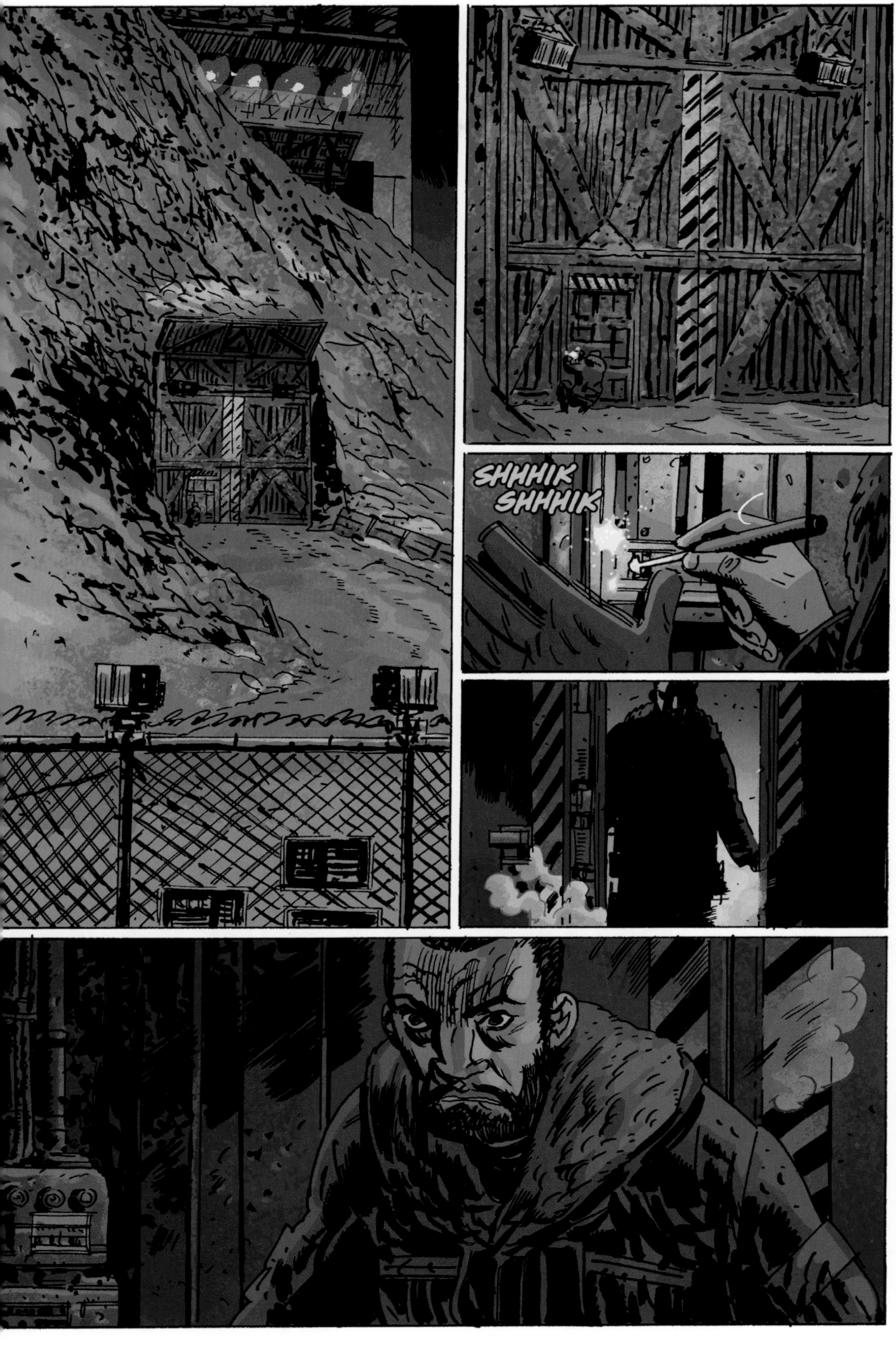
SHHHIK
SHHHIK

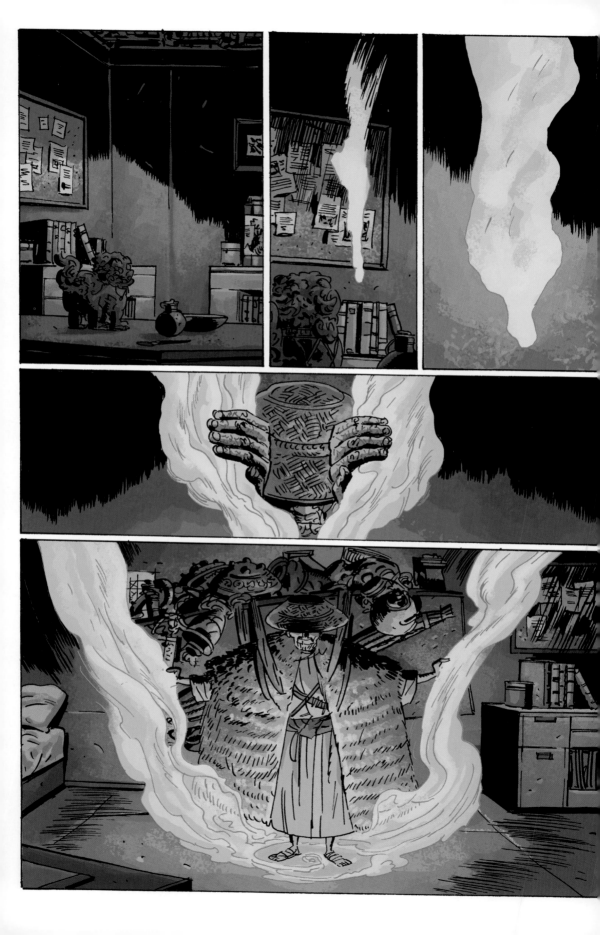

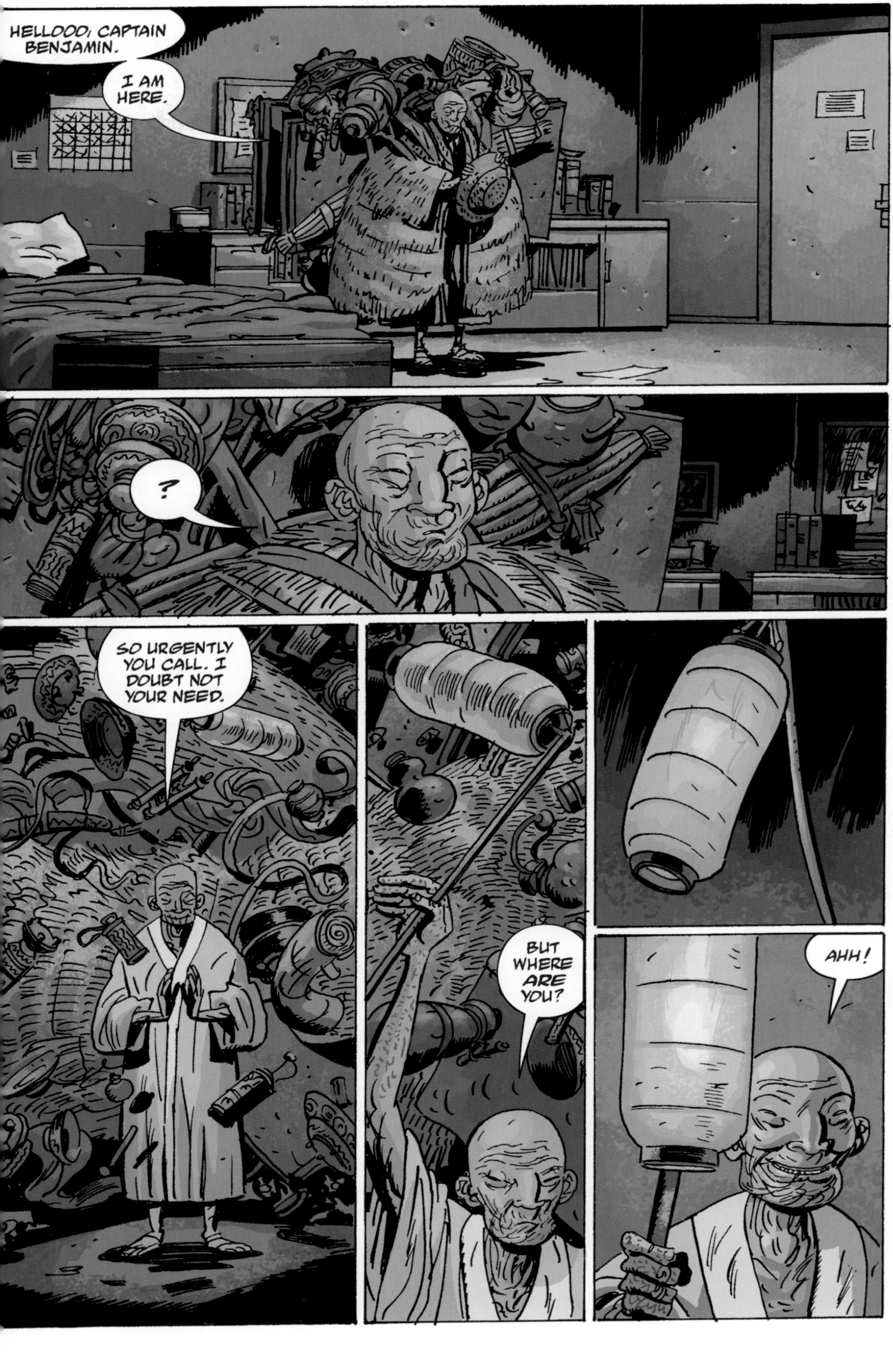
HELLOOO, CAPTAIN BENJAMIN.
I AM HERE.
?
SO URGENTLY YOU CALL. I DOUBT NOT YOUR NEED.
BUT WHERE ARE YOU?
AHH!

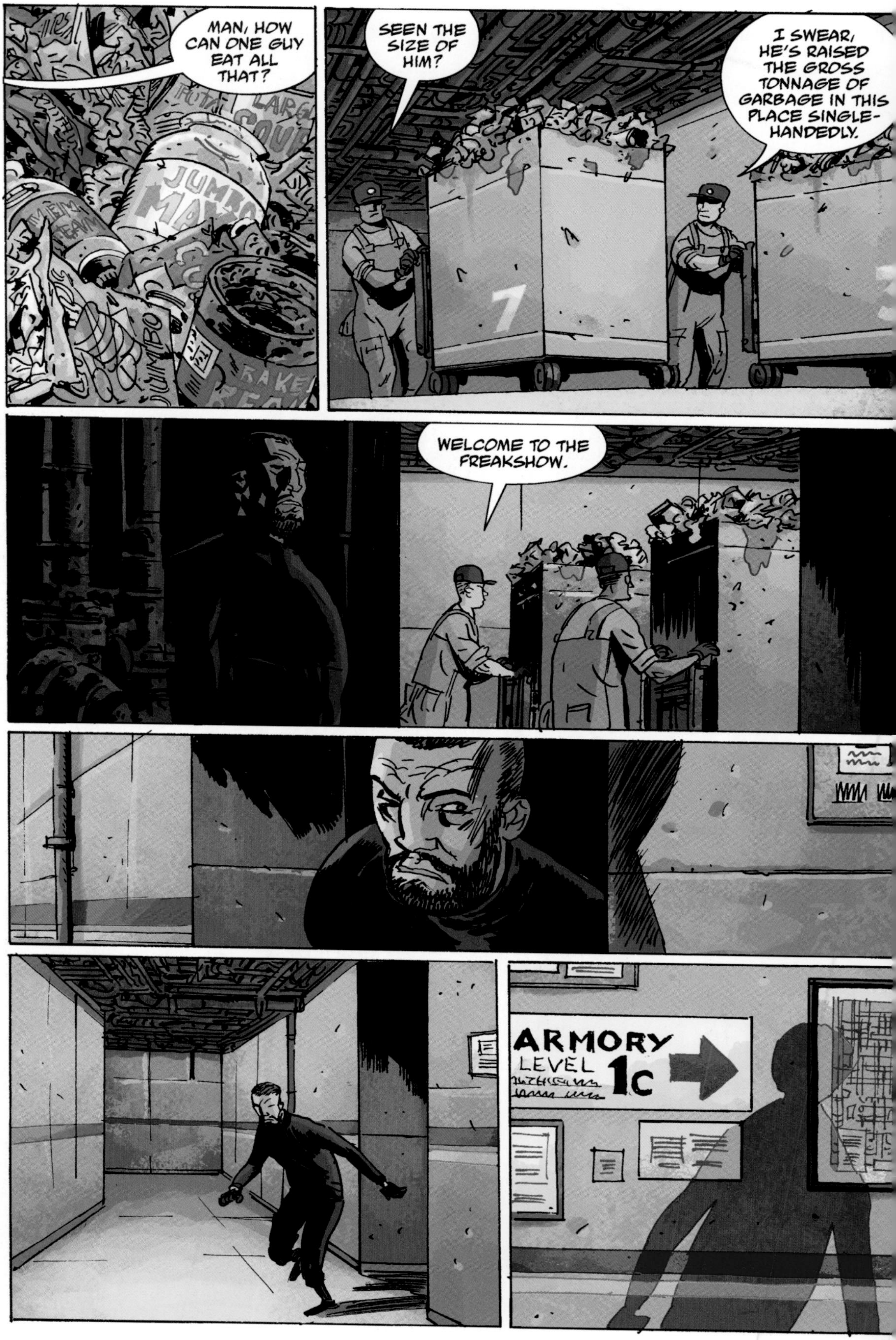
MAN, HOW CAN ONE GUY EAT ALL THAT?
SEEN THE SIZE OF HIM?
I SWEAR, HE'S RAISED THE GROSS TONNAGE OF GARBAGE IN THIS PLACE SINGLE-HANDEDLY.
WELCOME TO THE FREAKSHOW.
ARMORY
LEVEL 1C

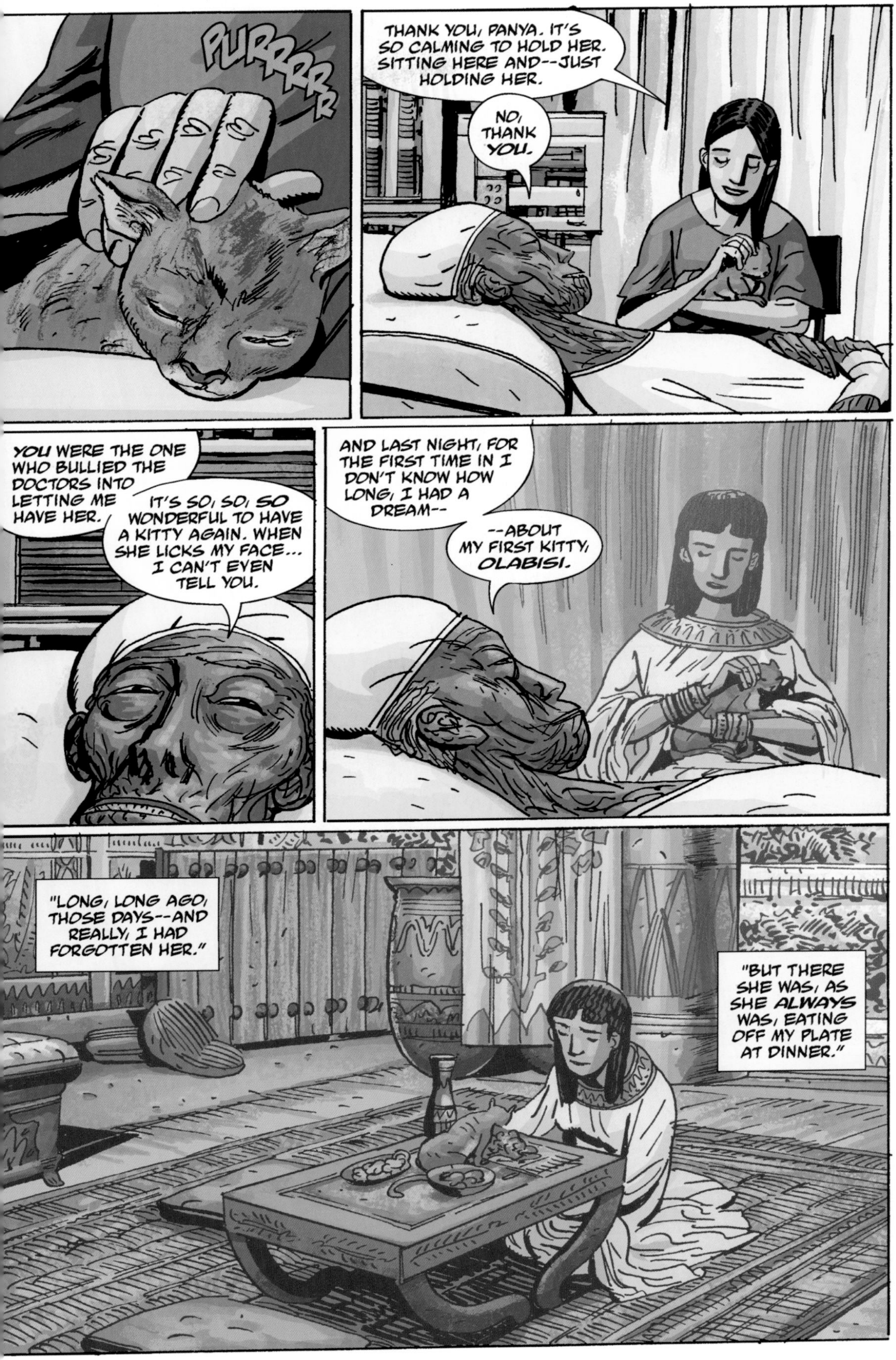
PURRRRR
THANK YOU, PANYA. IT'S SO CALMING TO HOLD HER. SITTING HERE AND--JUST HOLDING HER.
NO, THANK YOU.
YOU WERE THE ONE WHO BULLIED THE DOCTORS INTO LETTING ME HAVE HER.
IT'S SO, SO, SO WONDERFUL TO HAVE A KITTY AGAIN. WHEN SHE LICKS MY FACE... I CAN'T EVEN TELL YOU.
AND LAST NIGHT, FOR THE FIRST TIME IN I DON'T KNOW HOW LONG, I HAD A DREAM--
--ABOUT MY FIRST KITTY, OLABISI.
"LONG, LONG AGO, THOSE DAYS--AND REALLY, I HAD FORGOTTEN HER."
"BUT THERE SHE WAS, AS SHE ALWAYS WAS, EATING OFF MY PLATE AT DINNER."

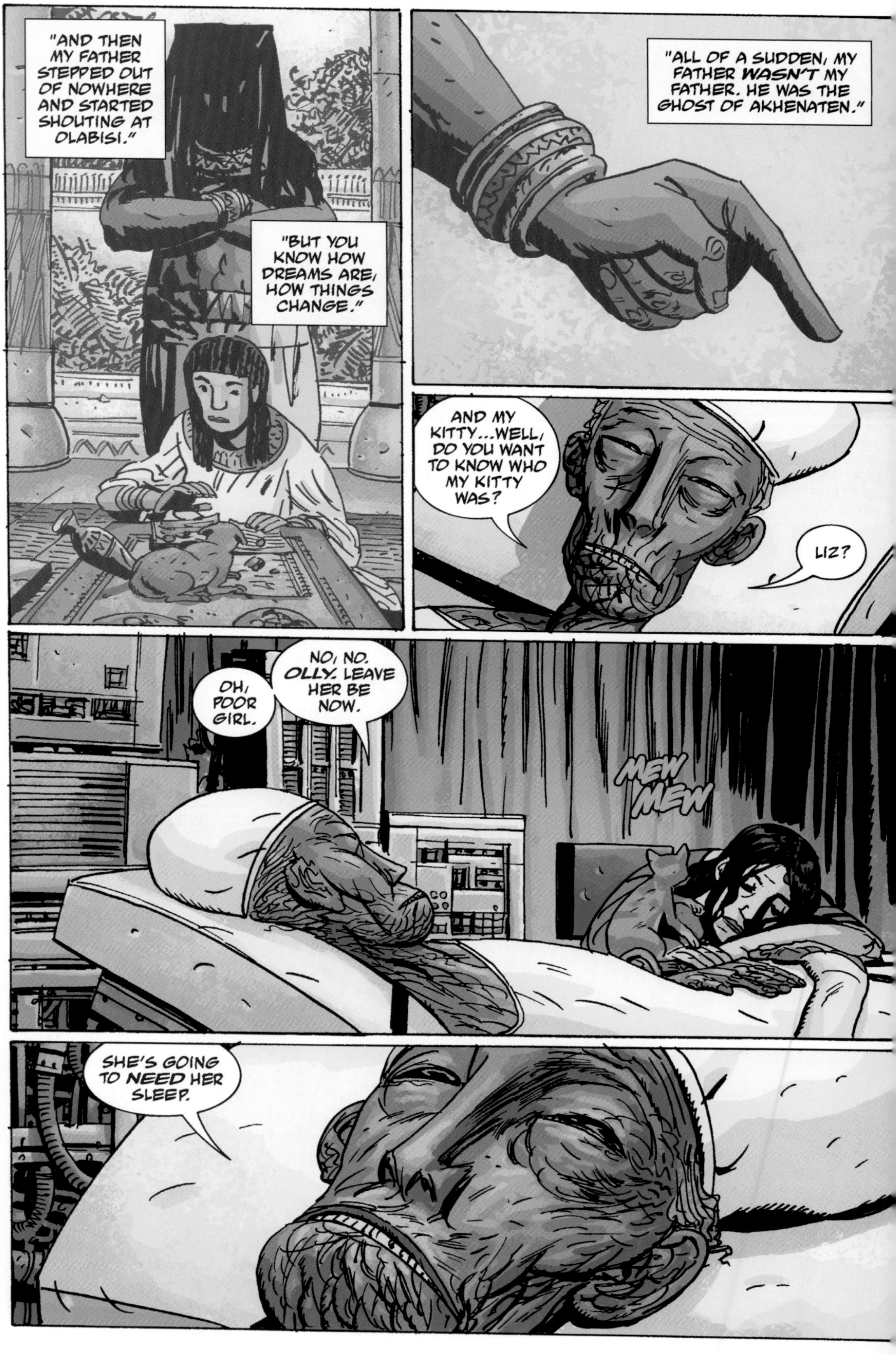
"AND THEN MY FATHER STEPPED OUT OF NOWHERE AND STARTED SHOUTING AT OLABISI."
"BUT YOU KNOW HOW DREAMS ARE, HOW THINGS CHANGE."
"ALL OF A SUDDEN, MY FATHER WASN'T MY FATHER. HE WAS THE GHOST OF AKHENATEN."
AND MY KITTY...WELL, DO YOU WANT TO KNOW WHO MY KITTY WAS?
LIZ?
OH, POOR GIRL.
NO, NO. OLLY. LEAVE HER BE NOW.
MEW MEW
SHE'S GOING TO NEED HER SLEEP.

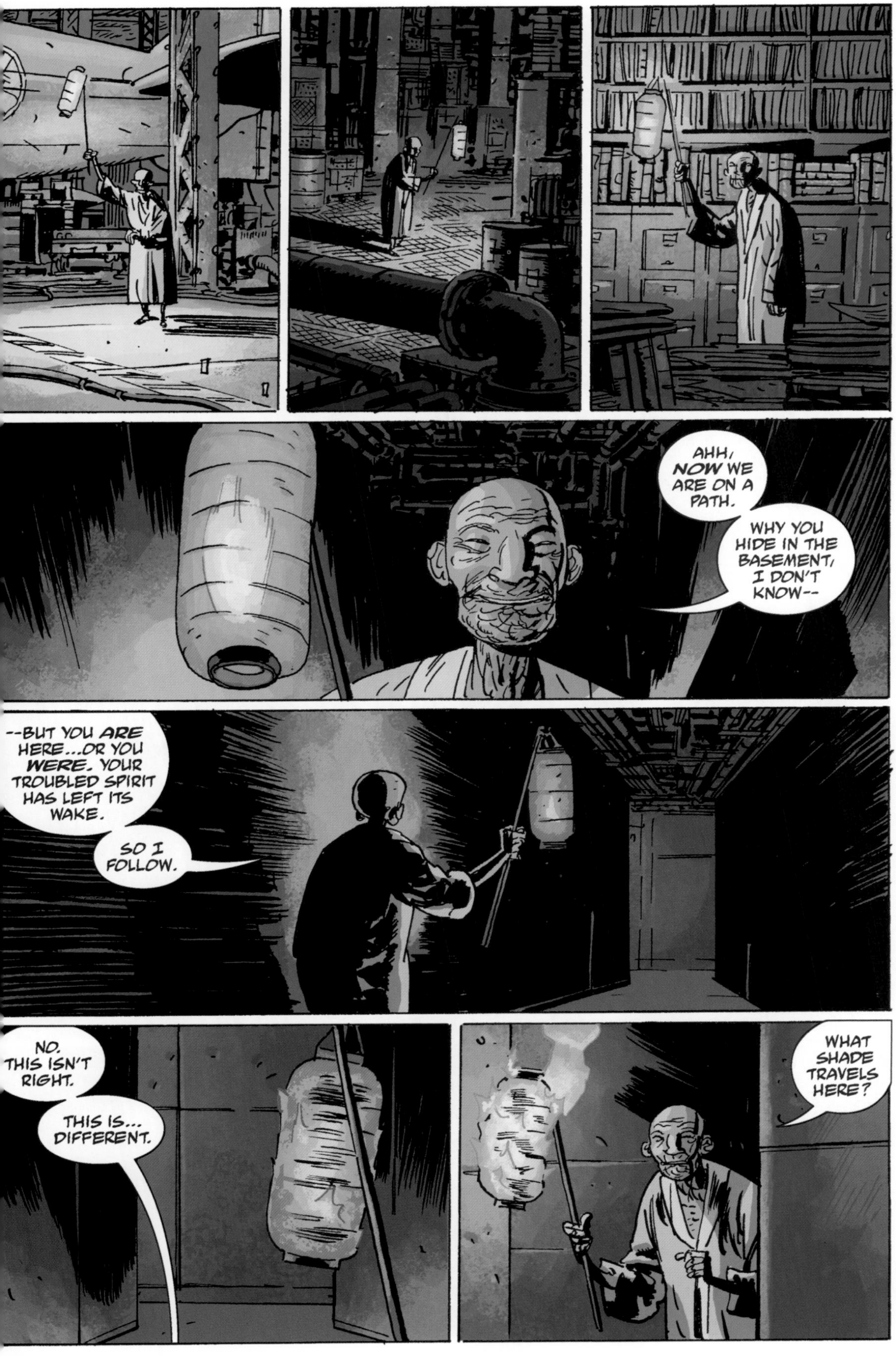
AHH, NOW WE ARE ON A PATH.
WHY YOU HIDE IN THE BASEMENT, I DON'T KNOW--
--BUT YOU ARE HERE...OR YOU WERE. YOUR TROUBLED SPIRIT HAS LEFT ITS WAKE.
SO I FOLLOW.
NO. THIS ISN'T RIGHT.
THIS IS... DIFFERENT.
WHAT SHADE TRAVELS HERE?

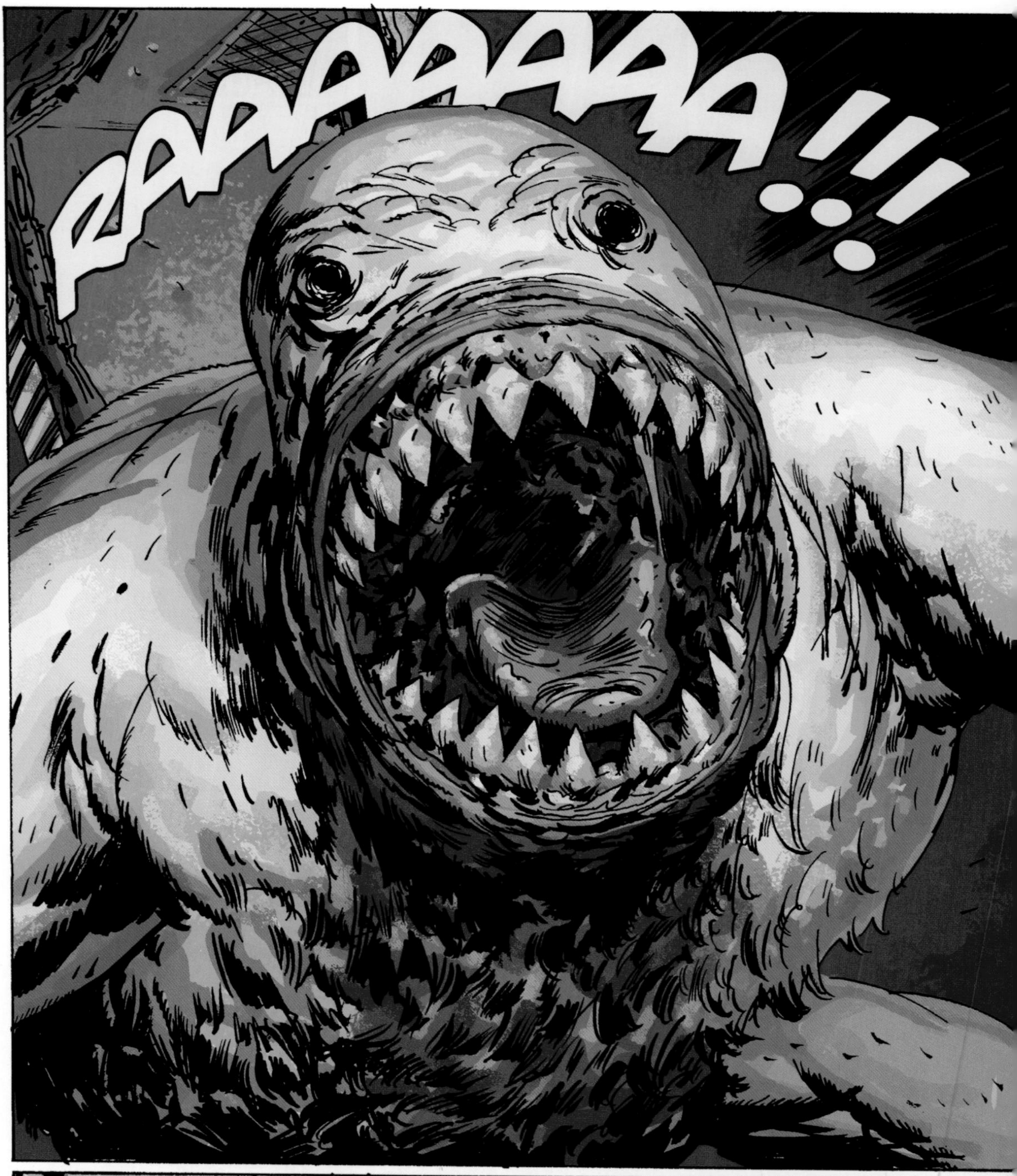
RAAAAAAA!!!

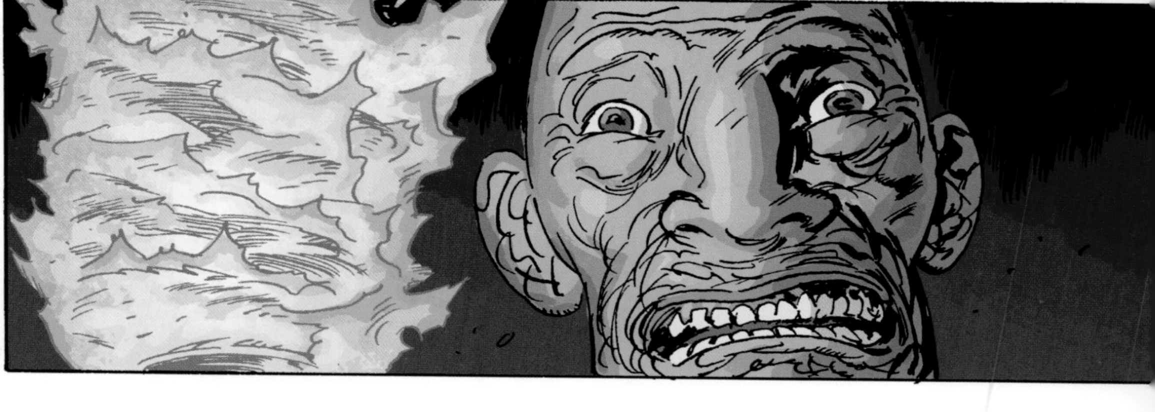

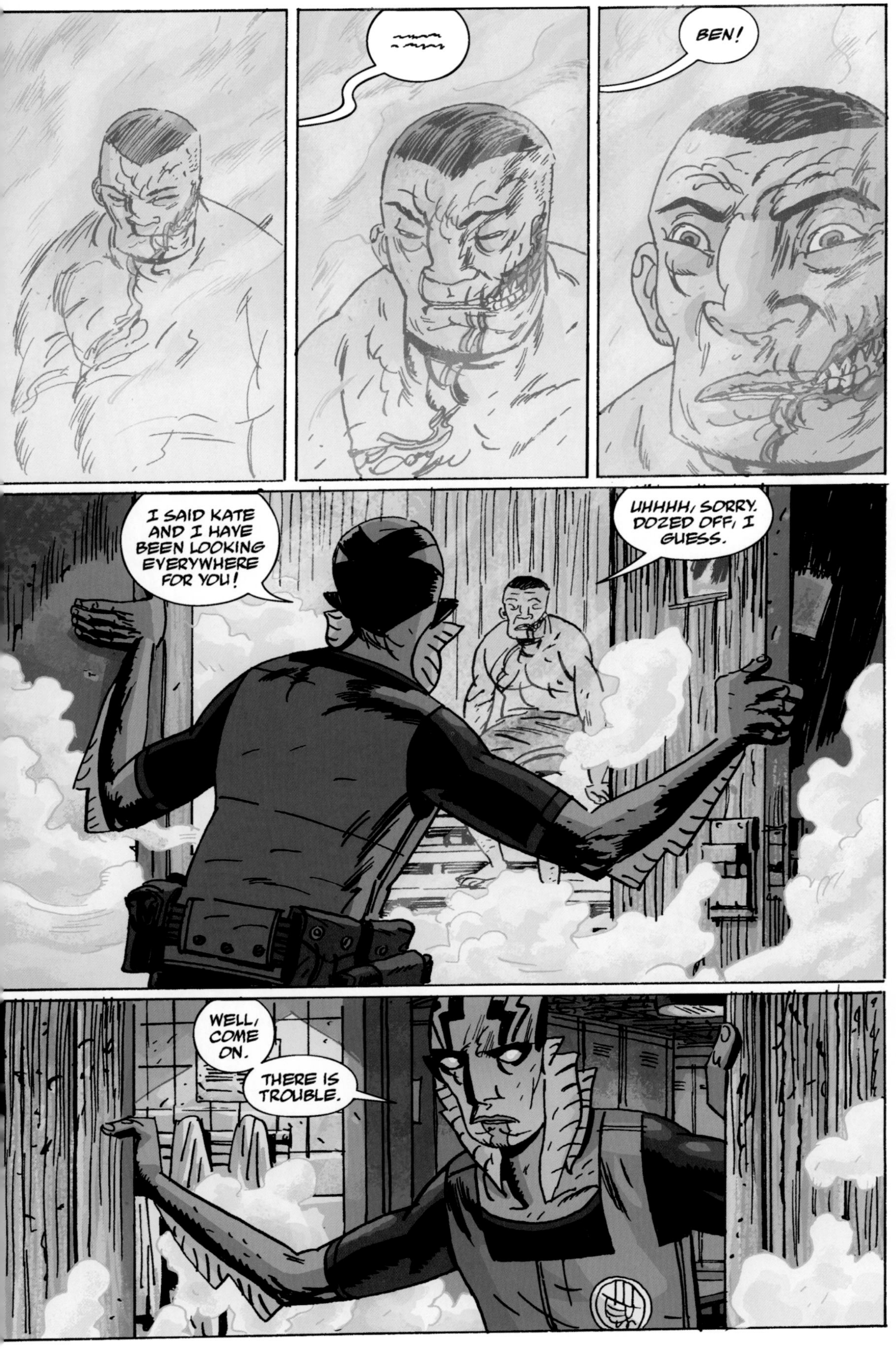
BEN!
I SAID KATE AND I HAVE BEEN LOOKING EVERYWHERE FOR YOU!
UHHHH, SORRY. DOZED OFF, I GUESS.
WELL, COME ON.
THERE IS TROUBLE.

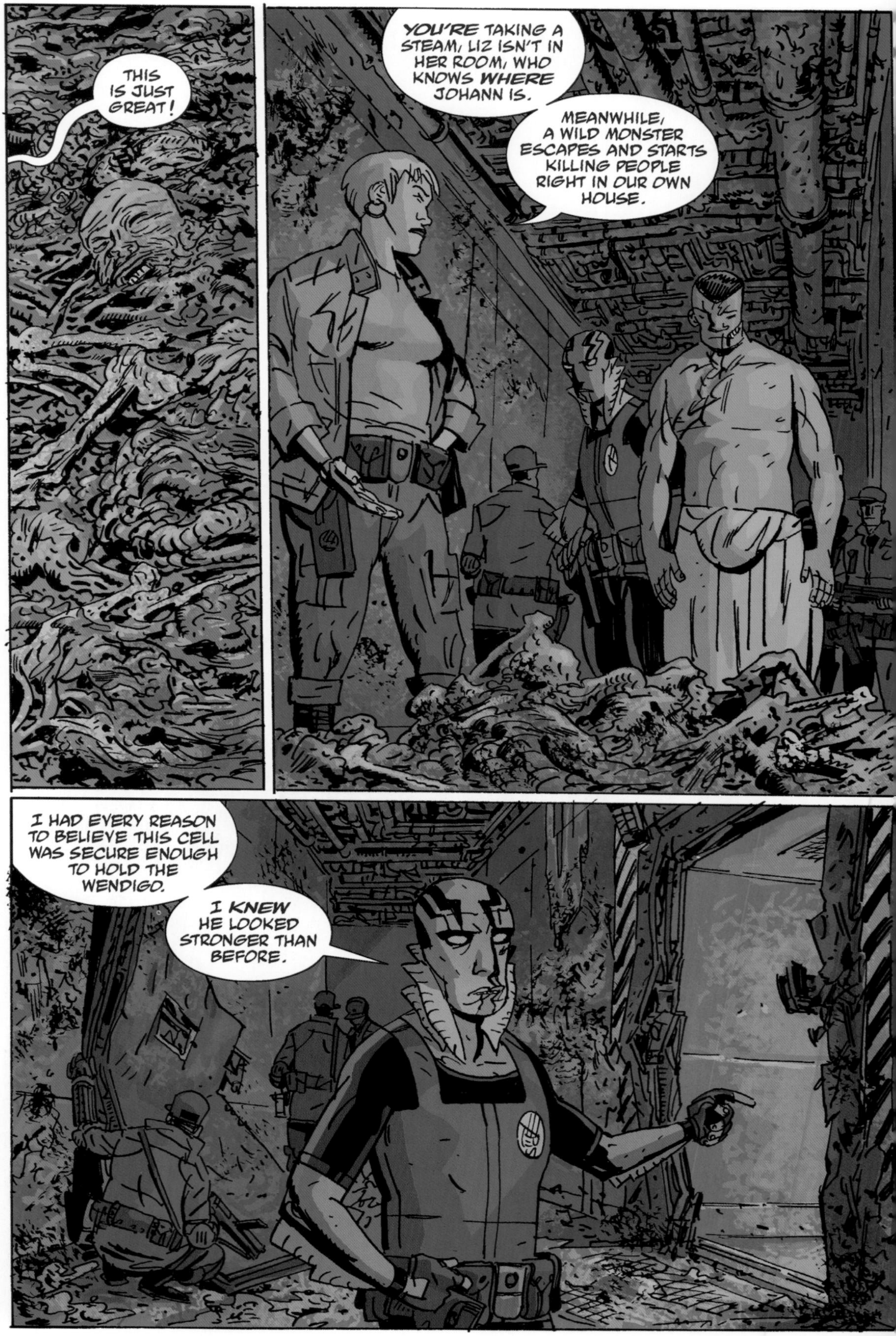
THIS IS JUST GREAT!
YOU'RE TAKING A STEAM, LIZ ISN'T IN HER ROOM, WHO KNOWS WHERE JOHANN IS.
MEANWHILE, A WILD MONSTER ESCAPES AND STARTS KILLING PEOPLE RIGHT IN OUR OWN HOUSE.
I HAD EVERY REASON TO BELIEVE THIS CELL WAS SECURE ENOUGH TO HOLD THE WENDIGO.
I KNEW HE LOOKED STRONGER THAN BEFORE.

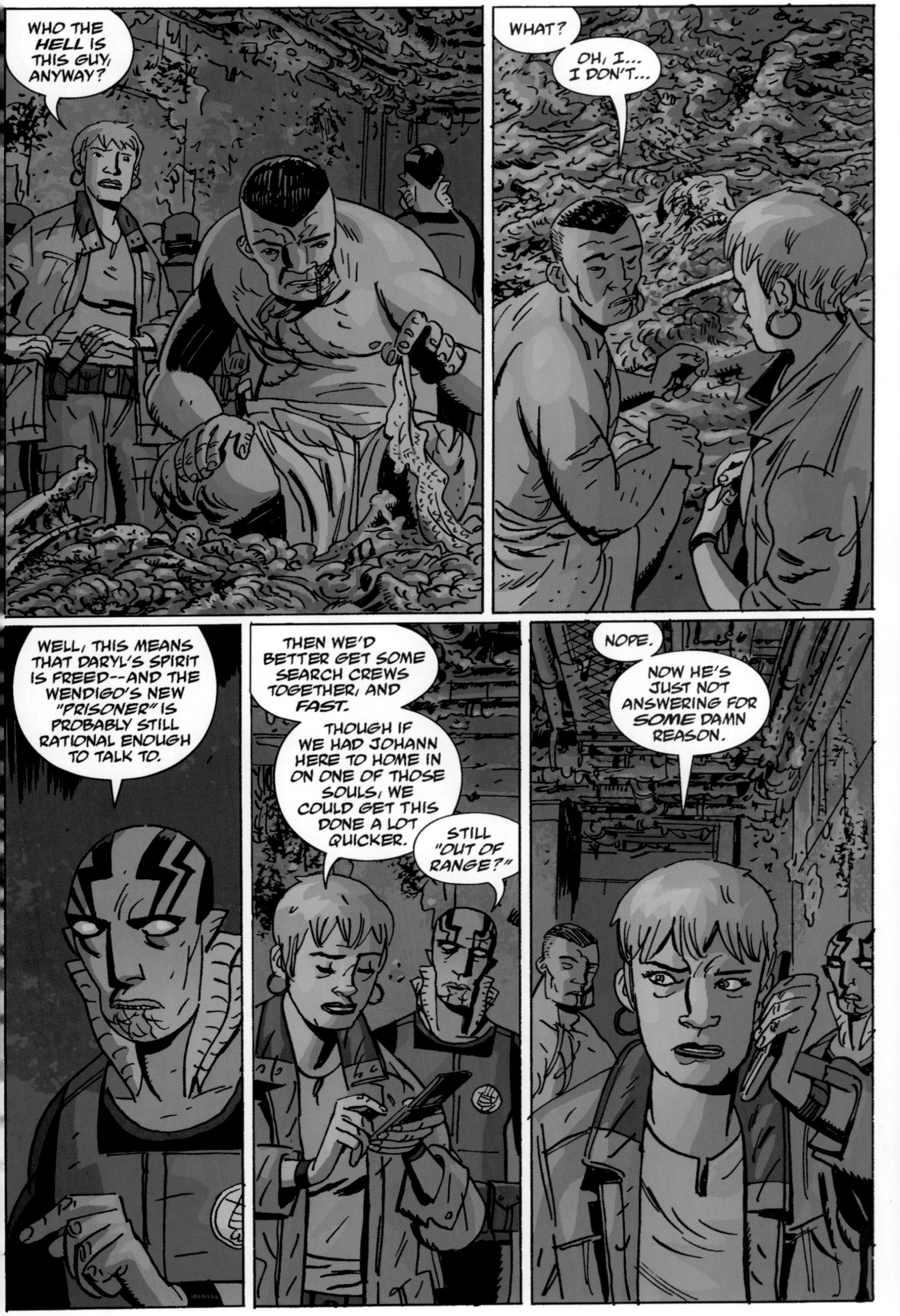
WHO THE HELL IS THIS GUY, ANYWAY?
WHAT?
OH, I... I DON'T...
WELL, THIS MEANS THAT DARYL'S SPIRIT IS FREED--AND THE WENDIGO'S NEW "PRISONER" IS PROBABLY STILL RATIONAL ENOUGH TO TALK TO.
THEN WE'D BETTER GET SOME SEARCH CREWS TOGETHER, AND FAST.
THOUGH IF WE HAD JOHANN HERE TO HOME IN ON ONE OF THOSE SOULS, WE COULD GET THIS DONE A LOT QUICKER.
STILL "OUT OF RANGE?"
NOPE.
NOW HE'S JUST NOT ANSWERING FOR SOME DAMN REASON.

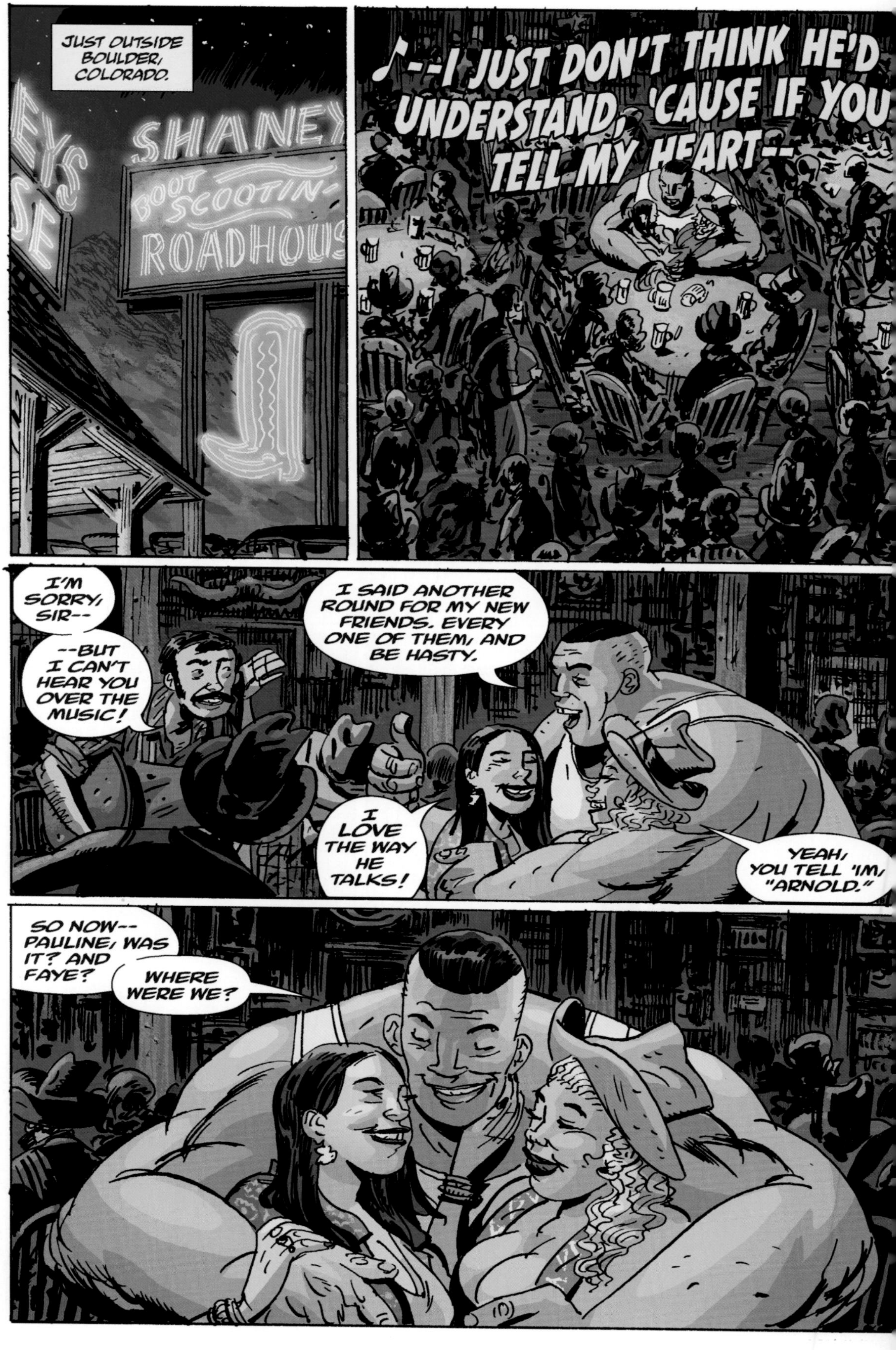
JUST OUTSIDE BOULDER, COLORADO.
SHANEY
BOOT SCOOTIN-
ROADHOUS
♪--I JUST DON'T THINK HE'D UNDERSTAND, 'CAUSE IF YOU TELL MY HEART--
I'M SORRY, SIR--
--BUT I CAN'T HEAR YOU OVER THE MUSIC!
I SAID ANOTHER ROUND FOR MY NEW FRIENDS. EVERY ONE OF THEM, AND BE HASTY.
I LOVE THE WAY HE TALKS!
YEAH, YOU TELL 'IM, "ARNOLD."
SO NOW-- PAULINE, WAS IT? AND FAYE?
WHERE WERE WE?

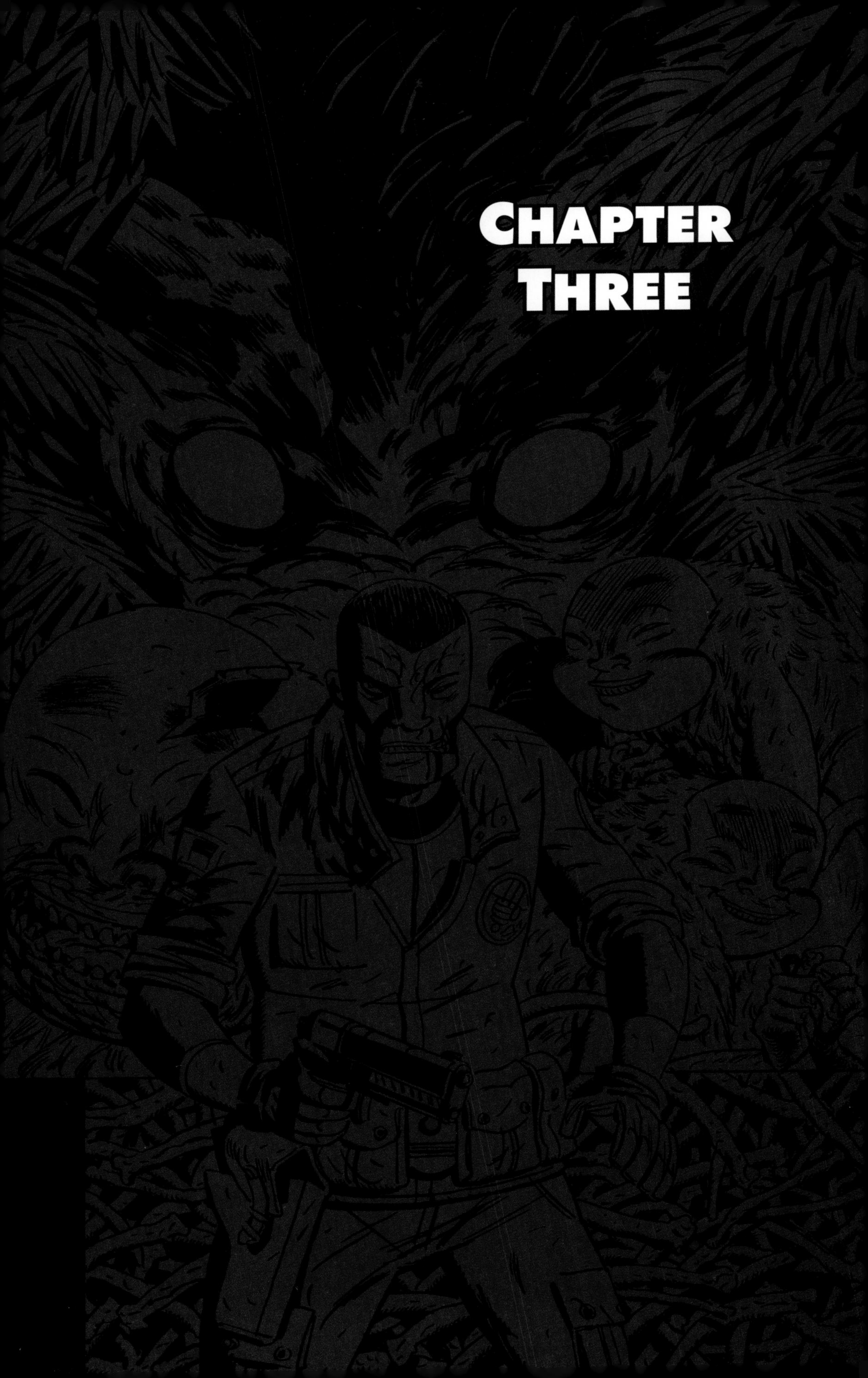
CHAPTER
THREE

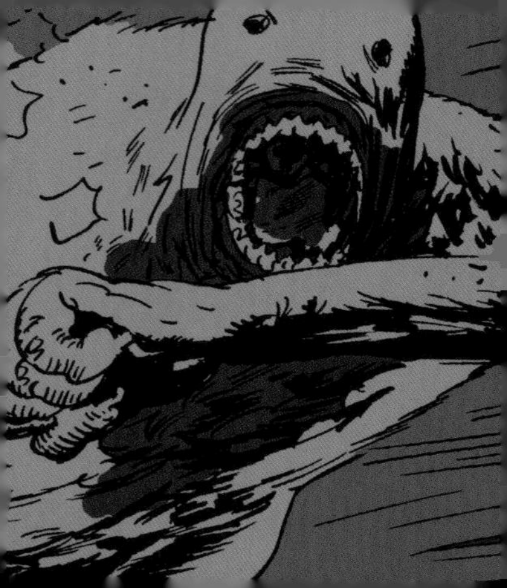

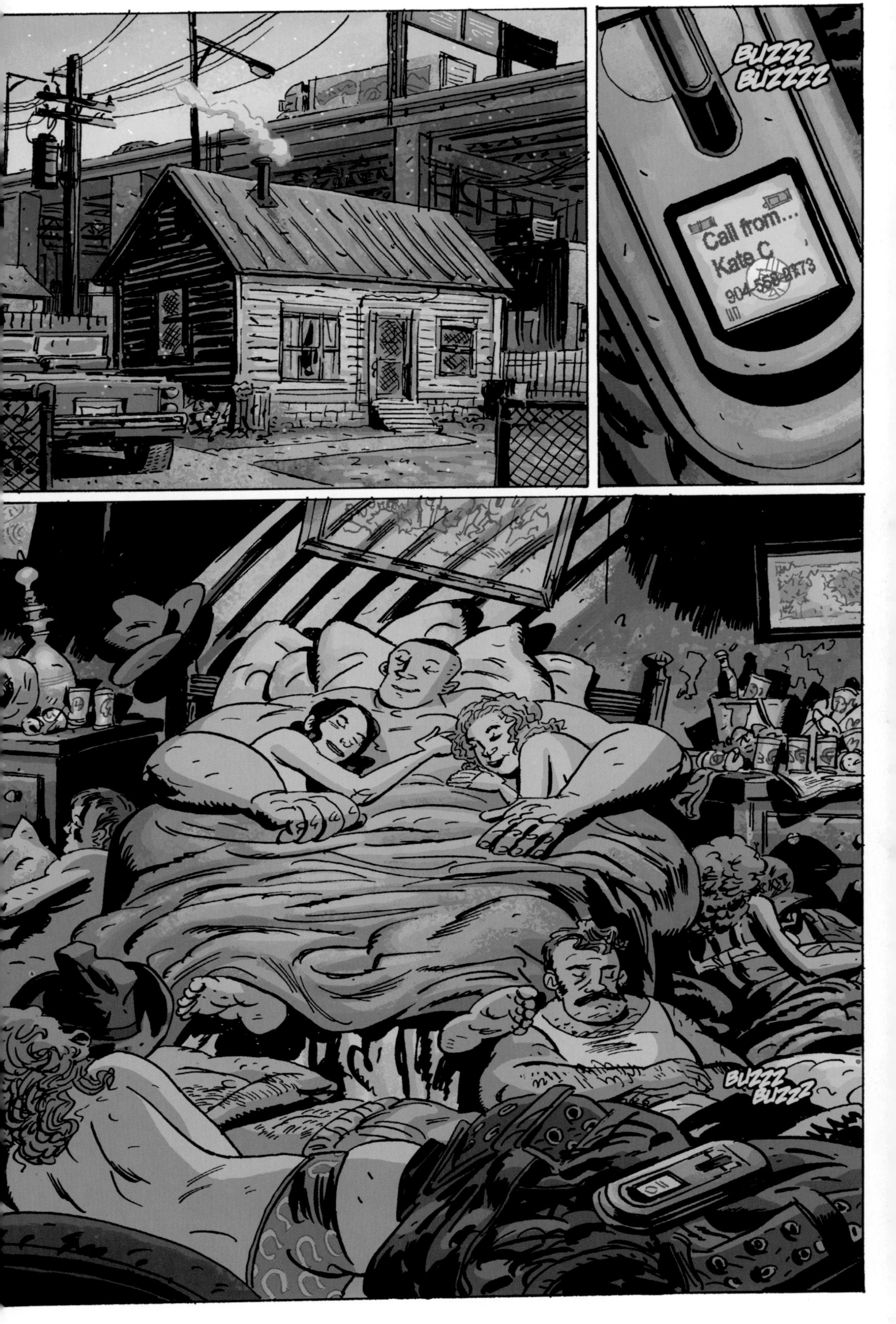
BUZZZ BUZZZZ
Call from...
Kate C
904-558-0173
BUZZZ BUZZZ

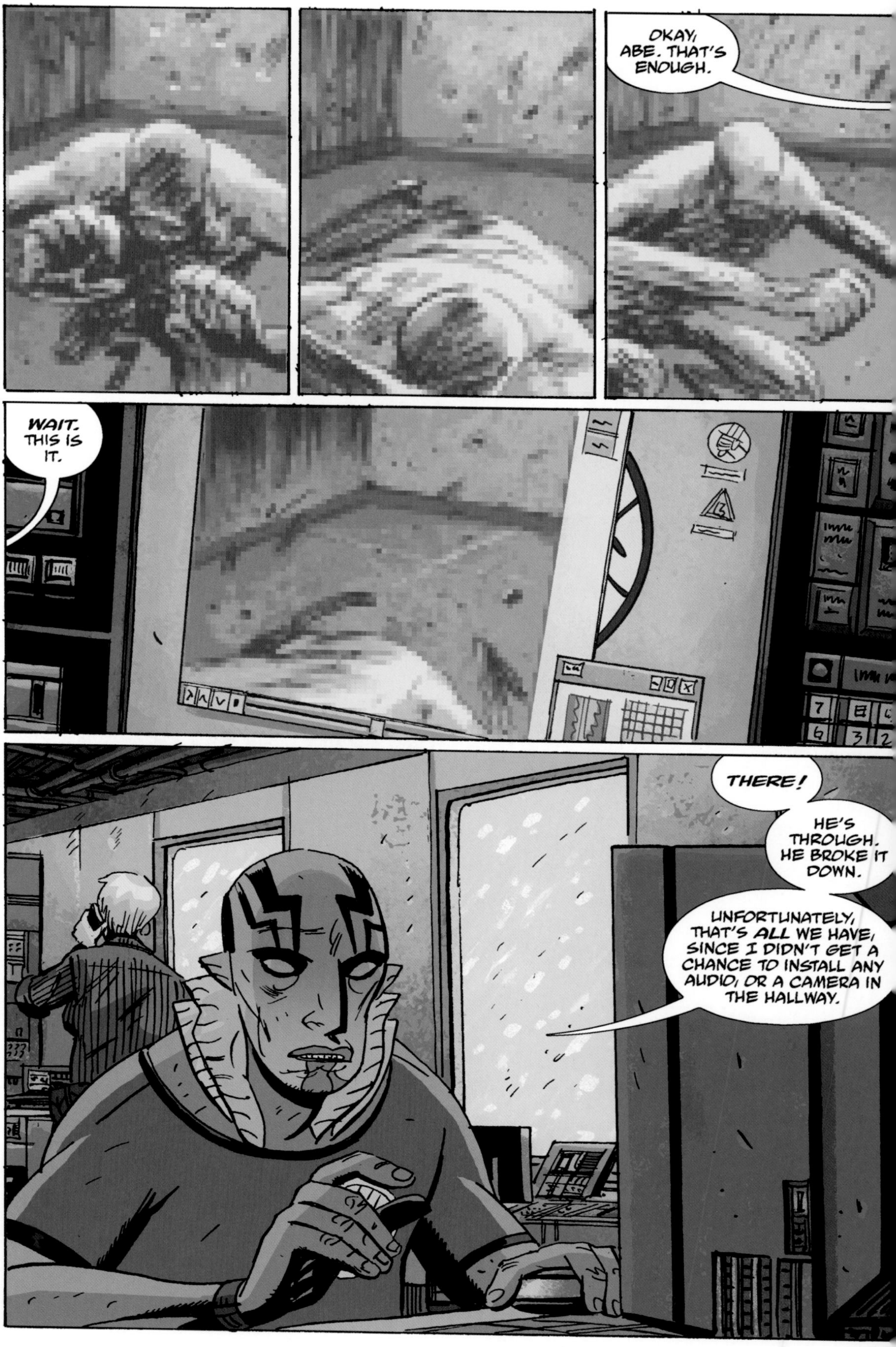
OKAY, ABE. THAT'S ENOUGH.
WAIT. THIS IS IT.
THERE!
HE'S THROUGH. HE BROKE IT DOWN.
UNFORTUNATELY, THAT'S ALL WE HAVE, SINCE I DIDN'T GET A CHANCE TO INSTALL ANY AUDIO, OR A CAMERA IN THE HALLWAY.

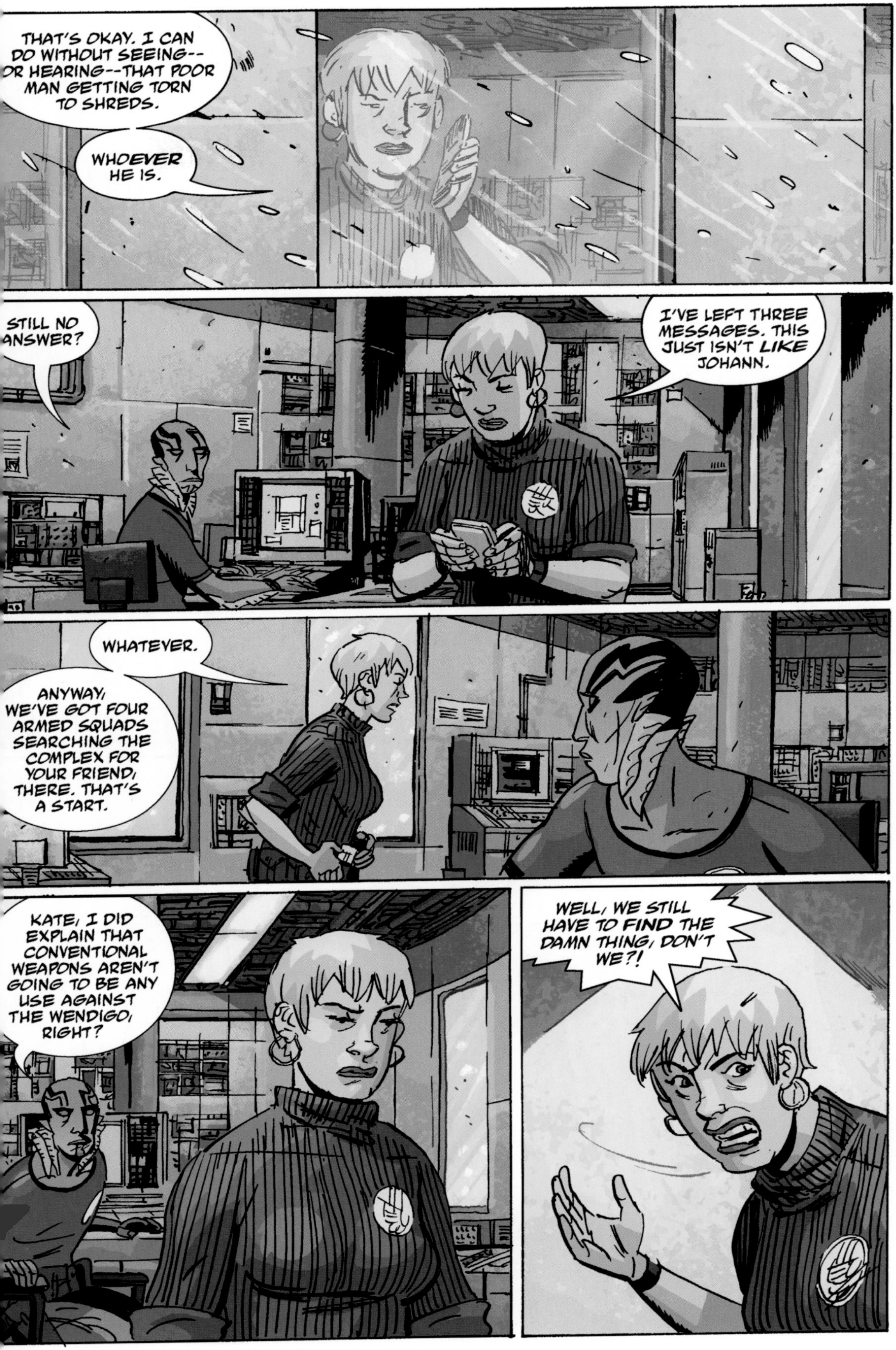
THAT'S OKAY. I CAN DO WITHOUT SEEING-- OR HEARING--THAT POOR MAN GETTING TORN TO SHREDS.
WHOEVER HE IS.
STILL NO ANSWER?
I'VE LEFT THREE MESSAGES. THIS JUST ISN'T LIKE JOHANN.
WHATEVER.
ANYWAY, WE'VE GOT FOUR ARMED SQUADS SEARCHING THE COMPLEX FOR YOUR FRIEND, THERE. THAT'S A START.
KATE, I DID EXPLAIN THAT CONVENTIONAL WEAPONS AREN'T GOING TO BE ANY USE AGAINST THE WENDIGO, RIGHT?
WELL, WE STILL HAVE TO FIND THE DAMN THING, DON'T WE?!

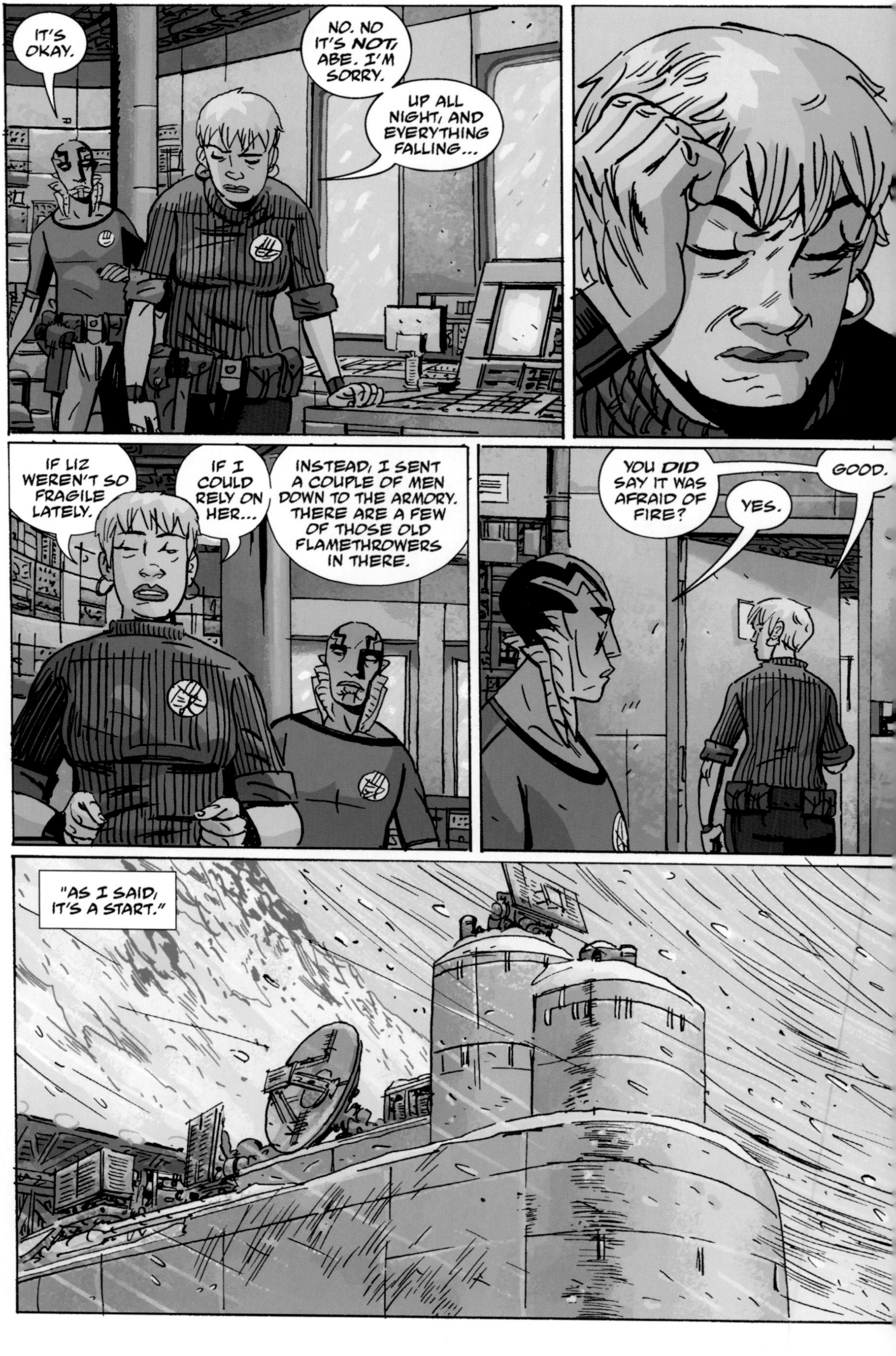
IT'S OKAY.
NO. NO IT'S NOT, ABE. I'M SORRY.
UP ALL NIGHT, AND EVERYTHING FALLING...
IF LIZ WEREN'T SO FRAGILE LATELY.
IF I COULD RELY ON HER...
INSTEAD, I SENT A COUPLE OF MEN DOWN TO THE ARMORY. THERE ARE A FEW OF THOSE OLD FLAMETHROWERS IN THERE.
YOU DID SAY IT WAS AFRAID OF FIRE?
YES.
GOOD.
"AS I SAID, IT'S A START."

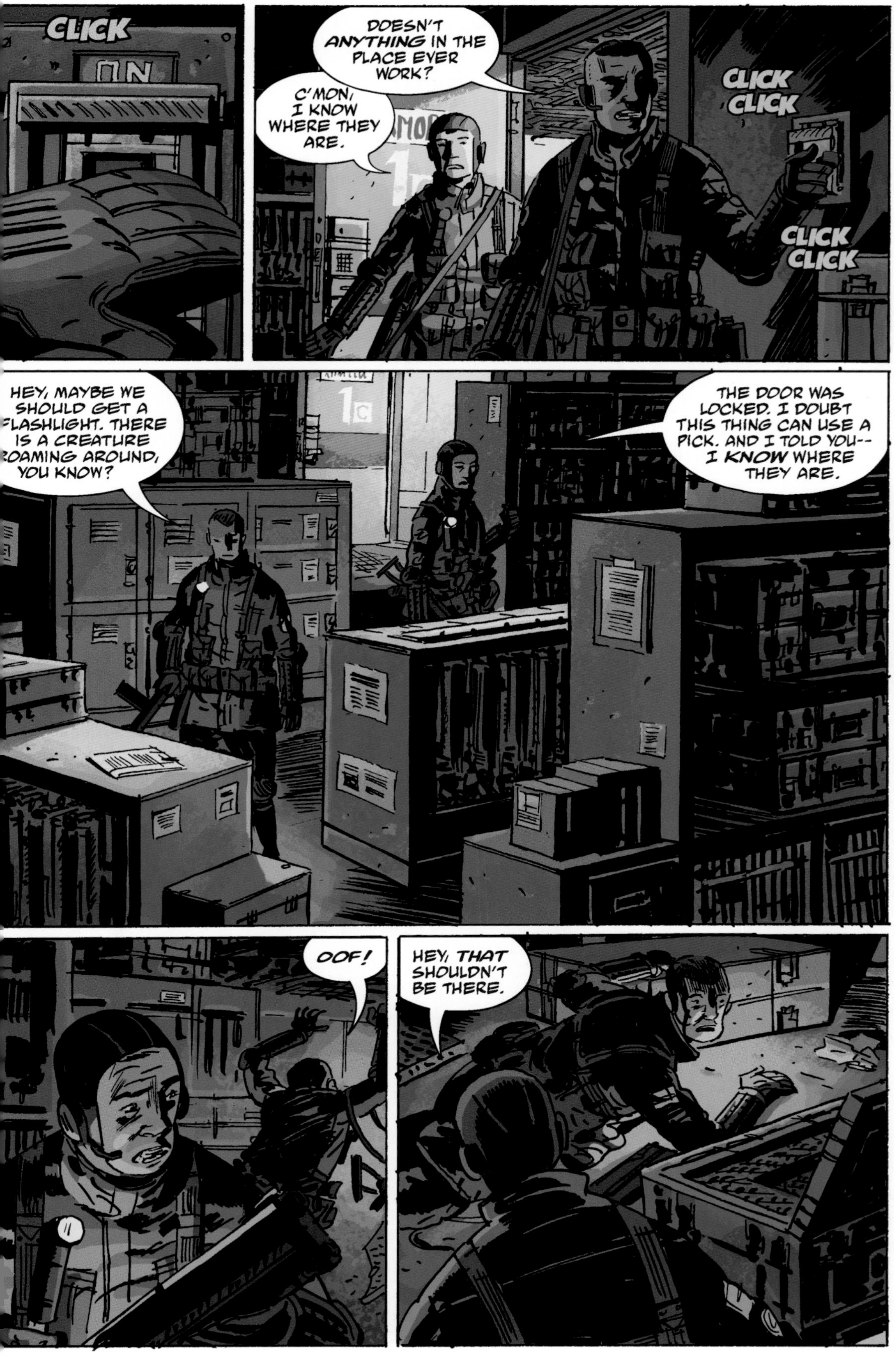
CLICK
ON
DOESN'T ANYTHING IN THE PLACE EVER WORK?
C'MON, I KNOW WHERE THEY ARE.
CLICK CLICK
CLICK CLICK
HEY, MAYBE WE SHOULD GET A FLASHLIGHT. THERE IS A CREATURE ROAMING AROUND, YOU KNOW?
THE DOOR WAS LOCKED. I DOUBT THIS THING CAN USE A PICK. AND I TOLD YOU-- I KNOW WHERE THEY ARE.
OOF!
HEY, THAT SHOULDN'T BE THERE.

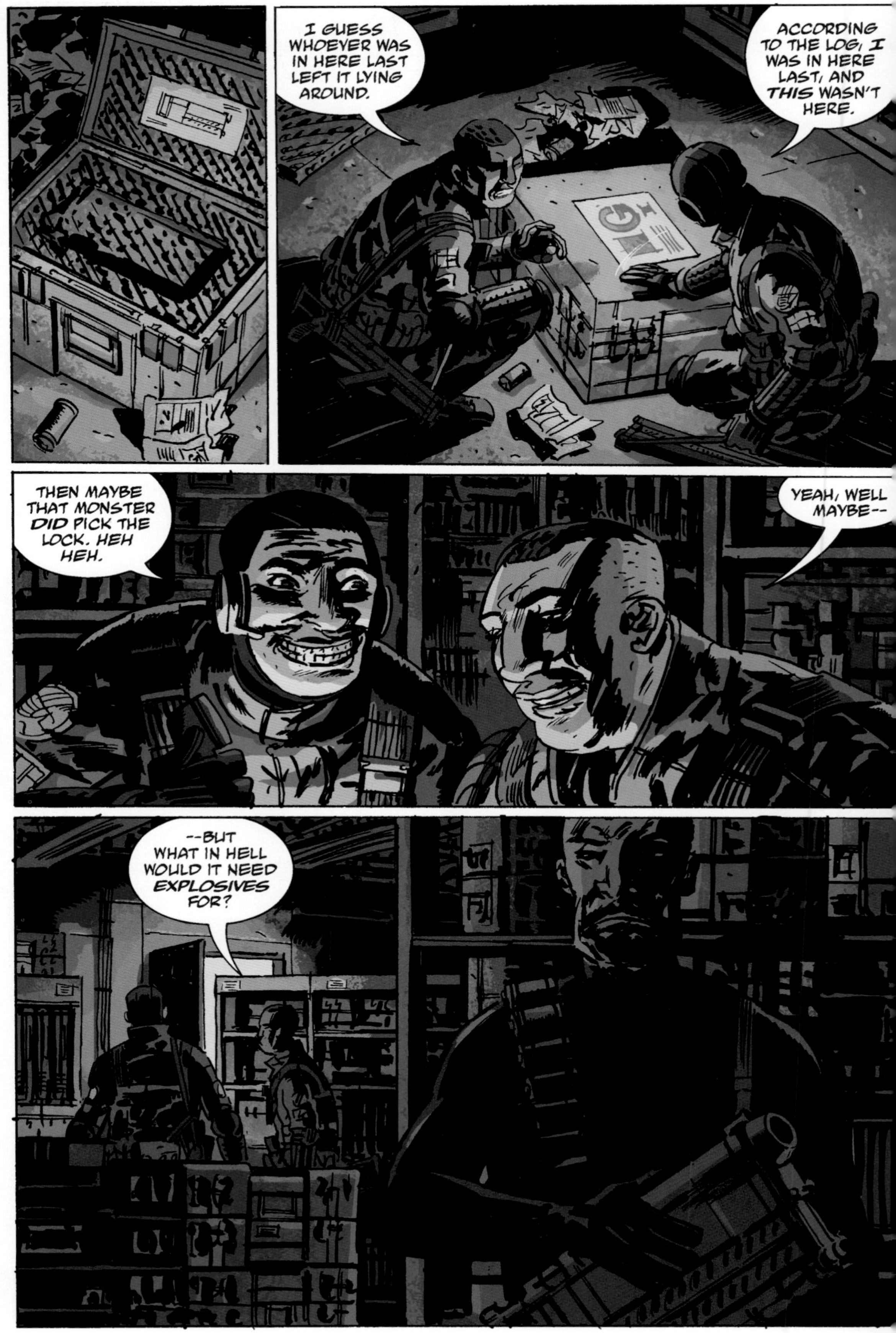
I GUESS WHOEVER WAS IN HERE LAST LEFT IT LYING AROUND.
ACCORDING TO THE LOG, I WAS IN HERE LAST, AND THIS WASN'T HERE.
THEN MAYBE THAT MONSTER DID PICK THE LOCK. HEH HEH.
YEAH, WELL MAYBE--
--BUT WHAT IN HELL WOULD IT NEED EXPLOSIVES FOR?

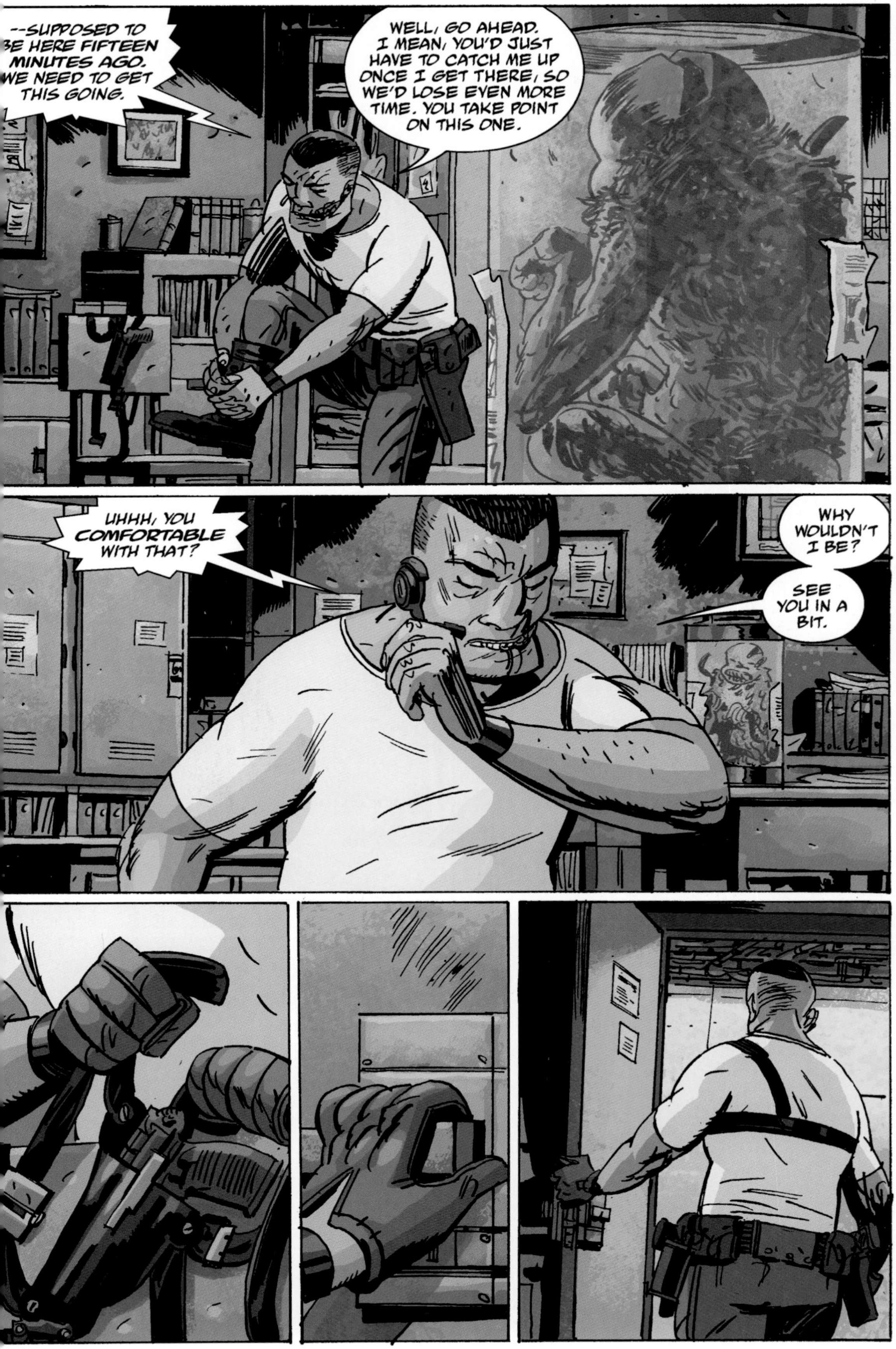
--SUPPOSED TO BE HERE FIFTEEN MINUTES AGO. WE NEED TO GET THIS GOING.
WELL, GO AHEAD. I MEAN, YOU'D JUST HAVE TO CATCH ME UP ONCE I GET THERE, SO WE'D LOSE EVEN MORE TIME. YOU TAKE POINT ON THIS ONE.
UHHH, YOU COMFORTABLE WITH THAT?
WHY WOULDN'T I BE?
SEE YOU IN A BIT.

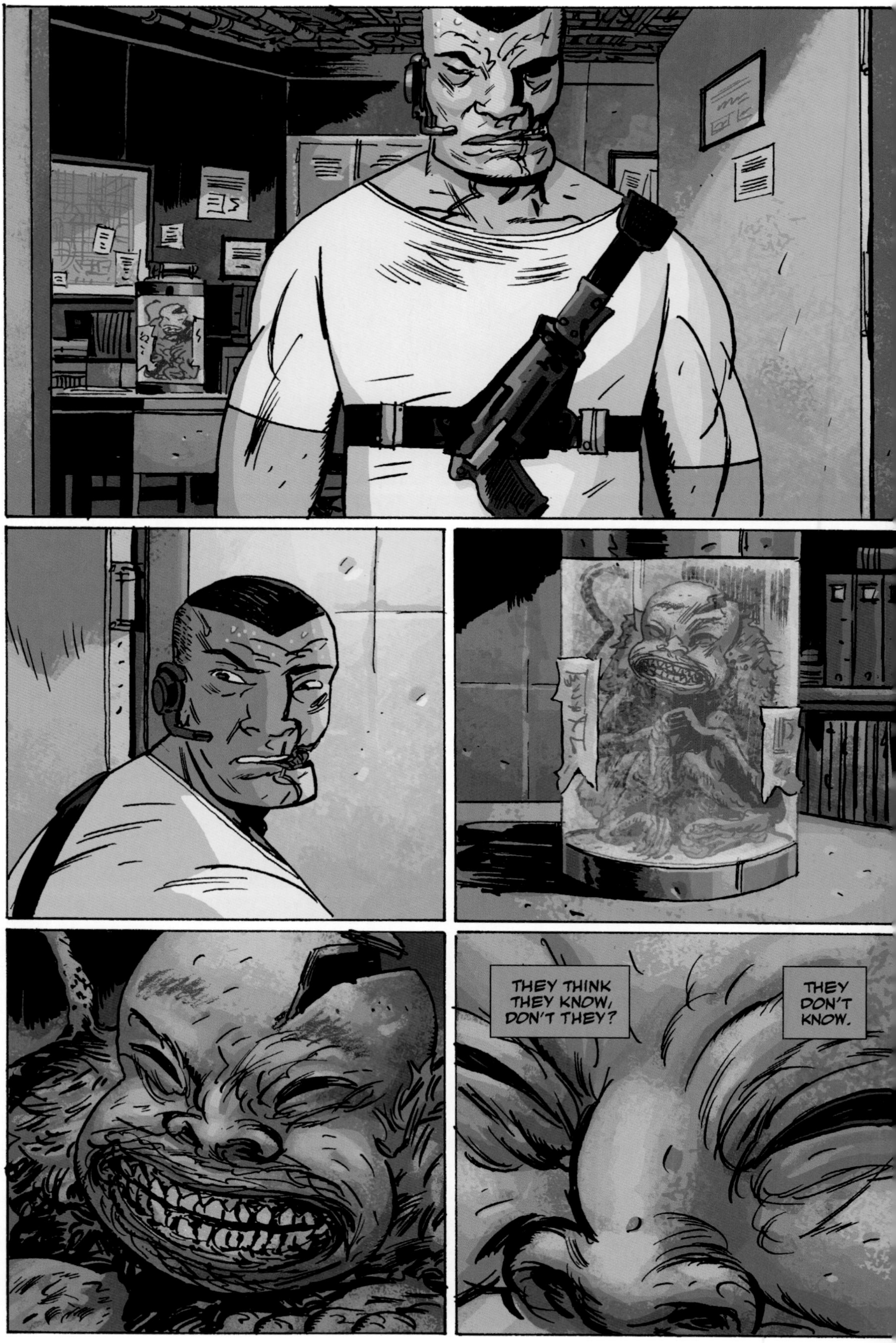
THEY THINK THEY KNOW, DON'T THEY?
THEY DON'T KNOW.

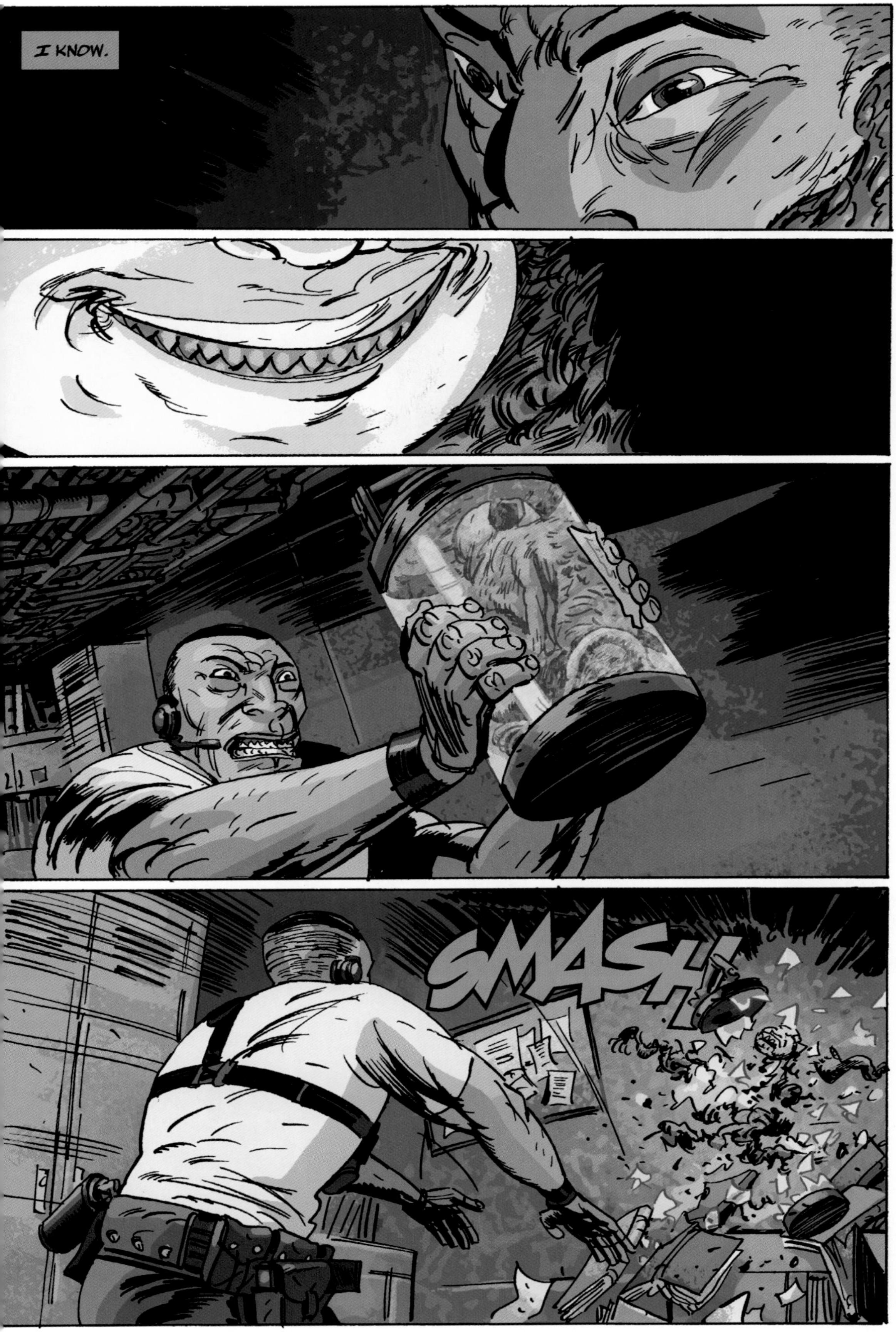
I KNOW.
SMASH!

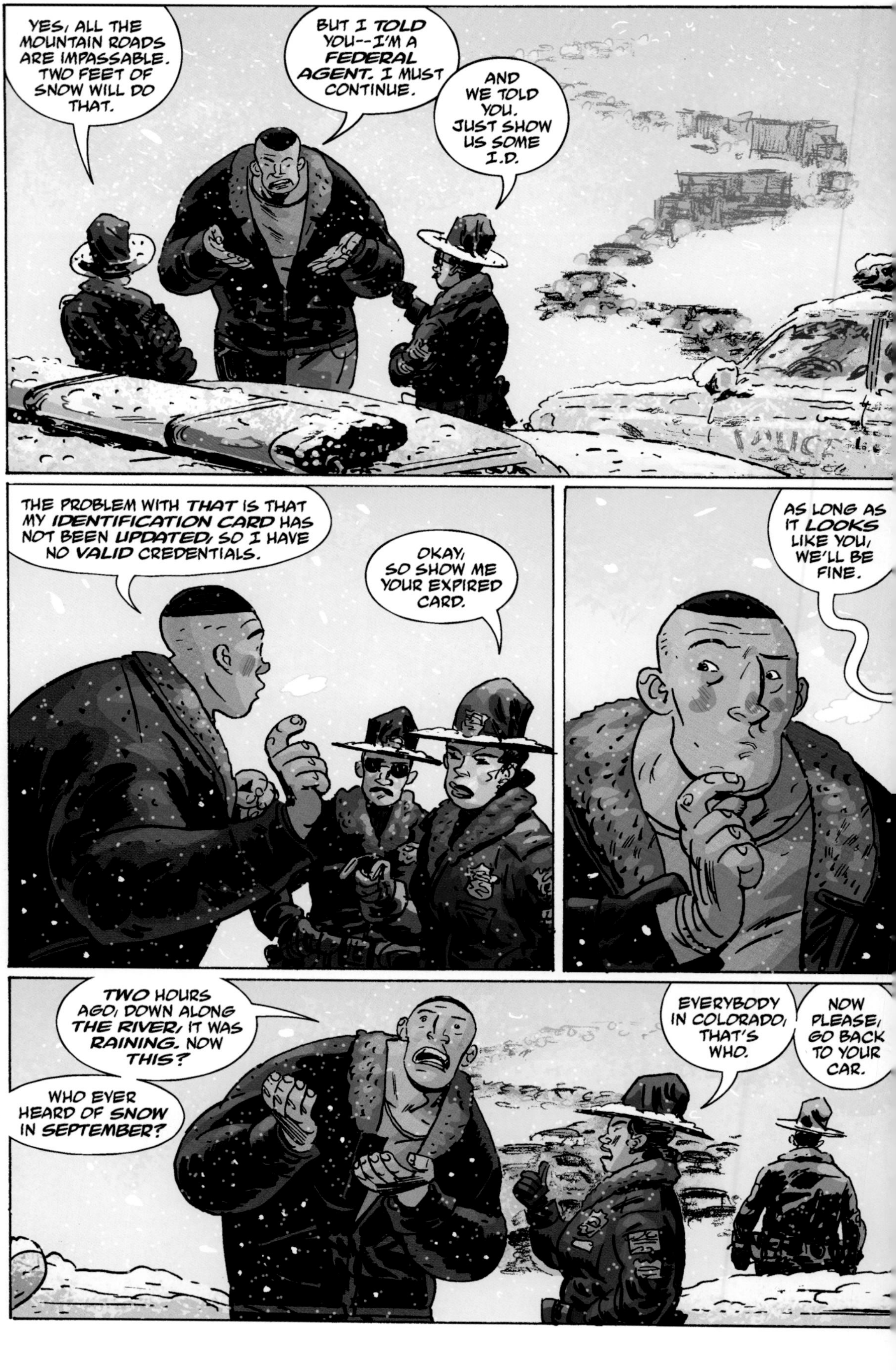
YES, ALL THE MOUNTAIN ROADS ARE IMPASSABLE. TWO FEET OF SNOW WILL DO THAT.
BUT I TOLD YOU--I'M A FEDERAL AGENT. I MUST CONTINUE.
AND WE TOLD YOU. JUST SHOW US SOME I.D.
THE PROBLEM WITH THAT IS THAT MY IDENTIFICATION CARD HAS NOT BEEN UPDATED, SO I HAVE NO VALID CREDENTIALS.
OKAY, SO SHOW ME YOUR EXPIRED CARD.
AS LONG AS IT LOOKS LIKE YOU, WE'LL BE FINE.
TWO HOURS AGO, DOWN ALONG THE RIVER, IT WAS RAINING. NOW THIS?
WHO EVER HEARD OF SNOW IN SEPTEMBER?
EVERYBODY IN COLORADO, THAT'S WHO.
NOW PLEASE, GO BACK TO YOUR CAR.

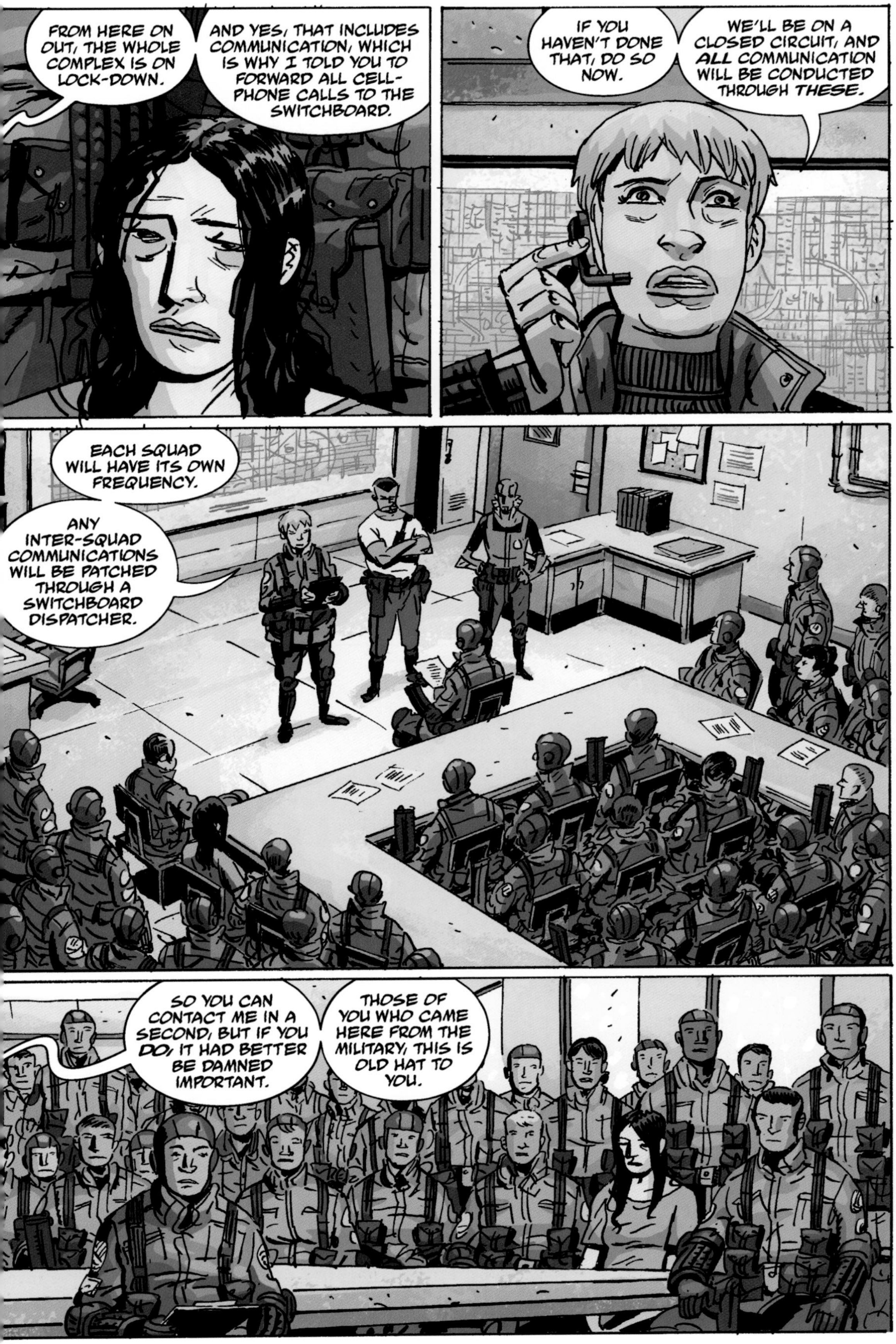
FROM HERE ON OUT, THE WHOLE COMPLEX IS ON LOCK-DOWN.
AND YES, THAT INCLUDES COMMUNICATION, WHICH IS WHY I TOLD YOU TO FORWARD ALL CELL-PHONE CALLS TO THE SWITCHBOARD.
IF YOU HAVEN'T DONE THAT, DO SO NOW.
WE'LL BE ON A CLOSED CIRCUIT, AND ALL COMMUNICATION WILL BE CONDUCTED THROUGH THESE.
EACH SQUAD WILL HAVE ITS OWN FREQUENCY.
ANY INTER-SQUAD COMMUNICATIONS WILL BE PATCHED THROUGH A SWITCHBOARD DISPATCHER.
SO YOU CAN CONTACT ME IN A SECOND, BUT IF YOU DO, IT HAD BETTER BE DAMNED IMPORTANT.
THOSE OF YOU WHO CAME HERE FROM THE MILITARY, THIS IS OLD HAT TO YOU.

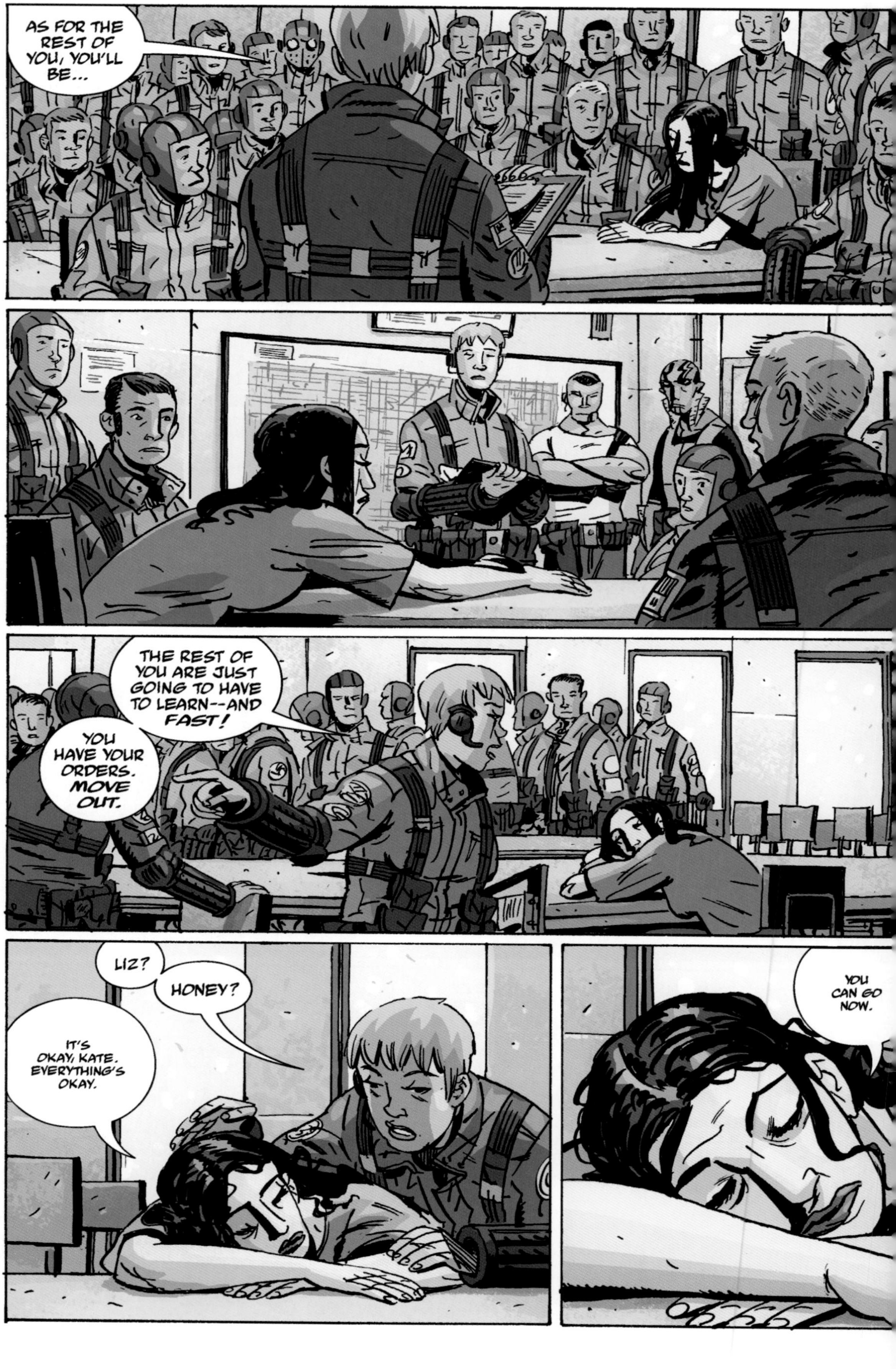
AS FOR THE REST OF YOU, YOU'LL BE...
THE REST OF YOU ARE JUST GOING TO HAVE TO LEARN--AND FAST!
YOU HAVE YOUR ORDERS. MOVE OUT.
LIZ?
HONEY?
IT'S OKAY, KATE. EVERYTHING'S OKAY.
YOU CAN GO NOW.

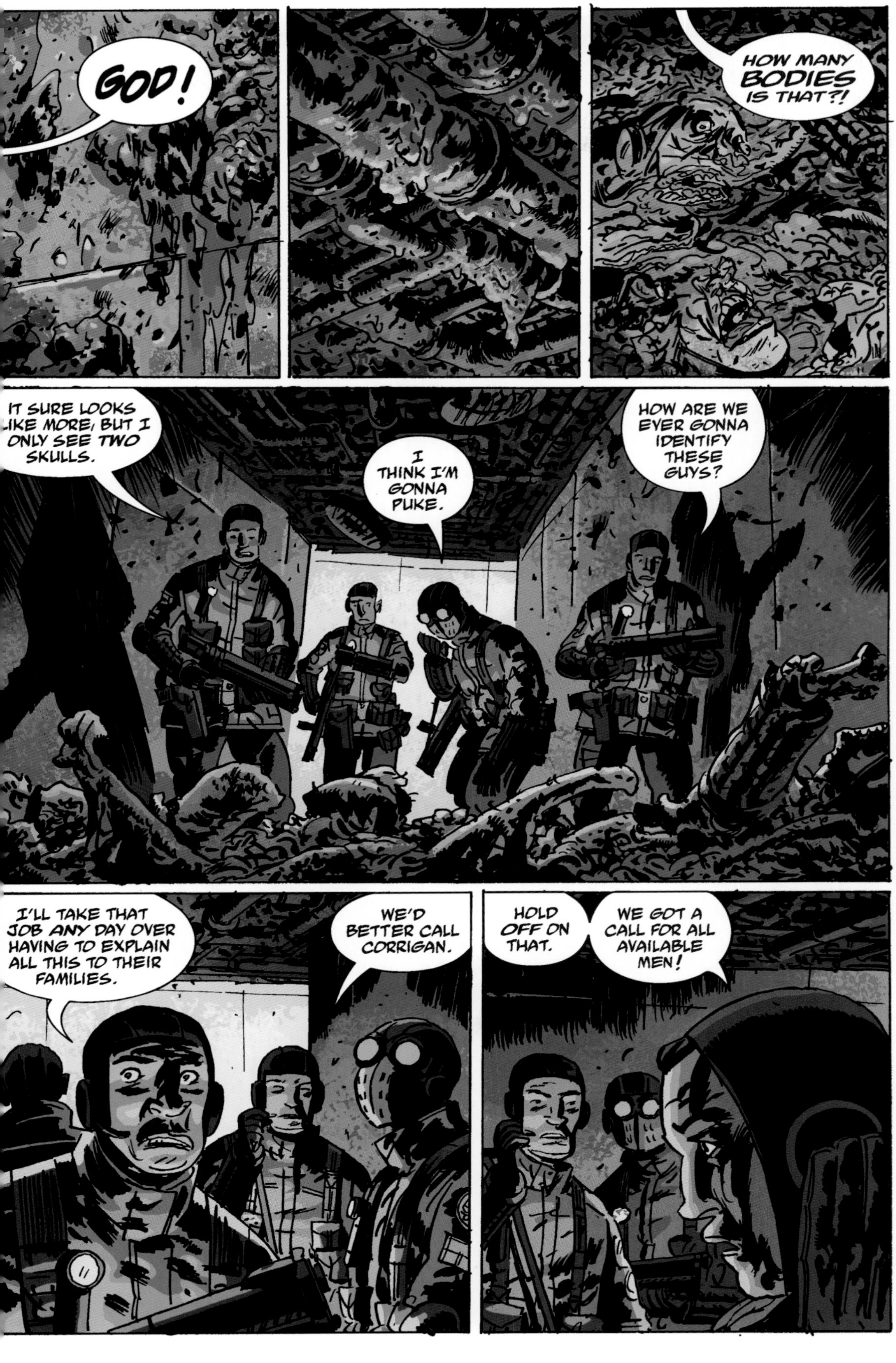
GOD!
HOW MANY BODIES IS THAT?!
IT SURE LOOKS LIKE MORE, BUT I ONLY SEE TWO SKULLS.
I THINK I'M GONNA PUKE.
HOW ARE WE EVER GONNA IDENTIFY THESE GUYS?
I'LL TAKE THAT JOB ANY DAY OVER HAVING TO EXPLAIN ALL THIS TO THEIR FAMILIES.
WE'D BETTER CALL CORRIGAN.
HOLD OFF ON THAT.
WE GOT A CALL FOR ALL AVAILABLE MEN!

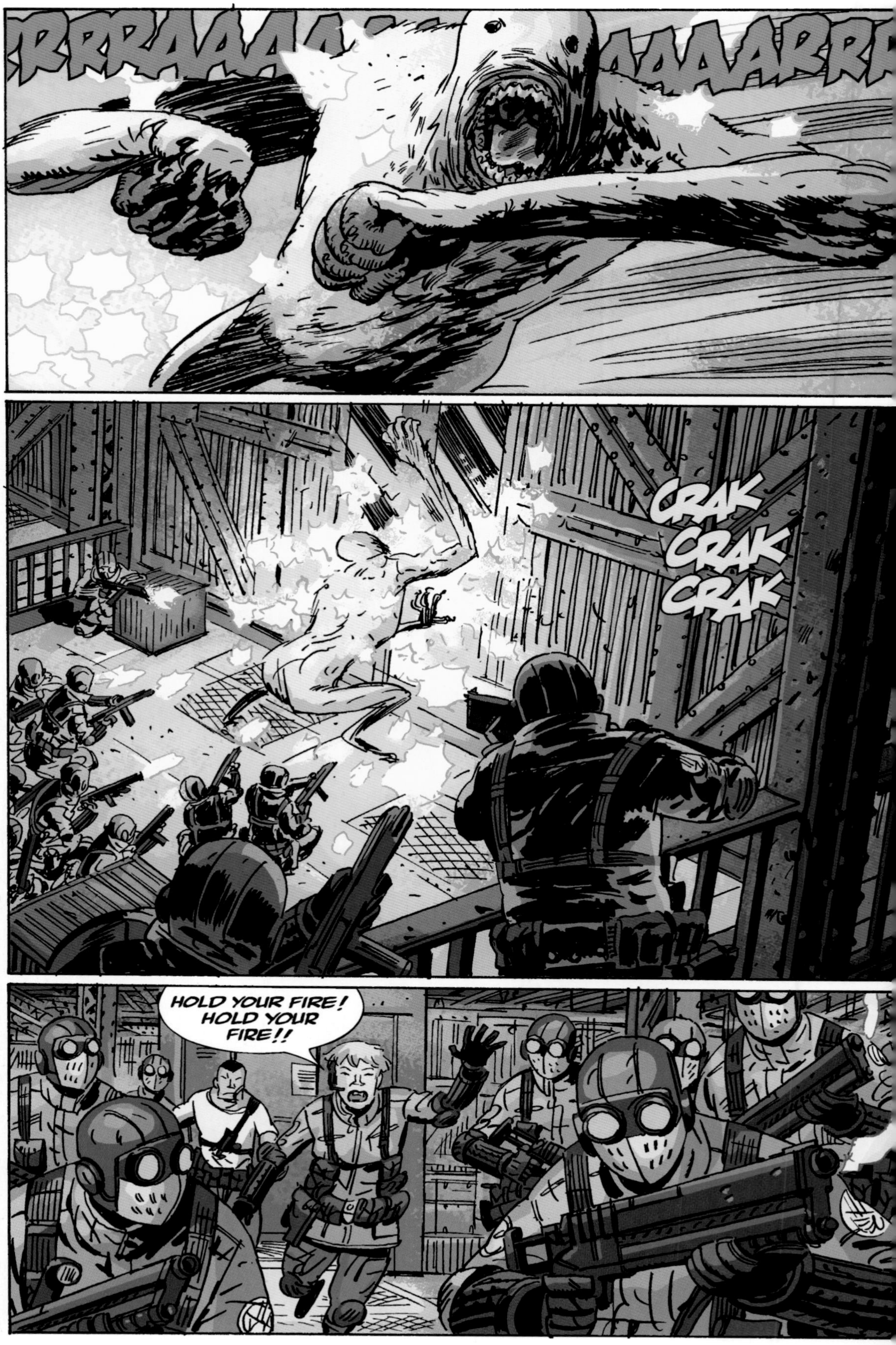
RRRAAAA... AAAAARRR
CRAK CRAK CRAK
HOLD YOUR FIRE! HOLD YOUR FIRE!!

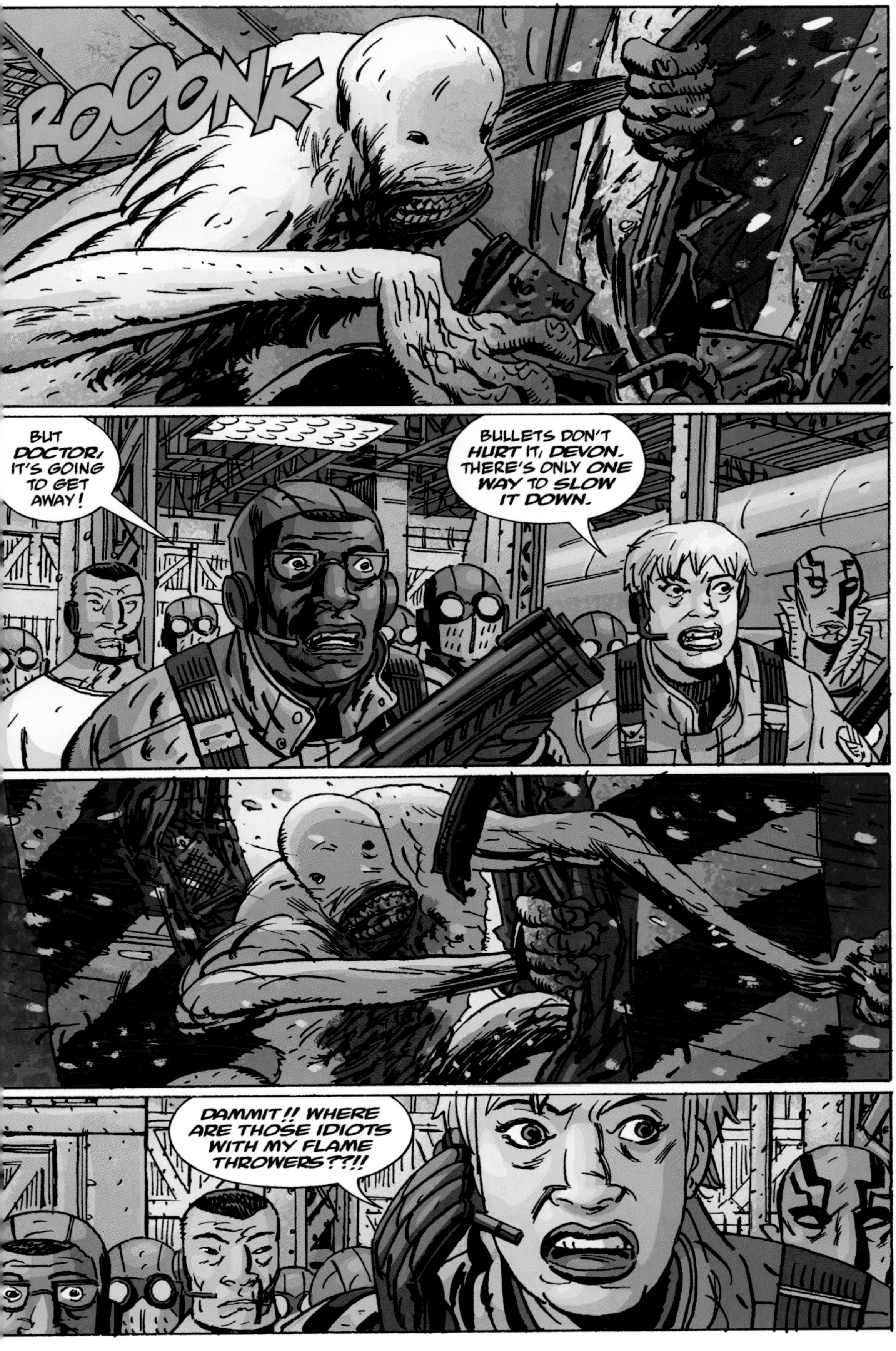
ROOONK
BUT DOCTOR, IT'S GOING TO GET AWAY!
BULLETS DON'T HURT IT, DEVON. THERE'S ONLY ONE WAY TO SLOW IT DOWN.
DAMMIT!! WHERE ARE THOSE IDIOTS WITH MY FLAME THROWERS??!!

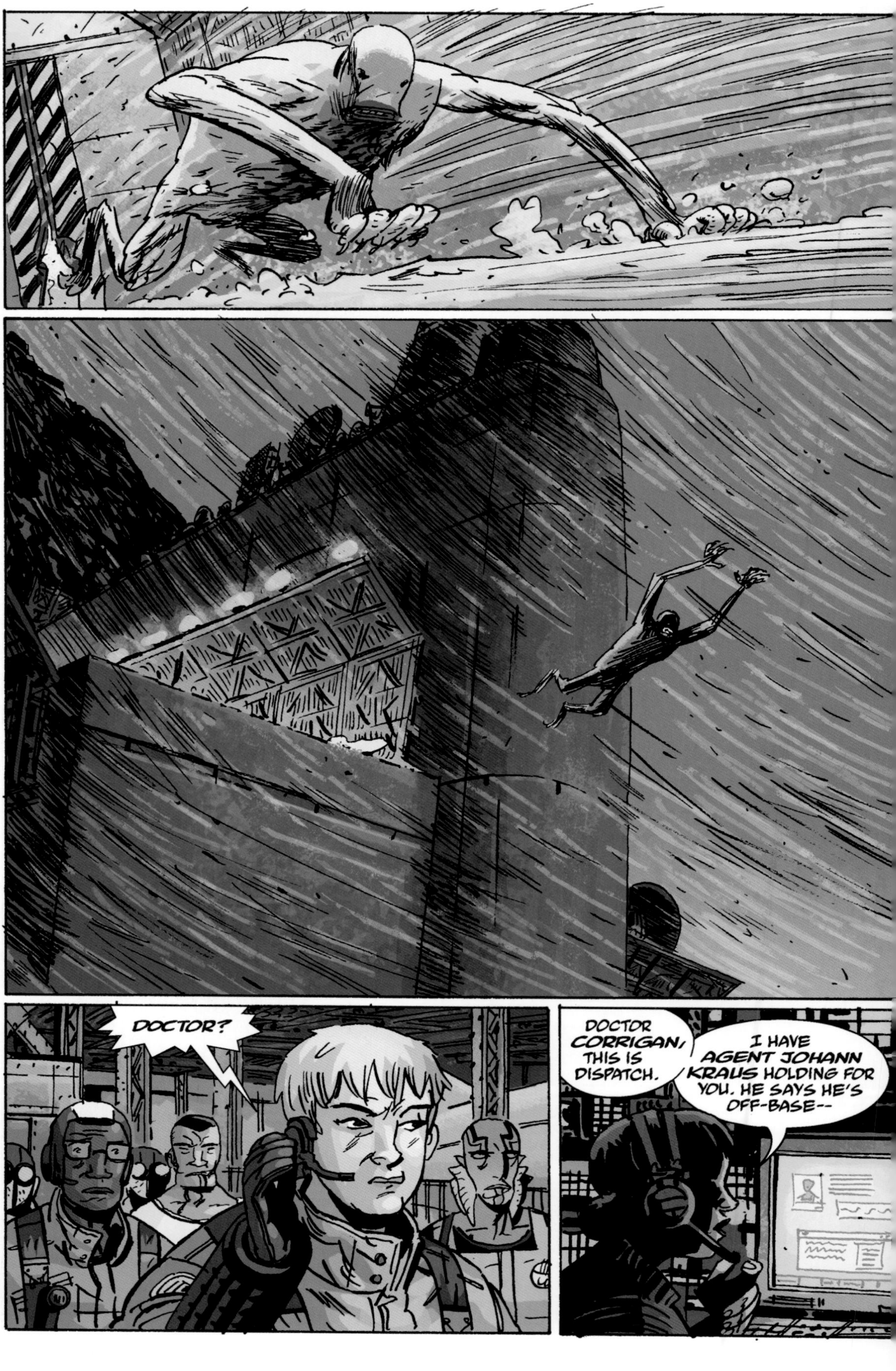
DOCTOR?
DOCTOR CORRIGAN, THIS IS DISPATCH.
I HAVE AGENT JOHANN KRAUS HOLDING FOR YOU. HE SAYS HE'S OFF-BASE--

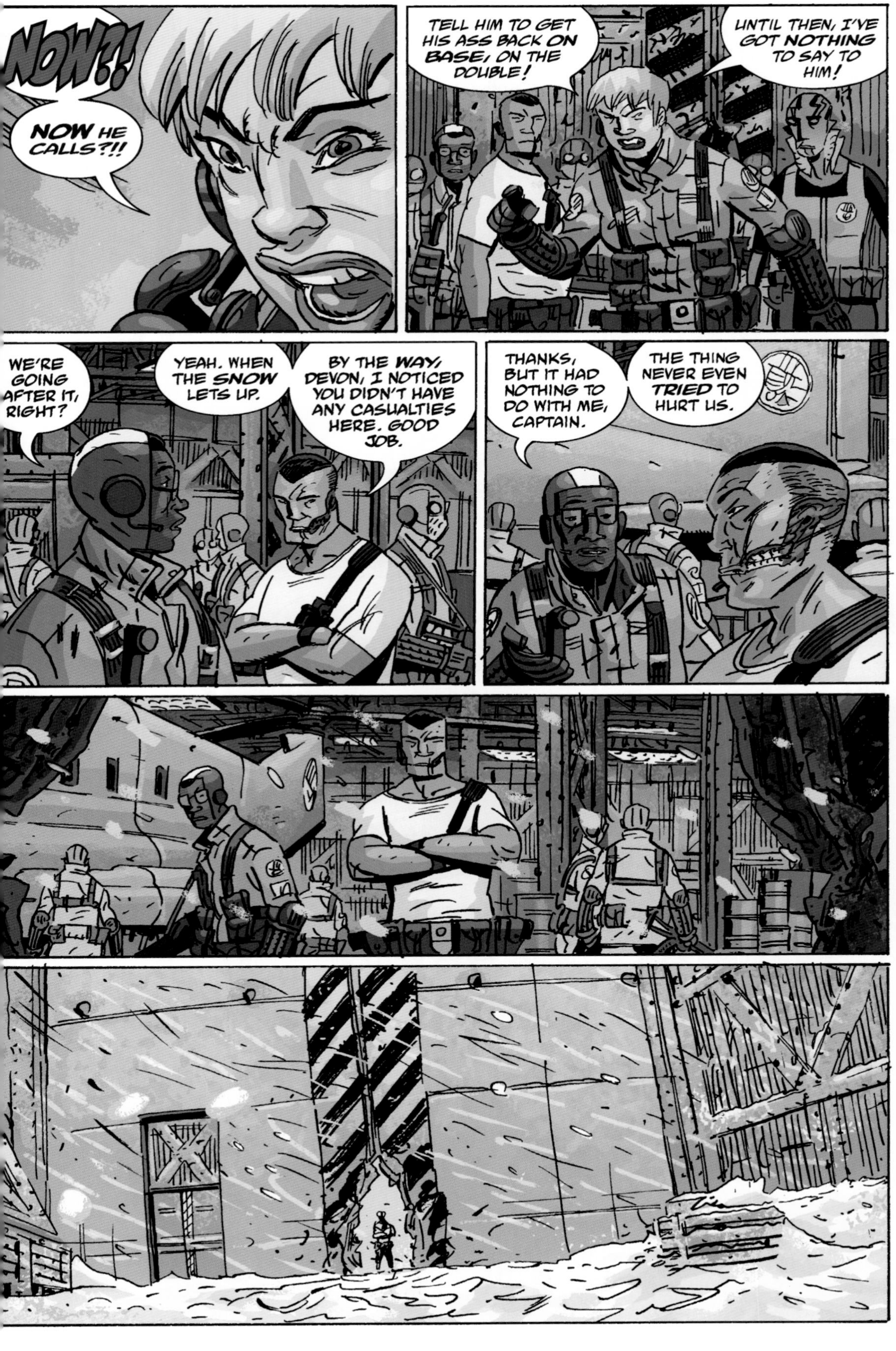
NOW?!
NOW HE CALLS?!!
TELL HIM TO GET HIS ASS BACK ON BASE, ON THE DOUBLE!
UNTIL THEN, I'VE GOT NOTHING TO SAY TO HIM!
WE'RE GOING AFTER IT, RIGHT?
YEAH. WHEN THE SNOW LETS UP.
BY THE WAY, DEVON, I NOTICED YOU DIDN'T HAVE ANY CASUALTIES HERE. GOOD JOB.
THANKS, BUT IT HAD NOTHING TO DO WITH ME, CAPTAIN.
THE THING NEVER EVEN TRIED TO HURT US.

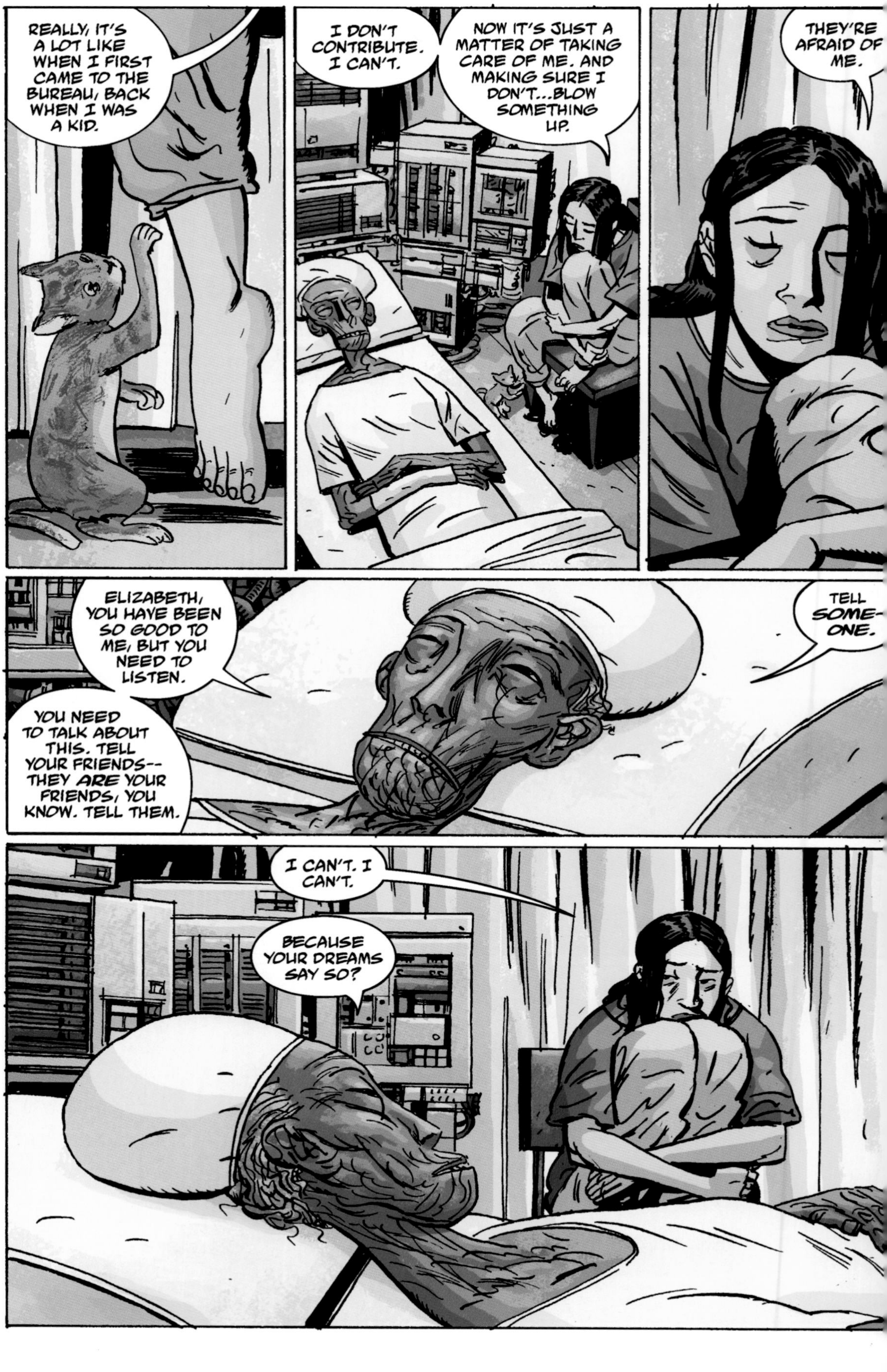
REALLY, IT'S A LOT LIKE WHEN I FIRST CAME TO THE BUREAU, BACK WHEN I WAS A KID.
I DON'T CONTRIBUTE. I CAN'T.
NOW IT'S JUST A MATTER OF TAKING CARE OF ME. AND MAKING SURE I DON'T...BLOW SOMETHING UP.
THEY'RE AFRAID OF ME.
ELIZABETH, YOU HAVE BEEN SO GOOD TO ME, BUT YOU NEED TO LISTEN.
YOU NEED TO TALK ABOUT THIS. TELL YOUR FRIENDS-- THEY *ARE* YOUR FRIENDS, YOU KNOW. TELL THEM.
TELL *SOME-ONE.*
I CAN'T. I CAN'T.
BECAUSE YOUR DREAMS SAY SO?

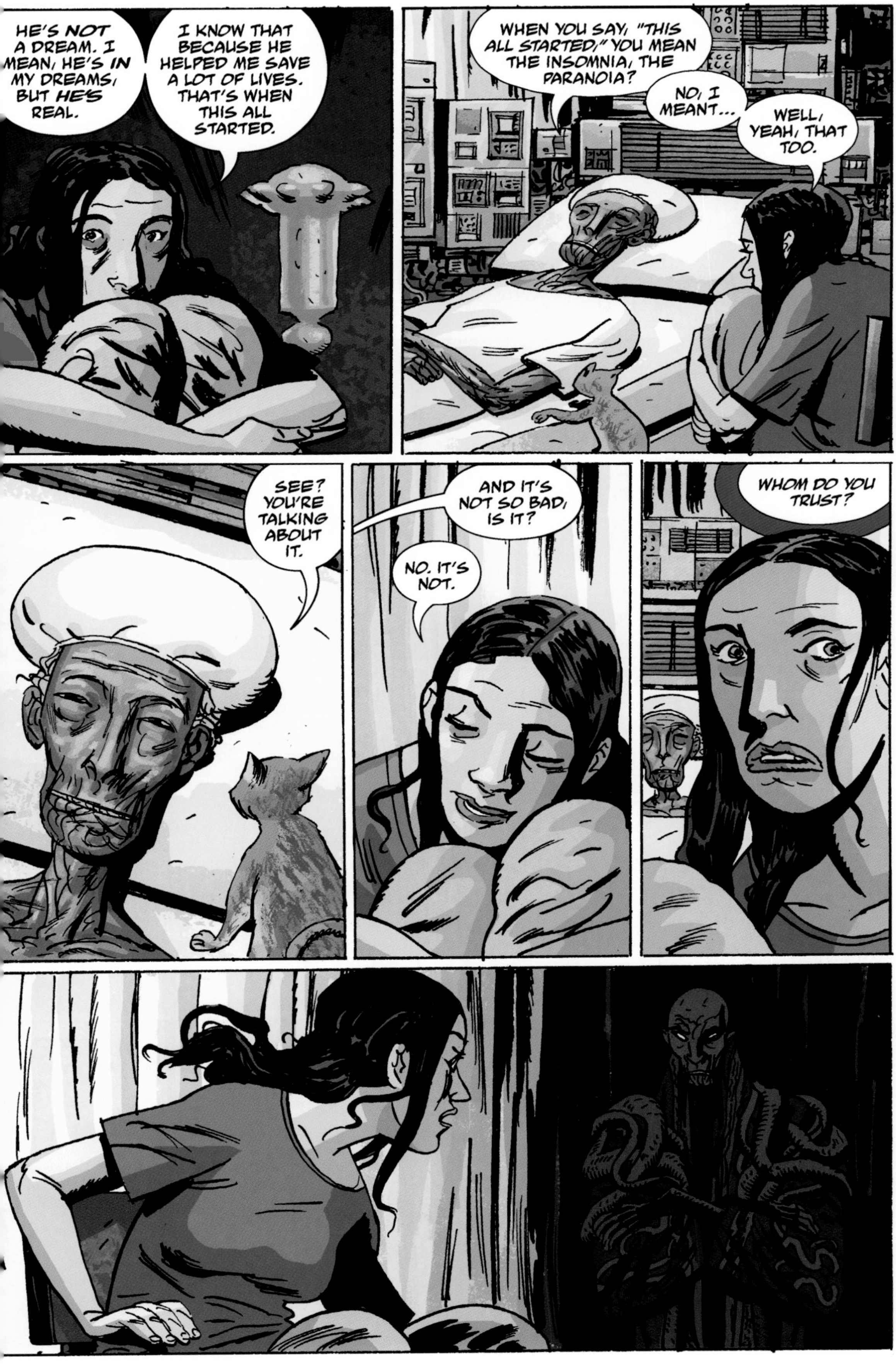
HE'S NOT A DREAM. I MEAN, HE'S IN MY DREAMS, BUT HE'S REAL.
I KNOW THAT BECAUSE HE HELPED ME SAVE A LOT OF LIVES. THAT'S WHEN THIS ALL STARTED.
WHEN YOU SAY, "THIS ALL STARTED," YOU MEAN THE INSOMNIA, THE PARANOIA?
NO, I MEANT...
WELL, YEAH, THAT TOO.
SEE? YOU'RE TALKING ABOUT IT.
AND IT'S NOT SO BAD, IS IT?
NO. IT'S NOT.
WHOM DO YOU TRUST?

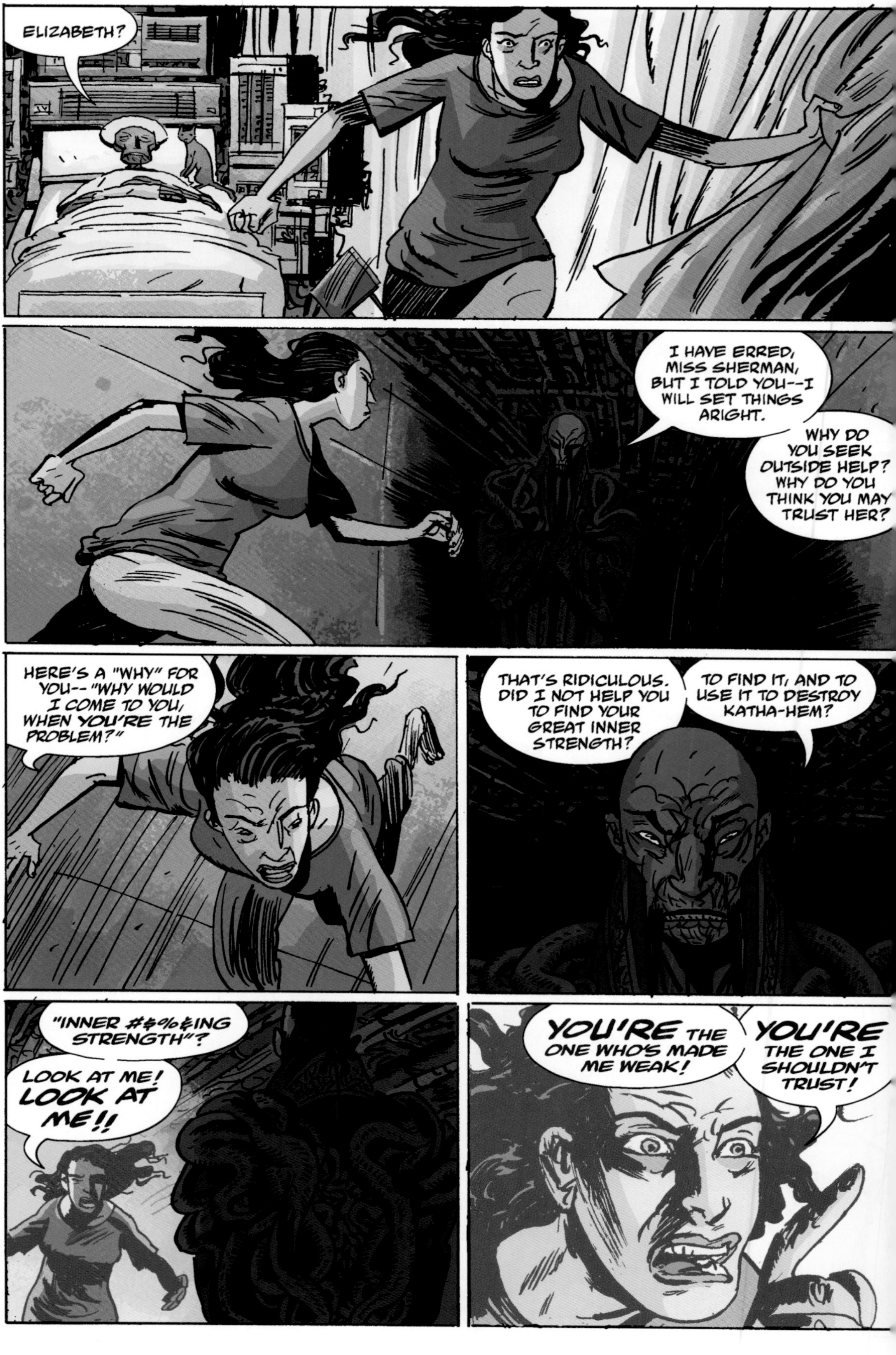
ELIZABETH?
I HAVE ERRED, MISS SHERMAN, BUT I TOLD YOU--I WILL SET THINGS ARIGHT.
WHY DO YOU SEEK OUTSIDE HELP? WHY DO YOU THINK YOU MAY TRUST HER?
HERE'S A "WHY" FOR YOU-- "WHY WOULD I COME TO YOU, WHEN YOU'RE THE PROBLEM?"
THAT'S RIDICULOUS. DID I NOT HELP YOU TO FIND YOUR GREAT INNER STRENGTH?
TO FIND IT, AND TO USE IT TO DESTROY KATHA-HEM?
"INNER #$%&ING STRENGTH"?
LOOK AT ME! LOOK AT ME!!
YOU'RE THE ONE WHO'S MADE ME WEAK!
YOU'RE THE ONE I SHOULDN'T TRUST!

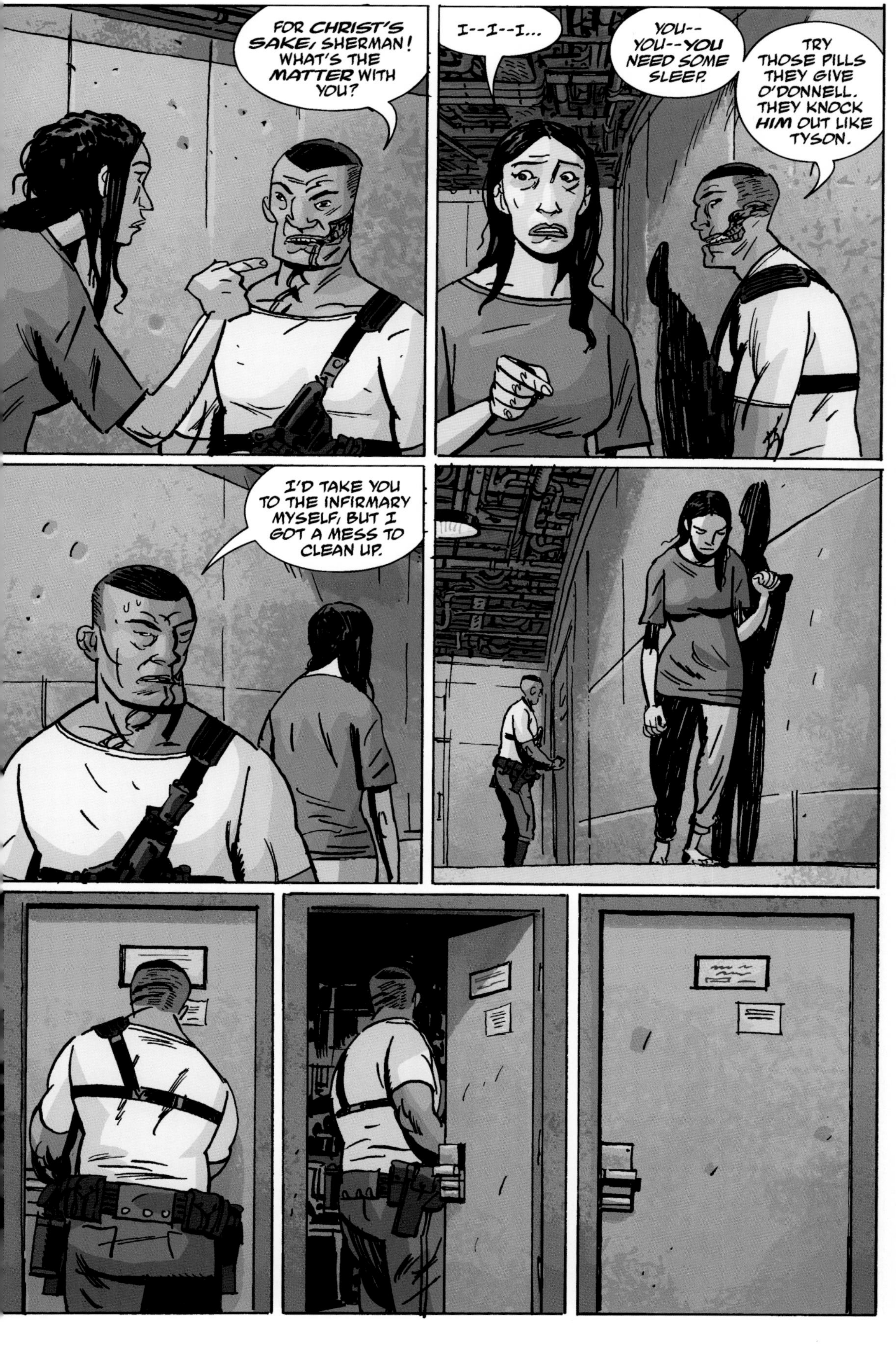
FOR CHRIST'S SAKE, SHERMAN! WHAT'S THE MATTER WITH YOU?
I--I--I...
YOU--YOU--YOU NEED SOME SLEEP.
TRY THOSE PILLS THEY GIVE O'DONNELL. THEY KNOCK HIM OUT LIKE TYSON.
I'D TAKE YOU TO THE INFIRMARY MYSELF, BUT I GOT A MESS TO CLEAN UP.

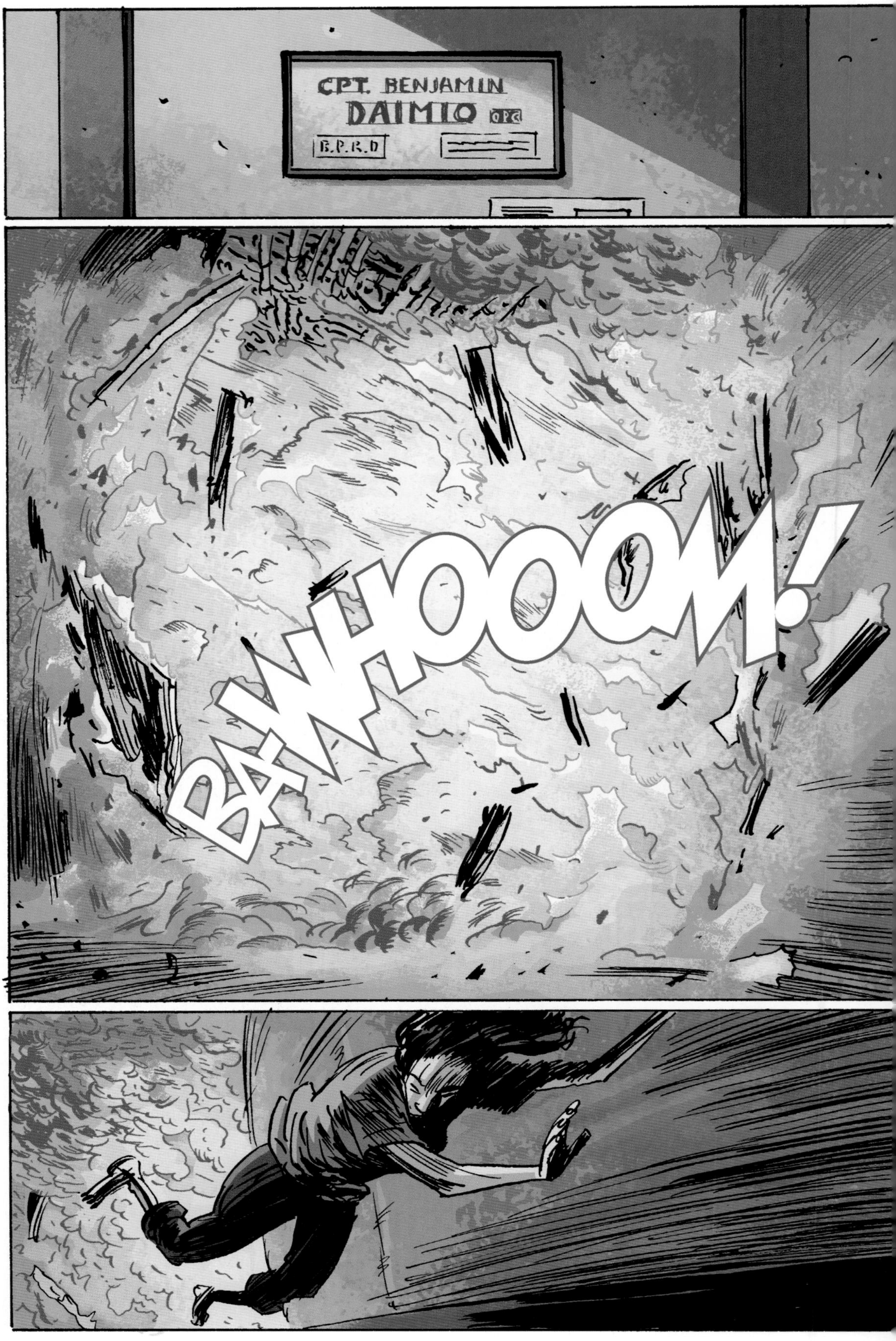
CPT. BENJAMIN
DAIMIO
B.P.R.D
BA-WHOOOM!

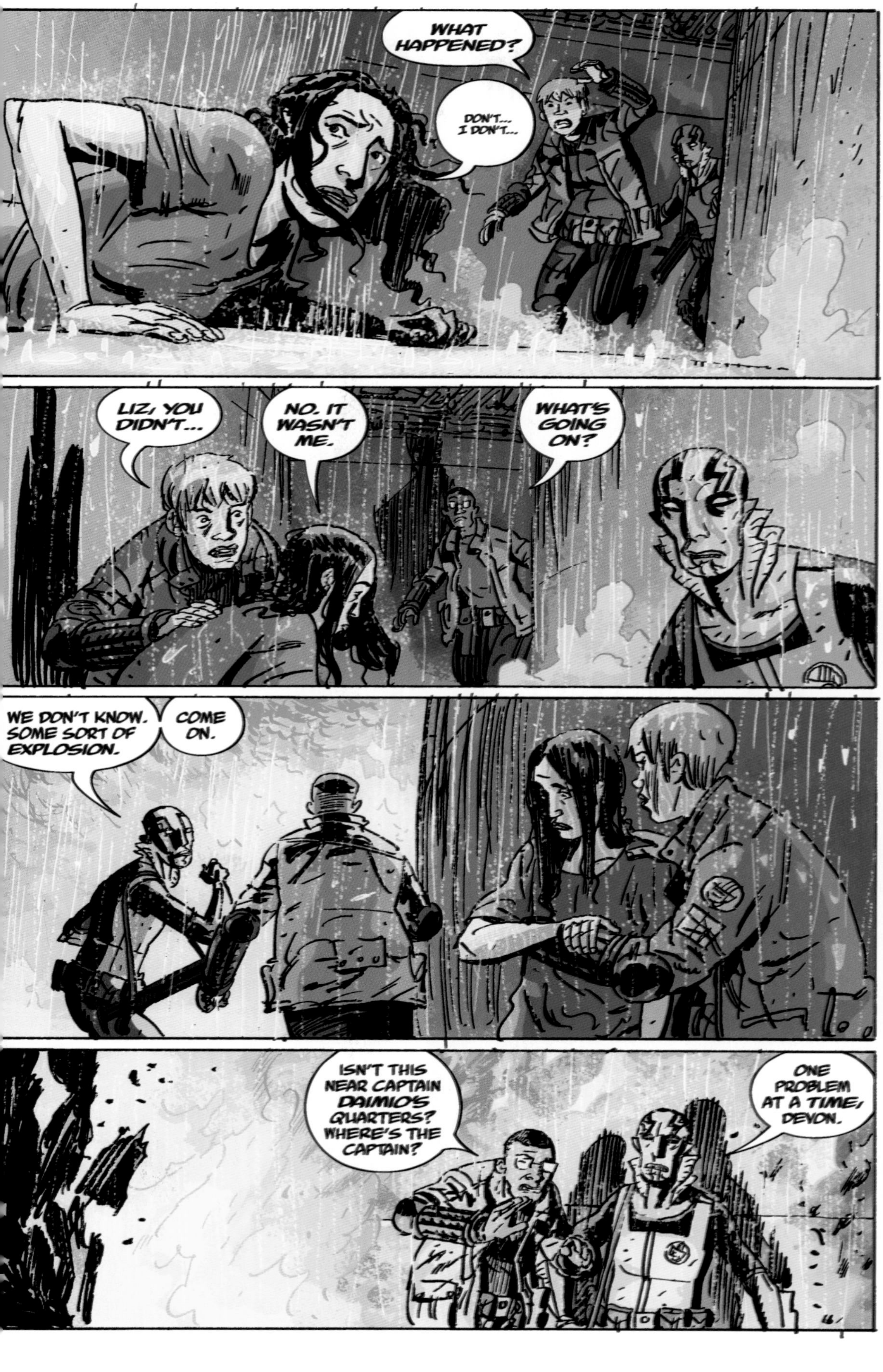
WHAT HAPPENED?
DON'T... I DON'T...
LIZ, YOU DIDN'T...
NO. IT WASN'T ME.
WHAT'S GOING ON?
WE DON'T KNOW. SOME SORT OF EXPLOSION.
COME ON.
ISN'T THIS NEAR CAPTAIN DAIMIO'S QUARTERS? WHERE'S THE CAPTAIN?
ONE PROBLEM AT A TIME, DEVON.

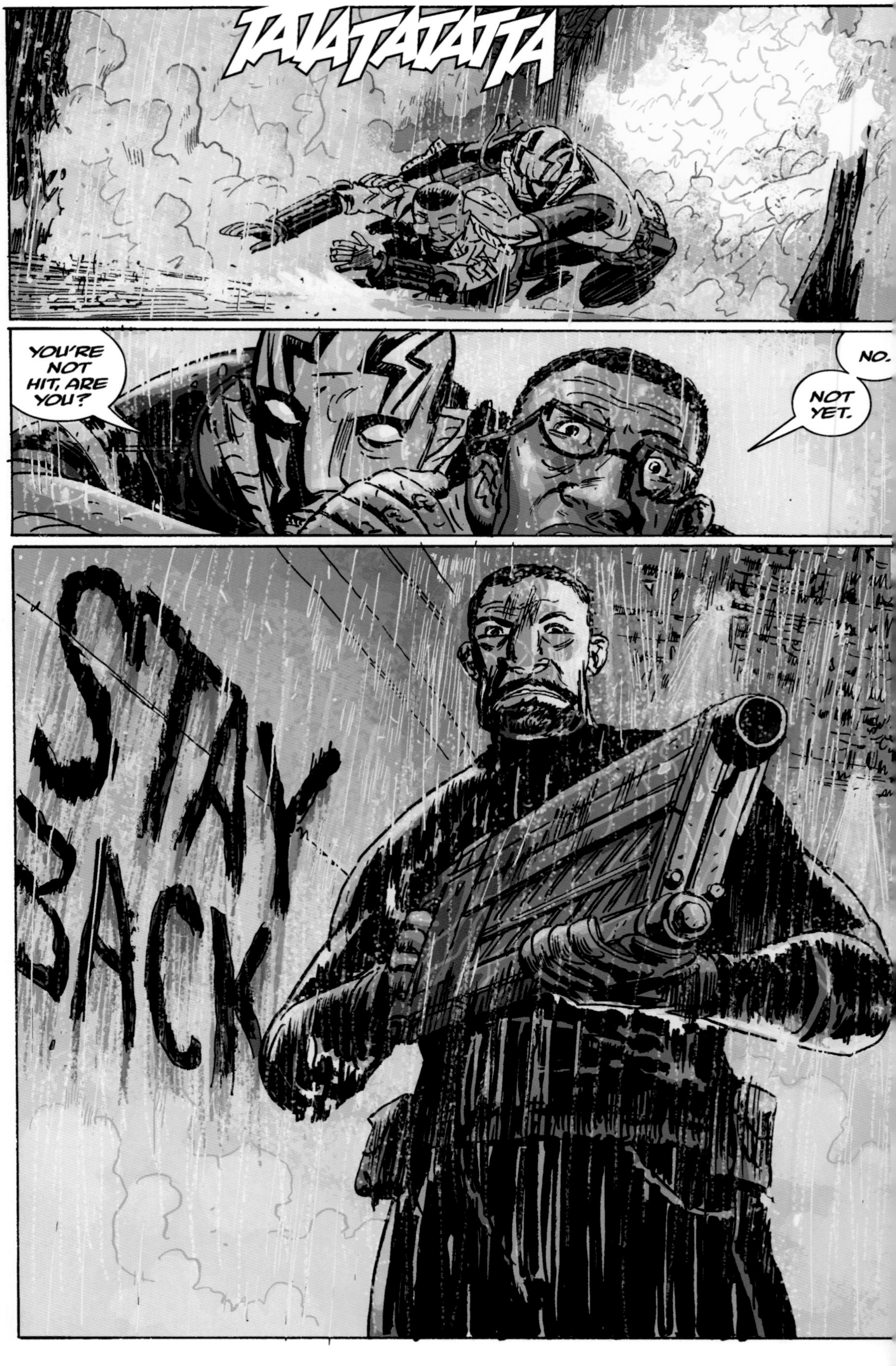
TATATATATTA
YOU'RE NOT HIT, ARE YOU?
NO.
NOT YET.
STAY BACK

CHAPTER FOUR

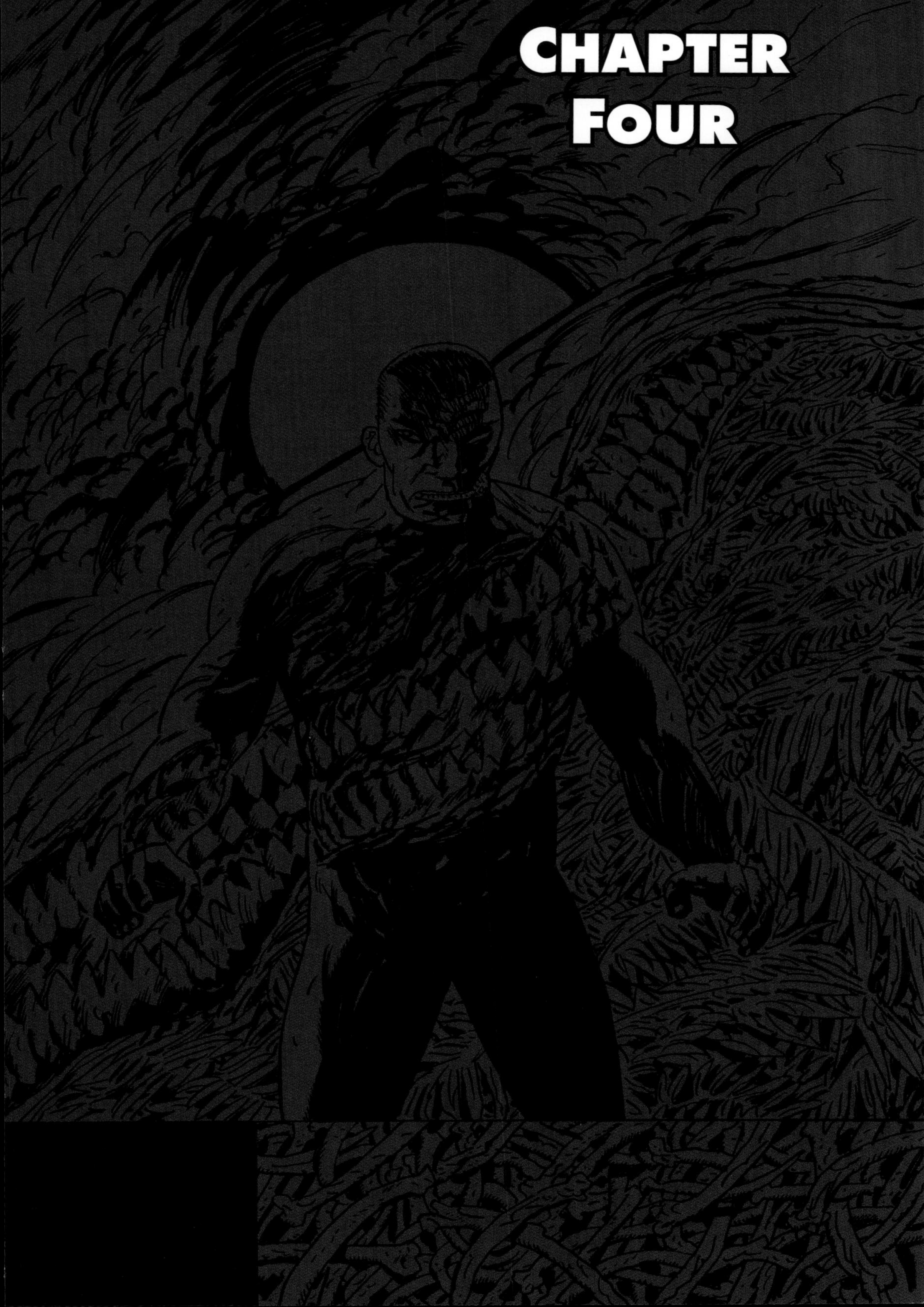

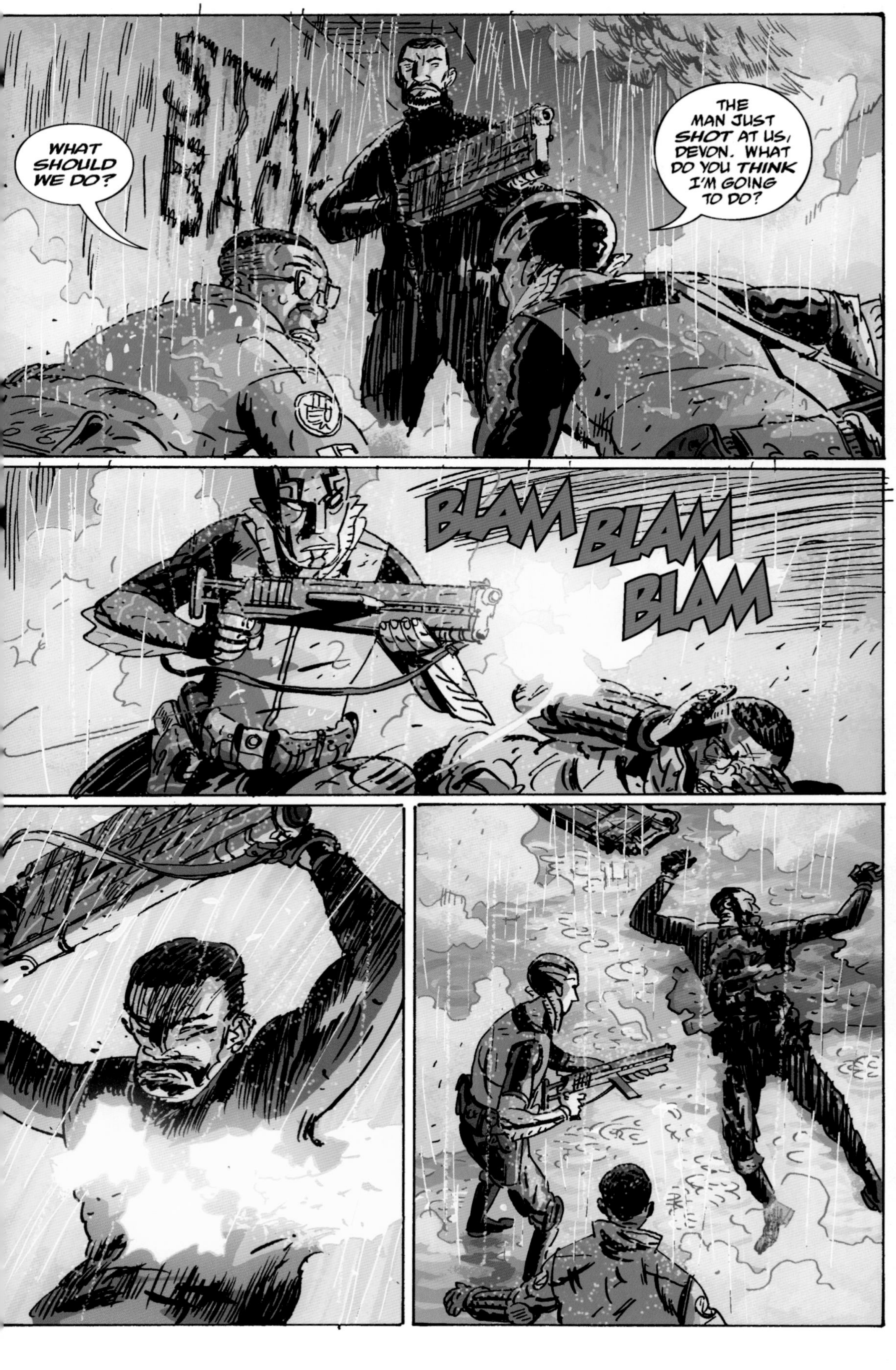
STAY BACK
WHAT SHOULD WE DO?
THE MAN JUST SHOT AT US, DEVON. WHAT DO YOU THINK I'M GOING TO DO?
BLAM BLAM BLAM

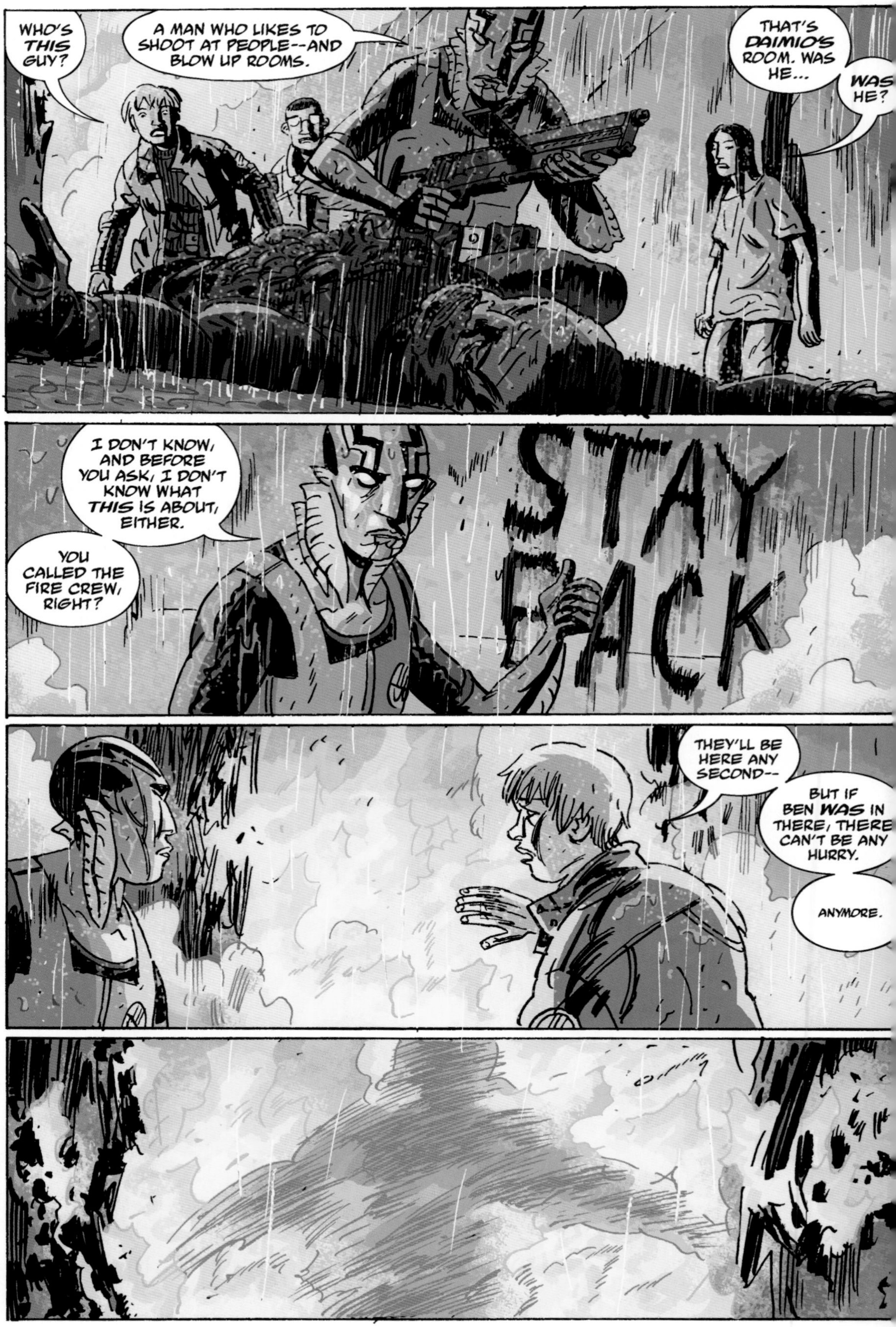
WHO'S THIS GUY?
A MAN WHO LIKES TO SHOOT AT PEOPLE--AND BLOW UP ROOMS.
THAT'S DAIMIO'S ROOM. WAS HE...
WAS HE?
I DON'T KNOW, AND BEFORE YOU ASK, I DON'T KNOW WHAT THIS IS ABOUT, EITHER.
YOU CALLED THE FIRE CREW, RIGHT?
STAY BACK
THEY'LL BE HERE ANY SECOND--
BUT IF BEN WAS IN THERE, THERE CAN'T BE ANY HURRY.
ANYMORE.

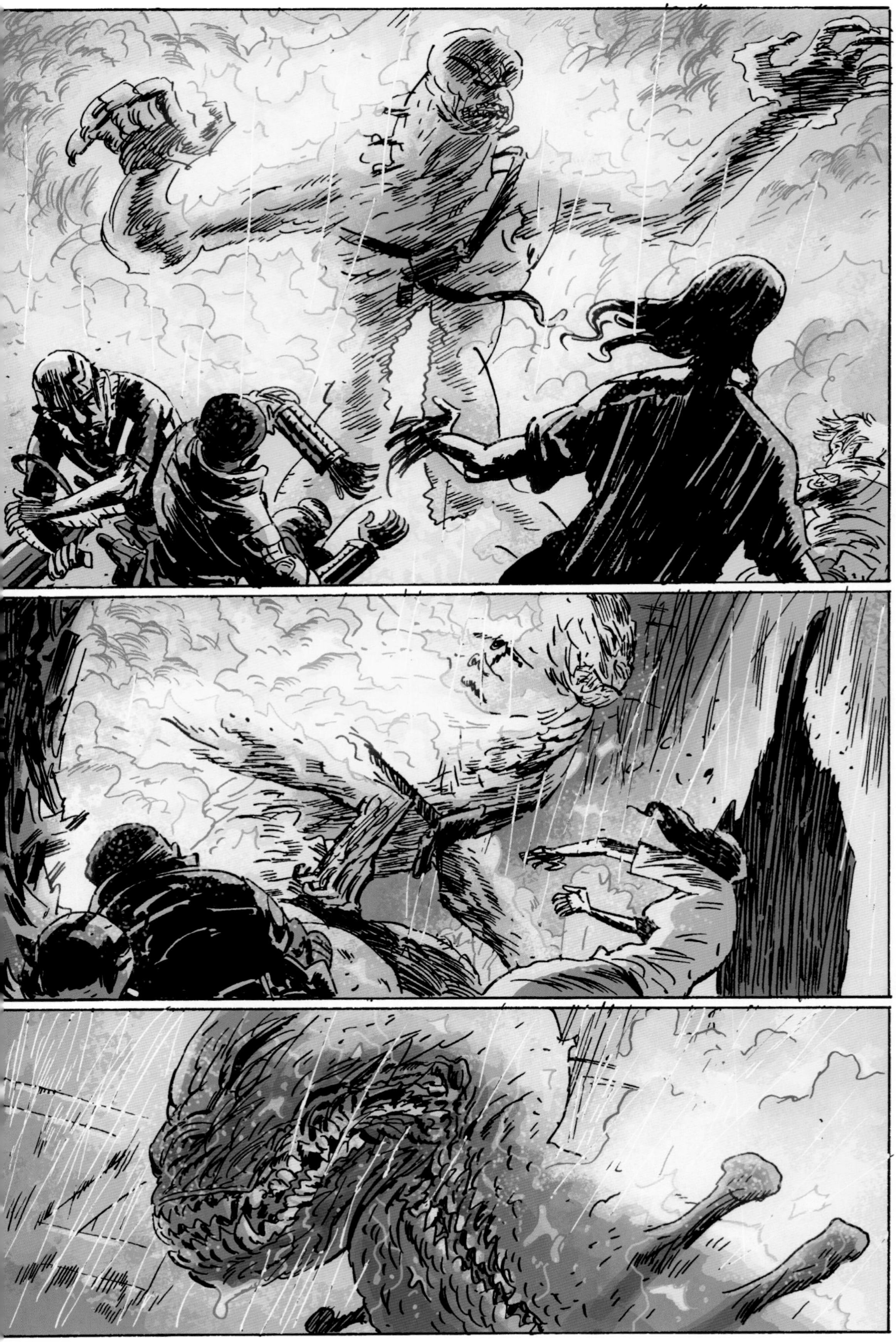

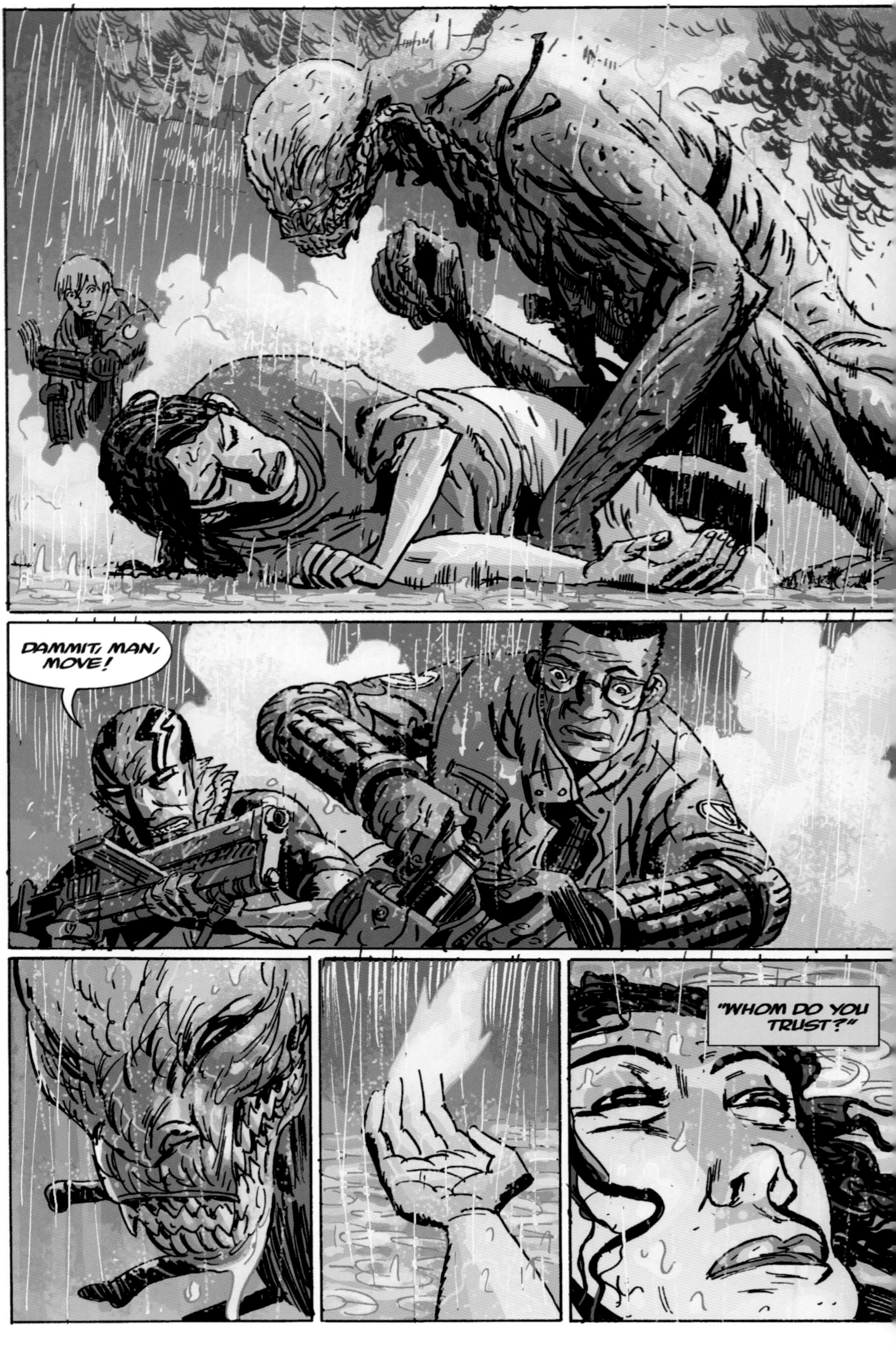
DAMMIT, MAN, MOVE!
"WHOM DO YOU TRUST?"

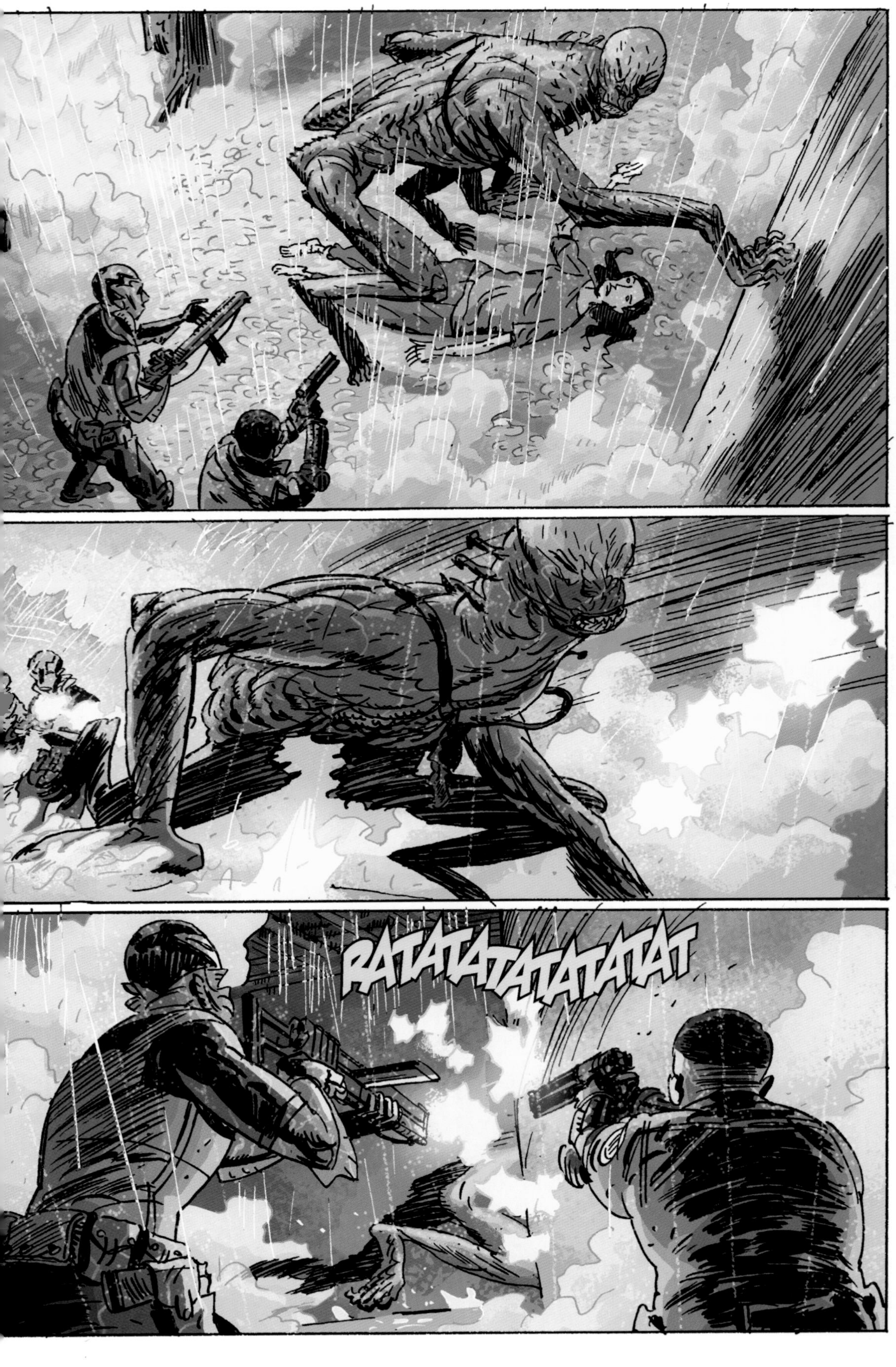
RATATATATATATATAT

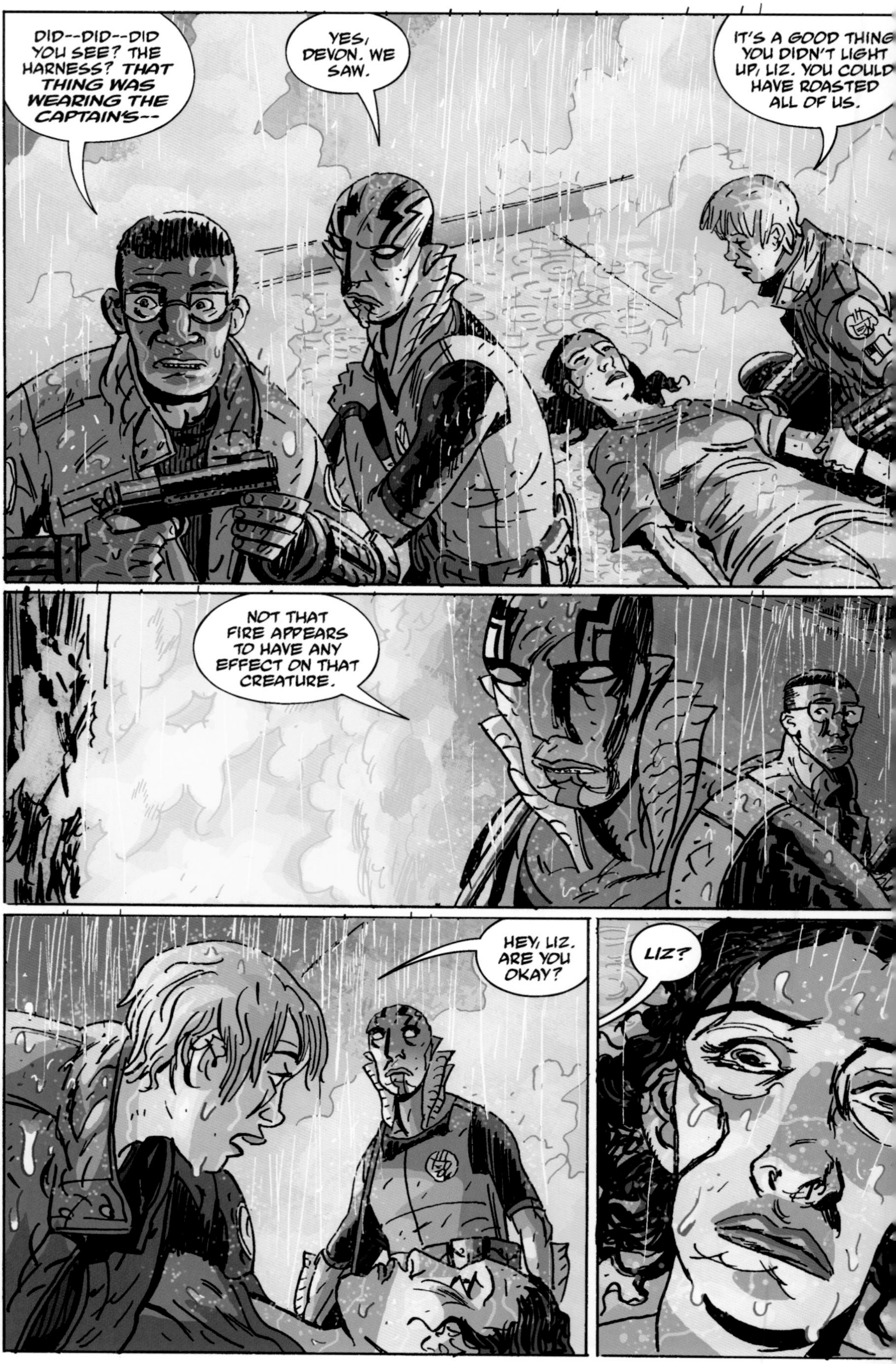
DID--DID--DID YOU SEE? THE HARNESS? THAT THING WAS WEARING THE CAPTAIN'S--
YES, DEVON. WE SAW.
IT'S A GOOD THING YOU DIDN'T LIGHT UP, LIZ. YOU COULD HAVE ROASTED ALL OF US.
NOT THAT FIRE APPEARS TO HAVE ANY EFFECT ON THAT CREATURE.
HEY, LIZ. ARE YOU OKAY?
LIZ?

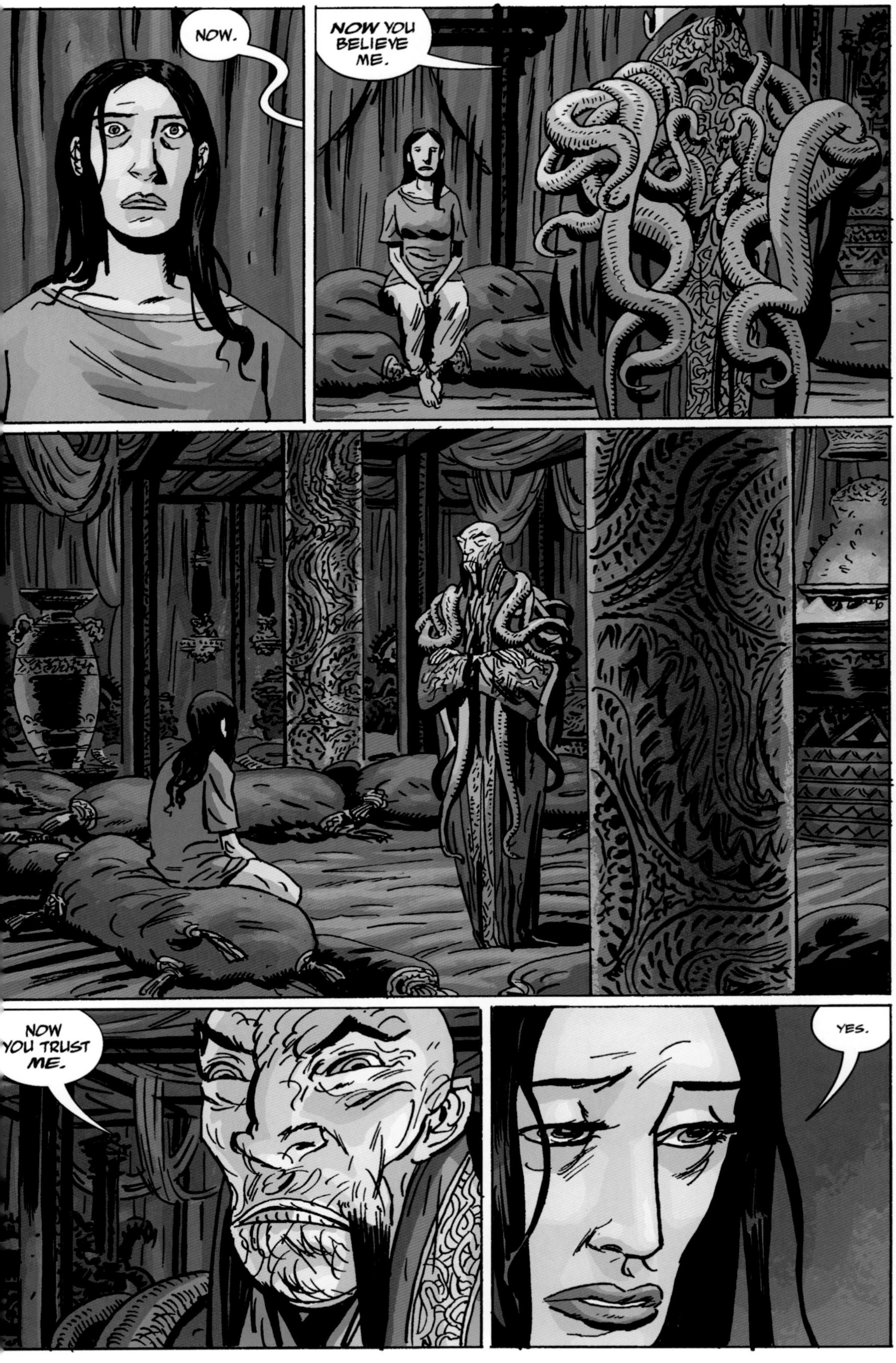
NOW.
NOW YOU BELIEVE ME.
NOW YOU TRUST ME.
YES.

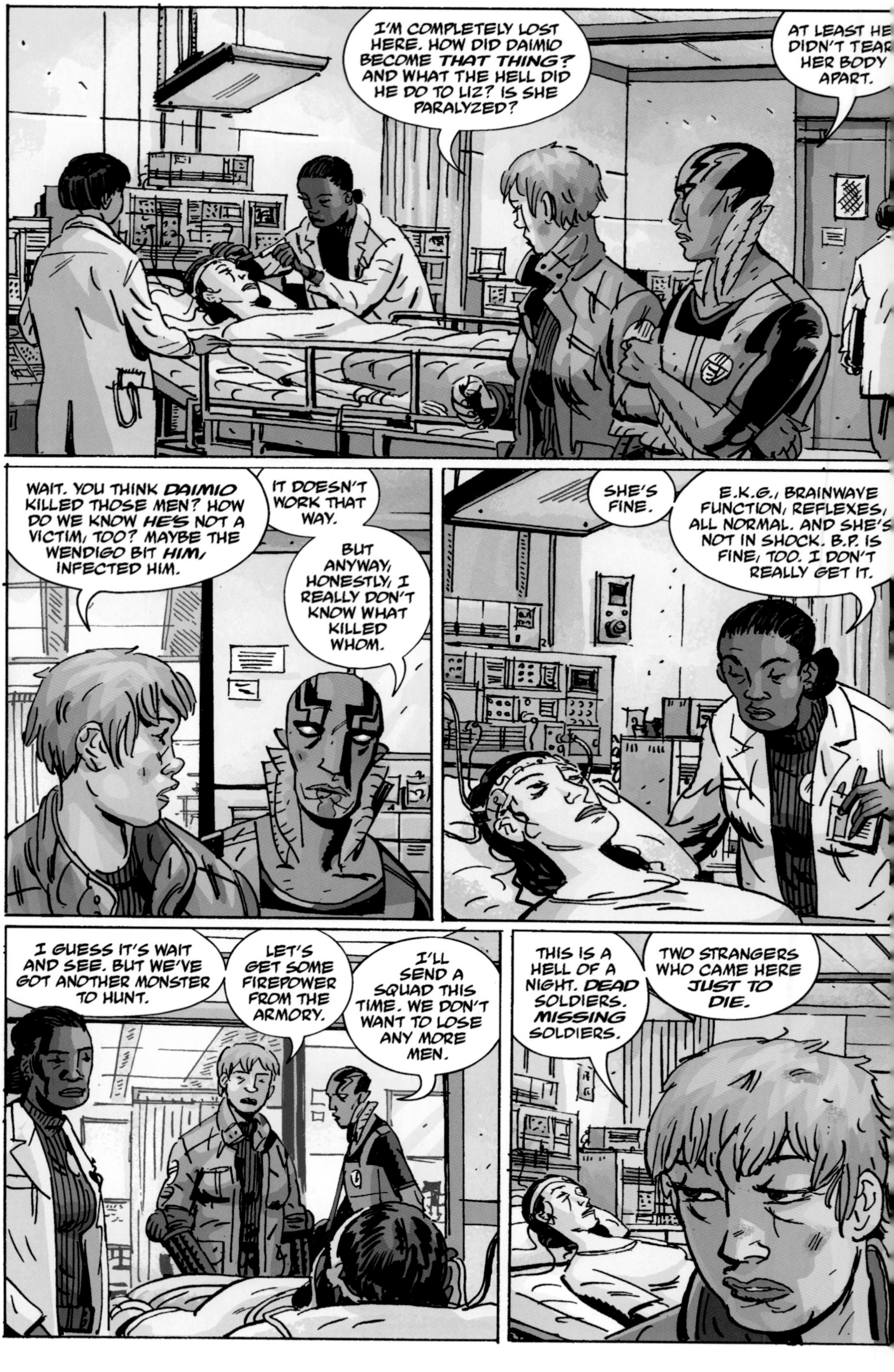
I'M COMPLETELY LOST HERE. HOW DID DAIMIO BECOME THAT THING? AND WHAT THE HELL DID HE DO TO LIZ? IS SHE PARALYZED?
AT LEAST HE DIDN'T TEAR HER BODY APART.
WAIT. YOU THINK DAIMIO KILLED THOSE MEN? HOW DO WE KNOW HE'S NOT A VICTIM, TOO? MAYBE THE WENDIGO BIT HIM, INFECTED HIM.
IT DOESN'T WORK THAT WAY.
BUT ANYWAY, HONESTLY, I REALLY DON'T KNOW WHAT KILLED WHOM.
SHE'S FINE.
E.K.G., BRAINWAVE FUNCTION, REFLEXES, ALL NORMAL. AND SHE'S NOT IN SHOCK. B.P. IS FINE, TOO. I DON'T REALLY GET IT.
I GUESS IT'S WAIT AND SEE. BUT WE'VE GOT ANOTHER MONSTER TO HUNT.
LET'S GET SOME FIREPOWER FROM THE ARMORY.
I'LL SEND A SQUAD THIS TIME. WE DON'T WANT TO LOSE ANY MORE MEN.
THIS IS A HELL OF A NIGHT. DEAD SOLDIERS. MISSING SOLDIERS.
TWO STRANGERS WHO CAME HERE JUST TO DIE.

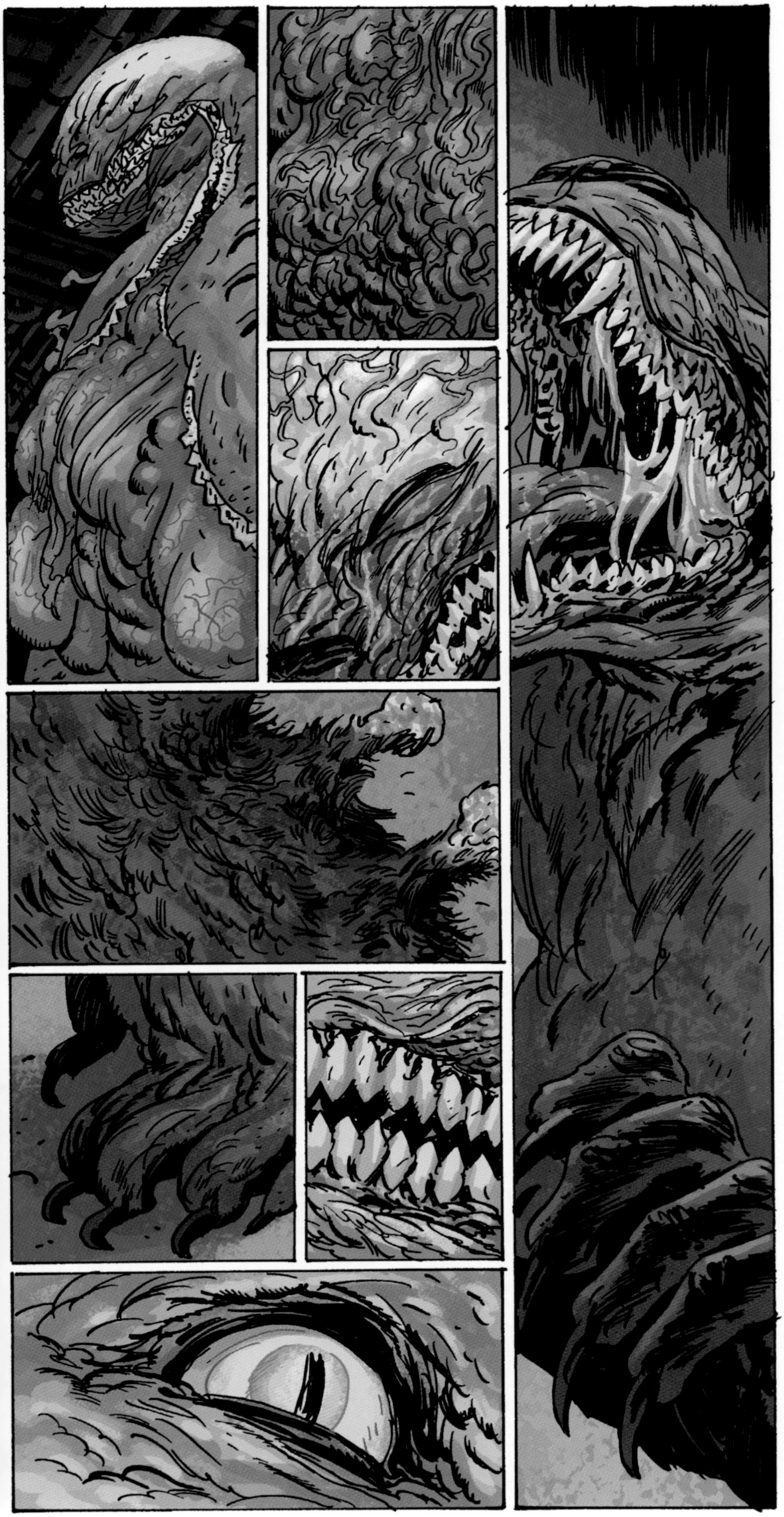

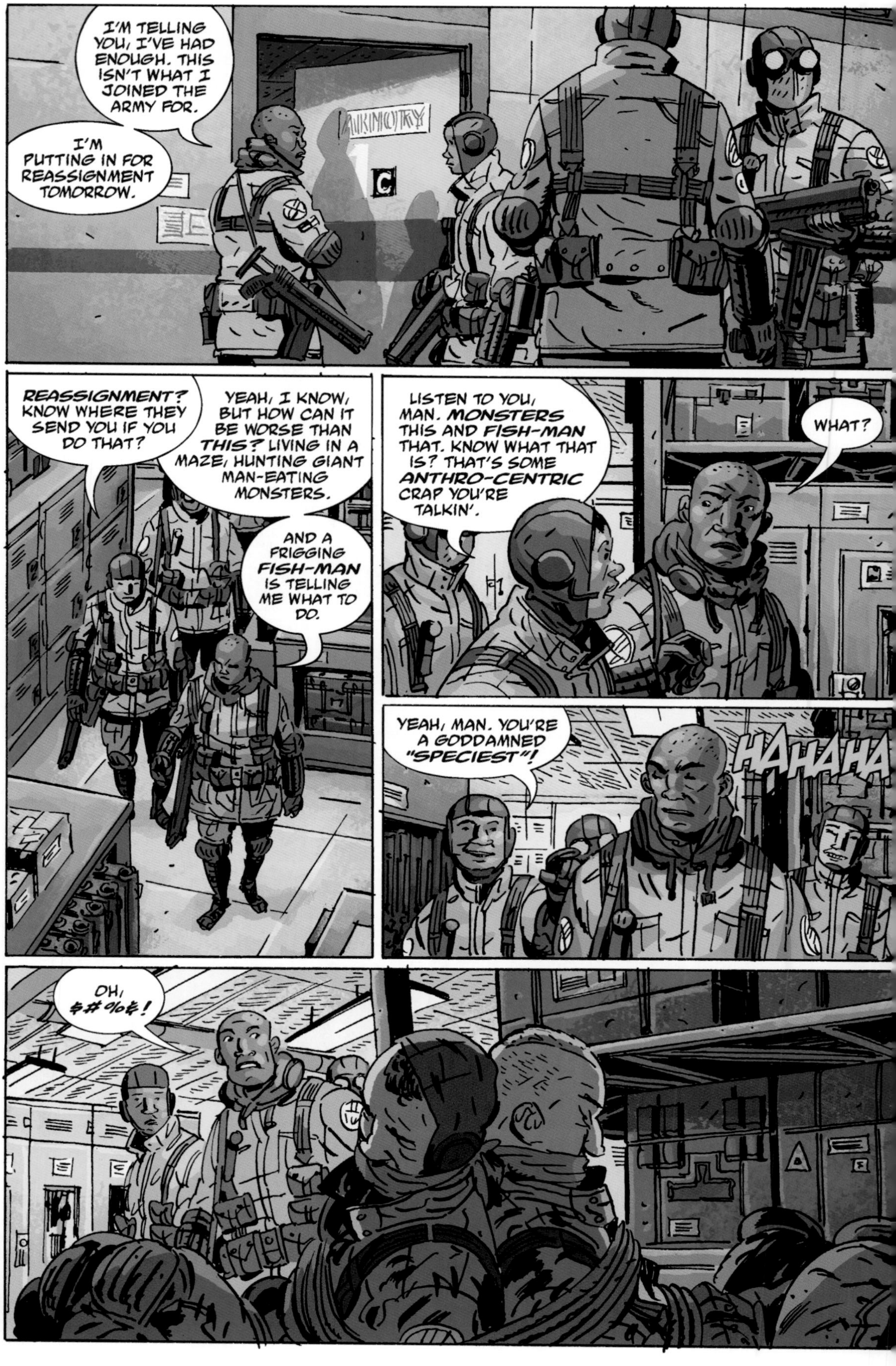
I'M TELLING YOU, I'VE HAD ENOUGH. THIS ISN'T WHAT I JOINED THE ARMY FOR.
I'M PUTTING IN FOR REASSIGNMENT TOMORROW.
C
REASSIGNMENT? KNOW WHERE THEY SEND YOU IF YOU DO THAT?
YEAH, I KNOW, BUT HOW CAN IT BE WORSE THAN THIS? LIVING IN A MAZE, HUNTING GIANT MAN-EATING MONSTERS.
AND A FRIGGING FISH-MAN IS TELLING ME WHAT TO DO.
LISTEN TO YOU, MAN. MONSTERS THIS AND FISH-MAN THAT. KNOW WHAT THAT IS? THAT'S SOME ANTHRO-CENTRIC CRAP YOU'RE TALKIN'.
WHAT?
YEAH, MAN. YOU'RE A GODDAMNED "SPECIEST"!
HAHAHA
OH, $#%&!

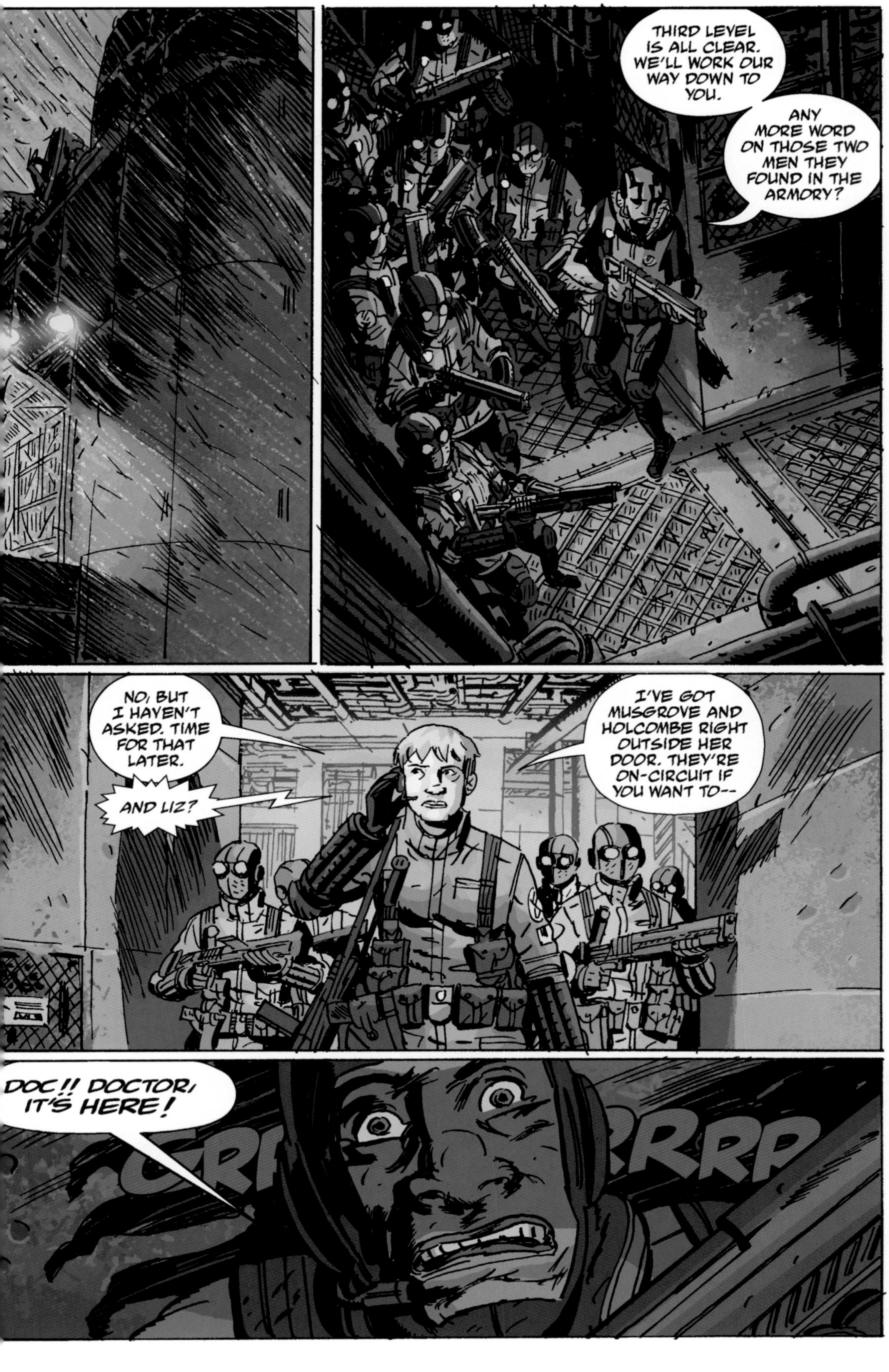
THIRD LEVEL IS ALL CLEAR. WE'LL WORK OUR WAY DOWN TO YOU.
ANY MORE WORD ON THOSE TWO MEN THEY FOUND IN THE ARMORY?
NO, BUT I HAVEN'T ASKED. TIME FOR THAT LATER.
AND LIZ?
I'VE GOT MUSGROVE AND HOLCOMBE RIGHT OUTSIDE HER DOOR. THEY'RE ON-CIRCUIT IF YOU WANT TO--
DOC!! DOCTOR, IT'S HERE!

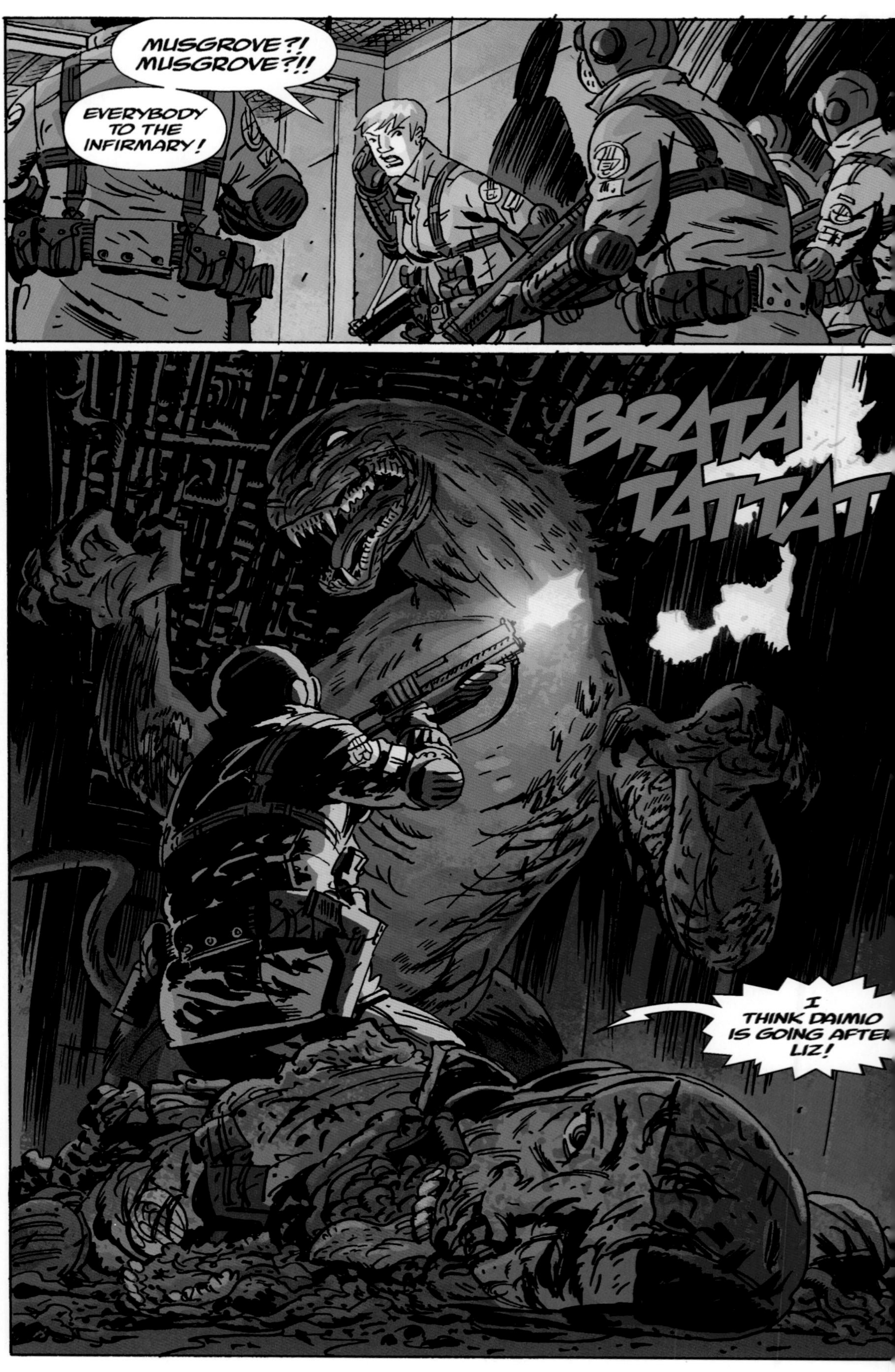
MUSGROVE?! MUSGROVE?!!
EVERYBODY TO THE INFIRMARY!
BRATA TATTAT
I THINK DAIMIO IS GOING AFTER LIZ!

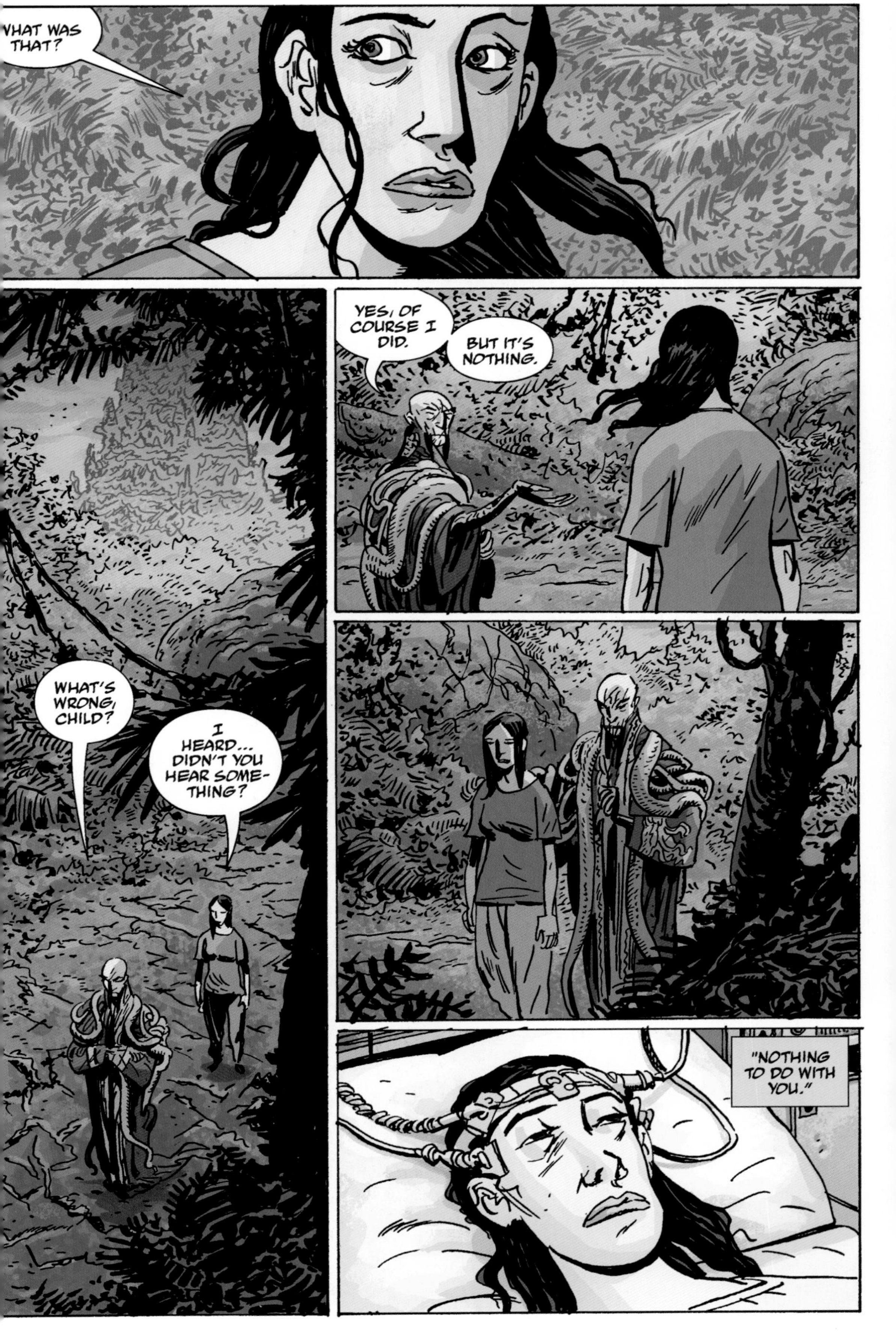
WHAT WAS THAT?
WHAT'S WRONG, CHILD?
I HEARD... DIDN'T YOU HEAR SOME-THING?
YES, OF COURSE I DID.
BUT IT'S NOTHING.
"NOTHING TO DO WITH YOU."

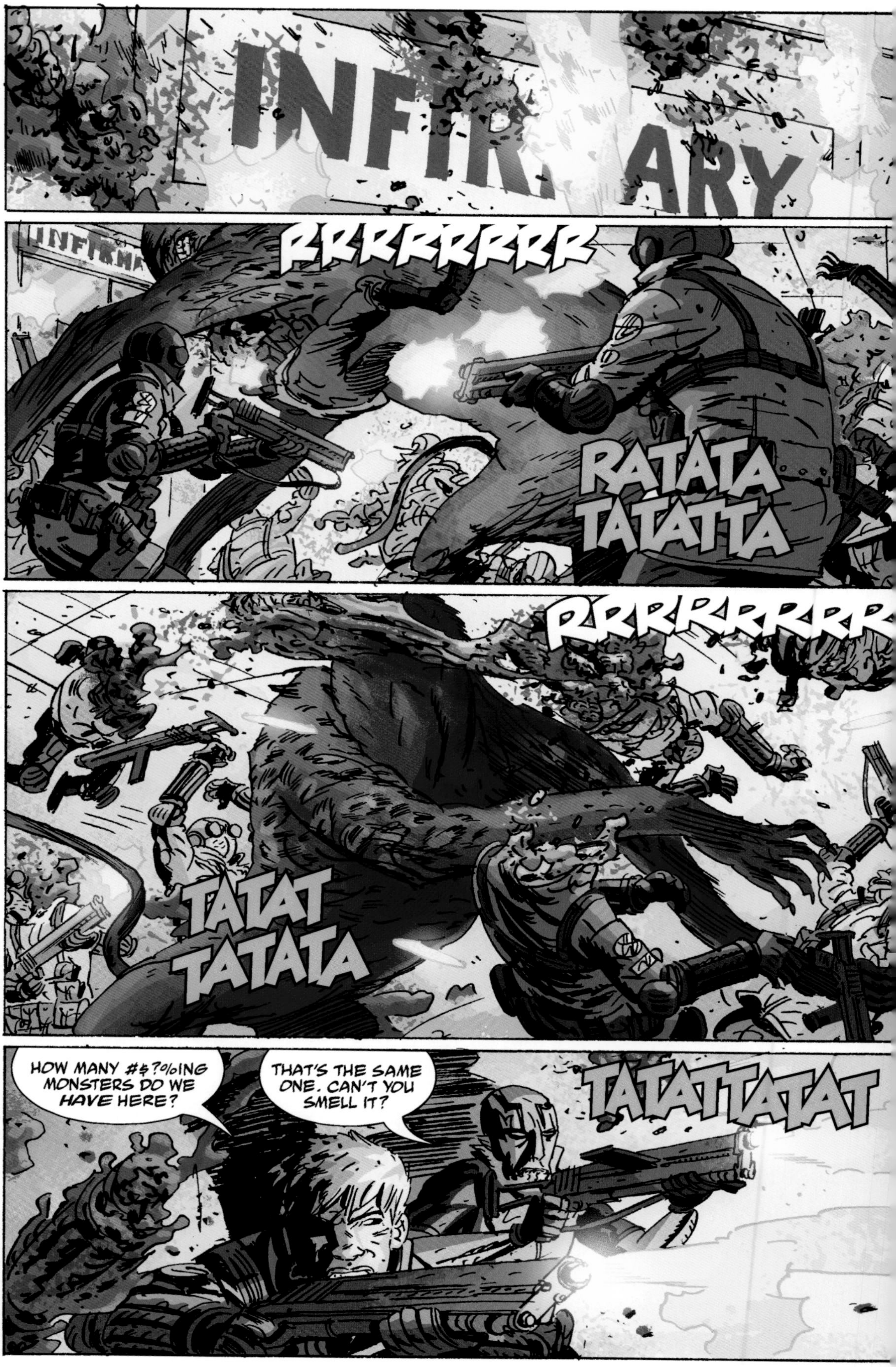
INFIR ARY
INFIRMA
RRRRRRRR
RATATA TATATTA
RRRRRRRRR
TATAT TATATA
HOW MANY #$?%ING MONSTERS DO WE HAVE HERE?
THAT'S THE SAME ONE. CAN'T YOU SMELL IT?
TATATTATAT

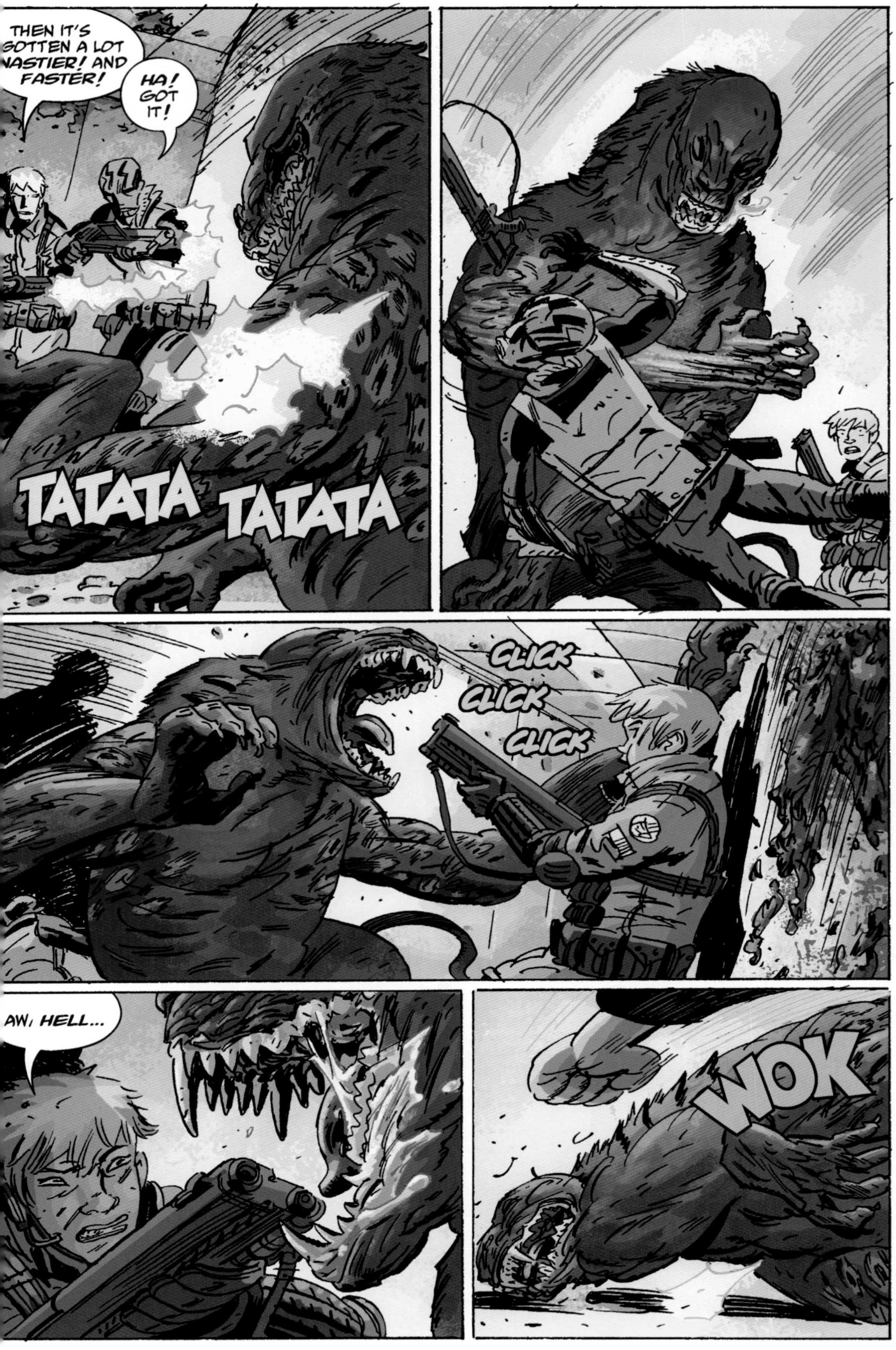

THEN IT'S GOTTEN A LOT NASTIER! AND FASTER!
HA! GOT IT!
TATATA TATATA
CLICK
CLICK
CLICK
AW, HELL...
WOK

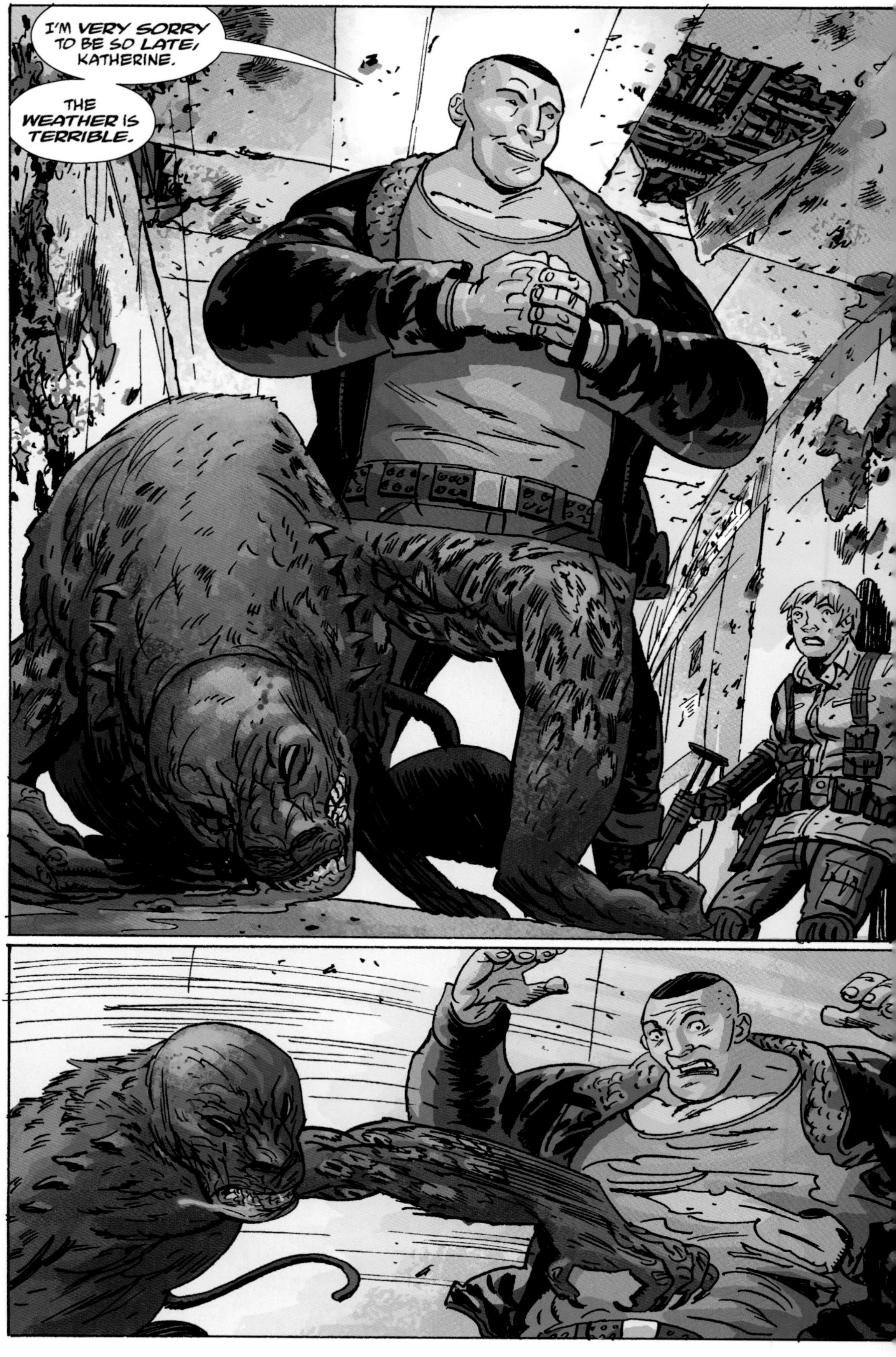
I'M VERY SORRY TO BE SO LATE, KATHERINE.
THE WEATHER IS TERRIBLE.

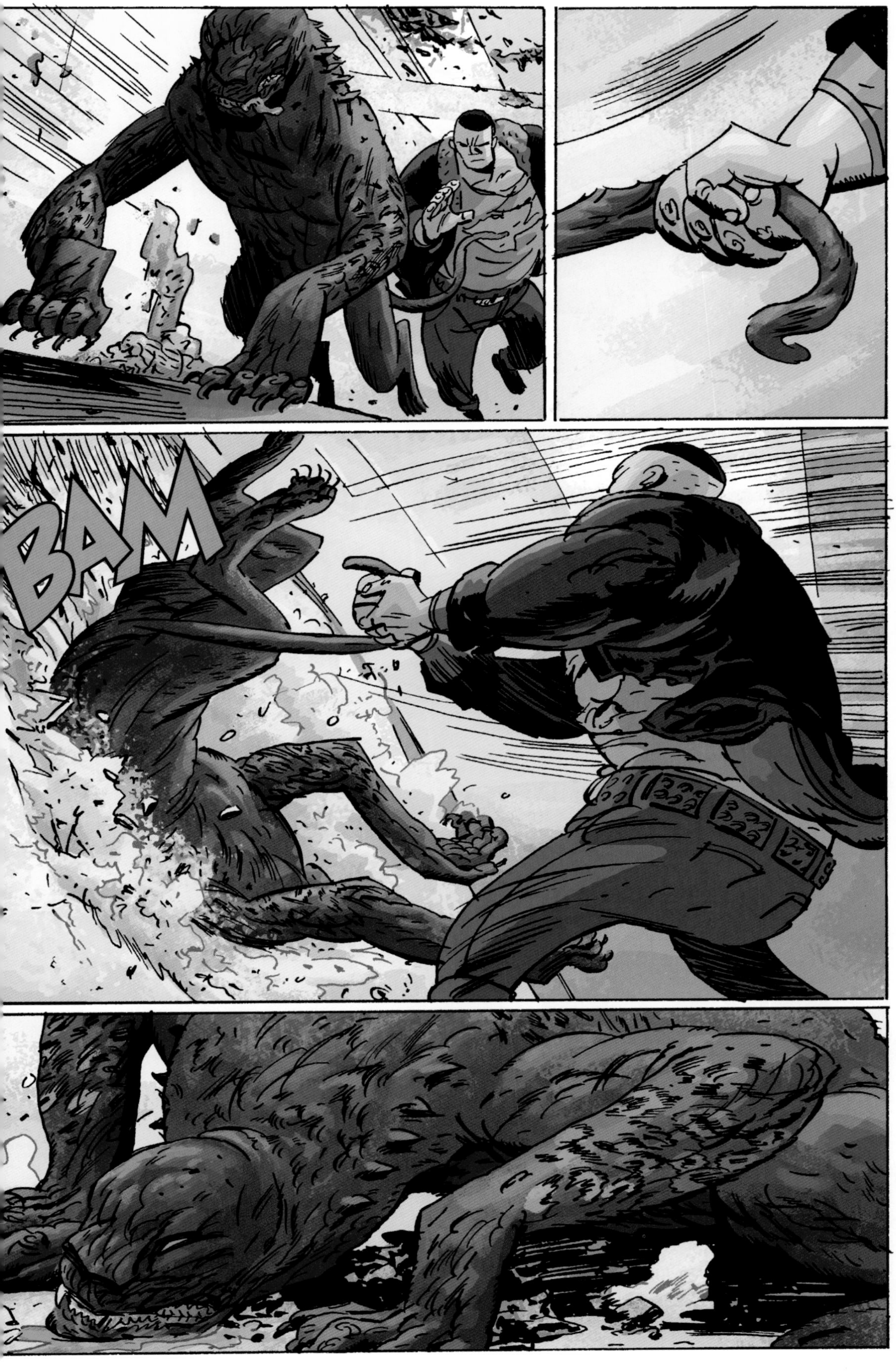
BAM

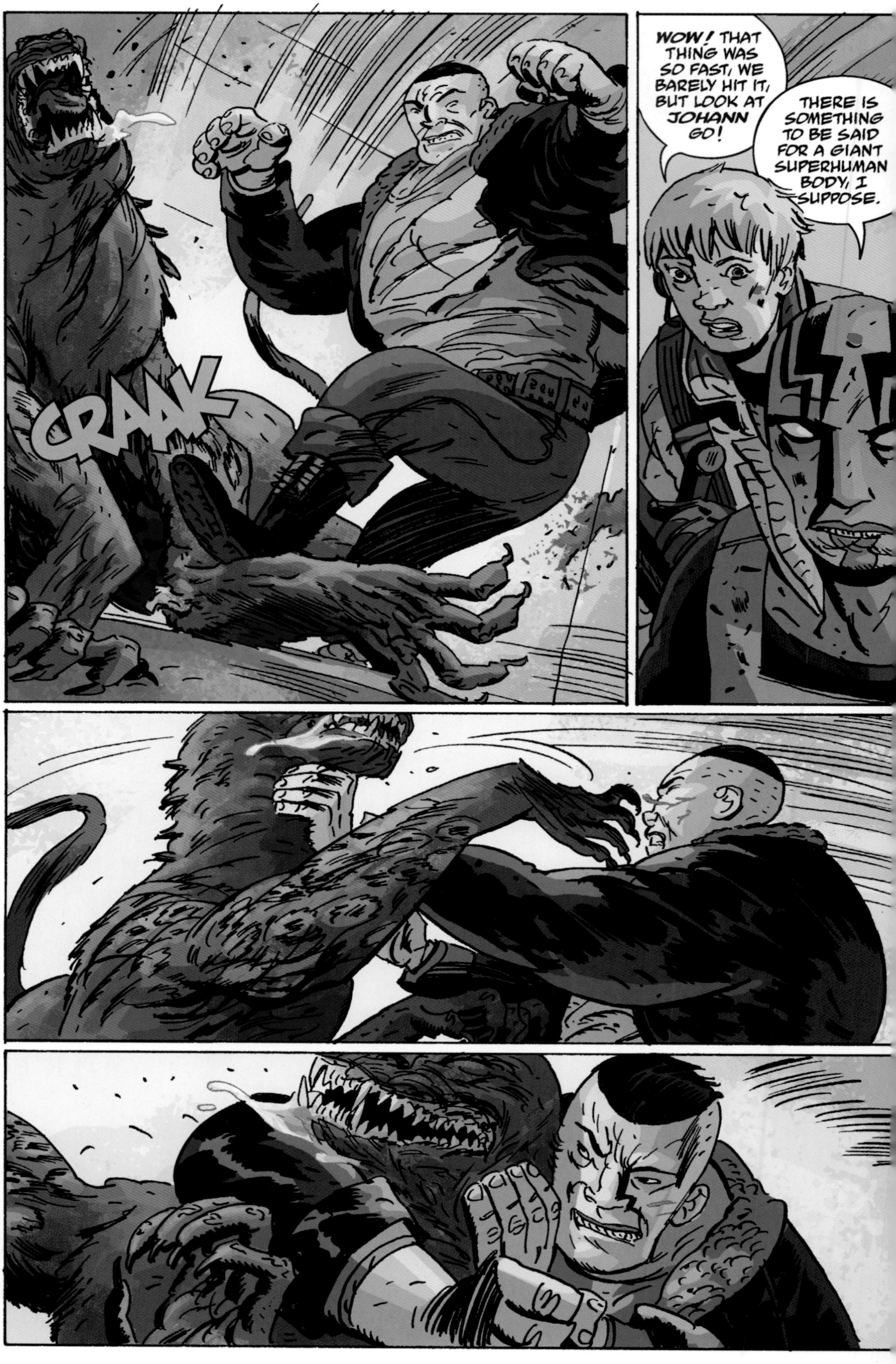
CRAAK
WOW! THAT THING WAS SO FAST, WE BARELY HIT IT, BUT LOOK AT JOHANN GO!
THERE IS SOMETHING TO BE SAID FOR A GIANT SUPERHUMAN BODY, I SUPPOSE.

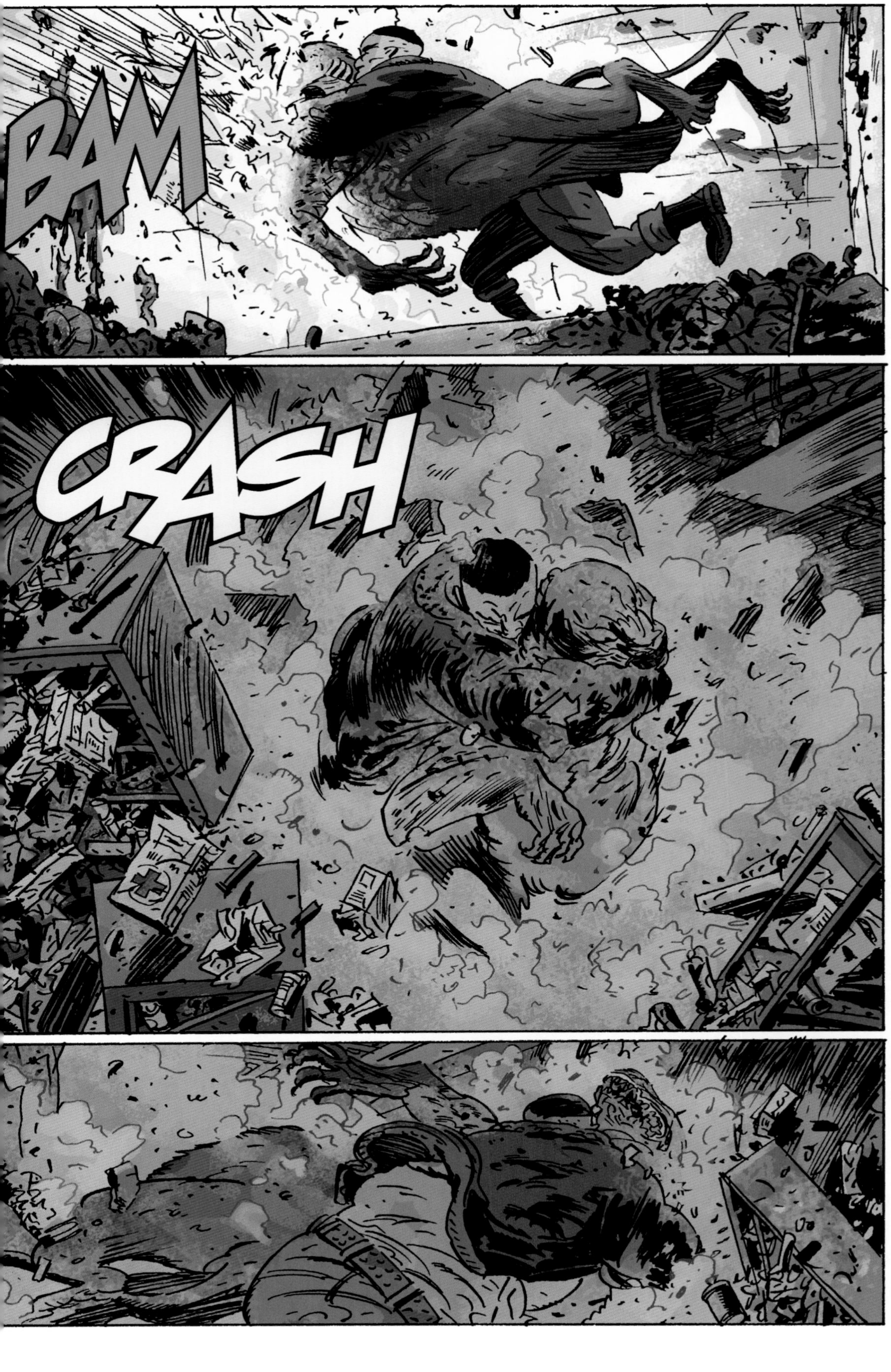
BAM
CRASH

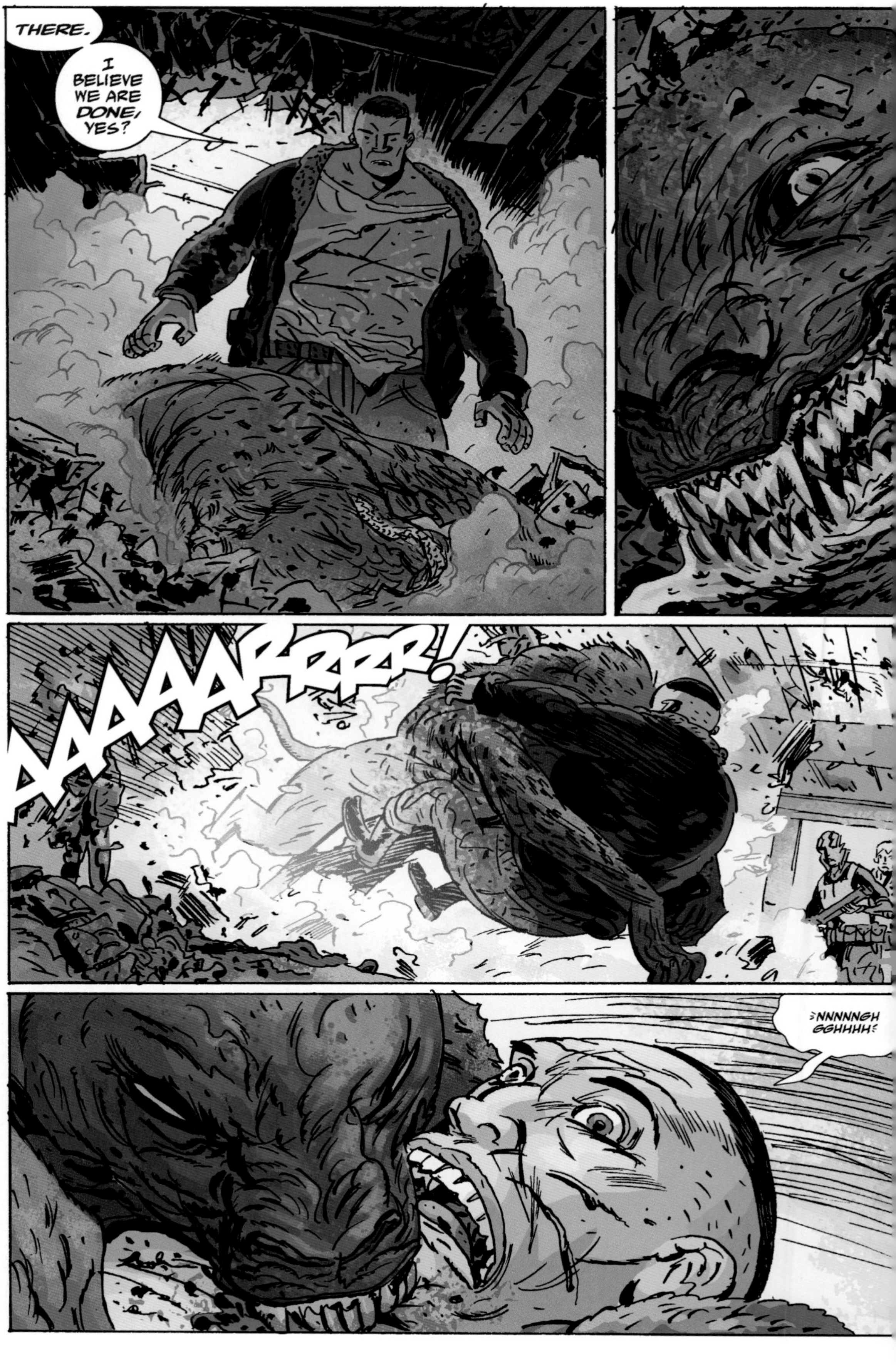
THERE.
I BELIEVE WE ARE DONE, YES?
AAAAARRRR!
NNNNNGH GGHHHH

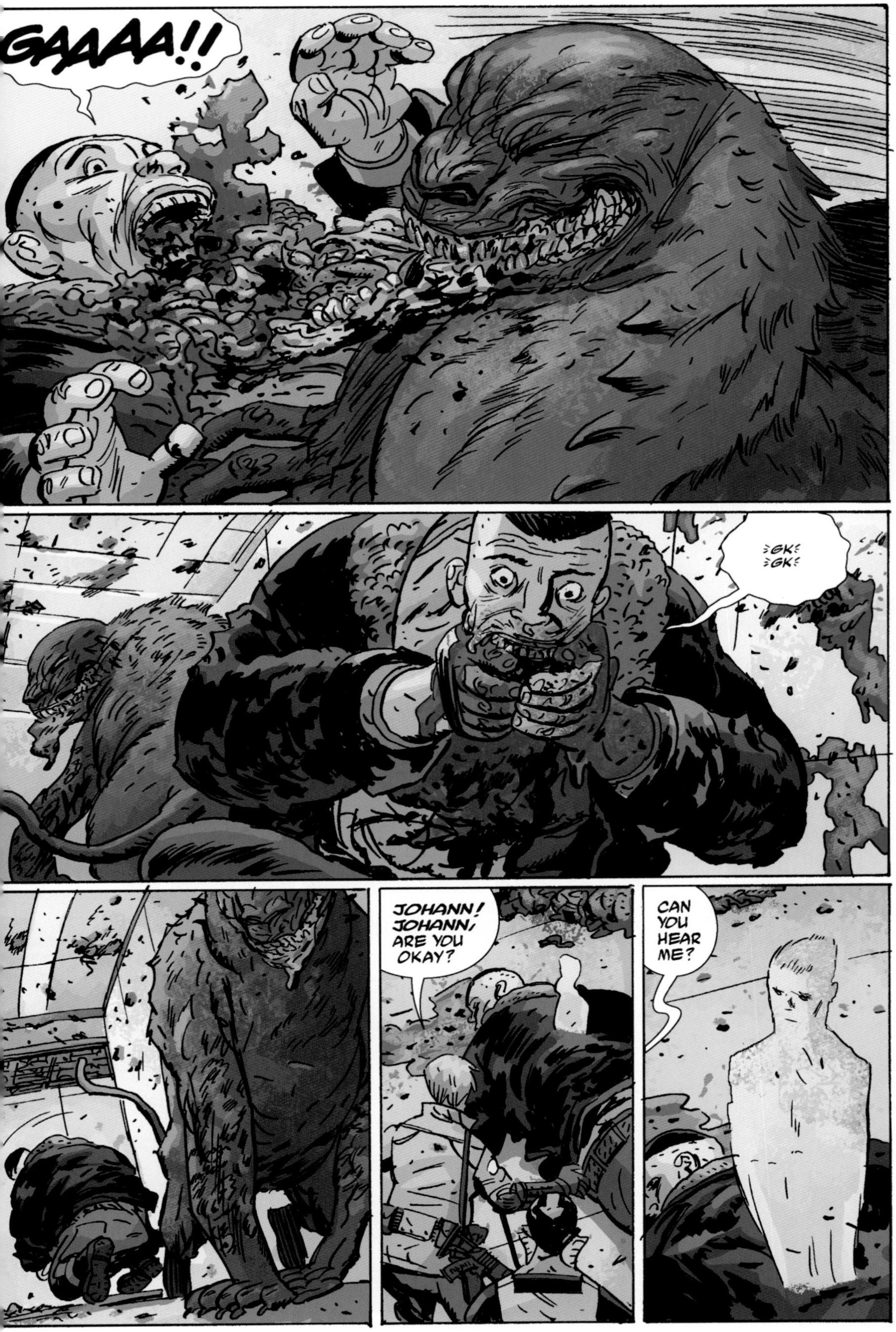
GAAAA!!
GK
GK
JOHANN! JOHANN, ARE YOU OKAY?
CAN YOU HEAR ME?

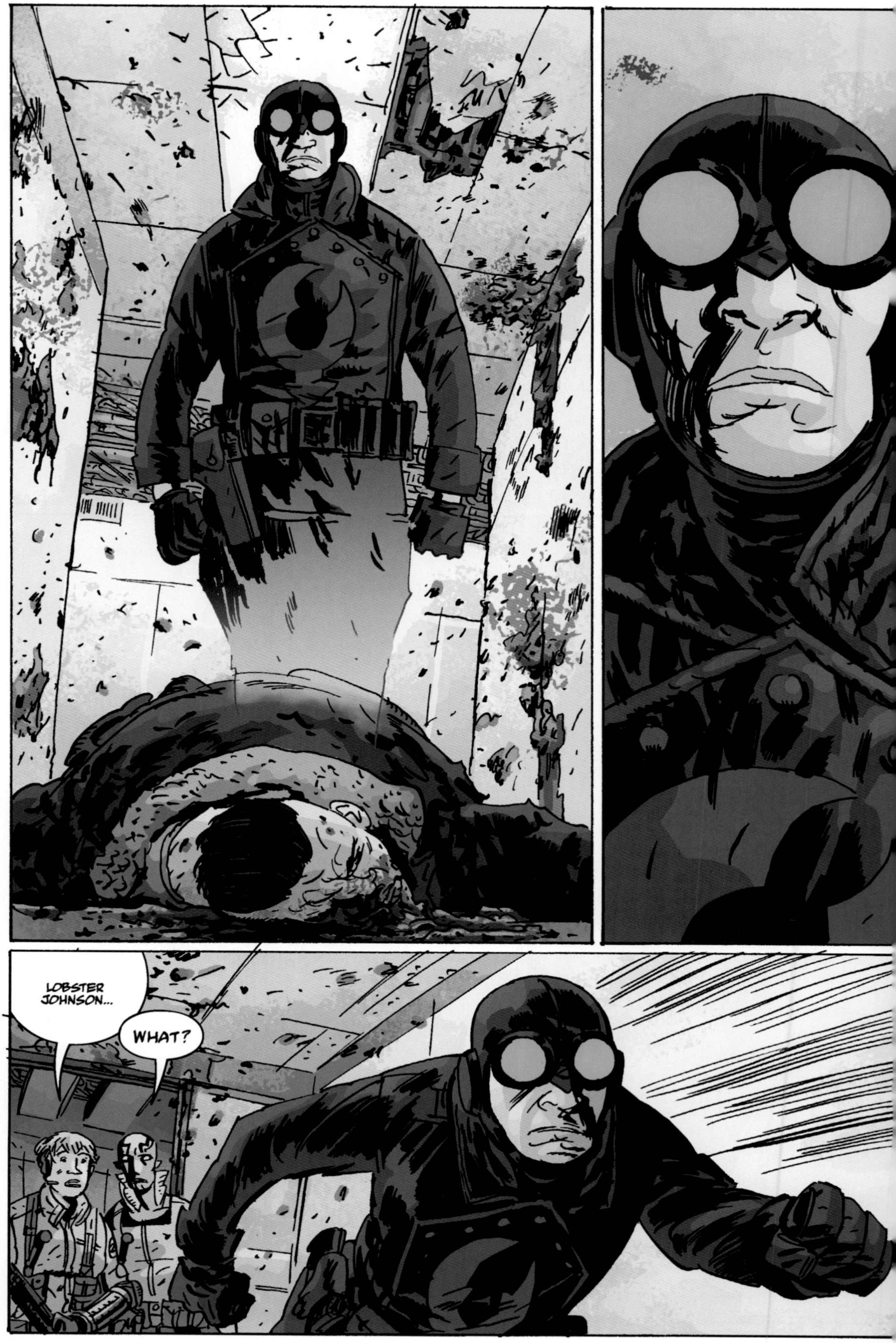
LOBSTER JOHNSON...
WHAT?

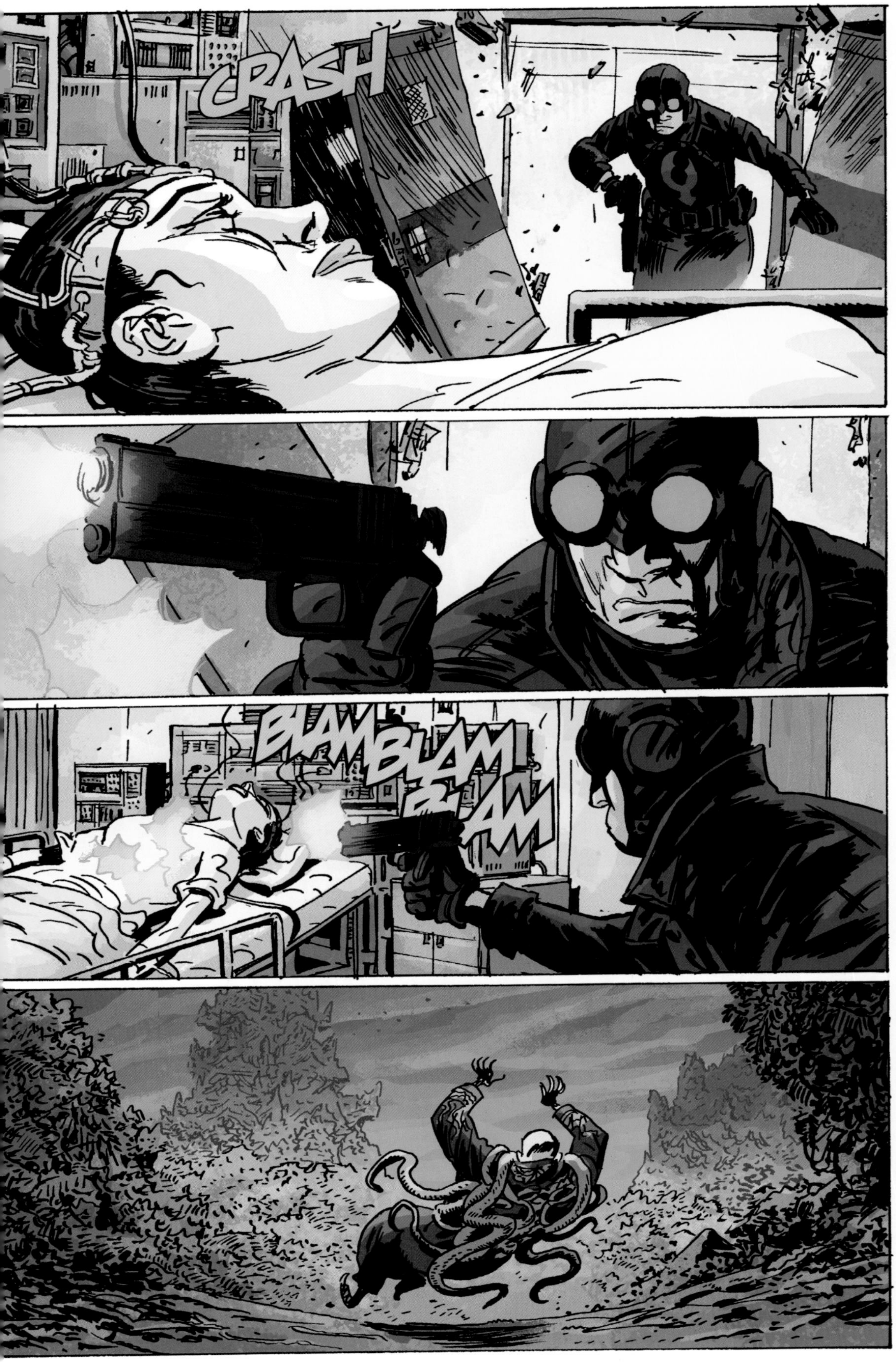
CRASH
BLAM BLAM
BLAM

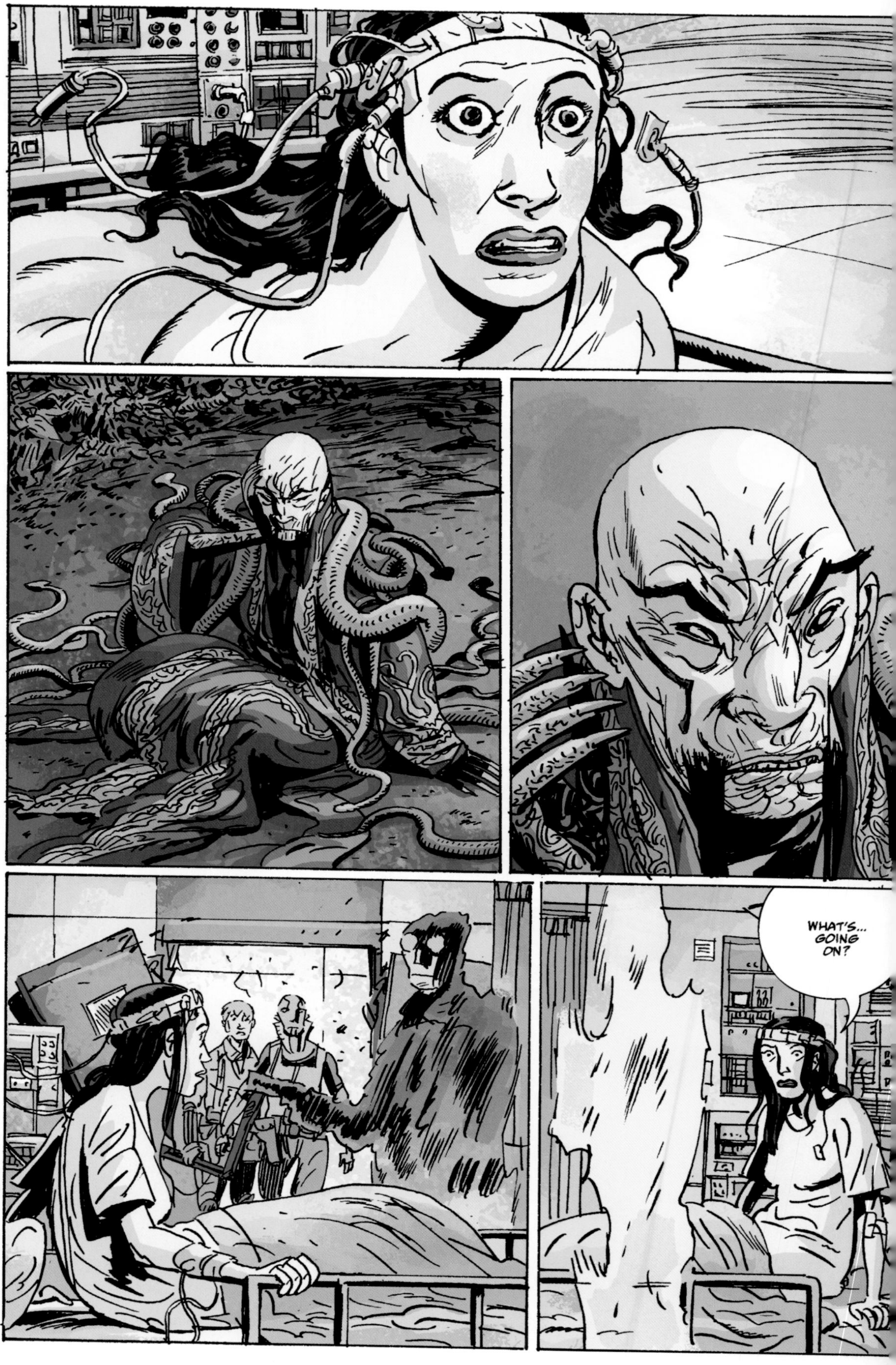
WHAT'S... GOING ON?

CHAPTER FIVE

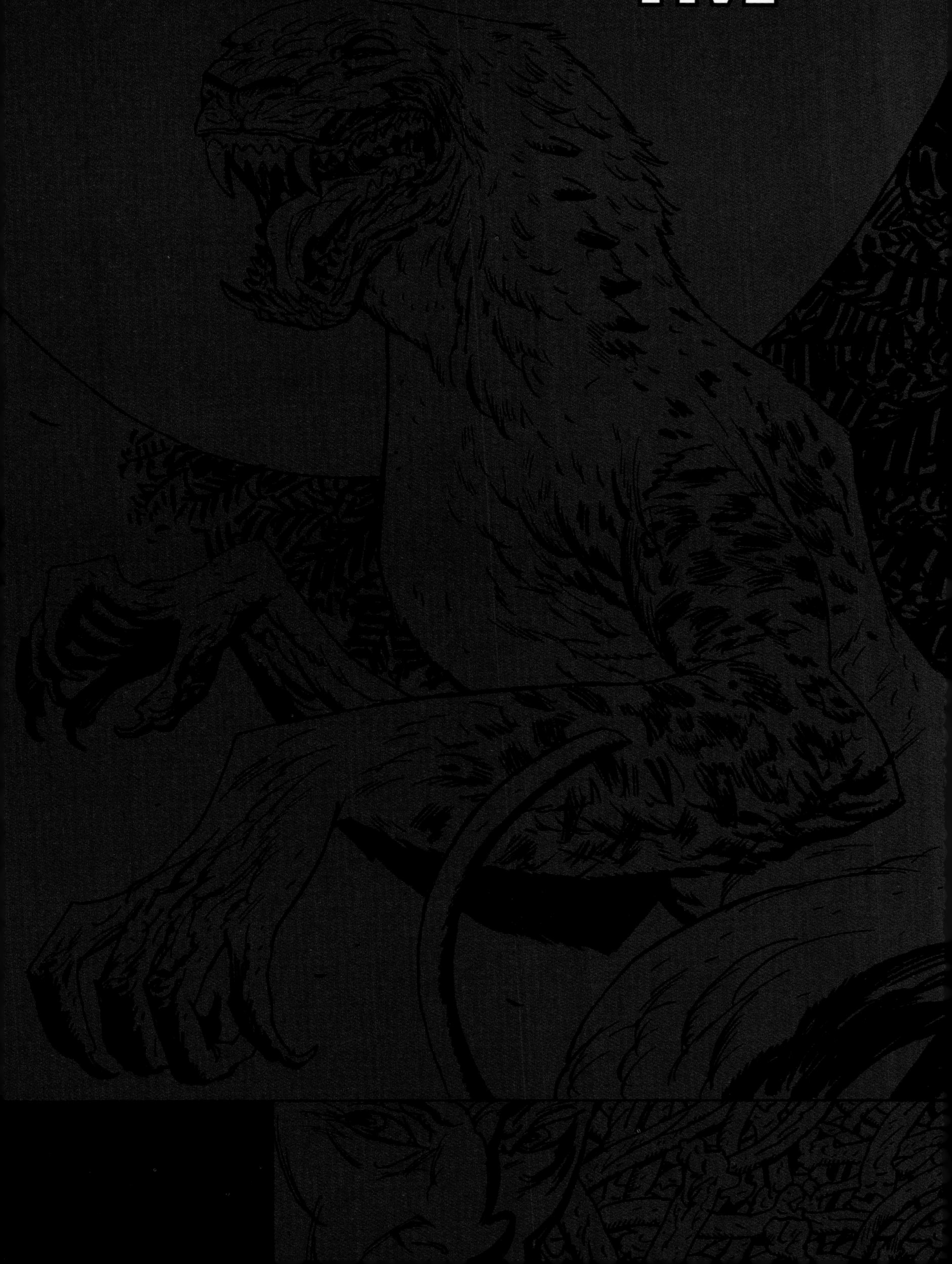

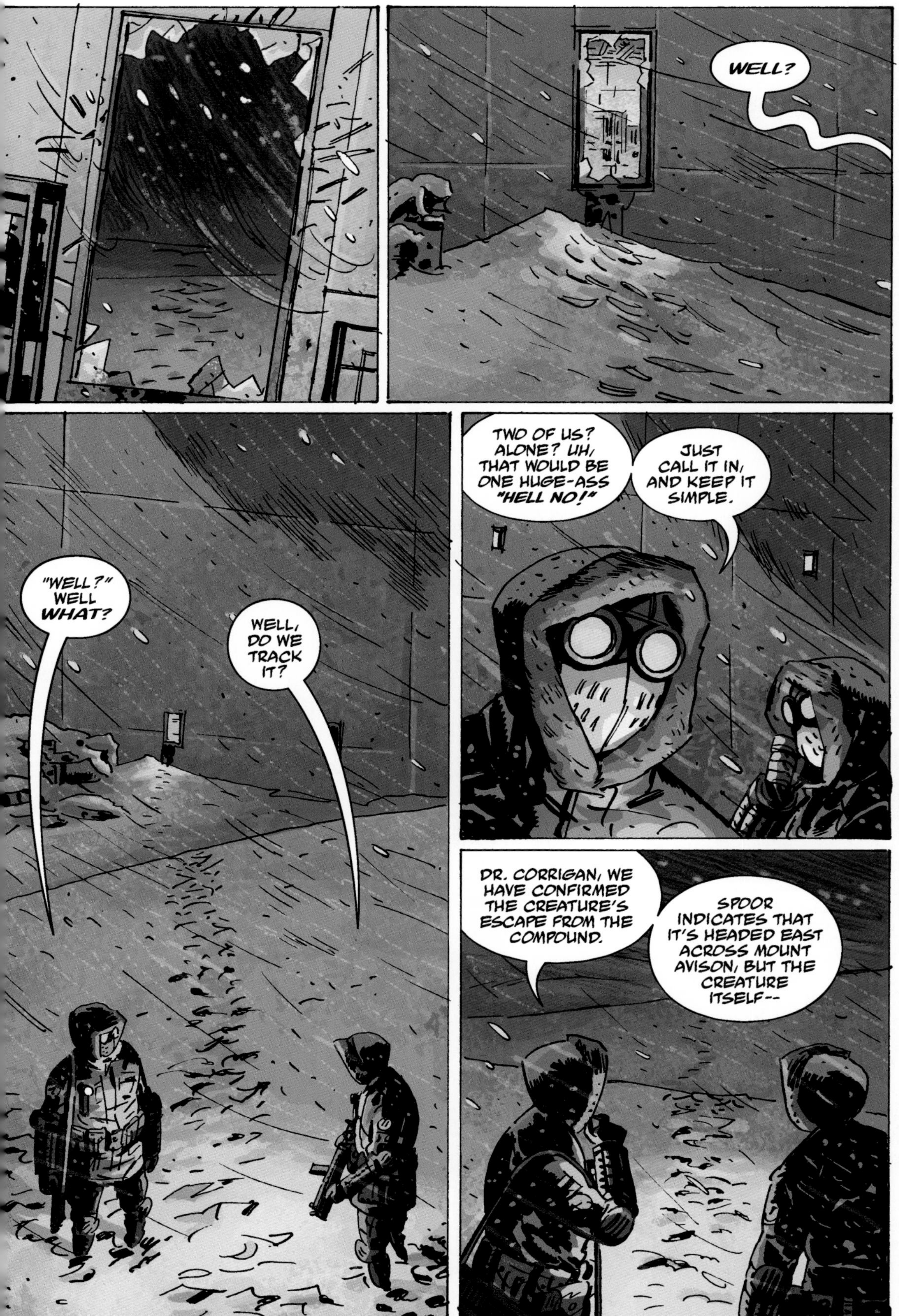
WELL?
"WELL?" WELL WHAT?
WELL, DO WE TRACK IT?
TWO OF US? ALONE? UH, THAT WOULD BE ONE HUGE-ASS "HELL NO!"
JUST CALL IT IN, AND KEEP IT SIMPLE.
DR. CORRIGAN, WE HAVE CONFIRMED THE CREATURE'S ESCAPE FROM THE COMPOUND.
SPOOR INDICATES THAT IT'S HEADED EAST ACROSS MOUNT AVISON, BUT THE CREATURE ITSELF--

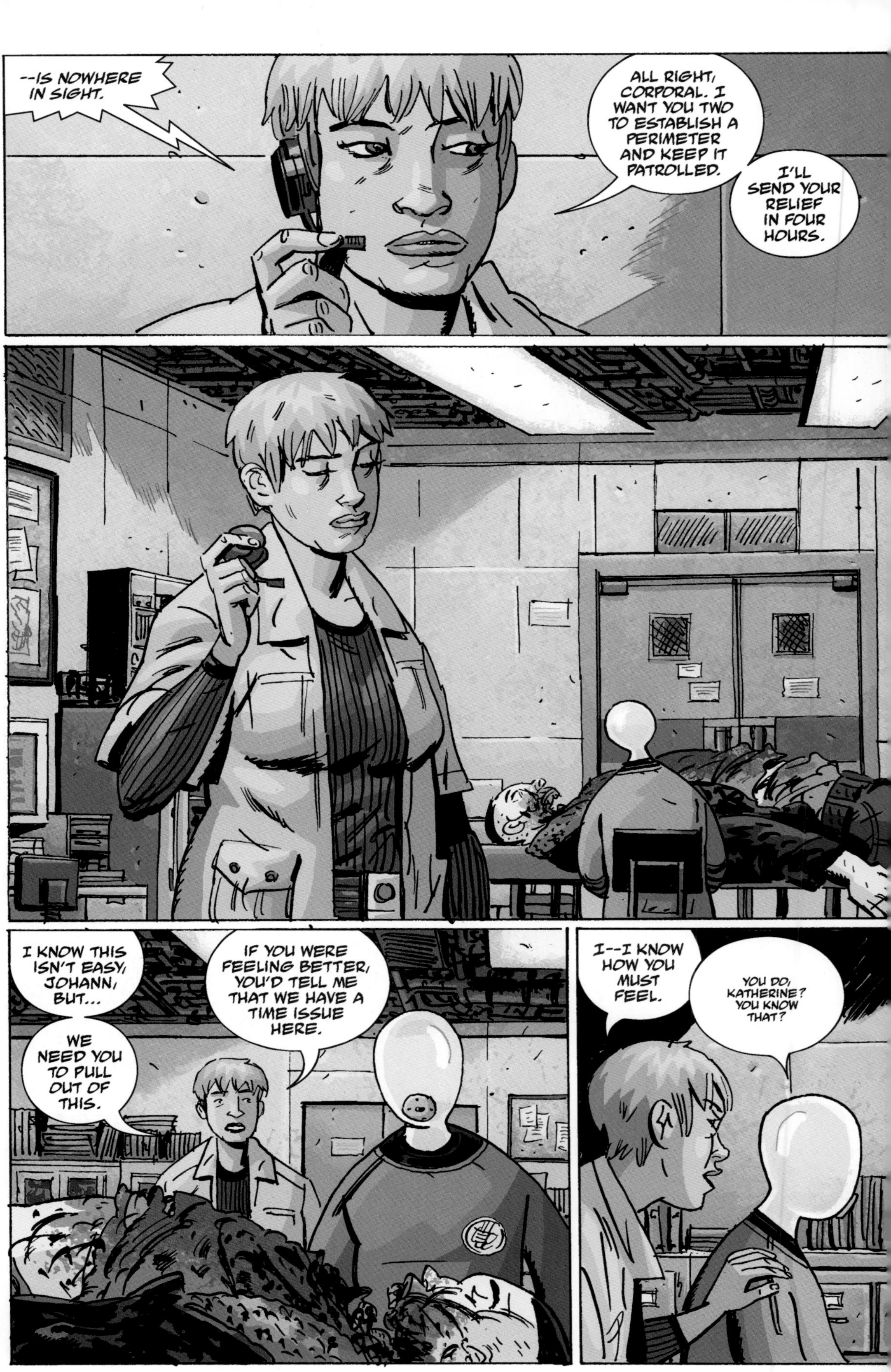
--IS NOWHERE IN SIGHT.
ALL RIGHT, CORPORAL. I WANT YOU TWO TO ESTABLISH A PERIMETER AND KEEP IT PATROLLED.
I'LL SEND YOUR RELIEF IN FOUR HOURS.
I KNOW THIS ISN'T EASY, JOHANN, BUT...
WE NEED YOU TO PULL OUT OF THIS.
IF YOU WERE FEELING BETTER, YOU'D TELL ME THAT WE HAVE A TIME ISSUE HERE.
I--I KNOW HOW YOU MUST FEEL.
YOU DO, KATHERINE? YOU KNOW THAT?

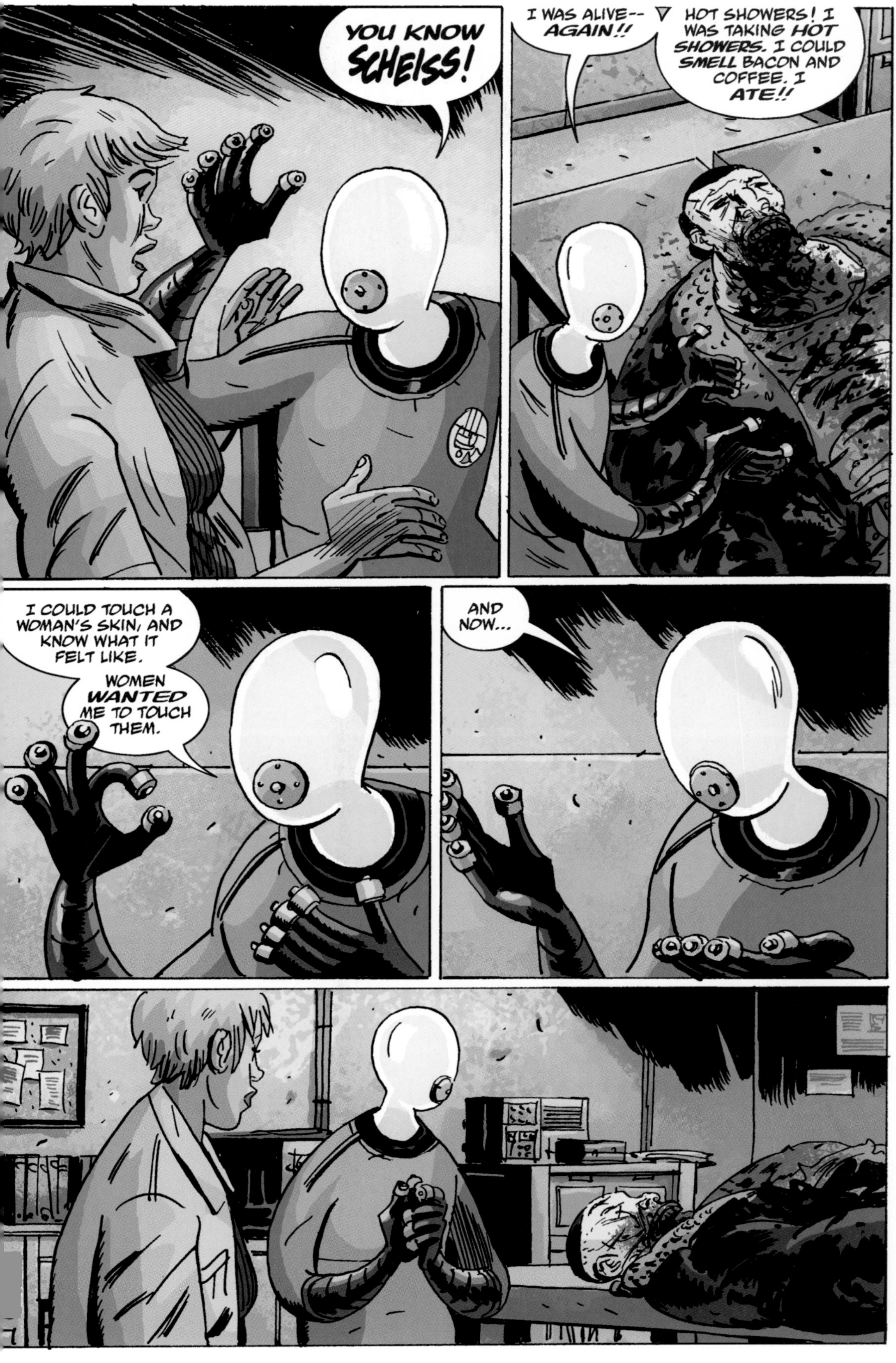
YOU KNOW SCHEISS!
I WAS ALIVE-- AGAIN!!
HOT SHOWERS! I WAS TAKING HOT SHOWERS. I COULD SMELL BACON AND COFFEE. I ATE!!
I COULD TOUCH A WOMAN'S SKIN, AND KNOW WHAT IT FELT LIKE.
WOMEN WANTED ME TO TOUCH THEM.
AND NOW...

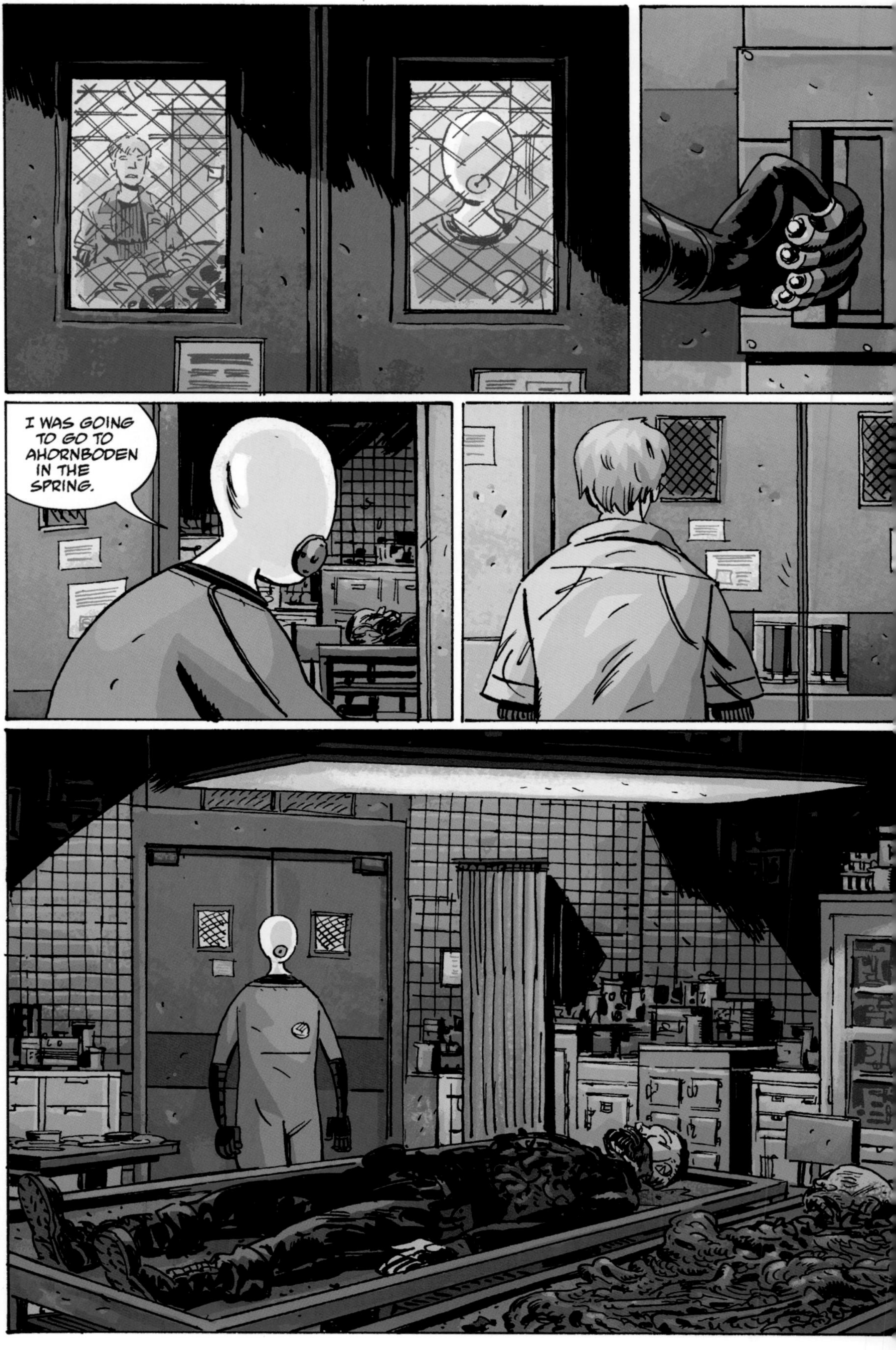
I WAS GOING TO GO TO AHORNBODEN IN THE SPRING.

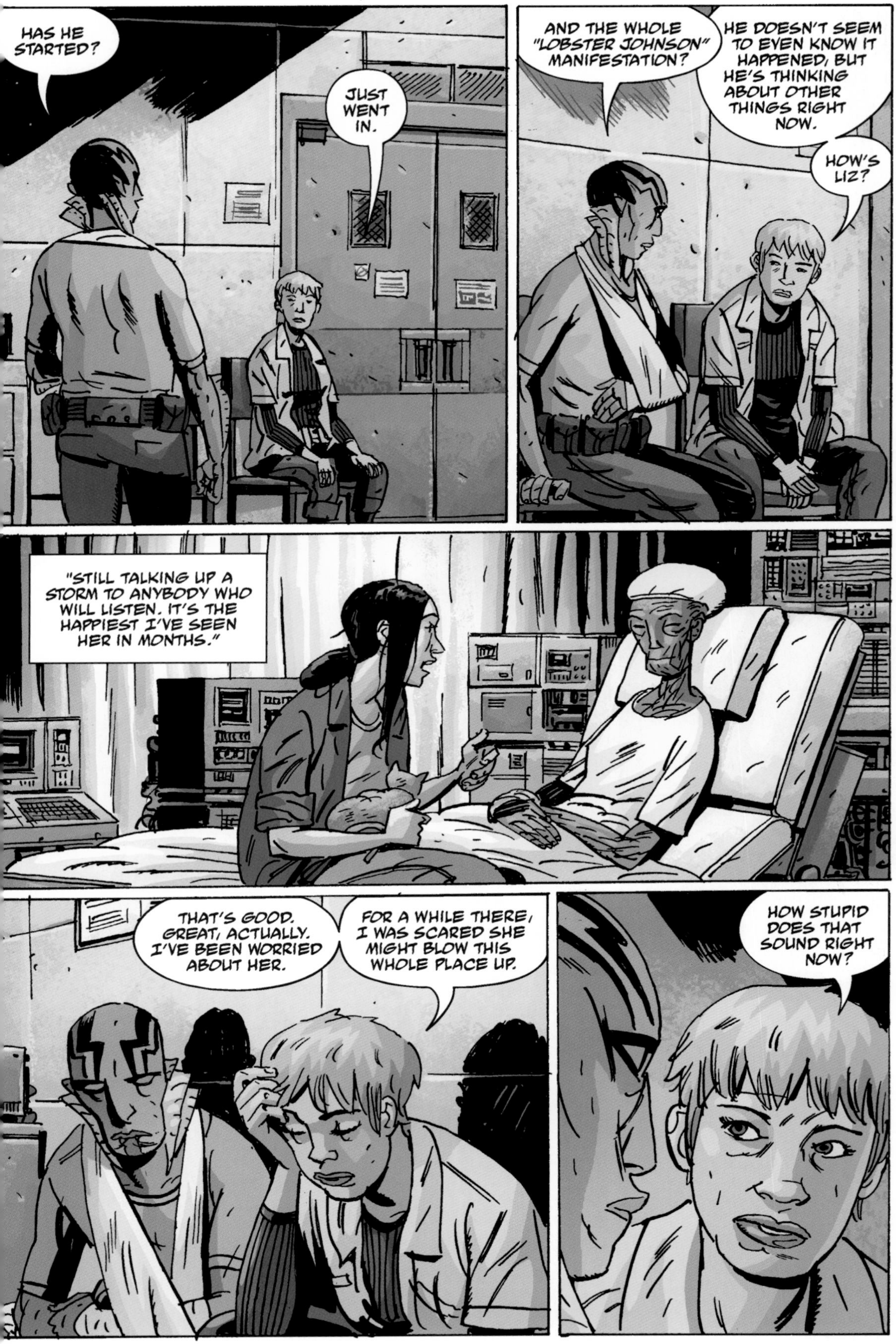
HAS HE STARTED?
JUST WENT IN.
AND THE WHOLE "LOBSTER JOHNSON" MANIFESTATION?
HE DOESN'T SEEM TO EVEN KNOW IT HAPPENED, BUT HE'S THINKING ABOUT OTHER THINGS RIGHT NOW.
HOW'S LIZ?
"STILL TALKING UP A STORM TO ANYBODY WHO WILL LISTEN. IT'S THE HAPPIEST I'VE SEEN HER IN MONTHS."
THAT'S GOOD. GREAT, ACTUALLY. I'VE BEEN WORRIED ABOUT HER.
FOR A WHILE THERE, I WAS SCARED SHE MIGHT BLOW THIS WHOLE PLACE UP.
HOW STUPID DOES THAT SOUND RIGHT NOW?

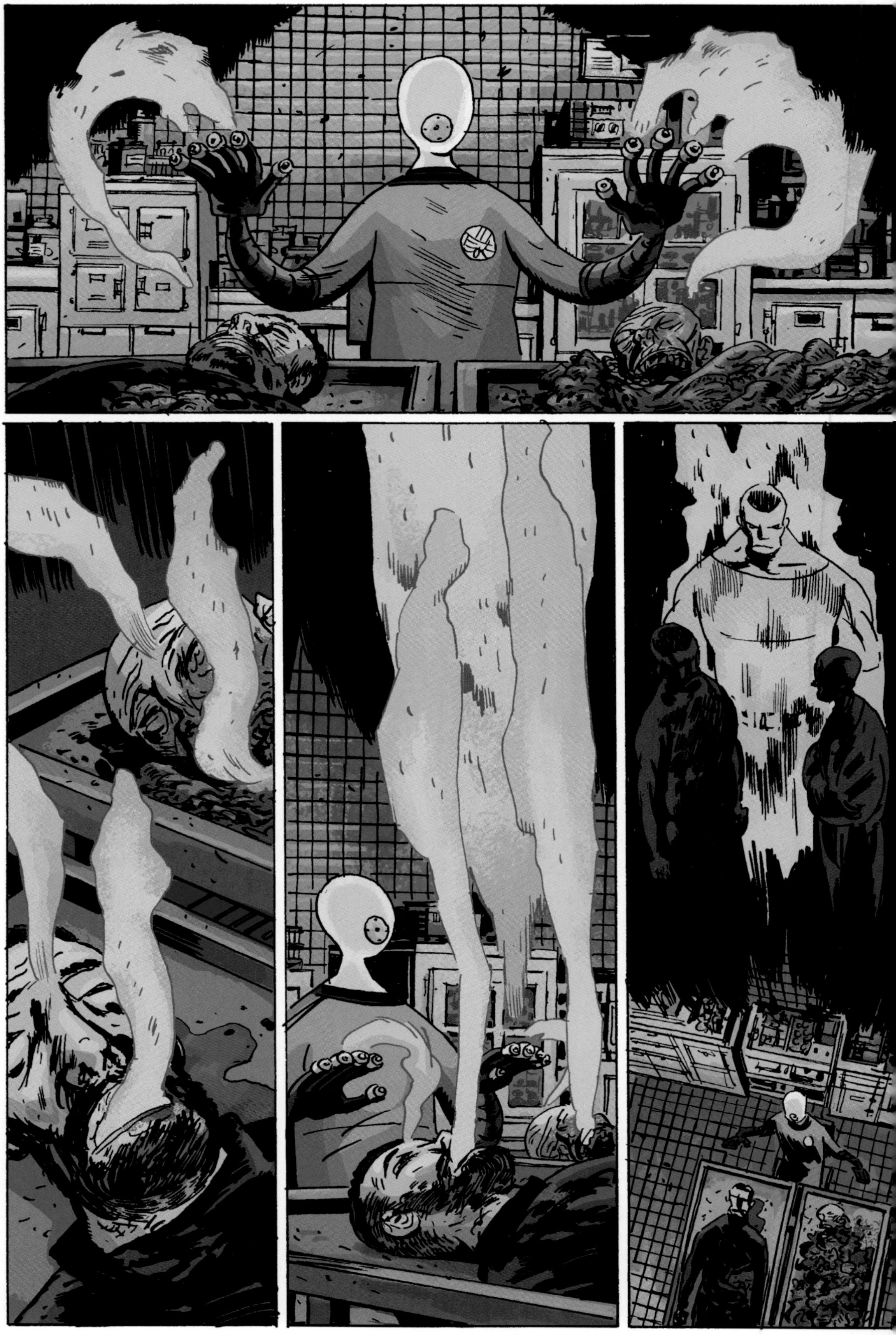

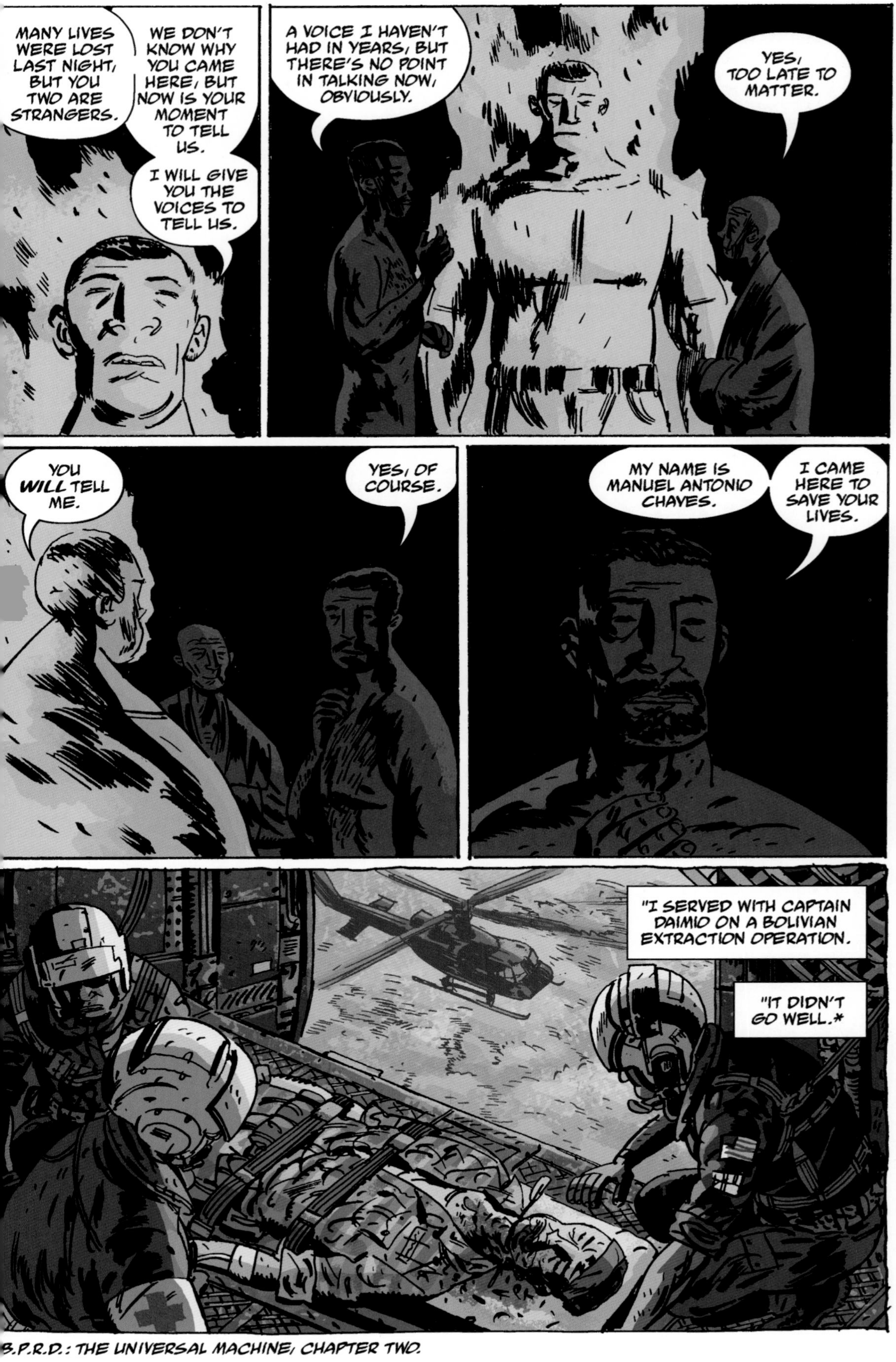
MANY LIVES WERE LOST LAST NIGHT, BUT YOU TWO ARE STRANGERS.
WE DON'T KNOW WHY YOU CAME HERE, BUT NOW IS YOUR MOMENT TO TELL US.
I WILL GIVE YOU THE VOICES TO TELL US.
A VOICE I HAVEN'T HAD IN YEARS, BUT THERE'S NO POINT IN TALKING NOW, OBVIOUSLY.
YES, TOO LATE TO MATTER.
YOU WILL TELL ME.
YES, OF COURSE.
MY NAME IS MANUEL ANTONIO CHAVES.
I CAME HERE TO SAVE YOUR LIVES.
"I SERVED WITH CAPTAIN DAIMIO ON A BOLIVIAN EXTRACTION OPERATION.
"IT DIDN'T GO WELL.*

*B.P.R.D.: THE UNIVERSAL MACHINE, CHAPTER TWO.

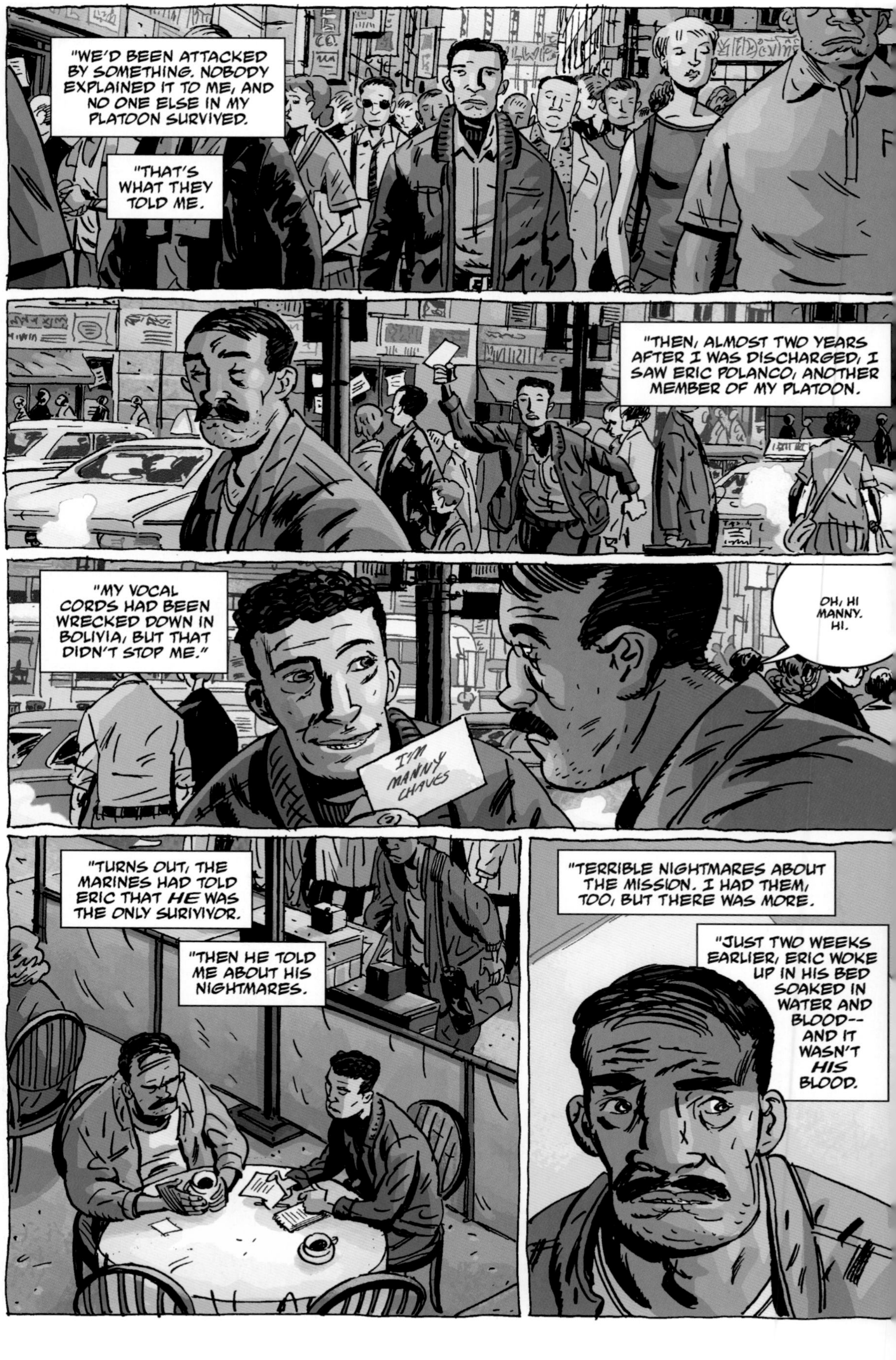
"WE'D BEEN ATTACKED BY SOMETHING. NOBODY EXPLAINED IT TO ME, AND NO ONE ELSE IN MY PLATOON SURVIVED.
"THAT'S WHAT THEY TOLD ME.
"THEN, ALMOST TWO YEARS AFTER I WAS DISCHARGED, I SAW ERIC POLANCO, ANOTHER MEMBER OF MY PLATOON.
"MY VOCAL CORDS HAD BEEN WRECKED DOWN IN BOLIVIA, BUT THAT DIDN'T STOP ME."
I'M MANNY CHAVES
OH, HI MANNY. HI.
"TURNS OUT, THE MARINES HAD TOLD ERIC THAT HE WAS THE ONLY SURIVIVOR.
"THEN HE TOLD ME ABOUT HIS NIGHTMARES.
"TERRIBLE NIGHTMARES ABOUT THE MISSION. I HAD THEM, TOO, BUT THERE WAS MORE.
"JUST TWO WEEKS EARLIER, ERIC WOKE UP IN HIS BED SOAKED IN WATER AND BLOOD-- AND IT WASN'T HIS BLOOD.

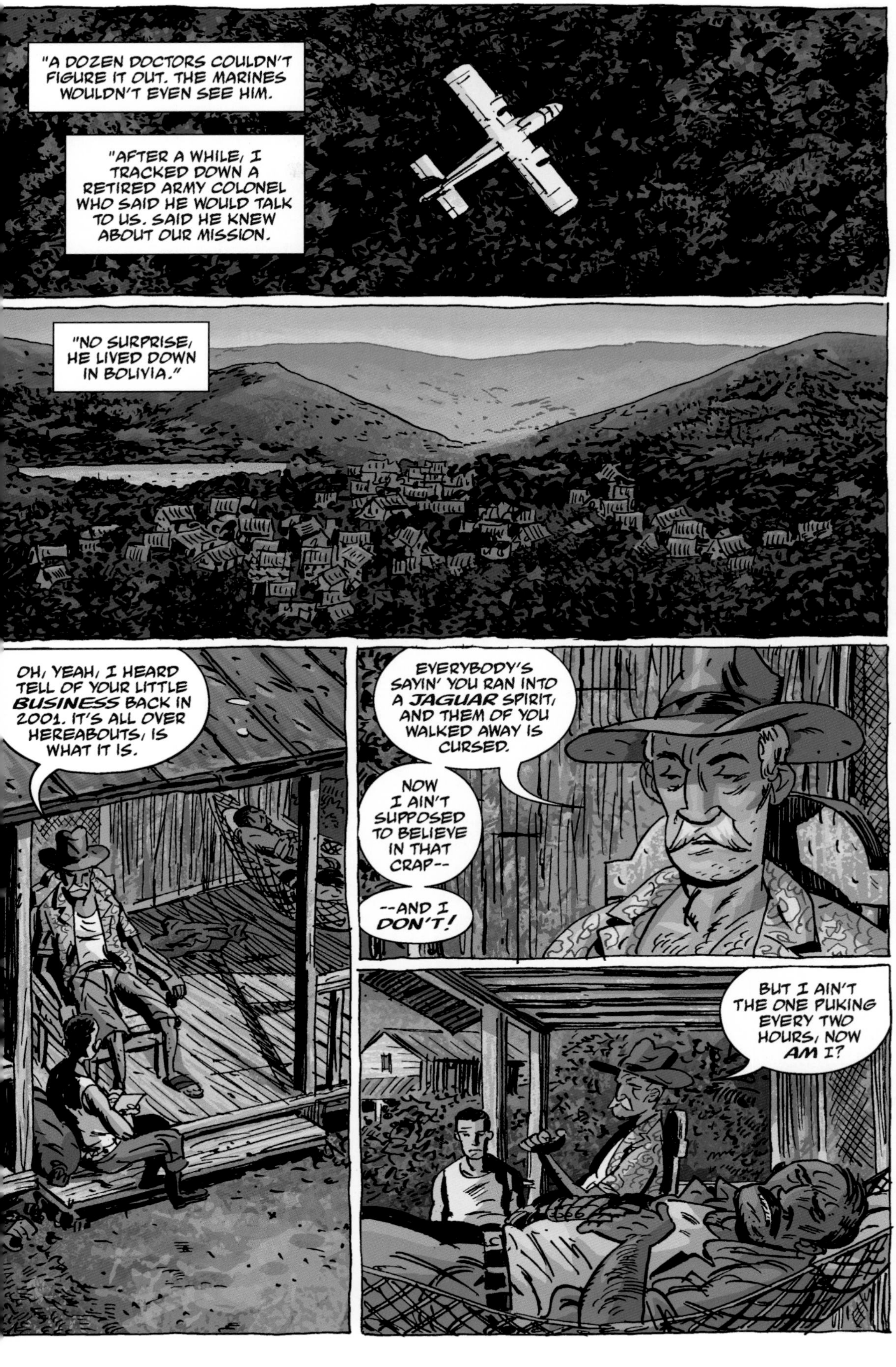
"A DOZEN DOCTORS COULDN'T FIGURE IT OUT. THE MARINES WOULDN'T EVEN SEE HIM.
"AFTER A WHILE, I TRACKED DOWN A RETIRED ARMY COLONEL WHO SAID HE WOULD TALK TO US. SAID HE KNEW ABOUT OUR MISSION.
"NO SURPRISE, HE LIVED DOWN IN BOLIVIA."
OH, YEAH, I HEARD TELL OF YOUR LITTLE BUSINESS BACK IN 2001. IT'S ALL OVER HEREABOUTS, IS WHAT IT IS.
EVERYBODY'S SAYIN' YOU RAN INTO A JAGUAR SPIRIT, AND THEM OF YOU WALKED AWAY IS CURSED.
NOW I AIN'T SUPPOSED TO BELIEVE IN THAT CRAP--
--AND I DON'T!
BUT I AIN'T THE ONE PUKING EVERY TWO HOURS, NOW AM I?

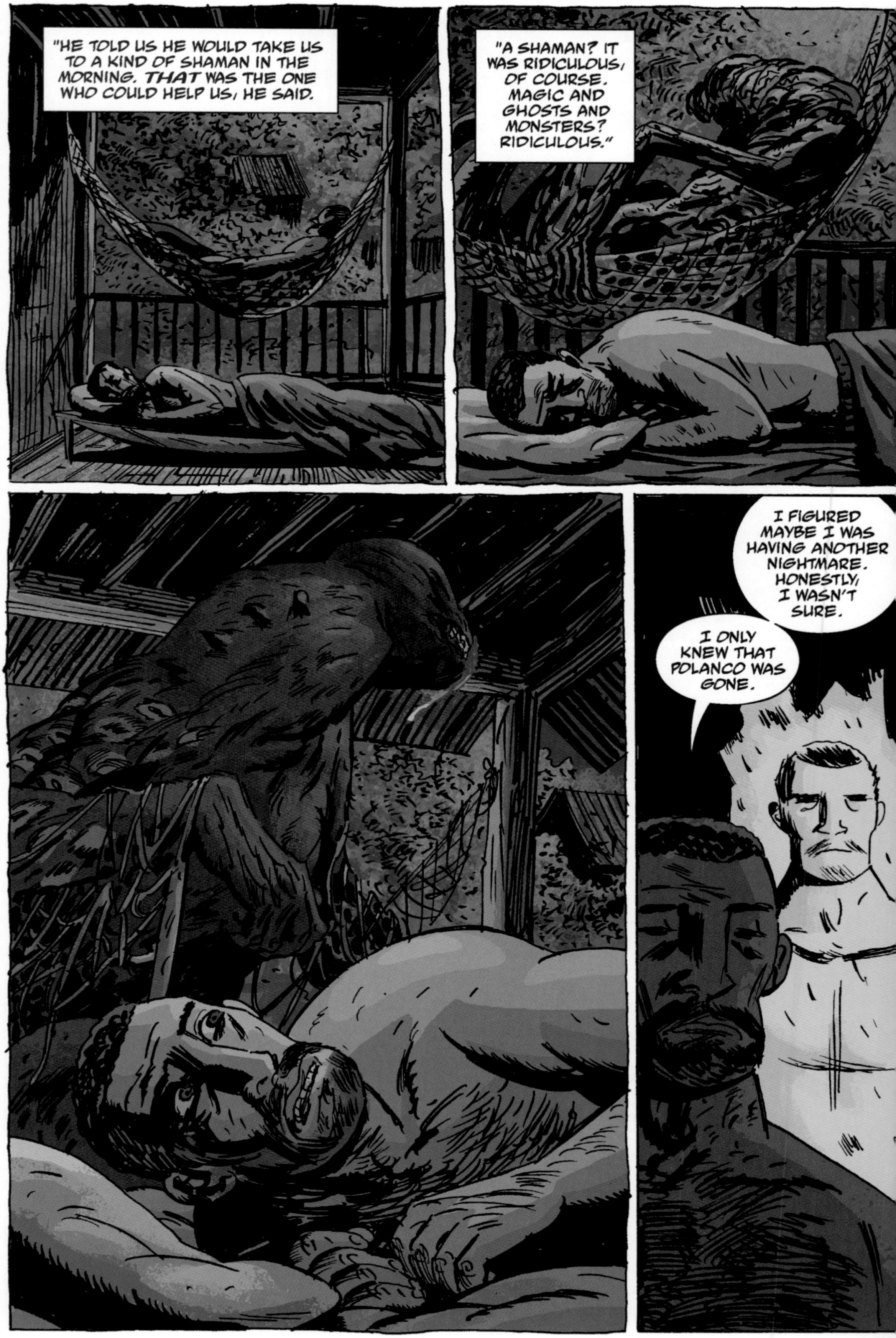
"HE TOLD US HE WOULD TAKE US TO A KIND OF SHAMAN IN THE MORNING. THAT WAS THE ONE WHO COULD HELP US, HE SAID.
"A SHAMAN? IT WAS RIDICULOUS, OF COURSE. MAGIC AND GHOSTS AND MONSTERS? RIDICULOUS."
I FIGURED MAYBE I WAS HAVING ANOTHER NIGHTMARE. HONESTLY, I WASN'T SURE.
I ONLY KNEW THAT POLANCO WAS GONE.

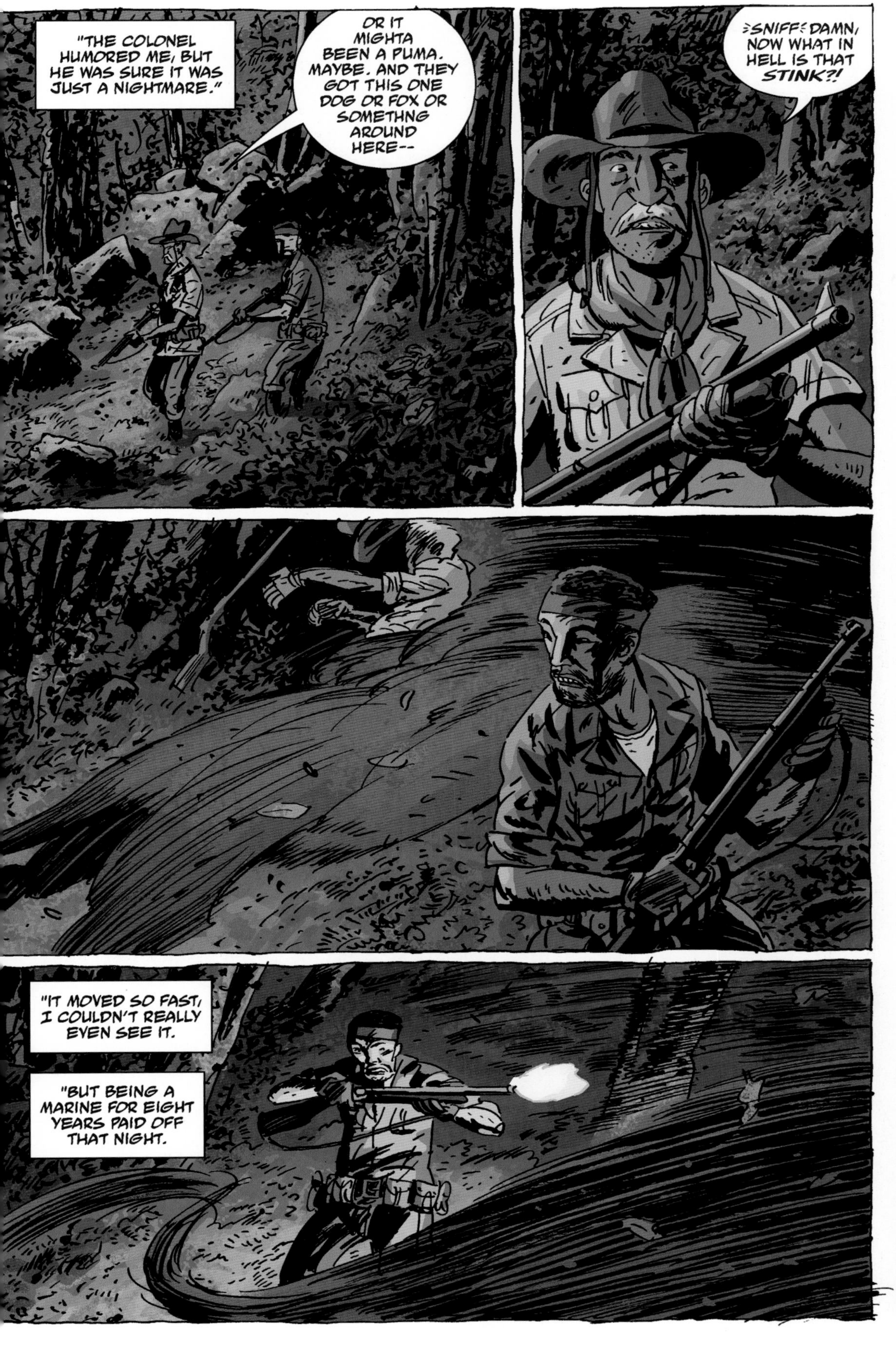
"THE COLONEL HUMORED ME, BUT HE WAS SURE IT WAS JUST A NIGHTMARE."
OR IT MIGHTA BEEN A PUMA. MAYBE. AND THEY GOT THIS ONE DOG OR FOX OR SOMETHNG AROUND HERE--
SNIFF DAMN, NOW WHAT IN HELL IS THAT STINK?!
"IT MOVED SO FAST, I COULDN'T REALLY EVEN SEE IT.
"BUT BEING A MARINE FOR EIGHT YEARS PAID OFF THAT NIGHT.

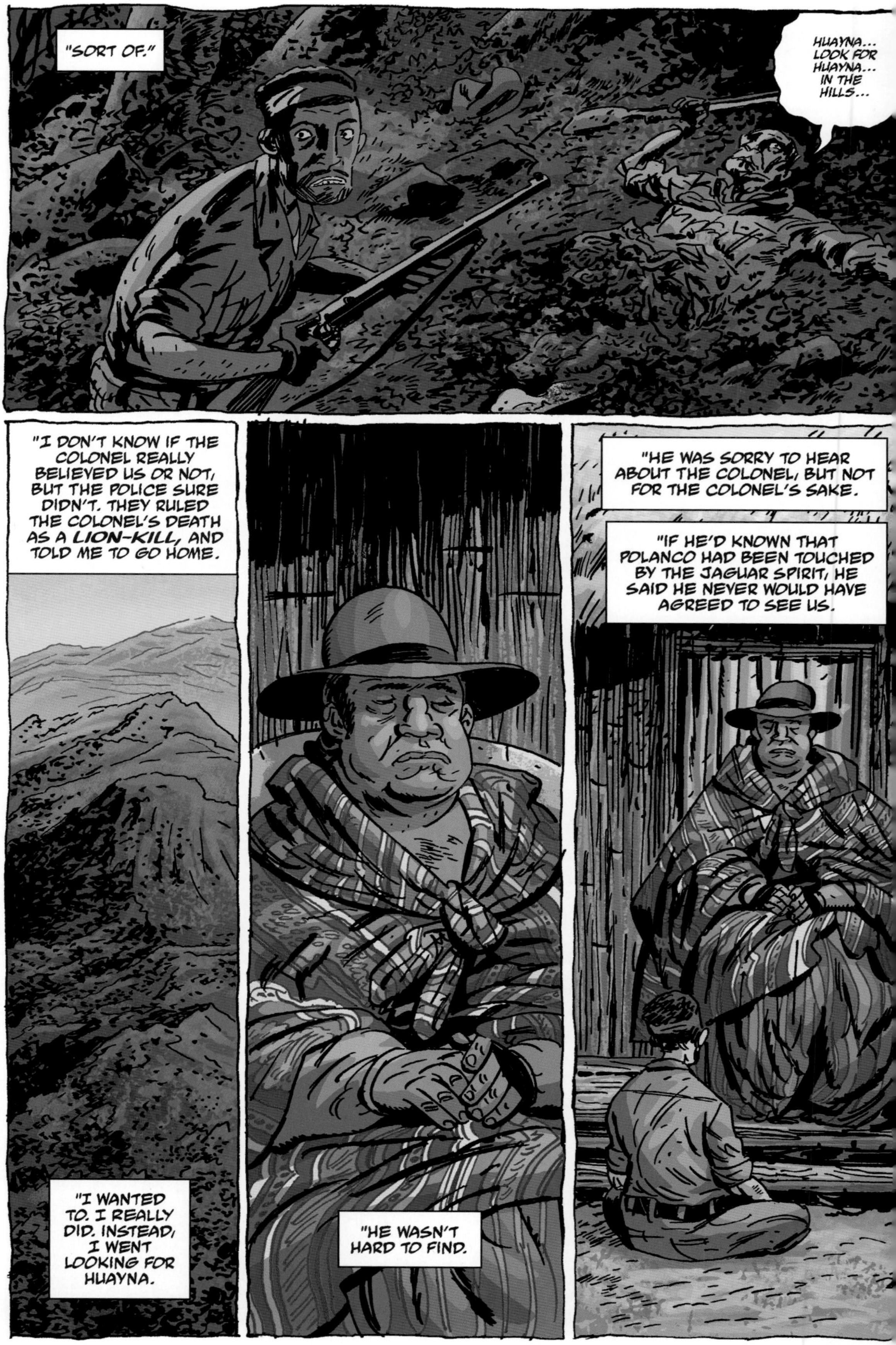
"SORT OF."
HUAYNA... LOOK FOR HUAYNA... IN THE HILLS...
"I DON'T KNOW IF THE COLONEL REALLY BELIEVED US OR NOT, BUT THE POLICE SURE DIDN'T. THEY RULED THE COLONEL'S DEATH AS A LION-KILL, AND TOLD ME TO GO HOME.
"I WANTED TO. I REALLY DID. INSTEAD, I WENT LOOKING FOR HUAYNA.
"HE WASN'T HARD TO FIND.
"HE WAS SORRY TO HEAR ABOUT THE COLONEL, BUT NOT FOR THE COLONEL'S SAKE.
"IF HE'D KNOWN THAT POLANCO HAD BEEN TOUCHED BY THE JAGUAR SPIRIT, HE SAID HE NEVER WOULD HAVE AGREED TO SEE US.

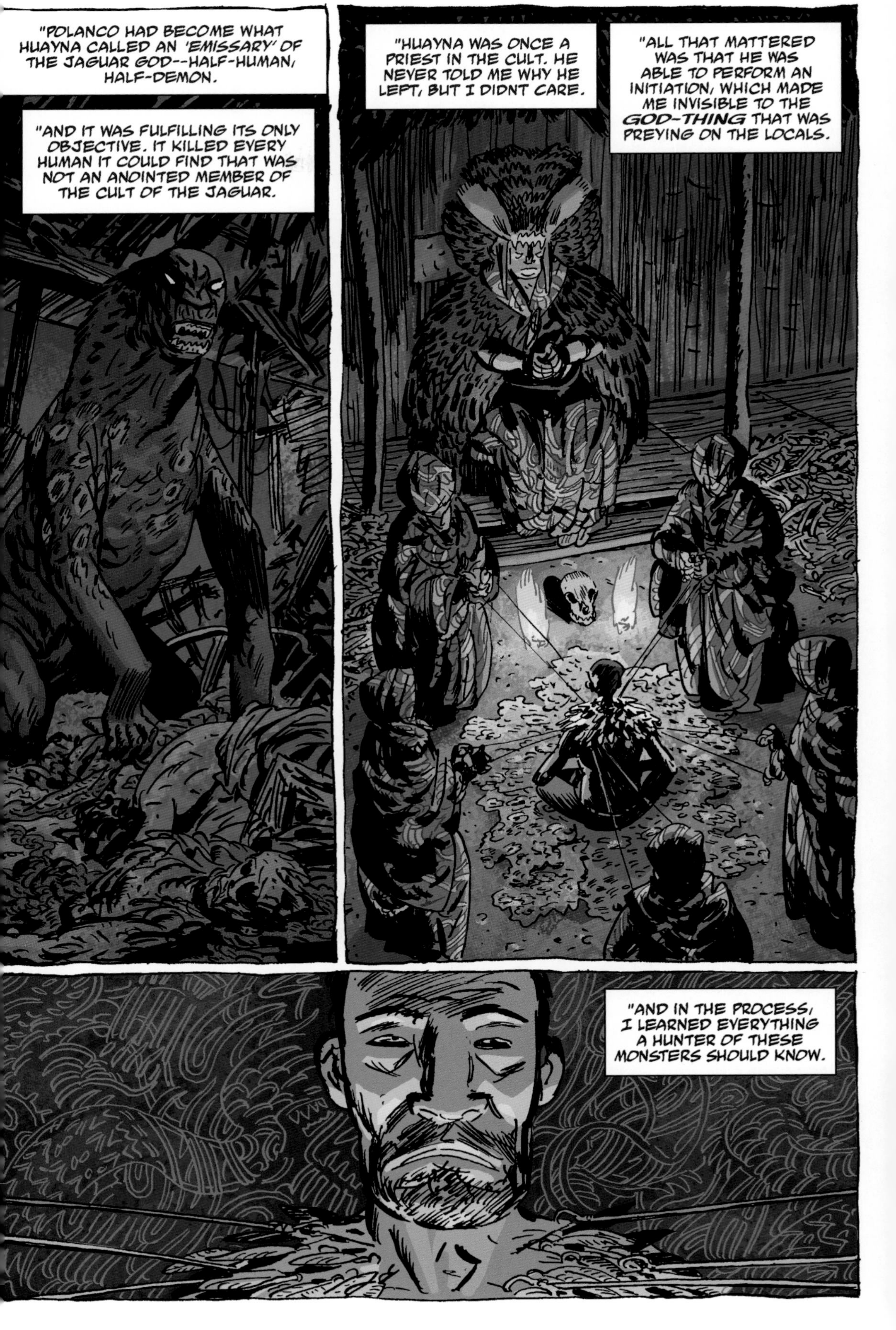
"POLANCO HAD BECOME WHAT HUAYNA CALLED AN 'EMISSARY' OF THE JAGUAR GOD--HALF-HUMAN, HALF-DEMON.
"AND IT WAS FULFILLING ITS ONLY OBJECTIVE. IT KILLED EVERY HUMAN IT COULD FIND THAT WAS NOT AN ANOINTED MEMBER OF THE CULT OF THE JAGUAR.
"HUAYNA WAS ONCE A PRIEST IN THE CULT. HE NEVER TOLD ME WHY HE LEFT, BUT I DIDNT CARE.
"ALL THAT MATTERED WAS THAT HE WAS ABLE TO PERFORM AN INITIATION, WHICH MADE ME INVISIBLE TO THE GOD-THING THAT WAS PREYING ON THE LOCALS.
"AND IN THE PROCESS, I LEARNED EVERYTHING A HUNTER OF THESE MONSTERS SHOULD KNOW.

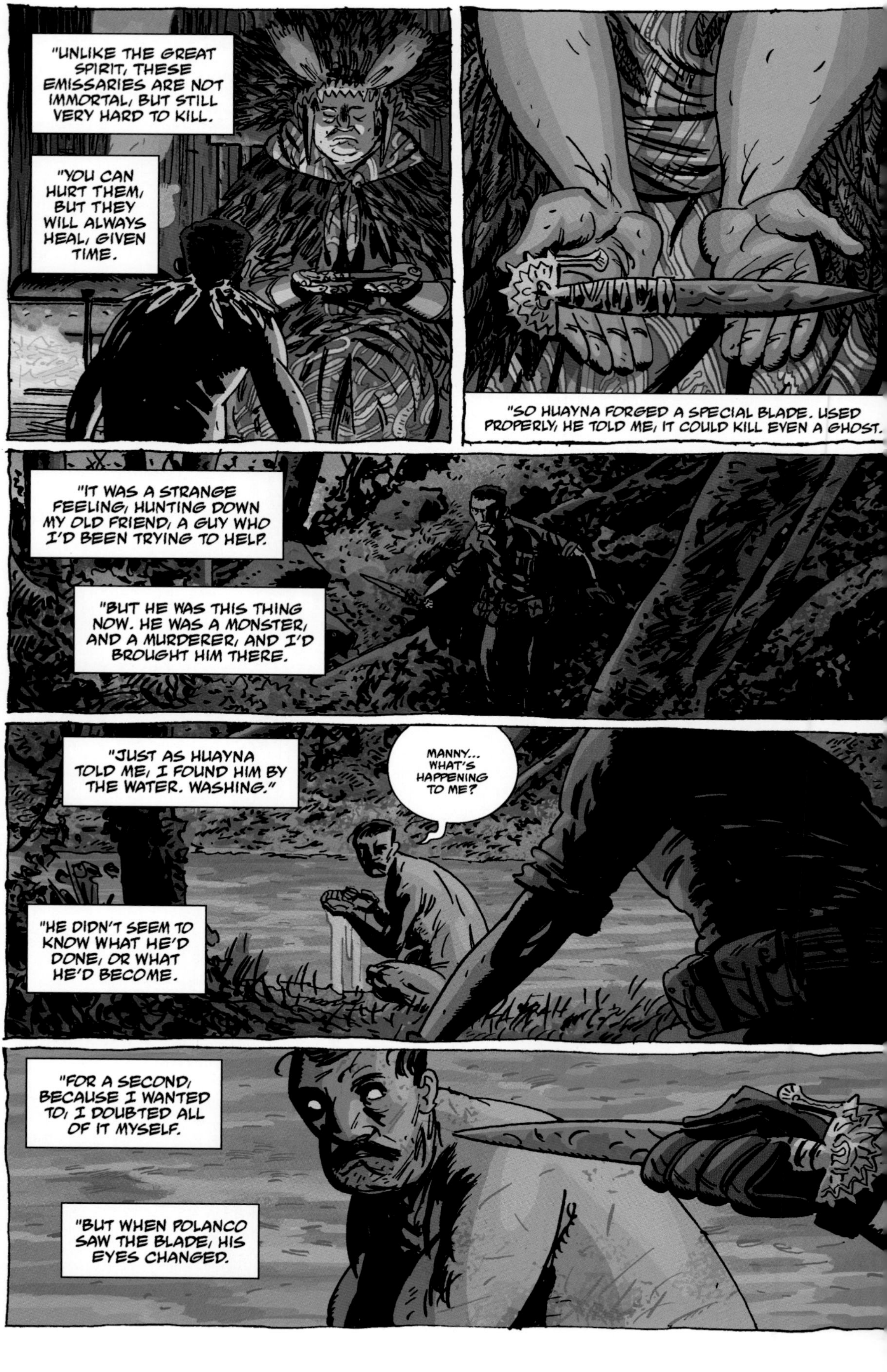
"UNLIKE THE GREAT SPIRIT, THESE EMISSARIES ARE NOT IMMORTAL, BUT STILL VERY HARD TO KILL.
"YOU CAN HURT THEM, BUT THEY WILL ALWAYS HEAL, GIVEN TIME.
"SO HUAYNA FORGED A SPECIAL BLADE. USED PROPERLY, HE TOLD ME, IT COULD KILL EVEN A GHOST.
"IT WAS A STRANGE FEELING, HUNTING DOWN MY OLD FRIEND, A GUY WHO I'D BEEN TRYING TO HELP.
"BUT HE WAS THIS THING NOW. HE WAS A MONSTER, AND A MURDERER, AND I'D BROUGHT HIM THERE.
"JUST AS HUAYNA TOLD ME, I FOUND HIM BY THE WATER. WASHING."
MANNY... WHAT'S HAPPENING TO ME?
"HE DIDN'T SEEM TO KNOW WHAT HE'D DONE, OR WHAT HE'D BECOME.
"FOR A SECOND, BECAUSE I WANTED TO, I DOUBTED ALL OF IT MYSELF.
"BUT WHEN POLANCO SAW THE BLADE, HIS EYES CHANGED.

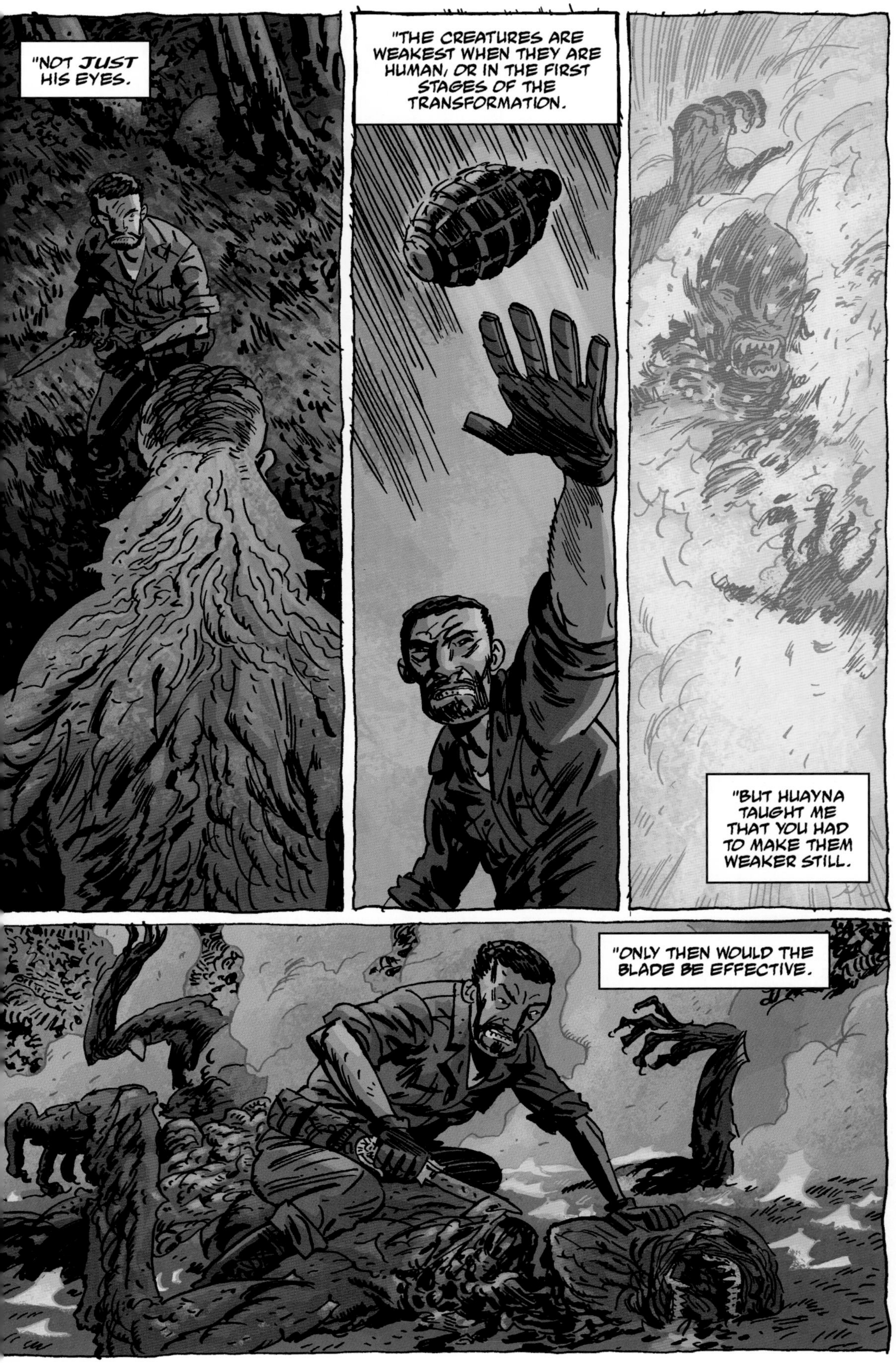
"NOT JUST HIS EYES.
"THE CREATURES ARE WEAKEST WHEN THEY ARE HUMAN, OR IN THE FIRST STAGES OF THE TRANSFORMATION.
"BUT HUAYNA TAUGHT ME THAT YOU HAD TO MAKE THEM WEAKER STILL.
"ONLY THEN WOULD THE BLADE BE EFFECTIVE.

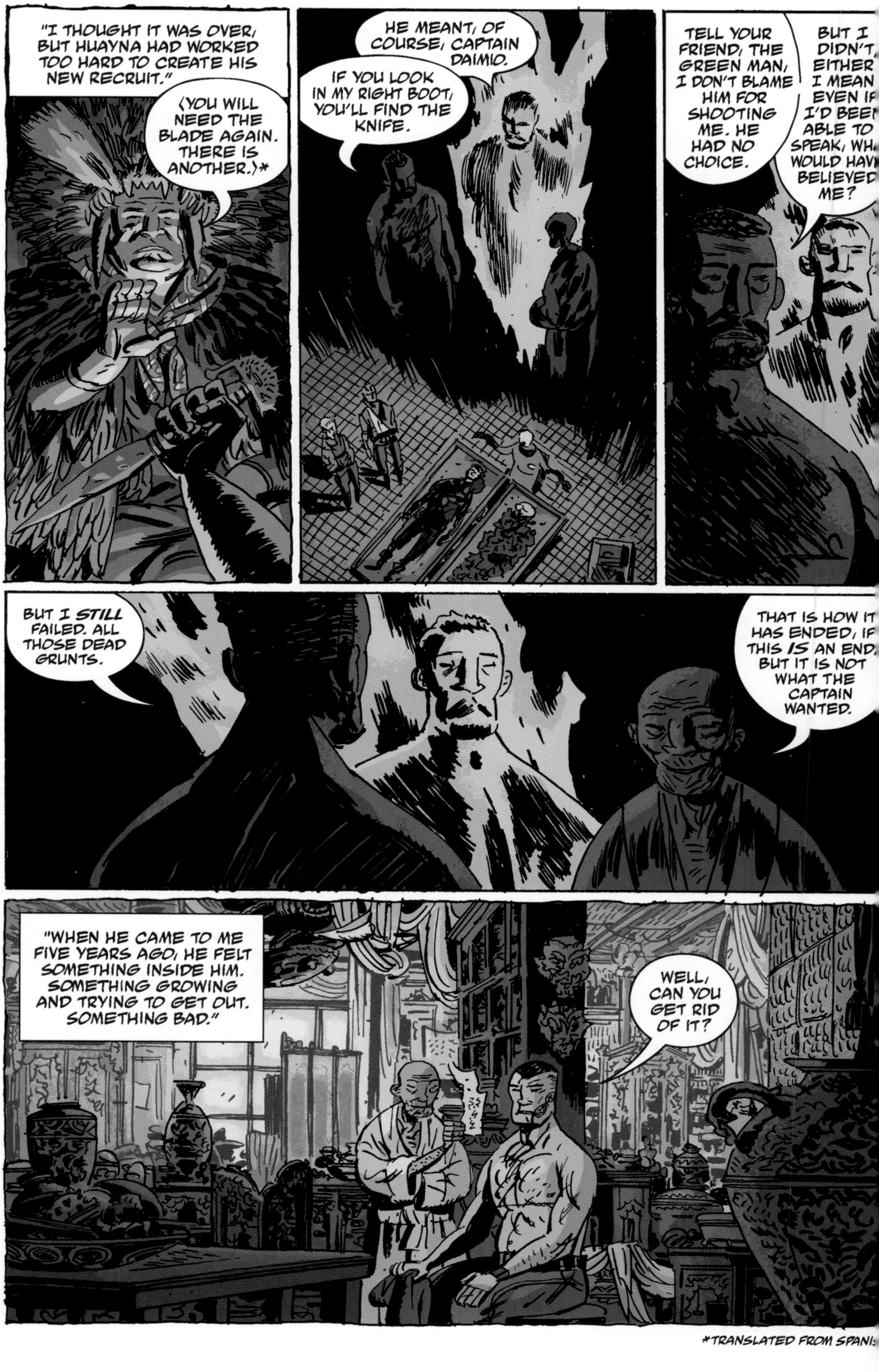
"I THOUGHT IT WAS OVER, BUT HUAYNA HAD WORKED TOO HARD TO CREATE HIS NEW RECRUIT."
‹YOU WILL NEED THE BLADE AGAIN. THERE IS ANOTHER.›*
HE MEANT, OF COURSE, CAPTAIN DAIMIO.
IF YOU LOOK IN MY RIGHT BOOT, YOU'LL FIND THE KNIFE.
TELL YOUR FRIEND, THE GREEN MAN, I DON'T BLAME HIM FOR SHOOTING ME. HE HAD NO CHOICE.
BUT I DIDN'T, EITHER I MEAN EVEN IF I'D BEEN ABLE TO SPEAK, WHA WOULD HAVE BELIEVED ME?
BUT I STILL FAILED. ALL THOSE DEAD GRUNTS.
THAT IS HOW IT HAS ENDED, IF THIS IS AN END. BUT IT IS NOT WHAT THE CAPTAIN WANTED.
"WHEN HE CAME TO ME FIVE YEARS AGO, HE FELT SOMETHING INSIDE HIM. SOMETHING GROWING AND TRYING TO GET OUT. SOMETHING BAD."
WELL, CAN YOU GET RID OF IT?
*TRANSLATED FROM SPANISH

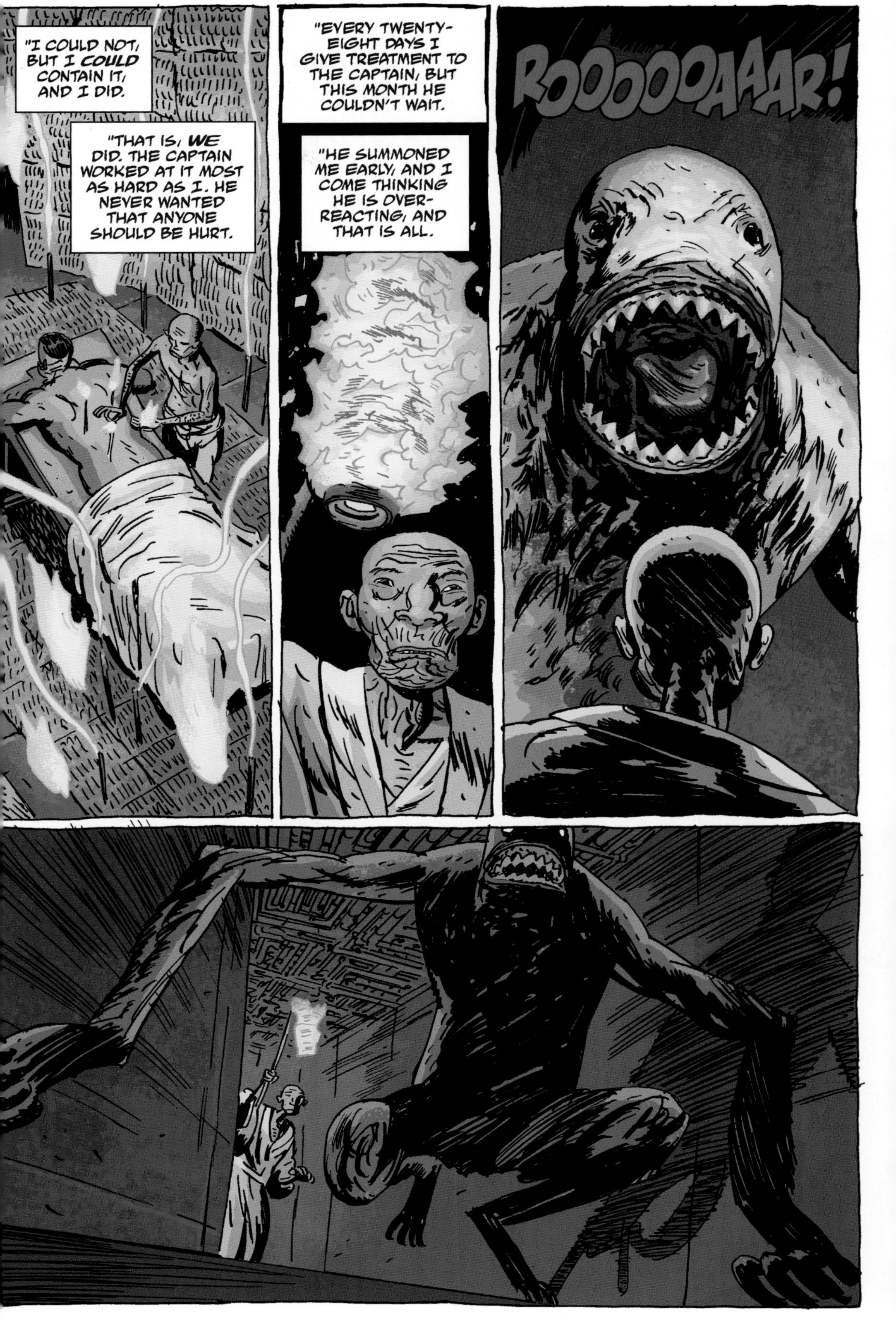
"I COULD NOT, BUT I *COULD* CONTAIN IT, AND I DID.
"THAT IS, *WE* DID. THE CAPTAIN WORKED AT IT MOST AS HARD AS I. HE NEVER WANTED THAT ANYONE SHOULD BE HURT.
"EVERY TWENTY-EIGHT DAYS I GIVE TREATMENT TO THE CAPTAIN, BUT THIS MONTH HE COULDN'T WAIT.
"HE SUMMONED ME EARLY, AND I COME THINKING HE IS OVER-REACTING, AND THAT IS ALL.
ROOOOOAAAR!

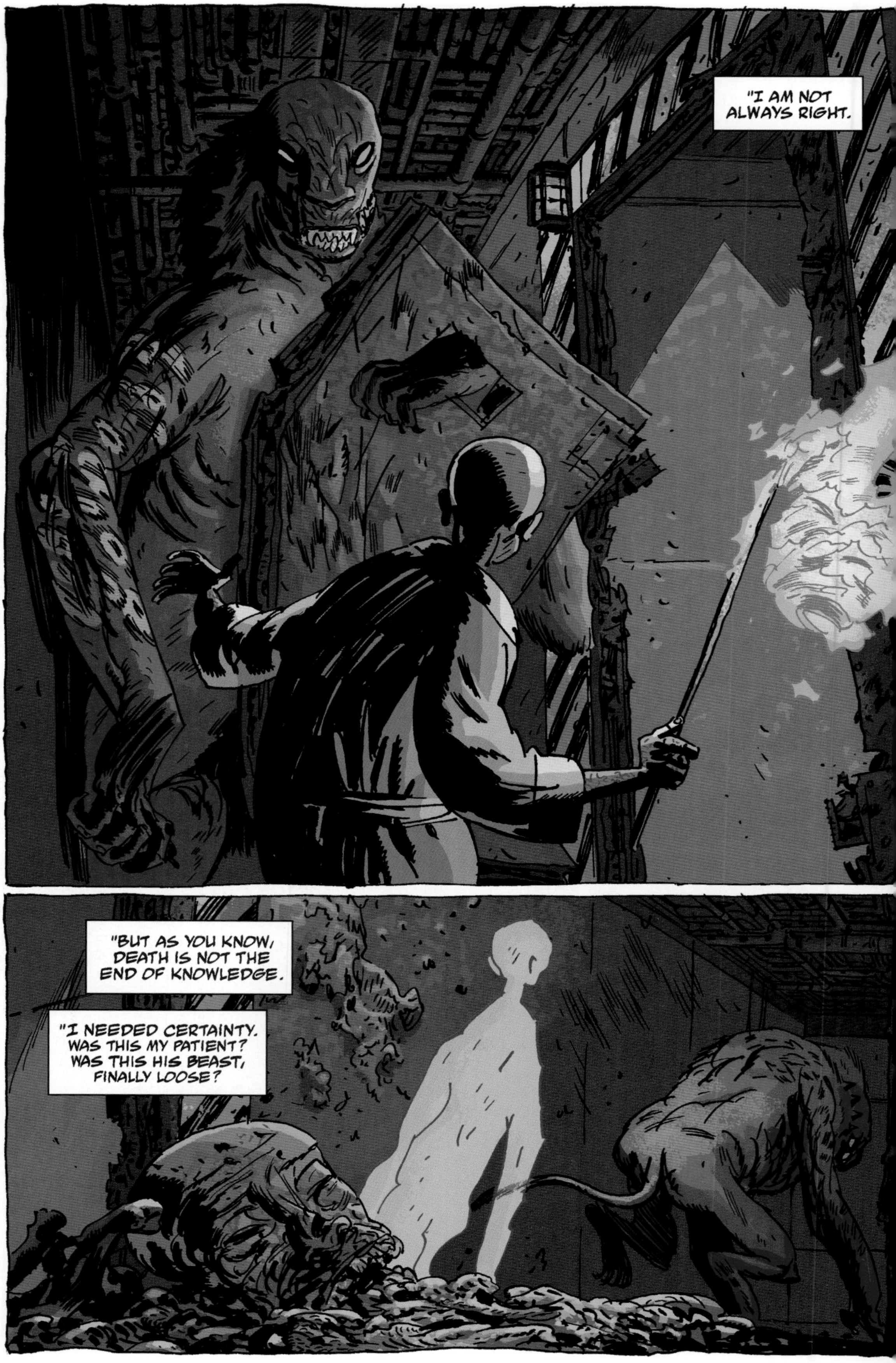
"I AM NOT ALWAYS RIGHT.
"BUT AS YOU KNOW, DEATH IS NOT THE END OF KNOWLEDGE.
"I NEEDED CERTAINTY. WAS THIS MY PATIENT? WAS THIS HIS BEAST, FINALLY LOOSE?

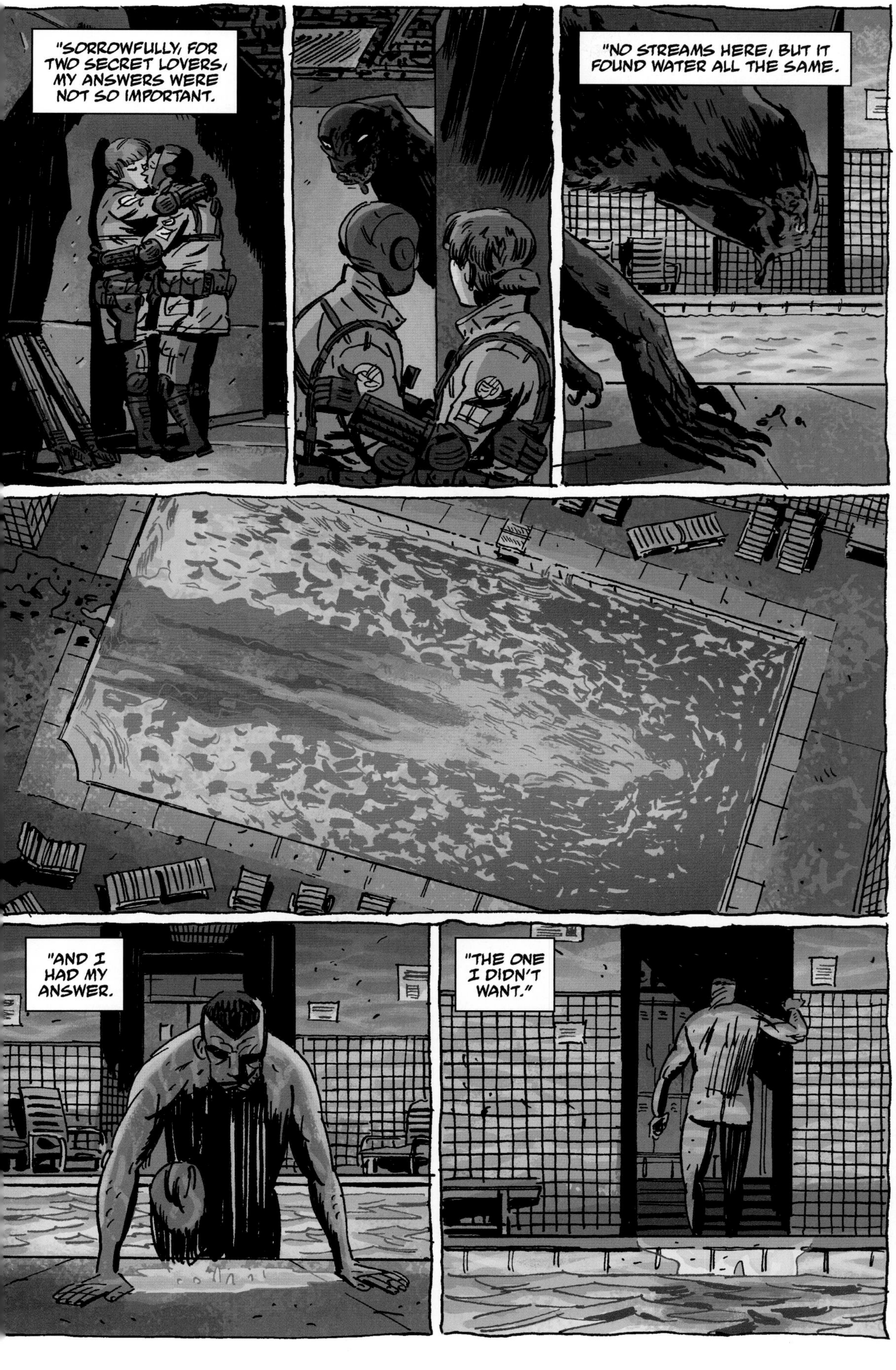
"SORROWFULLY, FOR TWO SECRET LOVERS, MY ANSWERS WERE NOT SO IMPORTANT.
"NO STREAMS HERE, BUT IT FOUND WATER ALL THE SAME.
"AND I HAD MY ANSWER.
"THE ONE I DIDN'T WANT."

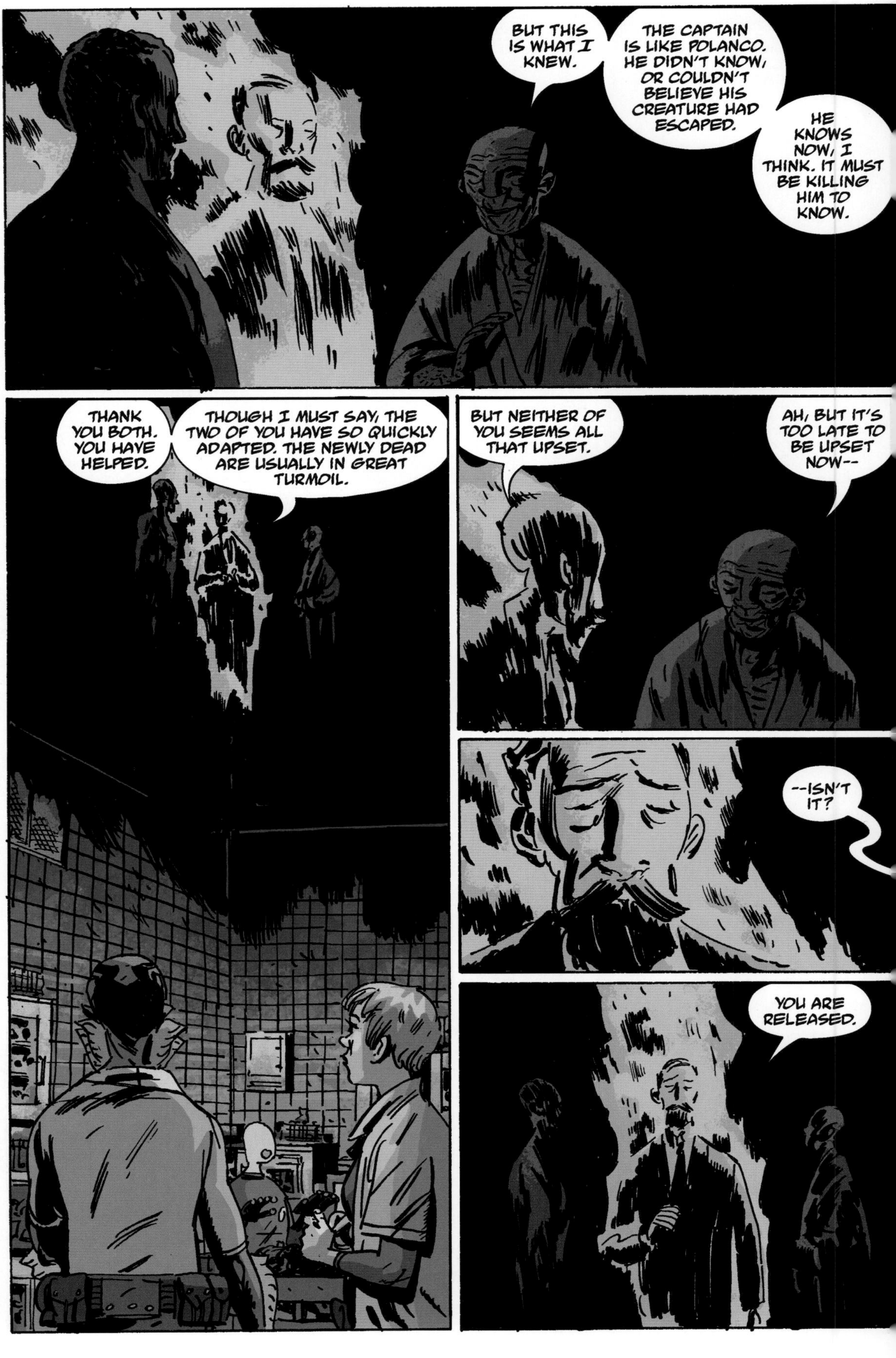
BUT THIS IS WHAT I KNEW.
THE CAPTAIN IS LIKE POLANCO. HE DIDN'T KNOW, OR COULDN'T BELIEVE HIS CREATURE HAD ESCAPED.
HE KNOWS NOW, I THINK. IT MUST BE KILLING HIM TO KNOW.
THANK YOU BOTH. YOU HAVE HELPED.
THOUGH I MUST SAY, THE TWO OF YOU HAVE SO QUICKLY ADAPTED. THE NEWLY DEAD ARE USUALLY IN GREAT TURMOIL.
BUT NEITHER OF YOU SEEMS ALL THAT UPSET.
AH, BUT IT'S TOO LATE TO BE UPSET NOW--
--ISN'T IT?
YOU ARE RELEASED.

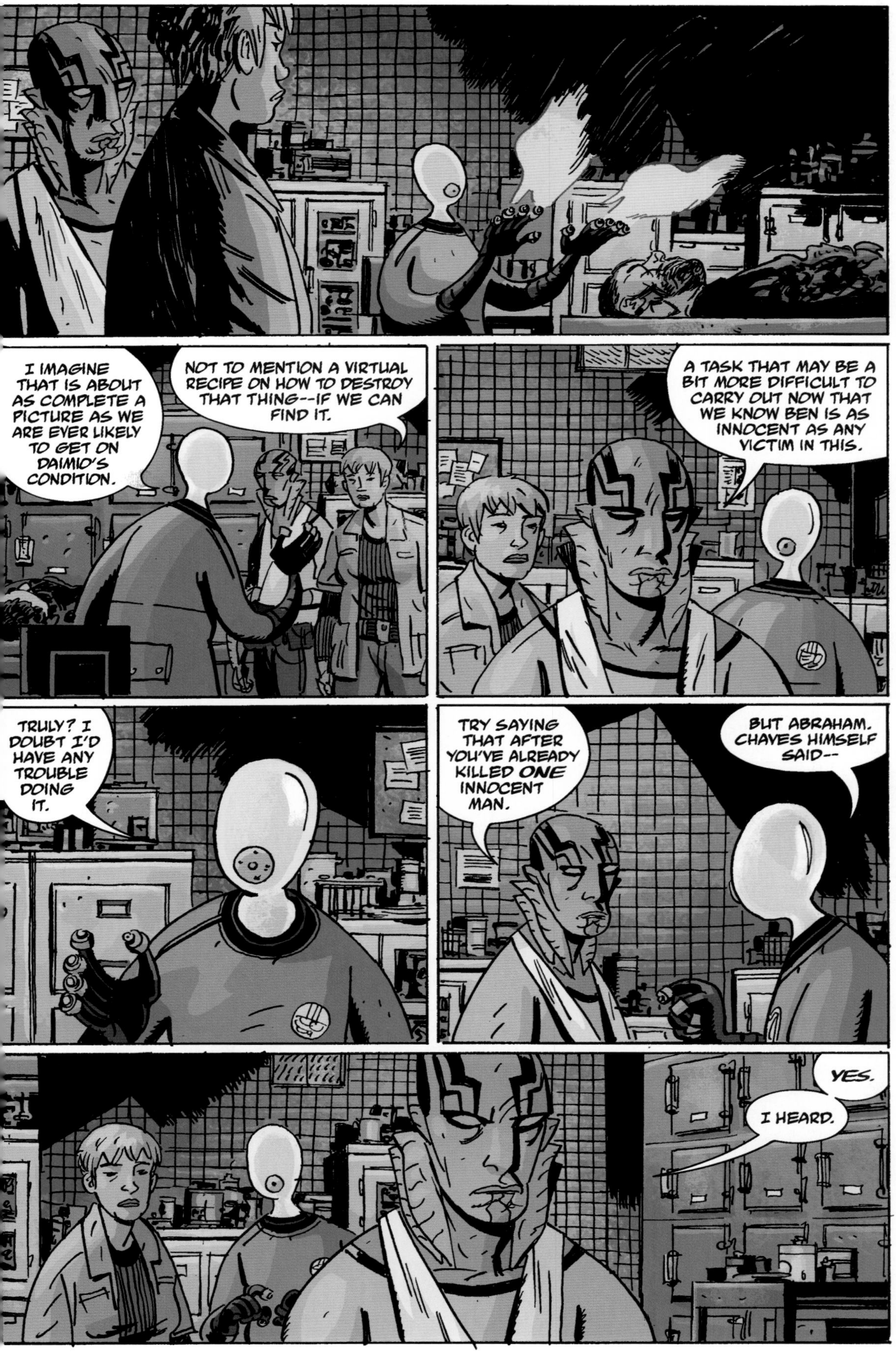
I IMAGINE THAT IS ABOUT AS COMPLETE A PICTURE AS WE ARE EVER LIKELY TO GET ON DAIMIO'S CONDITION.
NOT TO MENTION A VIRTUAL RECIPE ON HOW TO DESTROY THAT THING--IF WE CAN FIND IT.
A TASK THAT MAY BE A BIT MORE DIFFICULT TO CARRY OUT NOW THAT WE KNOW BEN IS AS INNOCENT AS ANY VICTIM IN THIS.
TRULY? I DOUBT I'D HAVE ANY TROUBLE DOING IT.
TRY SAYING THAT AFTER YOU'VE ALREADY KILLED ONE INNOCENT MAN.
BUT ABRAHAM. CHAVES HIMSELF SAID--
YES.
I HEARD.

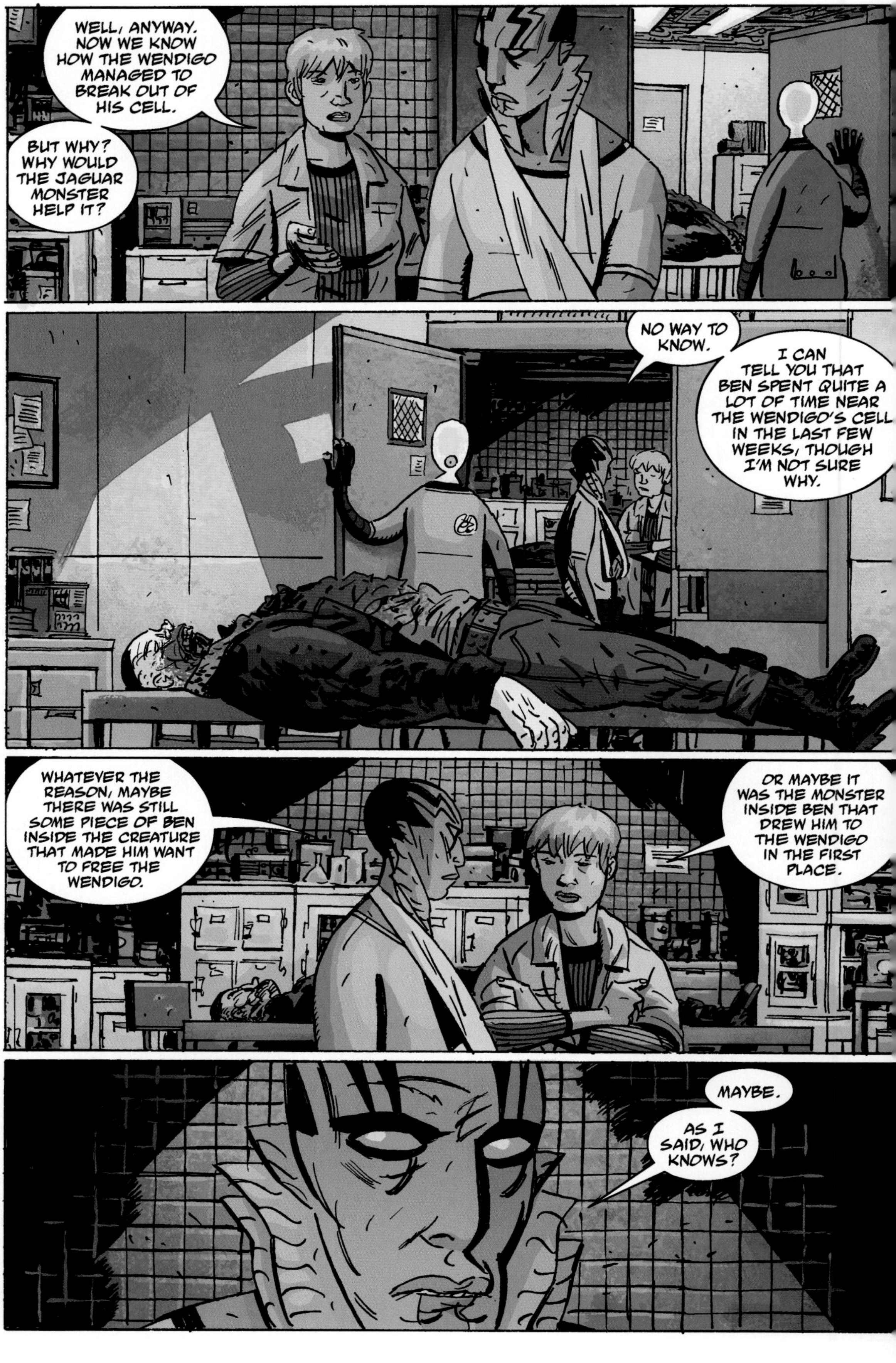
WELL, ANYWAY. NOW WE KNOW HOW THE WENDIGO MANAGED TO BREAK OUT OF HIS CELL.
BUT WHY? WHY WOULD THE JAGUAR MONSTER HELP IT?
NO WAY TO KNOW.
I CAN TELL YOU THAT BEN SPENT QUITE A LOT OF TIME NEAR THE WENDIGO'S CELL IN THE LAST FEW WEEKS, THOUGH I'M NOT SURE WHY.
WHATEVER THE REASON, MAYBE THERE WAS STILL SOME PIECE OF BEN INSIDE THE CREATURE THAT MADE HIM WANT TO FREE THE WENDIGO.
OR MAYBE IT WAS THE MONSTER INSIDE BEN THAT DREW HIM TO THE WENDIGO IN THE FIRST PLACE.
MAYBE.
AS I SAID, WHO KNOWS?

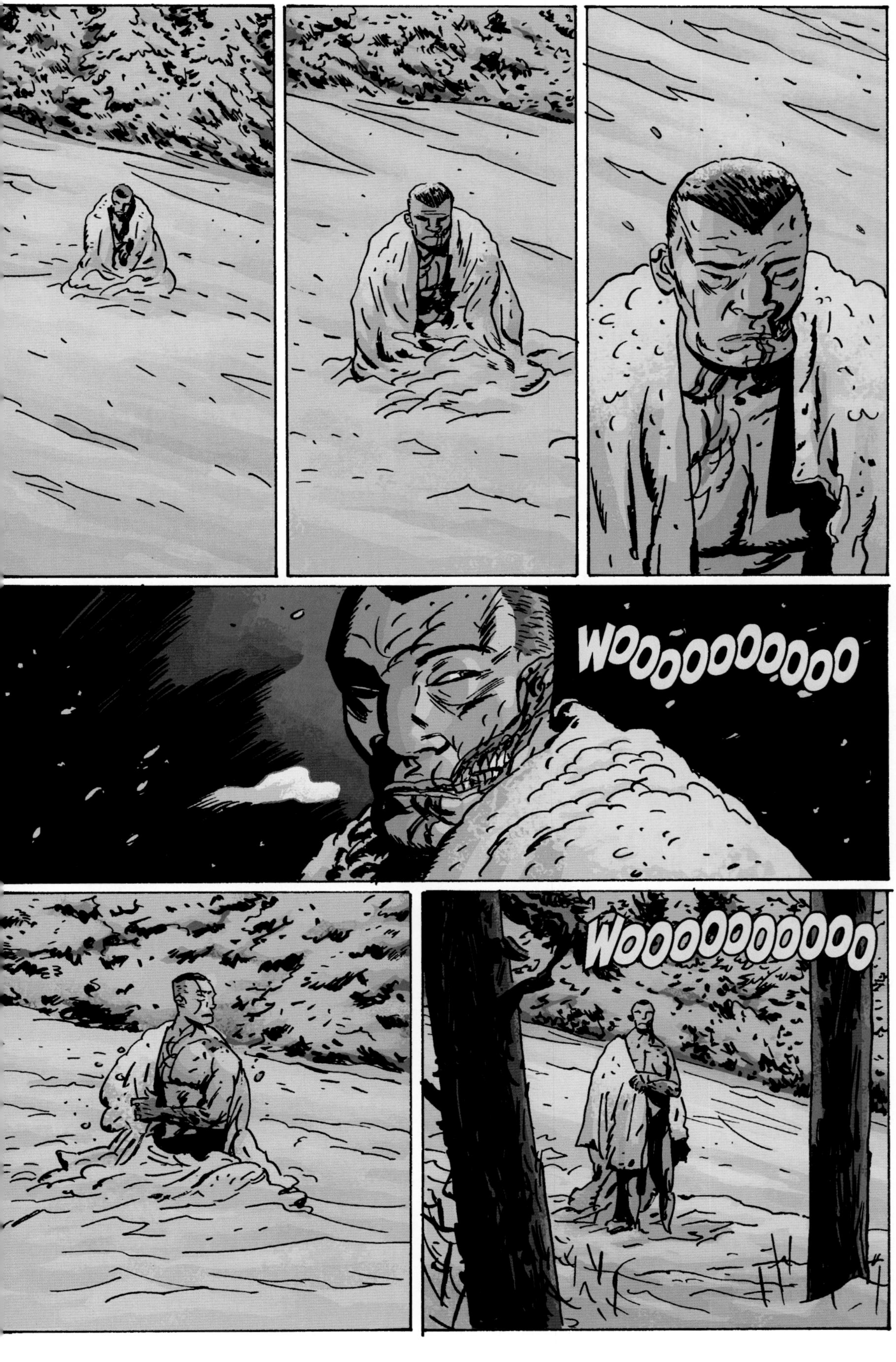
WOOOOOOOOOO
WOOOOOOOOOO

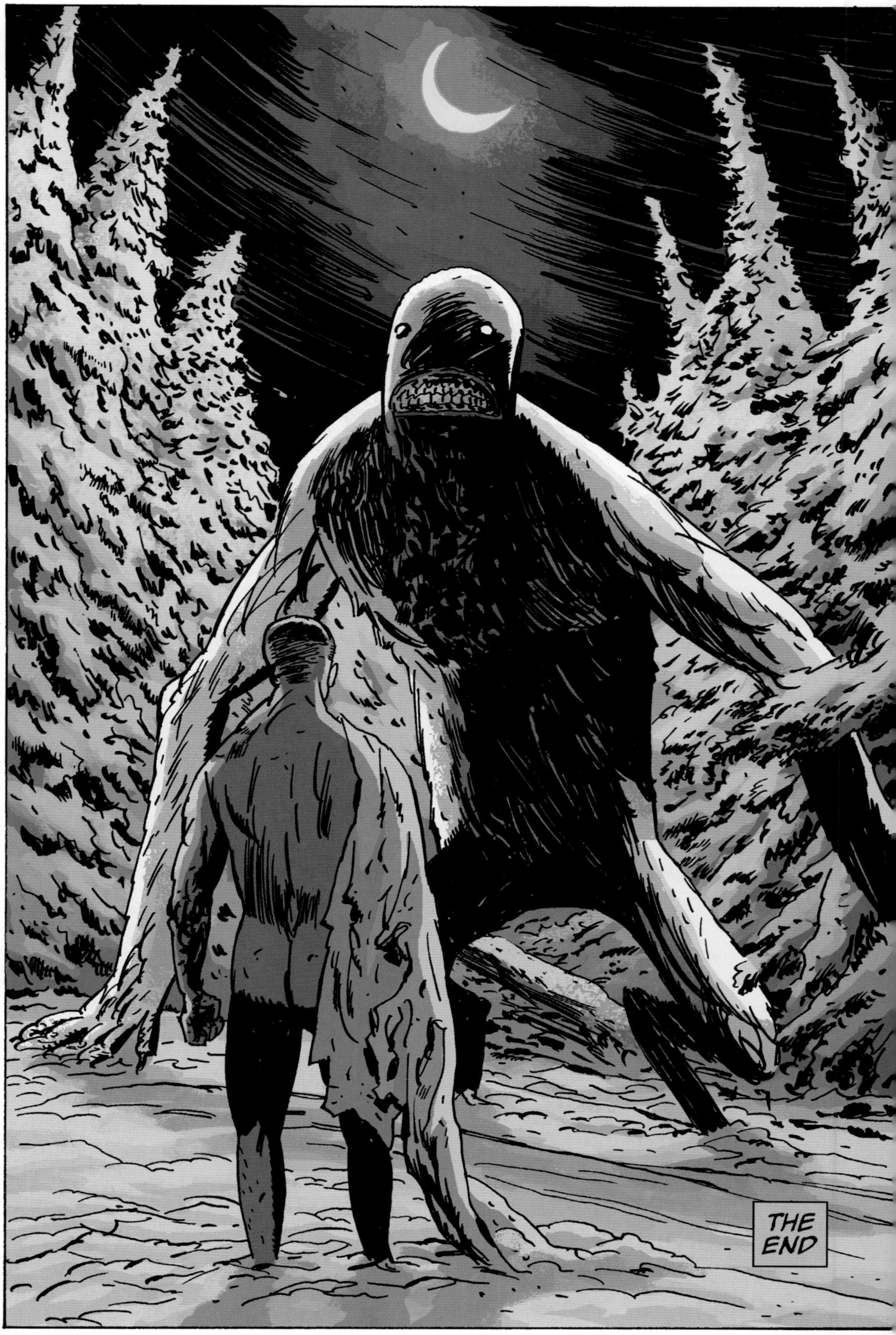
THE END

AFTERWORD

This one's been brewing for a while.

Ever since I first wrote the name "Benjamin Daimio," in fact. That's not to say that we knew all the way back in 2004 that it was going to play out just this way. For one thing, Guy Davis and I hadn't created Daryl yet, or any of the characters in *Garden of Souls,* including those spare giant bodies, so we didn't know the role that either Daryl or Johann would play. It's a process, after all. Well, it's more than that, really. It's almost a living, growing thing. It takes time, but if you nurture it properly, and don't force it, it grows naturally. But to complete this metaphor, and to bring it back to Ben, it grows from a seed.

When Mike asked me to work with him on *B.P.R.D.*, Hellboy was gone, and Abe was out of town. On the one hand, Mike knew Abe was coming back to the Bureau, and probably most of the readers *assumed* Abe was coming back, but as far as I could tell, none of the characters in the story knew it. So we thought to ourselves, "Wouldn't Tom Manning have a back-up plan?" and as it turns out, he did. That plan was Ben Daimio. Ben was meant to fill the void left by Hellboy and Abe; not so much for the readers, but for the other characters. He

was a man whom Roger could emulate, and Liz could resent, and Kate and Johann could respect, and Abe (when he returned) could even defer to. A strong man, and a good man who would do great work, but a man who was going to end up being one of the worst things that ever happened to the B.P.R.D.

That's what I was thinking right from day one, and not only was Mike okay with this, but if I remember correctly, it may have been half his idea. See, he didn't bring me on to help him create trademarks that were to be exploited and safeguarded in perpetuity. He didn't want a status quo for this team. He didn't want stagnation. His goal, our goal, was for us to develop characters that would be complex and interesting enough to generate their own stories. And, if we were lucky, the stories would be interesting enough to attract readers. So far, it looks as if we've been pretty lucky.

Oh, and by the way, if you're wondering what happened to Daimio right after the end of this story . . . good.

—John Arcudi
Philadelphia

B.P.R.D.™

SKETCHBOOK

With the action taking place in the already established B.P.R.D. headquarters, most of the designs for Killing Ground focused on the Daimio "were-jaguar" monster.

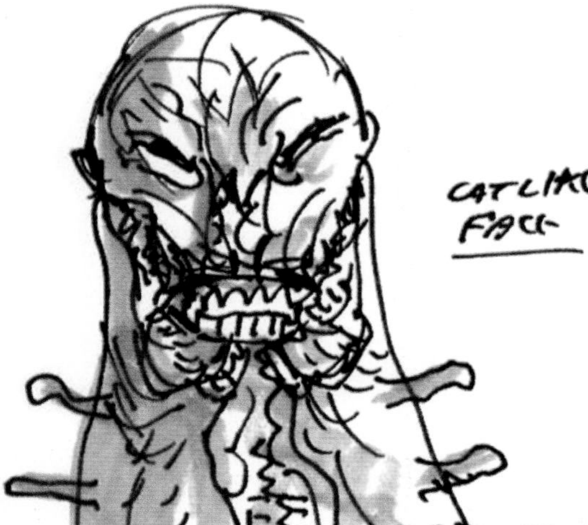
CAT LIKE FACE

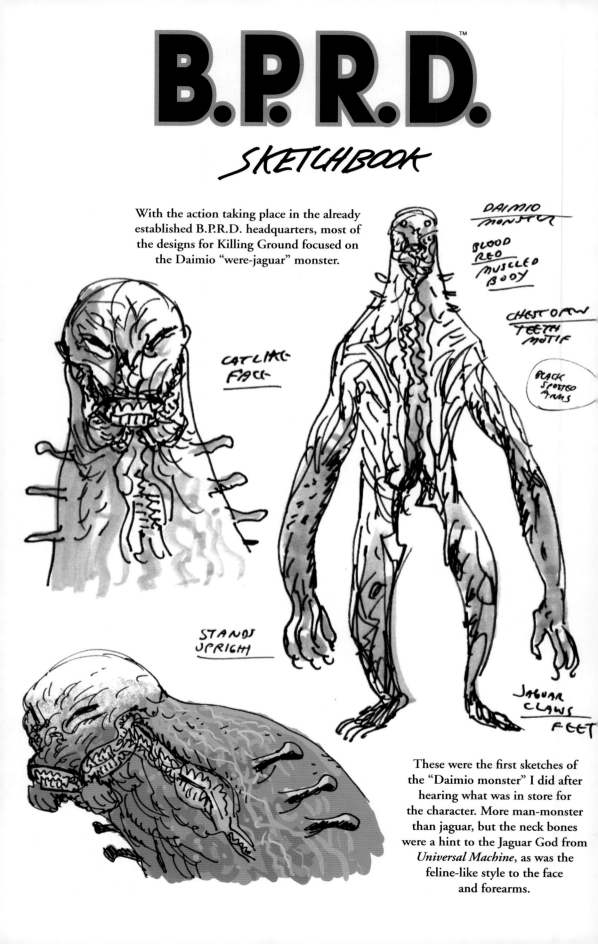

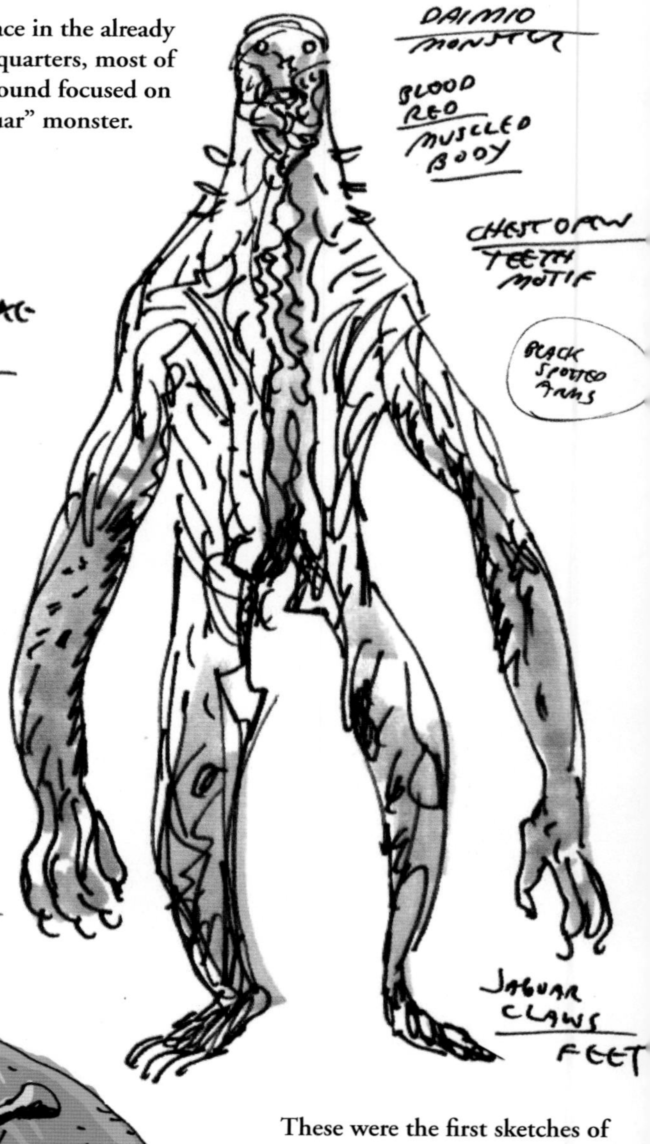
DAIMIO MONSTER
BLOOD RED MUSCLED BODY
CHEST OPEN TEETH MOTIF
BLACK SPOTTED ARMS
JAGUAR CLAWS FEET

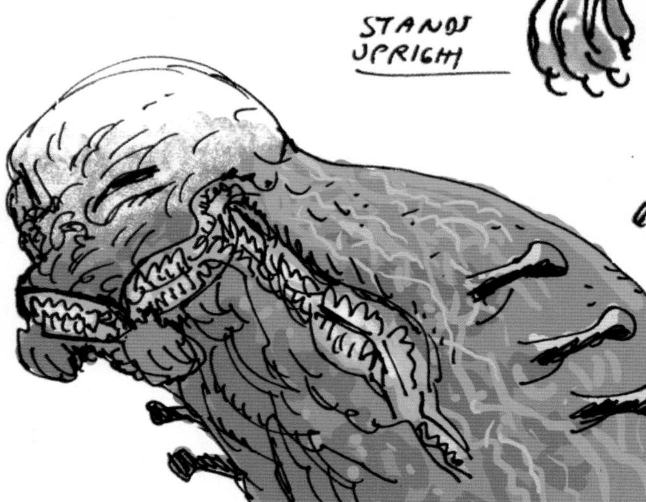
STANDS UPRIGHT

These were the first sketches of the "Daimio monster" I did after hearing what was in store for the character. More man-monster than jaguar, but the neck bones were a hint to the Jaguar God from *Universal Machine*, as was the feline-like style to the face and forearms.

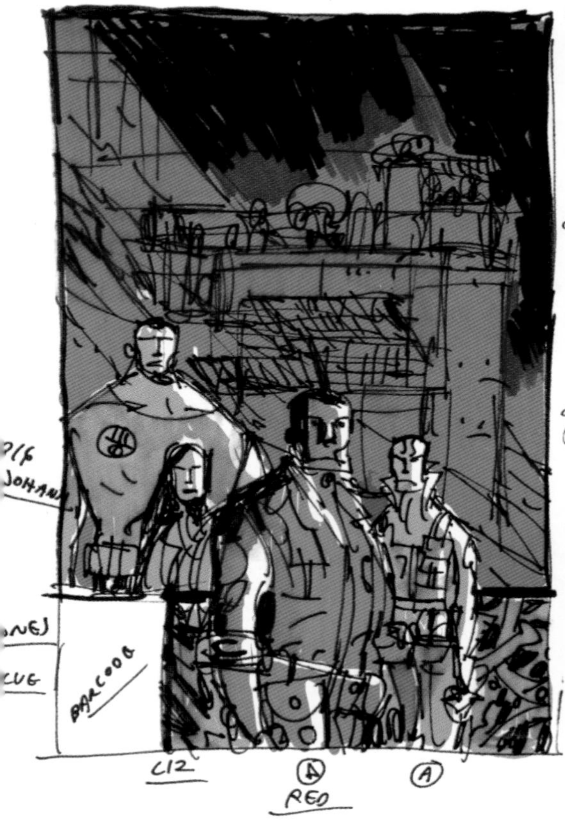
RED

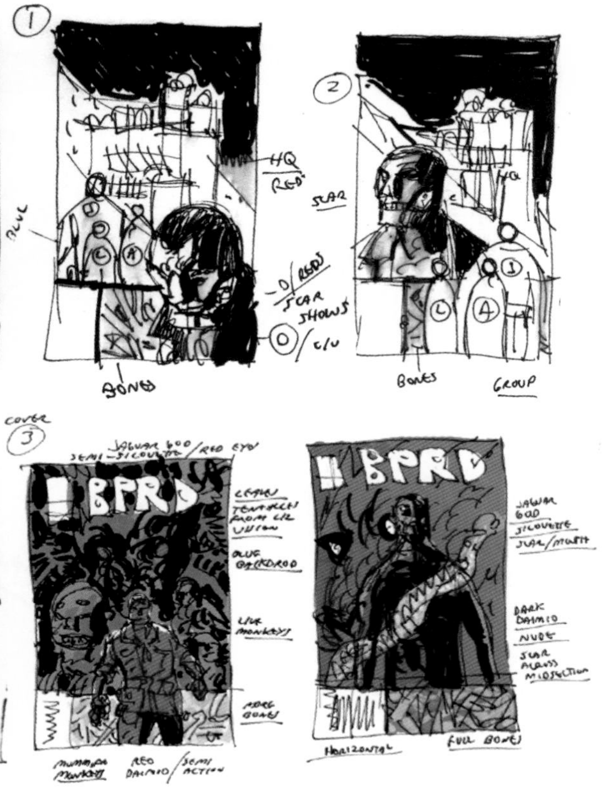
HQ
BONES
GROUP
COVER
BPRD
BPRD
HORIZONTAL
FULL BONES

Mike usually did the artwork for the series covers, but with the *Abe Sapien* and *Lobster Johnson* series keeping him busy, he let me step in to take over the cover chores for this series. Above are some of the first cover sketches for the single comic issues: red would play a big part of the color scheme and also tie into the color of Daimio's monster form. Below are unused penciled versions of the covers to #4 and #5.

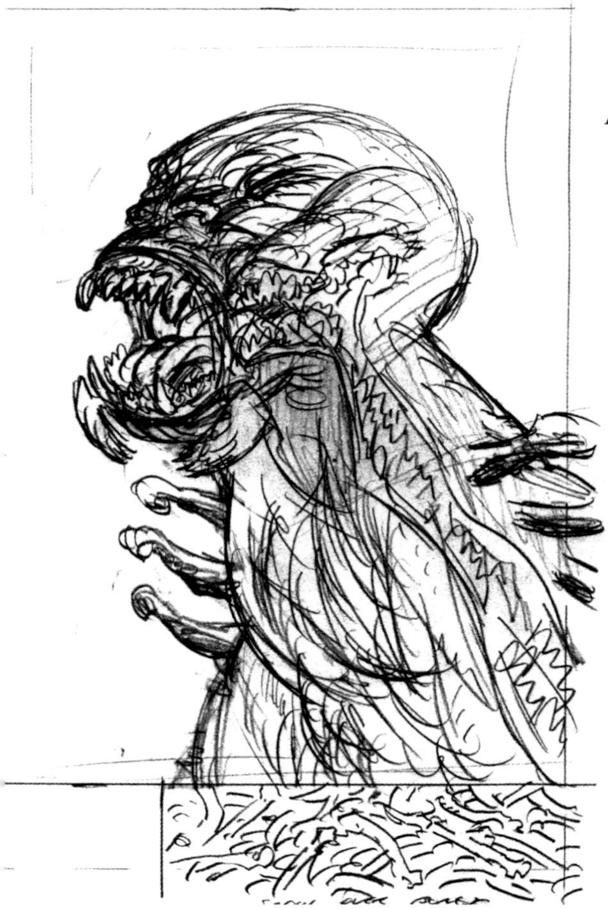

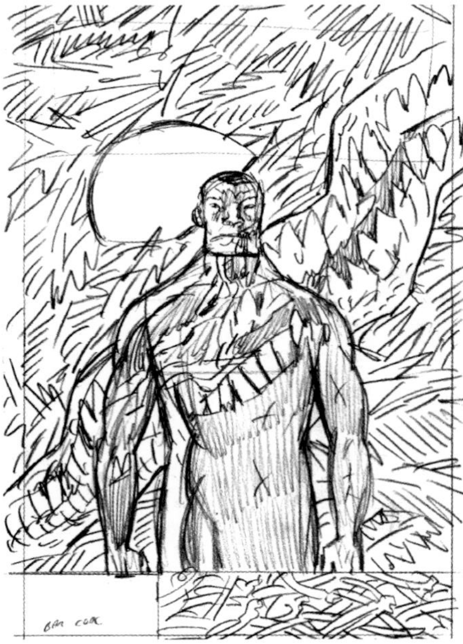

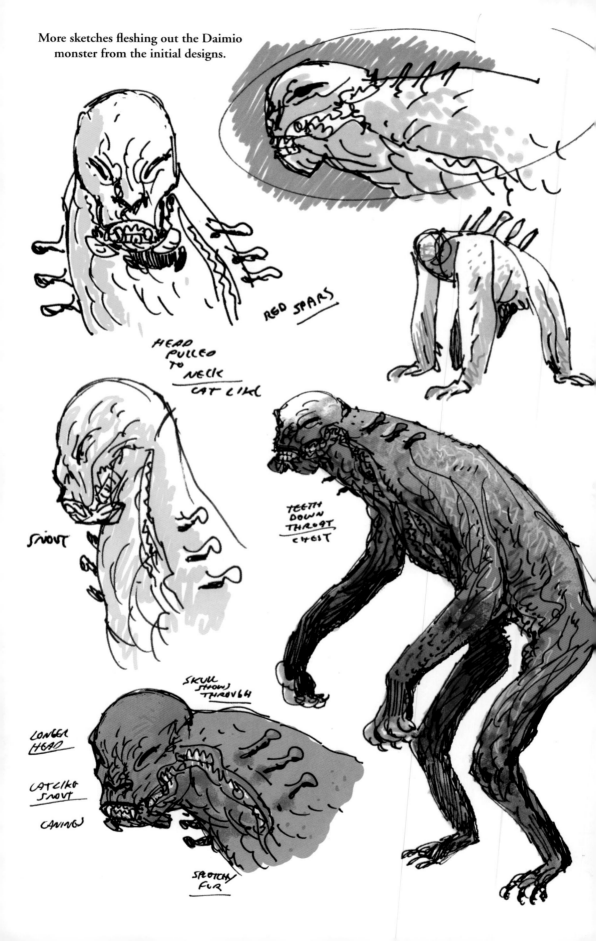

More sketches fleshing out the Daimio
monster from the initial designs.

RED SPARS

HEAD
PULLED
TO
NECK
CAT LIKE

SNOUT

TEETH
DOWN
THROAT
CHEST

SKULL
SHOW
THROUGH

LONGER
HEAD

CAT LIKE
SNOUT

CANINE

SPLOTCHY
FUR

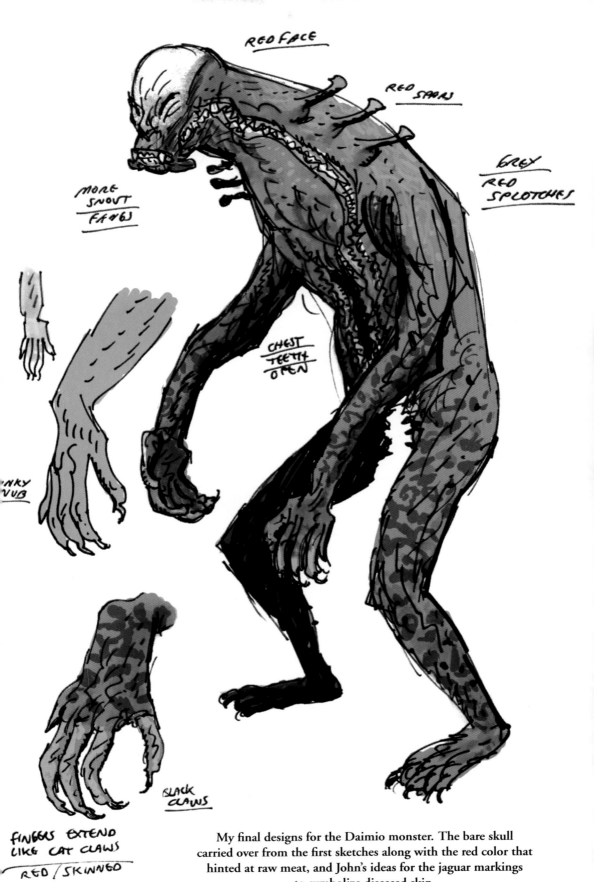

RED FACE

RED SPARS

GREY
RED
SPLOTCHES

MORE
SNOUT
FANGS

CHEST
TEETH
OPEN

~NKY
NUB

BLACK
CLAWS

FINGERS EXTEND
LIKE CAT CLAWS

RED / SKINNED

My final designs for the Daimio monster. The bare skull
carried over from the first sketches along with the red color that
hinted at raw meat, and John's ideas for the jaguar markings
to symbolize diseased skin.

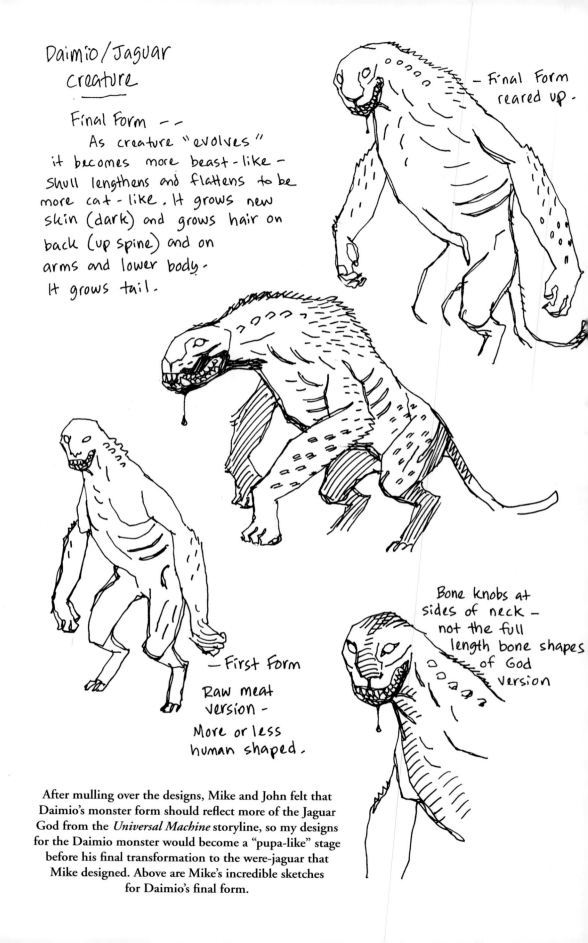

Daimio/Jaguar creature

Final Form --

As creature "evolves" it becomes more beast-like - Skull lengthens and flattens to be more cat-like. It grows new skin (dark) and grows hair on back (up spine) and on arms and lower body. It grows tail.

— Final Form reared up.

— First Form

Raw meat version -

More or less human shaped.

Bone knobs at sides of neck — not the full length bone shapes of God Version

After mulling over the designs, Mike and John felt that Daimio's monster form should reflect more of the Jaguar God from the *Universal Machine* storyline, so my designs for the Daimio monster would become a "pupa-like" stage before his final transformation to the were-jaguar that Mike designed. Above are Mike's incredible sketches for Daimio's final form.

More of Mike's design notes for the Daimio jaguar, along with his cover sketch for the last issue. To the right is my final inked version of the design.

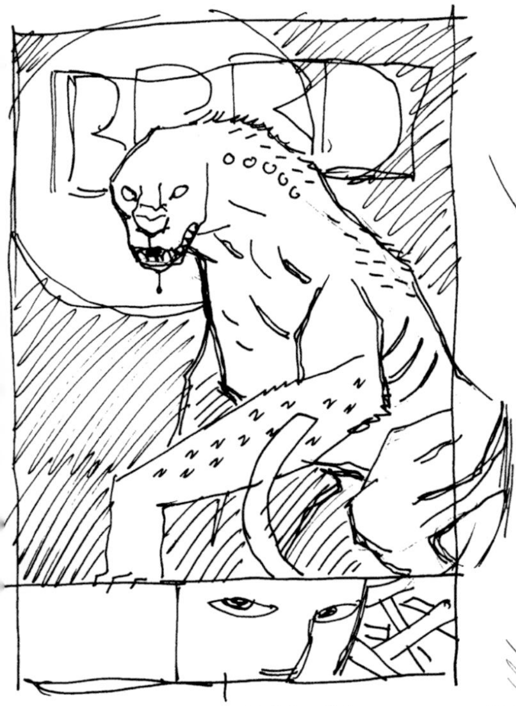
Idea for #5 cover
HUMAN DAMIO

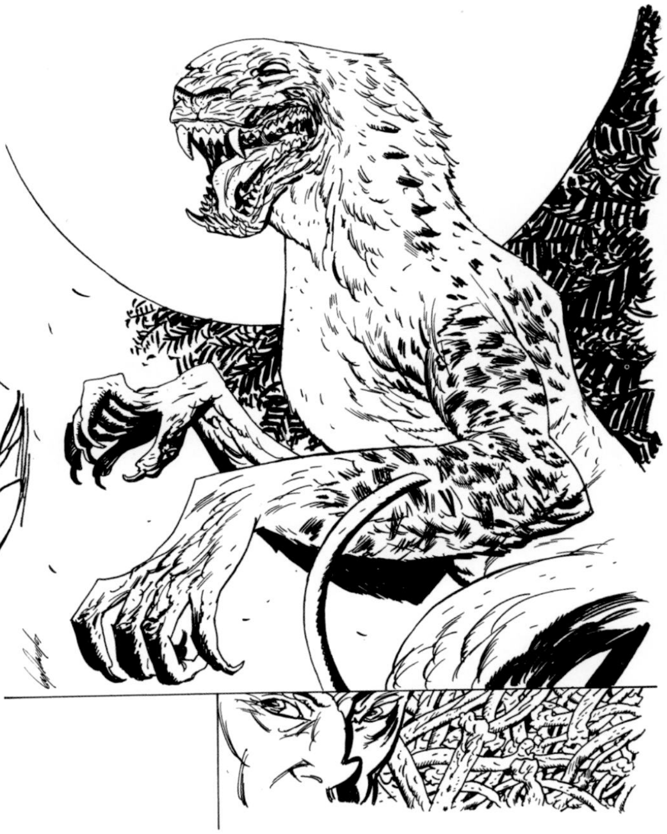

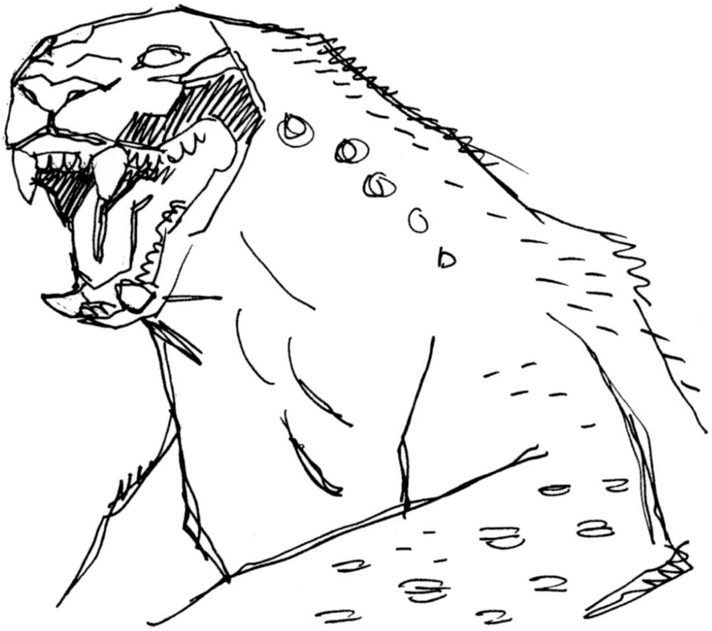
Final form of the creature - Noble - Majestic -
- Head lowered in growl or raised up in classic Lion/Tiger roar.

Some ideas on the shaman's feather headdress: giving the impression of a stylized jaguar face and the stone-bladed knife used by Chaves to hunt the were-jaguars.

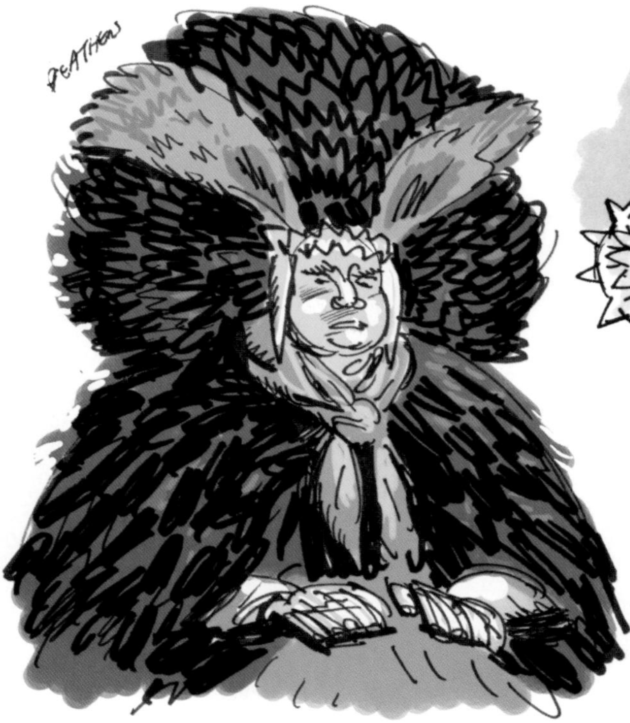
FEATHERS

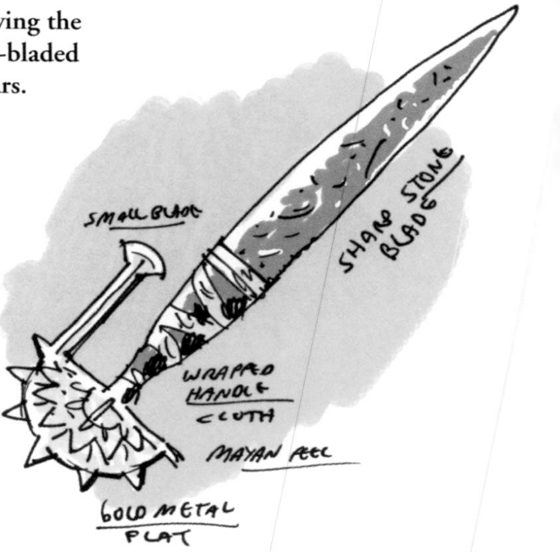
SMALL BLADE
SHARP STONE BLADE
WRAPPED HANDLE
CLOTH
MAYAN FEEL
GOLD METAL
PLAT

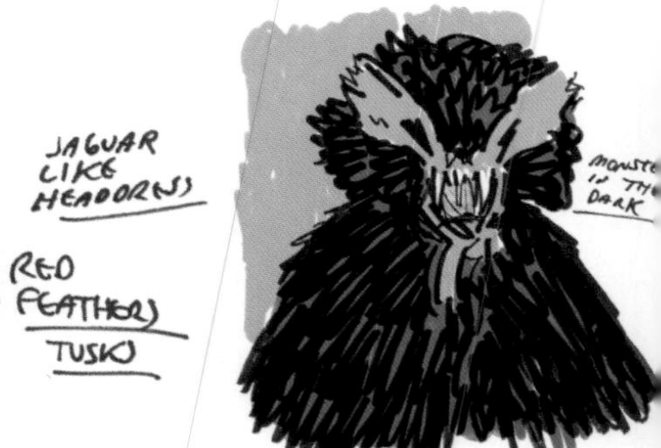
JAGUAR LIKE HEADDRESS
RED FEATHERS
TUSKS
MONSTE IN THE DARK

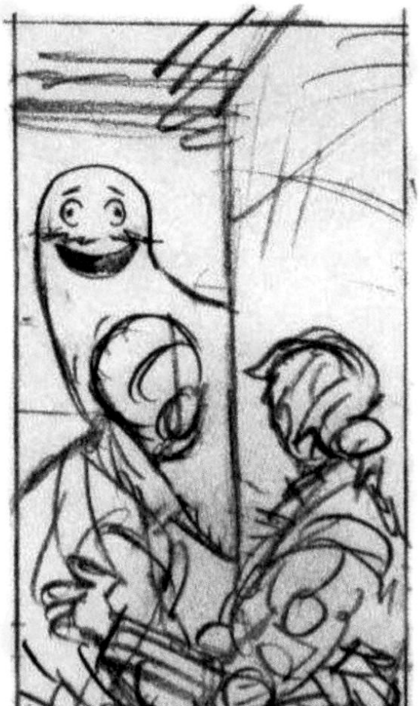

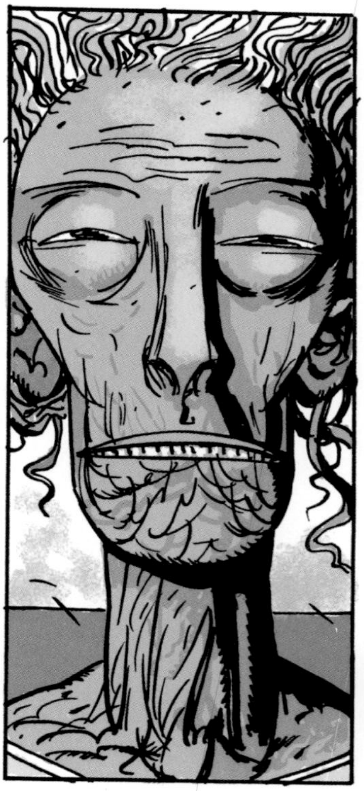

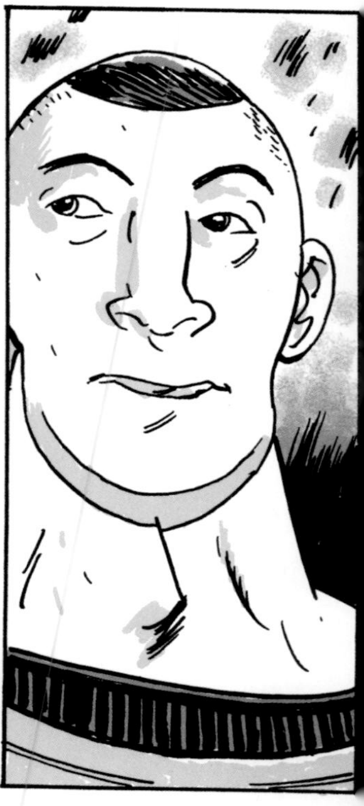

Above: Something sinister lurks through the B.P.R.D. HQ—a bit of sillyness hidden in the pencils to chapter five. Right: Unused bio drawings of Panya and "fleshy" Johann that were done for the inside front covers to the single comic issues.

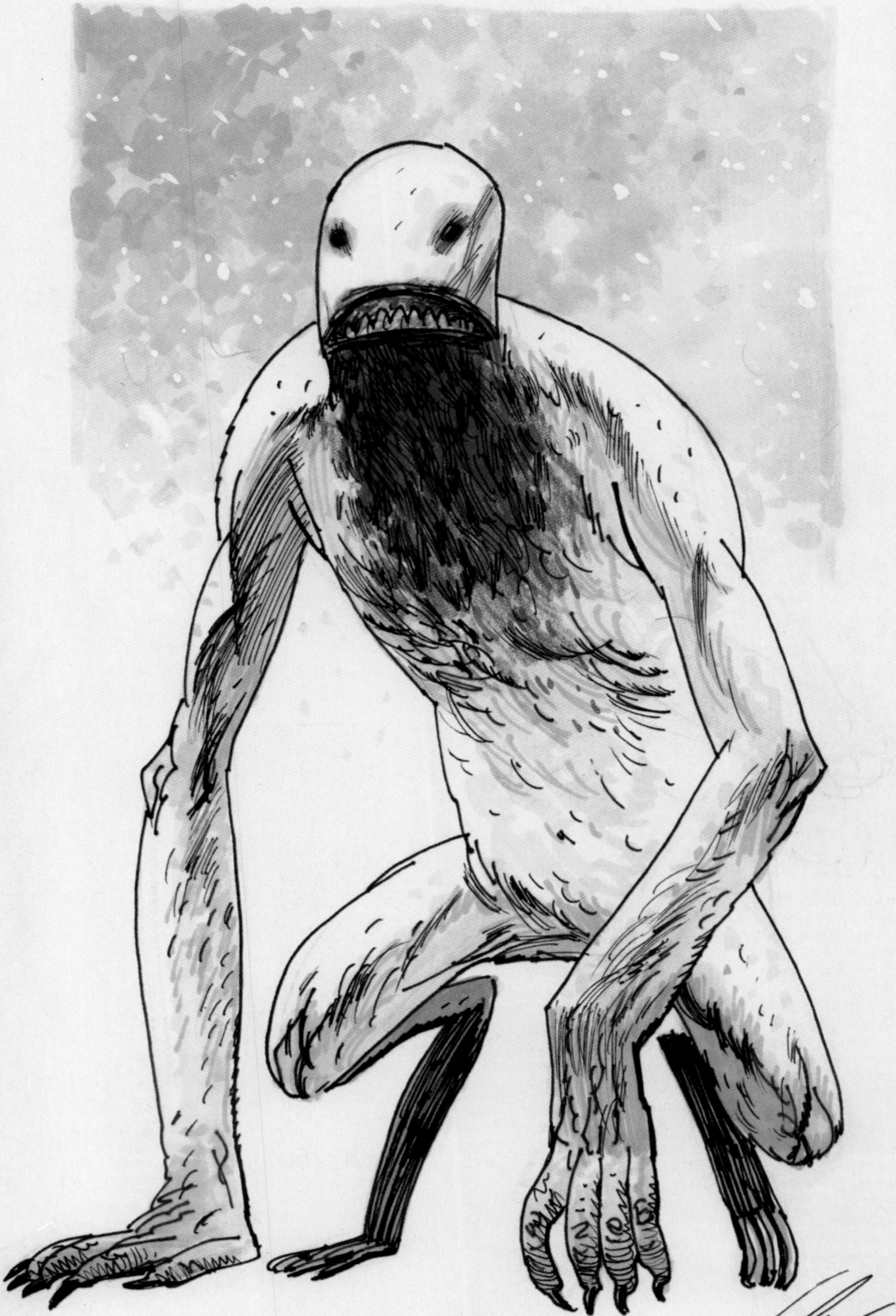

Feral Daryl, the wendigo from *Universal Machine*, returned more menacing and bestial than his first sympathetic appearance.

HELLBOY™

by MIKE MIGNOLA

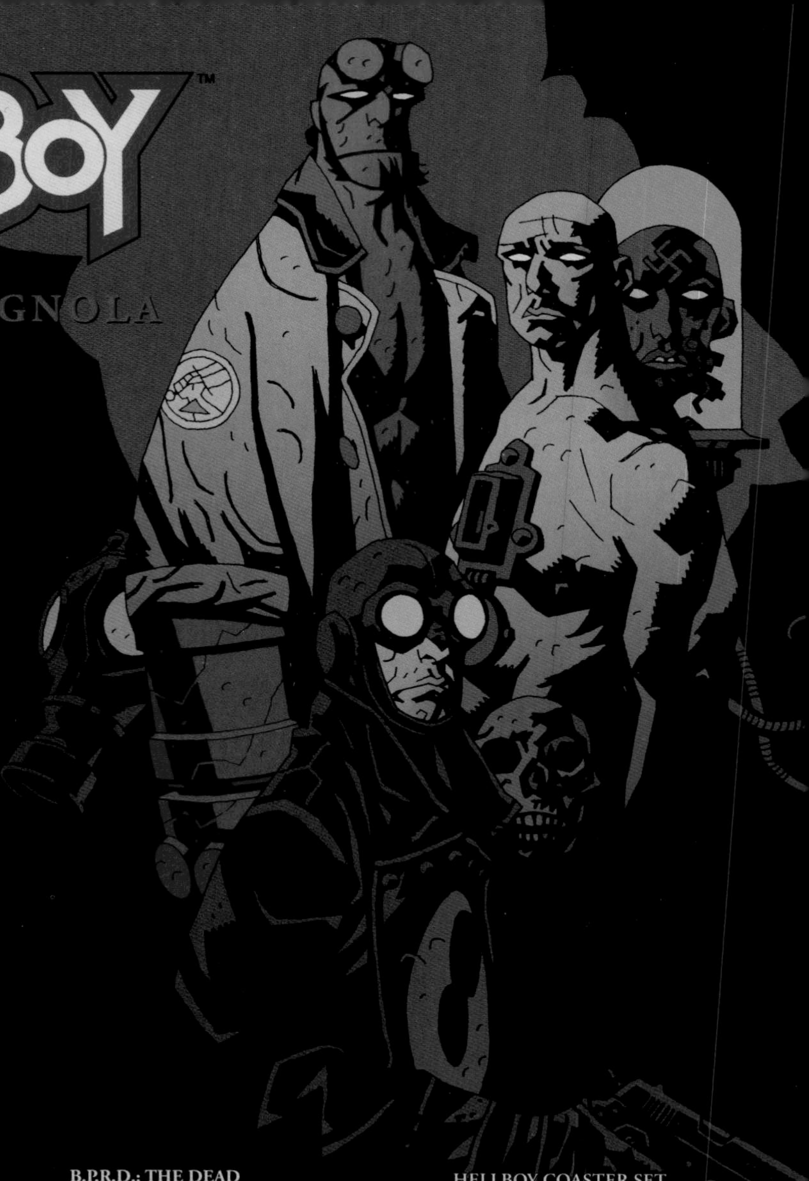

SEED OF DESTRUCTION
with John Byrne
ISBN: 978-1-59307-094-6 | $17.95

WAKE THE DEVIL
ISBN: 978-1-59307-095-3 | $17.95

THE CHAINED COFFIN AND OTHERS
ISBN: 978-1-59307-091-5 | $17.95

THE RIGHT HAND OF DOOM
ISBN: 978-1-59307-093-9 | $17.95

CONQUEROR WORM
ISBN: 978-1-59307-092-2 | $17.95

STRANGE PLACES
ISBN: 978-1-59307-475-3 | $17.95

THE TROLL WITCH AND OTHERS
By Mignola, Corben, and Russell
ISBN: 978-1-59307-860-7 | $17.95

THE ART OF HELLBOY
ISBN: 978-1-59307-089-2 | $29.95

HELLBOY WEIRD TALES
Volume 1
ISBN: 978-1-56971-622-9 | $17.95

Volume 2
ISBN: 978-1-56971-953-4 | $17.95

ODD JOBS
Short stories by Mignola, Poppy Z. Brite, Chris Golden, and others
Illustrations by Mignola
ISBN: 978-1-56971-440-9 | $14.95

ODDER JOBS
Short stories by Frank Darabont, Guillermo del Toro, and others
Illustrations by Mignola
ISBN: 978-1-59307-226-1 | $14.95

B.P.R.D.: HOLLOW EARTH
By Mignola, Chris Golden, Ryan Sook, and others
ISBN: 978-1-56971-862-9 | $17.95

B.P.R.D.: THE SOUL OF VENICE
By Mignola, Mike Oeming, Guy Davis, Scott Kolins, Geoff Johns, and others
ISBN: 978-1-59307-132-5 | $17.95

B.P.R.D.: PLAGUE OF FROGS
By Mignola and Guy Davis
ISBN: 978-1-59307-288-9 | $17.95

B.P.R.D.: THE DEAD
By Mignola, John Arcudi, and Guy Davis
ISBN: 978-1-59307-380-0 | $17.95

B.P.R.D.: THE BLACK FLAME
By Mignola, Arcudi, and Davis
ISBN: 978-1-59307-550-7 | $17.95

B.P.R.D.: THE UNIVERSAL MACHINE
By Mignola, Arcudi, and Davis
ISBN: 978-1-59307-710-5 | $17.95

B.P.R.D.: GARDEN OF SOULS
By Mignola, Arcudi, and Davis
ISBN: 978-1-59307-882-9 | $17.95

HELLBOY ZIPPO LIGHTER
#17-101 $29.95

HELLBOY TALKING BOARD
#10-248 $24.99

HELLBOY DELUXE TALKING BOARD
#10-380 $99.99

HELLBOY COASTER SET
#13-252 $9.99

HELLBOY QEE FIGURE: HELLBOY
#13-821 $7.99

HELLBOY QEE FIGURE: ABE SAPIEN
#13-822 $7.99

To find a comics shop in your area, call 1-888-266-4226
For more information or to order direct:
• On the web: darkhorse.com
• E-mail: mailorder@darkhorse.com
• Phone: 1-800-862-0052
Mon.–Fri. 9 AM to 5 PM Pacific Time

DARK HORSE COMICS™ darkhorse.com *drawing on your nightmares*